I0762163

BITTER CHOICES

A STAN TURNER MYSTERY

BITTER CHOICES

A STAN TURNER MYSTERY

By

William Manchee

Top Publications, Ltd.

TOP PUBLICATIONS, LTD.
PLANO, TEXAS

Bitter Choices
A Stan Turner Mystery
Volume 13

Top Publications, Ltd.
Plano, Texas

Library Edition
ISBN 978-1-7333283-4-0

To my sister Darline

Table of Contents

1
Trustee

Stan

Planning for a career is a challenging endeavor for high school students as their perception of what a particular occupation might be like isn't always realistic. This was the case with Stan Turner. In high school he was set on going into politics and went to law school to further that ambition. But once he got a taste of politics, he decided it wasn't for him and decided to practice law instead.

Unfortunately, coming from a lower middle-class family he had to work his way through college and law school. Being married with four children didn't help his financial situation either, although his wife Rebekah was a RN and worked part time to help out. They both agreed her main focus had to be the children. Desperately needing cash and unwilling to continue selling insurance, Stan felt he had no choice but to start his law practice even though the only funding he could get was a $2,000 cash advance on his American Express card.

Upon graduation, it had been his intention to specialize in estate planning since he'd already been trained in that specialty at Cosmopolitan Life where he worked while he went through SMU law school.

At that time estate planning was a very lucrative area of the law, so with a wife and four children to support, he thought he'd made a sound choice. Unfortunately, his plans didn't quite work out the way he had hoped.

Shortly after he started practice, Congress radically changed the estate tax laws making estate planning unnecessary for all but the very rich. So, his once thriving estate planning business soon was producing less than ten percent of his revenue. Stan quickly learned that with little or no capital to fall back on, he couldn't be choosy about what business to accept.

Before he knew it, he found himself doing real estate, probate, corporate law, contracts, bankruptcy, and even criminal law on occasion. He'd taken all the right courses in law school but had no practical experience in any area of the law other than estate planning. This meant he often found himself over his head on a case and scrambling to get the result his clients expected; clients he often didn't like or respect.

As he sat at his desk 20 years later and gazed out at the Dallas skyline from his 9th-floor office window, he lamented how quickly the years had gone by. His children were grown now and the eldest, Reggie, had graduated from law school and joined the firm, Turner & Waters, Attorneys, and Counselors at Law. Since they both had graduated from SMU Law School, Stan was able to participate in the hooding ceremony at Reggie's graduation. Stan's wife Rebekah and he were very proud of their law school graduate that day, but Stan had misgivings about him joining the law firm.

Practicing law wasn't as glamorous a job as most people thought. It was incredibly challenging, stressful, and dangerous. Perfect strangers came into an attorney's office every day expecting miracles and if the attorney couldn't perform them, they often blamed the attorney rather than accept the fact that they had made bad decisions or simply had bad luck.

But Reggie had his heart set on becoming a lawyer and joining the firm, so Stan had no choice but to accept his desires and feel grateful that Reggie would be such an integral part of his life for years to come.

It was near the turn of the century and the world was dealing with the Y2K scare. On January 1, 2000, computers all over the world were expected to malfunction, thanks to short-sighted programmers who didn't count on their coding still being utilized in the next century. Until the 1990s many computer programs were designed to abbreviate four-digit years as two digits to save memory space. The world had been alerted to the problem for several years and had spent a lot of money supposedly fixing it, but many in the media, on Wall Street, and some on the pulpit still predicted a calamity, which was now less than a month away. Planes would fall from the sky, banks would be unable to open their vaults, electric grids would fail, and the economies all over the world would crater.

Static on his intercom awakened Stan from his daydreaming. His attention turned to his calendar where he noticed his next client was Ruben Acosta, a referral from an accountant friend, Roger Moore, whom he'd met at an estate planning conference years earlier. Referrals from friends were great and much appreciated, but they came with double the usual stress because if the attorney disappointed the client, the friend would be disappointed as well. Stan sighed deeply, hoping this wouldn't be one of those impossible cases that no attorney could solve and would end badly. It seemed to Stan like he had gotten a lot of those lately.

His intercom came to life. "Mr. Acosta is here to see you," Maria, Stan's secretary, announced.

Maria had been Stan's secretary for over fifteen years and had always diligently and efficiently performed her very demanding job. Stan appreciated that she executed every task effectively with little or no supervision. He didn't have the time or patience to micromanage his employees.

In addition to his law partner, Paula Waters, who he met and befriended in law school, the firm had one other lawyer, Jodie Marshall. Jodie had been Stan's first secretary when he first started practice. She loved the law and wanted to become a lawyer, so Stan let her go part-time to law school while she worked as an investigator for the firm. Stan hired Maria as his secretary to replace her and when Jodie graduated from law school, Jodie joined the firm as an associate.

Jodie was knock-out gorgeous in addition to being smart, ambitious, and cunning. Although Stan always managed to keep their relationship professional, his heart always beat a little faster when they were working together. Over time Jodie became like another daughter to Stan and he worried about her a lot. Jodie was a tenacious and fearless fighter and showed no mercy to her opponents. In fact, she had angered a Mexican cartel boss so much on one occasion that he had her kidnapped. She survived but the entire ordeal took its toll on her and Stan. And there had been other close calls, too.

Stan stood up, went out to the reception area and observed a tall, trim, man with black hair and a mustache standing in front of Maria's desk. As Stan approached their eyes met, Stan smiled and said, "Come on back."

Ruben followed Stan into his office clutching a large, thick envelope. Stan motioned for Ruben to take a seat across from him. Ruben seemed a bit nervous, quickly scanning the room from one end to the other and avoiding eye contact. After they chatted for a while about trivial matters, Stan smiled and asked, "So, what can I do for you today?"

"Ah. Well. I heard you are an expert in asset protection."

Asset protection was an area of estate planning that hadn't been impacted by the change in the estate tax laws. Small business owners, contractors, architects, doctors, lawyers, accountants, and many others were often in the cross hairs of unhappy clients, competitors, creditors, governmental agencies, or scam artists trying to make a fast buck. Sometimes these were legitimate claims, but just as often they were blatant attempts to extort money from the business owner who they believed had deep pockets.

Stan shook his head and replied, "No. I don't claim to be an expert in anything. I'm a general practitioner. The Texas State Bar doesn't let you call yourself and expert unless they have certified you as such. I get bored easily, so I don't want to specialize in just one field of the law. Is someone after you or are you just preparing for the worst?"

"Well, no one has sued me yet, but there have been threats. They may be coming after me soon."

"What kind of threats?" Stan asked. "Do you own a business?"

"Yes, several, in fact. My main business is managing medical offices so doctors, dentists, and other professionals can concentrate on practicing their profession and not running a business."

"Right. I've noticed doctors and dentists doing more of that lately. It makes sense."

"Yes," Ruben said. "Doctors and dentists are very smart people, but they often are overwhelmed by the intricacies of managing a business. I saw that with my own dentist, so I asked him if I could run his practice for him. He was skeptical at first, but I convinced him I could do it. I have an MBA in finance from the University of Dallas. It's worked out well, so now I have a string of professional clients."

"Are you a dentist?"

He laughed. "God, no. I'm a number cruncher. I can't stand the sight of blood. After I got my degree, I worked for a while for a small CPA firm here in Dallas whose clientele were primarily small businesses, so I was familiar with the challenges that I'd be facing. This is why I need asset protection. People are so litigious nowadays that the cost of malpractice and workmen's compensation insurance has gotten out of hand, particularly if you've had a claim."

"You're right about that," Stan agreed.

"So, many of my professionals want to self-insure to save money. They think having insurance makes them a target. I have advised against it but some of them still want to do it."

"Yeah, I hate it when client's pay for my advice and then don't take it."

"That's right," Ruben replied. "But if they get sued then guess who is going to get caught in the crossfire one way or another?"

"Right. The first rule of litigation is to sue as many defendants as you possibly can, even if their liability is questionable. The more entities you sue the quicker you'll get a settlement. Nobody wants to throw the dice."

"Exactly, so if this self-insuring nonsense doesn't work out, I need some protection."

"Yes, that makes a lot of sense," Stan agreed. Self-insuring against malpractice and workplace accidents was very dangerous, if not outright foolish. The cost of defending the litigation could be devastating by itself even if the employer was successful, but it was clear Ruben knew that but was being forced to do it anyway to make his clients happy. "Sure, I can help you with that."

For the next hour, Ruben explained his businesses in more detail, and they discussed various ways to restructure each entity to make them less vulnerable to attack. This involved setting up a personal trust, a limited partnership to own his real estate, equipment, and investment assets, and transferring assets out of his personal name to the appropriate entities. These were all legal methods of protection, but they would greatly complicate Ruben's life, so Stan wanted to make sure he understood that.

"Now, doing all this will require your careful attention. All these new entities have to deal with each other at arm's length. You can't cut corners and commingle assets. Your accounting costs are going to increase substantially with all the additional accounting and tax preparation that will be necessary."

"That's okay," Ruben replied. "It will be a lot less expensive than the cost of insurance."

"Maybe, but nothing is foolproof, and you will still have to hire an attorney and defend yourself if you or one of your business entities are sued."

"If that happens, can you defend me?"

"I don't personally do that, but we have an associate, Jodie Marshall, who could handle it."

"Is she any good?"

"Oh yes, she's very capable. I'll introduce you to her here in a minute."

"Good. I don't want to have to be searching for a litigation attorney if I get sued."

"Not a problem," Stan assured him. "As I mentioned, you could set up an irrevocable trust or even go offshore, if you wanted complete protection, but then you would lose control over your assets."

"No, I'm not turning everything over to some trustee in the Cayman Islands that I have never met."

"Right. That's a bit risky, but you will need one or more alternate trustees and executors to handle your affairs in case you die or become incapacitated. Do you know who that would be? A family member, friend, or business associate, perhaps?"

"That's a problem. I don't really have anyone to do that."

"You don't have any family members or friends who would be willing to step in should you die or be unable to act?"

"No. My parents are dead, and I don't have any brothers or sisters."

"What about your wife."

He laughed. "I'm divorced and my ex-wife can't balance a checkbook. She has about as much business sense as my cat."

Stifling a laugh, Stan said, "Alright. What about a bank?"

Ruben shook his head irritably. "No! Are you kidding me? Bankers are a bunch of thieves."

"Okay," Stan said letting out a long breath while he wracked his brain for another suggestion.

"How about you or your firm doing it?" Ruben suggested.

Stan frowned. "No. Sorry, we don't take on fiduciary appointments. We can only act as your attorneys."

"Why not? One of my friends has a trust and his attorney is his trustee."

Stan cringed. "Yes. Some attorneys do that, but I don't have any investment expertise or training." The truth was a lot of attorneys did take trustee appointments and then employed themselves or their firms to act as the trust or estate's attorney. It was a very lucrative arrangement that allowed attorneys to legally double charge. Stan didn't think it was ethical. "Plus, it's very expensive to have an attorney as a trustee because they won't agree to serve unless they can charge their standard rates. Rates that would be much higher than what an individual trustee would charge."

"Well, I'm not worried about your fees. I just want to make sure my affairs are in good hands."

Stan felt his resolve floundering. "So, you're sure there isn't someone else who could do it?"

"Positive. Will you do it?"

"I suppose, for now. But you should be on the lookout for a friend or business associate who you can substitute for me down the road."

"Right. I'll do that."

Stan wasn't convinced about Ruben's sincerity but there was no point in pressing the issue. It was unlikely he would ever actually serve as a trustee since the life expectancy of a small business was less than seven years. When the business was sold or shut down Ruben would no longer need such a complex asset protection plan, so he'd probably revoke the trust and restructure his estate plan. And, of course, a trustee could always refuse to serve if he felt the situation warranted it. But deep-down Stan knew that wouldn't be an option for him. He found it very difficult to break a promise, let a client down or run away from a challenge.

"One last thing," Stan said. "At your death who do you want to get your property? You don't have any children, right?"

"Not that I know of," he replied with a grin.

Stan smiled. "So, a charity?"

Ruben thought for a moment and then replied, "I may have children down the road if I get married again, so leave everything to my wife and then my children. If I don't end up having a wife or any children at my death then give everything to ... ah ... let's see ... the NHLC, I guess."

"What's that?" Stan asked.

"Oh, its legal name is New Hope Legal Clinics, Inc. It's a non-profit legal clinic. They help undocumented aliens living in the United States with their myriad of legal issues."

Stan raised his eyebrows. "Wow! How did you get interested in that?"

"It's a long story," Ruben replied without elaboration.

"Hmm. Okay. I bet they are busy."

Ruben laughed. "That's for sure."

"Alright," Stan said. "That sounds good."

Before he left, Ruben went through his financial statements with Stan. Stan needed to know what kind of investment assets needed to be protected. Pension, profit sharing, IRAs, and 401K retirement plans would be the easiest. They all were generally exempt from seizure by creditors in Texas. Cash, business interests, stock, bonds, mutual funds, and non-homesteaded real estate were more problematic.

Ruben had an impressive inventory of residential real estate and commercial properties that he leased out to the dental practices he managed. He also owned their equipment and leased it to them. This simplified each professional's operation and eliminated the need for them to borrow large sums of money to start and operate their practices. These assets were all held in Ruben's name as a sole proprietorship with the DBA of Acosta Less Leasing. Stan laughed when he read the name. The truth was that leasing while it had its advantages usually ended up being much more expensive in the long run than buying.

Ruben's most lucrative business was his employee leasing operation, Medical Network, Inc. or MedNet as he called it. This company handled all the staffing needs of each location, payroll, human resources, insurance, and billing. Billing and dealing with insurance claims were a professional's biggest nightmare but Acosta's clients didn't have to worry about that. Every meticulous detail was handled by Acosta's company.

Before Ruben left, Stan introduced him to Jodie and filled her in on what they would be doing for him. After Ruben had gone, Stan made a list of all the documents he would need to prepare and a checklist of the steps necessary to implement the plan. While he was working, Reggie walked in.

"Hey, Dad. You got time for lunch?"

Stan looked up and smiled. "Sure, if we go somewhere close. I'm up to my eyeballs with work that needed to be done yesterday."

"Downstairs in the Deli in ten minutes?" Reggie suggested.

Stan looked at his watch and nodded. His attention then went back to his To-do list. There would be many documents to prepare, get signed, and then file with the Secretary of State. Next, all the assets would have to be transferred to each entity. The most difficult part would be making sure Ruben understood how everything was supposed to work and monitoring things for a while to be sure the plan was being properly implemented. If it wasn't, not only would the asset protection plan fail and Ruben's assets lost, but Stan would be blamed for its failure.

Reggie had brought Jodie with him and they were talking as Stan walked into the Deli. Like Stan, Reggie had been infatuated with Jodie from the first time they met. While he was in college at UT he started working at the office during the summer and at school breaks. Jodie wasn't married but she always had a boyfriend and didn't give Reggie a second thought. She was too old for him, of course, but Stan doubted Reggie cared much about that. It occurred to him that Reggie's unexpected decision to go to law school might have had something to do with being around Jodie.

After they had gotten their orders, they found a table and sat down. Midway through the meal, Reggie informed them he'd been referred a personal injury case. "Personal injury?" Stan questioned. "We don't do personal injury cases."

Reggie shrugged. "I know, but we should. It can be very lucrative."

"Or, you can spend hundreds of hours on a case and get nothing. Believe me, I have been down that road before."

Early on in Stan's career, he had been referred to a wrongful death case. A man was crossing a busy highway and was run over by a driver who had stopped on the way home for Happy Hour. Stan shouldn't have taken it, but it looked like a slam dunk and a gift from God. The defendant was even arrested for being under the influence. So, Stan assumed it would be a gold mine, but he was wrong. Stan's client was the man's only son. The only problem was the son had never met his father! Once Stan found that out the case went south in a hurry.

Reggie continued, "Dirk Bennett's father is a personal injury attorney, and he says his father never takes a case unless he knows it will settle, so there is no risk."

"Right," Stan said. "Sadly, there are a lot of attorneys who think like that, but the way I look at it, if you take on a case it's like a marriage, for better or for worse."

Reggie slumped in his chair and frowned. "So, you don't even want to hear about it?"

Jodie gave Stan a disapproving stare. Stan shook his head and turned back to Reggie. "No. I didn't say that. Tell me about it."

Reggie leaned forward and began, "Remember my suitemate, Josh Rich? You met him at the open house last year."

"Right," Stan said trying to picture him in his mind.

"Well, his half-sister, Amanda Rich, and her six-year-old daughter, Julie, were in a car wreck up in McKinney last week. She had just gotten off work, picked up Julie from daycare, and were on their way home when she suddenly lost control of the car, crossed the center line, and hit a pickup truck head-on."

"Oh, my god!" Stan said. "How badly were they hurt?"

"Amanda died on the operating table twice but somehow they brought her back to life. She's got two broken legs, broken hands, fingers, and wrists, head injuries, a ruptured spleen, and the list of injuries goes on and on. Julie wasn't hurt as badly, thank God. She has a broken arm, lots of cuts and bruises."

"Geez. That's terrible, but it sounds like it might have been her fault since she crossed the center line?"

"Maybe," Reggie said. "I don't know. I haven't talked to them yet."

"If it is her fault, the only thing you could help her with would be negotiating with her insurance company to make sure she gets the policy maximums."

"I'm not sure she has insurance, but even if she does it will be a minimum $20,000 policy."

"That won't even begin to pay her medical expenses," Jodie interjected thoughtfully. "Maybe she hit something, her tire ruptured, and she lost control of the car. If so, they may have a claim against the tire manufacturer."

Stan shook his head. "Products liability is very complicated and would be a huge undertaking. We couldn't possibly take on such a case."

Reggie glared at Stan. "But Dad, can't Jodie and I, at least, go meet with them and the family and get the facts. It might turn out to be a good case."

Stan stifled a laugh. Took a deep breath and replied, "Jodie is too busy with paying clients. If you want to meet with them, knock yourself out, but don't get your hopes up and don't promise them anything. This is fact-finding only. Okay?"

"Okay," Reggie conceded and gave Jodie a triumphant smile. She winked back at him.

2
The Accident

Reggie

Most of Reggie's friends in college and law school complained incessantly about their parents. The complaints were all over the map from being too strict, overbearing, and controlling, to not giving a shit. Since half of their parents were divorced, another complaint was that they were always at each other's throats and life at home was hell. Bottom line, Reggie's friends couldn't wait to leave home and be out on their own.

Reggie couldn't relate to his friends. Stan and Rebekah were happily married and rarely even argued. If their four children were reasonably obedient and respectful, they trusted them and didn't feel the need for close monitoring. Even so, life was not perfect in the Turner household. When they did argue, it was usually about money, or the lack thereof. Neither of Reggie's grandparents had money, so Stan and Rebekah had started out with nothing. They worked their way through college, and both worked while Stan was in law school. Rebekah hated being poor, but it didn't seem to bother Stan as much. Not that Rebekah was materialistic. She wasn't at all. She didn't spend money on expensive clothes or cosmetics and rarely wore jewelry. She worried a lot about Reggie, his siblings, and Stan, but often neglected her own needs. The financial burden of four children and making ends meet while Stan was going to law school weighed heavily on her.

When Stan started his law practice, he worked long hours and the family didn't see him as much as they'd have liked, but he still managed to spend time with them at night and on the weekends and took them on great vacations each summer. If Stan neglected anyone, it was Rebekah. But she never complained if Stan was spending his little spare time with the children. She was unselfish that way.

So, Reggie's big complaint with his father was that he never made much money even though he was a lawyer and, as he often joked, had a license to steal. Rebekah often complained that he was too laid back and easygoing. If a client didn't pay his bill, Stan would say, "Well, I guess he needs the money more than I do."

Reggie hated it when his father bragged that he'd never sued a client over an unpaid bill and had written off hundreds of thousands of dollars over the years like it was a badge of honor. Reggie resented the struggle his family always had to endure on account of being in dire financial straits. He believed if they'd had that extra money life would have been so much easier, particularly for Mom.

That's one reason Reggie wanted to go into law practice with his father. It was time Turner & Waters made some real money and he knew just how to make that happen. He was going to start practicing personal injury law. He'd hung around with several friends in law school who either had parents who were PI attorneys or had summer internships in personal injury firms. They all agreed PI work was very lucrative and definitely the ticket to financial security. Now all Reggie had to do was convince his father that this was a good move for the firm.

Being offered a shot at getting Amanda and Julie's case was a stroke of good luck in Reggie's mind and couldn't have come at a better time. He figured if he'd let his dad saddle him with a bunch of bankruptcy cases at the start of his career, he'd never make any decent money. So, Reggie was nervous as he got out of his white 2002 Mercury Montego in front of the Mercy Hospital in McKinney. He needed to convince Amanda and her mother that they should hire Turner & Waters to handle Amanda and Julie's personal injury cases. He knew he couldn't actually sign them up yet without his dad's approval, but he had to convince them today that Turner & Waters was the best firm for the job. If he didn't, he figured another firm would scoop up the lucrative case within days and he'd miss his chance to kick-start his legal career.

Reggie entered the hospital through the Emergency Room entrance. It was crowded with patients and families waiting uncomfortably to be seen by the next available ER doctor. Fortunately, Reggie knew where he was going so he bypassed the crowd and went straight to the elevators. On the 5th floor, he got out and went to the nurses' station. Julie was in Room 524, but he wanted to be sure it was okay for him to go right in. The nurse in charge gave him a hard look.

"Are you family?" she asked.

"No. Legal counsel. They are expecting me."

She frowned but nodded her assent. Reggie thanked her and headed for Julie's room. He knew he wouldn't be able to see Amanda yet as she was still in ICU and would be there for some time. But Amanda's mother Stella would be with Julie, so that was the best he could do now. As he walked into the room Julie was sitting up in her bed with a coloring book on her tray table. She was busy coloring while her grandmother was reading a book.

Julie looked up and smiled. She had a black eye, cuts and bruises on the left side of her face, and a cast on her left arm. An IV tube had been inserted in a vein in her right arm and a heart monitor clip was attached to her right index finger. Reggie smiled back at her.

"Hi. I'm Reggie."

"Oh, you're Josh's friend," Julie noted.

"That's right. He asked me to come to visit you."

"My mother died in the accident," Julie said, "but they brought her back to life!"

Tears began to well in Reggie's eyes," Yes, so I heard. She was lucky she had good doctors."

Julie nodded. "But she's very sick. She can't talk to us right now."

"Alright, Julie," her grandmother said. "That's enough. Let Reggie talk."

"Sorry," Julie said and went back to her coloring.

"So, Mr. Turner," Stella said, "Josh says you want to handle Amanda and Julie's cases."

"Yes. I just joined my father's law firm, Turner & Waters. You may have heard of them; they've been involved in several high-profile murder cases."

Recognition suddenly came over Stella's face. "Oh, your father is Stan Turner."

"Yes," Reggie acknowledged.

"And what's his partner's name?"

"Paula Waters."

"Right. I've heard of them," Stella said. "So, you're not going to follow in your father's footsteps and practice criminal law?"

"Actually, my dad doesn't do much criminal law these days. That's Paula's passion. He helps her if she needs it, but he does mostly civil law."

"I see."

Reggie looked over at Julie who had stopped coloring. "How are you feeling, Julie?"

She shrugged. "Okay, I guess."

"Do you remember anything about the accident?"

Julie wrinkled up her face like she was trying hard to remember and then shook her head.

"Well, the mind often represses unpleasant memories." Reggie turned to Stella and asked. "So, how is Amanda? Is she still in a coma?"

Stella grimaced. "Yes, the doctor thought a medically induced coma was best for a while. Her brain suffered so much trauma it needed time to heal."

"Has Amanda been conscious at all?"

"She was right after the accident. She talked to one of the Care Flite paramedics on her way to McKinney National Airport."

"Do you know what she told the paramedic?"

"No. All I know is his name is Stuart Green."

Reggie wrote down the name and then started his well-rehearsed pitch, "So, Amanda and Julie are going to need a lawyer."

"That's what Josh told us, too," Stella said. "But I don't know what an attorney will be able to do for them. It wasn't the other driver's fault. He was a victim too."

"Well, these cases are complicated, and it will take time to sort out the facts to find out what caused the accident and determine if someone is at fault. Amanda's car might have been defective and malfunctioned, another car might have been involved in the accident that we don't know about, or an object may have fallen from the sky. Who knows? The important thing is that you get an attorney on the case right now to start an investigation before the evidence gets lost and witnesses disappear."

"So, you think your father would take this case?" Stella asked.

"Well, the firm would. I'd be handling it but, of course, if I needed help either he or Paula would help me out."

She frowned. "But you just joined the firm. You don't have any experience."

"That's true, but I have been working on and off at the firm for the last seven years while I was in college and then in law school. I have learned so much from my helping and observing my dad and Paula handle their cases that I feel like an experienced attorney already."

"Well, when Amanda is better and able to talk, I will tell her about you and the other attorneys who want to handle her case."

"The other attorneys?" Reggie questioned.

Stella sighed. "Yes, they've been in and out of here all day." She pointed to a stack of business cards at least a half-inch thick.

Reggie's heart sank. He looked away so she wouldn't see the disappointment on his face. "Oh. Okay, well then...ah...when do you think Amanda will be brought out of the coma?"

"In a week or so, I think."

Reggie grimaced. "That's a long time to wait. I'd hate for her case to be compromised because we let critical evidence or witnesses disappear. Don't you have a power of attorney?"

"I do, but I'm not comfortable using it unless it is absolutely necessary. I want to wait a while to see what Amanda's mental state is like. It would be better if she made her own decision."

Reggie nodded. "Right. I understand. So, call me if I can be of assistance or if Amanda wants to talk to me. Thank you for seeing me."

Stella smiled warmly. "Thank you for coming out to see us."

Disappointed, Reggie turned and left the room. The big stack of attorney business cards Stella had accumulated had shaken him. He knew he shouldn't have been surprised, but he'd hoped knowing Josh would have given him a leg up.

When he got back to the office, he went looking for Jodie to report on the interview. She and Reggie had always gotten along well, and Reggie enjoyed working with her. Although she was quite a bit older than him, she had only graduated from law school a few years before him, making it seem they were closer in age.

Reggie found Jodie in the law library and took a seat across from her. She looked up and smiled. "So, how did it go?"

"I didn't get to see Amanda. She's in a medically induced coma. She had pretty extensive head injuries."

Jodie nodded. "So, did you learn any more about the cause of the accident?"

"No. Julie doesn't know or remember how it happened. So, I guess we'll have to wait until Amanda gains consciousness to get any answers."

"What about the police report? When will it be available?"

"I don't know. I haven't been hired yet, so I don't have any authority to request it."

Jodie frowned. "You haven't? I thought Josh...?"

"Apparently, Josh doesn't have as much clout with his family as he led on. His mother has a power of attorney but she's reluctant to use it. She also has a stack of business cards from other attorneys interested in the case."

"That's because of the article that came out in the *Dallas Morning News* this morning," Jodie said.

"What article?"

Jodie handed Reggie the Metro Section of the newspaper. "Look at Page 3."

Reggie flipped to the page and began scanning the article. When he finished, he looked up and shook his head. "What? They think she fell asleep?"

"It's just speculation on the part of the police officer at this point," Jodie replied. "I wouldn't take it as gospel yet."

"I know, but what if he is right? That kills our case."

"Sorry, Reggie. Maybe this is for the best. You don't want to waste a lot of time on a hopeless case."

Reggie got up and dragged himself back to his office. He looked at the stack of bankruptcy files that needed to be processed and let out a silent scream. Then he sighed deeply, rolled up his sleeves, and got to work. As he worked, he wondered what Amanda would do if she were out of work for weeks or months or, God forbid, permanently disabled. How could she take care of Julie?

Josh had told him his mother lived in a mobile home and lived on welfare and food stamps. He wasn't sure her mother would be able to take them in, but even if she could, what kind of life would that be for Amanda and Julie? Amanda might be able to get Social Security Disability but that wouldn't be much, and it would take years to process. But then he reminded himself that it wasn't his problem since he hadn't been retained and when his father found out Amanda probably had fallen asleep at the wheel, he wouldn't let him take the case anyway.

Then Reggie recalled that there was a paramedic he needed to interview. He flipped open his notepad and saw his name, Stuart Green.

"Well, Mr. Green. You better have something good to tell me."

3
Intruder

Stan

On the way to work on Friday, Stan found himself following a DART bus that had a legal ad painted bumper to bumper on both sides of the bus. It read:

AUTO / TRUCK ACCIDENTS ... HIRE THE BEST IN TEXAS ... TOM 'THE TORNADO' TYSON ... YOUR INSURANCE COMPANY'S WORST NIGHTMARE ... CALL NOW! ... WE BLOW AWAY THE COMPETITION.

Stan cringed at the obnoxious advertisement and couldn't believe Reggie was dragging the firm into the sleazy personal injury business. He wondered if he should put his foot down and reject the idea immediately.

Upon arrival at the office, Maria reminded him that Ruben Acosta had a 9:30 a.m. appointment. When a client comes in for asset protection, they generally want the work done yesterday because they fear, or know, the hammer is about to fall on them. Ruben Acosta was no exception. He hadn't said it, but Stan suspected from his body language that he needed immediate protection, so he worked all weekend and got drafts ready for him to review. Once Ruben approved everything, Stan figured he'd be up in running by the end of the week.

On Friday Ruben came in and signed all the documents and Stan faxed the entity formation documents to the Secretary of State. By Tuesday, December 21st, all the new entities had been approved and were ready to be set up and put in operation. It was Ruben's plan to have each entity start on January 1, 2000, to simplify tax filings even though there could be chaos due to Y2K. On Wednesday Ruben and Roger came in for a final strategy session.

Roger, an immigrant from South Africa, had a charming British accent that all the girls loved, including Maria who always stopped what she was doing to talk to him whenever he visited. Roger had referred Stan a lot of business over the years and always came in with his clients to meet to be sure he understood and agreed with the estate plan being set up. He said he did it because he wanted to make sure proper consideration to the tax ramifications of the plan had been considered, and that the accounting would be done properly, which made sense to Stan.

"So, if the world's economies come to a screeching halt on Saturday and airplanes fall from the sky, none of this will make any difference," Ruben said half-jokingly.

Roger smiled. "Don't worry about any of that nonsense. That's media hype. The government and corporate America will never let that happen."

Stan shook his head. "Yeah. I haven't lost any sleep over it, nor should you, what you do need to worry about is the importance of respecting all these new entities and not to comingle each other's assets or cut corners for expediency. Each business has to stand on its own two feet and act in its own self-interest."

"Don't worry, Stan, I'll be supervising everything," Roger reminded him. "Ruben's got an actuary, too who will be getting quarterly reports."

Ruben smiled, "Yeah, these guys are worse than my ex-wife, always bitching about something."

They all laughed.

"Now. I also want to remind you of the Fraudulent Conveyances Act. Any assets we've been moving around to fund this new estate plan can still be attacked for four more years, if the creditor can prove you were trying to evade or avoid paying a lawful debt."

They both looked at Ruben. He shrugged. "I think all my bills are up to date for now, but I do think someone is following me."

Stan glanced at Roger then back to Ruben. "What! What makes you think that?"

Ruben took a deep breath. "It's probably nothing. Forget it."

"No. Tell us about it," Stan pressed.

"Well, there's been a silver car tailing me. I've seen it several times in my rearview mirror."

"What kind of car?" Stan asked.

"A late model Mercedes Benz, I think. It's hard to tell for sure from the rearview mirror, but I recognized the hood ornament. I owned a Mercedes once."

"Did you try and shake him to be sure he was following you?" Roger asked.

Ruben nodded. "Yes. I tried to lose him but couldn't. He finally followed me into a gas station."

"Did you confront him?" Stan asked.

"No. I just got the hell out of there and didn't look back. But when I got home my front door was ajar."

Roger and Stan didn't say anything. They just stared at Ruben trying to make sense of what he was saying. Finally, Stan asked. "Did you call the police?"

He shook his head. "Ah. No. I just closed the door, locked it, and went to a hotel. I didn't want to confront anyone who might be in there."

"Oh, my god!" Stan exclaimed. "You should have reported it to the police."

"No, the cops would just think I'm crazy."

Roger frowned. "No, they won't. People break into houses all the time."

"Did they take anything?" Stan asked.

Ruben shrugged. "I don't know. I haven't been back there yet."

Stan couldn't believe Ruben had been followed, his home invaded, and he hadn't done anything about it. A jolt of concern shot through him. He thought for a moment. "Roger, why don't we follow Ruben back to his house and check it out. I need to take pictures of his interior anyway to make an inventory for his living trust and to give to his insurance agent. "

"That sounds good," Roger said turning to Ruben. "How about it, Ruben? You want to give us the tour?"

"No. That's alright. Whoever was there is gone by now. I'm planning to go back there tomorrow to see if anything was stolen. It's possible I did leave the door open. Don't worry about it," Ruben said looking at his watch. "Oh, geez, I need to get to Arlington by 11:00 a.m. Thanks for getting all this set up for me."

Ruben stood abruptly and Roger and Stan followed his lead. Ruben gave them both a forced smile and walked out of Stan's office. After he was gone, Stan shook his head and asked, "So, do you think someone was following him?"

Roger laughed. "No. he's always been a little paranoid."

"A little paranoid? Do you think he might be illegal?"

"He is from Mexico. Maybe that's why he didn't want to call the police."

"Right. So, what else do you know about his past?" Stan asked.

"Well, his ex-wife took him to the cleaners and left him penniless about ten years ago. As a result, he doesn't trust anyone and is a bit secretive."

"So, why in the hell is he trusting me. If he dies tomorrow, I'll control everything."

"I don't know."

"What do you mean, you don't know? You referred him to me, right?"

"Not exactly. The last time he was in my office he asked about you. I told him you were a good guy and could be trusted, but he'd already had you under consideration for doing his estate plan."

"What?" Stan exclaimed, wracking his brain to remember if they'd met before.

"You must have crossed paths before, or one of your clients told him about you."

Roger left, leaving Stan a bit unsettled not knowing what was up with Ruben Acosta. A bad feeling had come over him and he didn't like it.

As Stan was contemplating the situation, Reggie walked in. Stan looked up expectantly.

"Hey, Dad. I'm going to interview the paramedic who accompanied Amanda and Julie on the Care Flite after their accident."

Stan grimaced. "I thought that case was dead. Didn't Amanda fall asleep at the wheel?"

"So, the police officer says, but how does he know?" Reggie responded.

"What about the stack of cards from all the personal injury firms in town?"

"Amanda has come out of a coma and wants me to handle the case."

"Really?" Stan asked. "Why you?"

"Ah, ... well, because none of those other firms want the case."

"Oh, Jesus! Come on Reggie. If they don't want it, it's a loser. You won't be able to collect anything but Amanda's insurance, which I imagine will be minimum limits."

"So, it will be something."

"What have you told Amanda? I hope you haven't promised her anything. She needs to realize there's not going to be a pot of gold at the end of the case."

Stan knew Reggie tended to be over-optimistic and imagine unrealistic outcomes. Stan sighed deeply. "Okay. I'll go with you, but I can't see this being a viable case."

"Well, let's just check it out for Amanda's sake."

Stan rolled his eyes. "Alright. Whatever."

After a thirty-minute drive north on Central Expressway, they were at McKinney National Airport in front of the Care Flite terminal. They went inside and walked up to the reception desk. A young lady in a blue and white uniform looked up. Reggie told her they were looking for Stuart Green.

"He's on his way in from a call. He should be here any minute."

They thanked her and took a seat in the waiting room. A few minutes later they heard a helicopter overhead and went to the window to see a red and white chopper with blue diagonal stripes land. A nurse and a paramedic lowered their heads as they walked to a side entrance to the terminal. The big blades slowly came to a halt and a few seconds later the engine shut down. A minute later, they turned and saw a paramedic walking toward them with a file in his hand.

"Hi. Mr. Turner?" he asked.

"Yes, I'm Reggie Turner and this is my dad, Stan."

They shook hands and Green directed them to a coffee room where they took a seat around a small table. Green poured himself a cup of coffee and asked if they wanted one. Stan took one and Reggie got a soda from a vending machine.

"So, how can I help you?" Green asked.

Reggie looked at Stan and then began, "So, I understand you were called to the scene of a head-on collision on Highway 383 near McKinney a couple weeks ago."

Green nodded, "Yes, that was a nasty accident. I've never seen such a devastating wreck. I'm surprised anybody survived."

"We represent," Reggie began, "I mean, we're thinking of representing Amanda Rich and her daughter and we wondered if you would tell us what you saw out there that afternoon."

"Well, sure. Of course, I didn't see the accident itself, but it was obvious that Ms. Rich's car went across the center line."

"How do you know that?" Reggie asked.

"Well, the two cars were directly in front of each other in the southbound lane. So, that made me think Amanda's car had gone across the center line into the lane for vehicles traveling South."

"But that's just your impression," Reggie argued. "They could have hit in the northbound lane and spun into the southbound lane."

"Possibly, Green admitted warily, "but I didn't see any tire tracks to support that theory."

Reggie's face dropped.

Stan asked, "Were there any witnesses at the scene that might have actually seen the accident?"

"Yes, there was a pickup truck following your client's car about a thousand yards behind. I have his name in the file. He's the one who called 911."

"Did you talk to him?" Reggie asked

"No, but I couldn't help but hear him talking to the police officer on the scene. He didn't see the accident, but he did see your client cross the center line earlier and thought she was either drunk or having trouble staying awake."

Reggie's face went pale. He turned to Stan with disappointment in his eyes. Stan took a deep breath and asked, "Was it windy that day? Maybe the wind made it difficult for her to stay in her lane."

Green thought a moment. "I can check our flite log."

He opened the file and flipped through some pages. "Ah, the wind speed was 12 mph which is a bit windy."

"Okay, anything else you can tell us?" Stan asked.

He shook his head. "No. But let me give you the name of that witness." He looked through the file and said, "Thomas Stillwater."

Green gave Stan Stillwater's contact information, and he forced a smile and stood up. "Thank you very much for talking with us."

Reggie just sat there in a daze. "Come on, Reggie, Mr. Green's got work to do, I'm sure."

They all shook hands, and Stan and Reggie left the terminal. On the way home, Stan felt bad because he knew how much Reggie had counted on this being a good case. He knew Reggie hated bankruptcy law and wanted to find something less tedious and more lucrative. The thought occurred to Stan that this case might be a good learning experience for him. It might make him more realistic in his future assessment of these type cases.

"Well, if you have your heart set on handling this case, I guess it couldn't hurt," Stan heard himself saying.

Reggie sat up and looked at Stan with a big grin. "Really?"

"Yeah. You know it's probably a loser, right?"

"Maybe," he conceded.

"Well, just promise me you won't go nuts and spend all your time on it. You will still need to handle your bankruptcy cases."

He nodded. "Sure, but if I get a bunch of PI cases can you find someone else to do that crap?"

Stan laughed. "Well, if that happens, sure, but you know how competitive the PI business is and don't think we have much money for advertising."

"You won't be sorry, Dad. I have a good feeling about this case."

Stan laughed. "I don't know why. I haven't seen anything positive so far."

Reggie just kept grinning at Stan as they drove south on Central Expressway. When they walked into their offices, Maria stood up with concern in her eyes.

"What?" Stan asked.

"You know the driver of the car Amanda hit?"

"Yeah," Reggie asked. "Dr. Kenneth Short, M.D. What about him?"

"He just died."

"How do you know?" Stan asked.

"Reggie's friend Josh just called. He saw it on the news."

Stan turned to Reggie. His eyes had glazed over. Stan put his arm around him and guided him to his office. Stan could see his mind was racing to understand the implications of this news. Reggie just stared out the window. They sat there in silence until Paula walked in.

"I heard the news," Paula said. "Do you think they might charge Amanda with negligent homicide?"

Reggie whirled around and spat, "No! That can't happen! It wasn't her fault for god's sake. She's the victim here. Come on!"

4
Negligent Homicide

Paula

Reggie's fixation on money and the law being his ticket to wealth amused Paula. If only Stan had thought the same way when they first started the firm, she was sure they would both have a lot more money in the bank. That was for sure. Paula liked Reggie and supported his idea that the firm branch out into personal injury.

Jodie had been keeping Paula abreast of the Amanda Rich case and she was disappointed it hadn't been going well. When Maria told Paula about Josh's call, she immediately reached out to one of her contacts at the Collin County DA's office to see if it was on their radar. She was a firm believer in cutting off potential problems before they got a head of steam.

Paula's husband Bart had worked there at the DA's office for a while and she'd defended plenty of defendants in the Collin County courts over the years, so she'd developed many valuable friendships herself. Wendy Pierce, a legal secretary there who she'd once helped beat a DUI charge, confirmed that a file had been made and turned over to one of the prosecutors for review. She indicated the file was sparse for the moment but that there was an inventory of Amanda's purse taken from the accident scene and it showed she was carrying open bottles of valerian root, Tylenol, and Xanax.

In doing some online research on these drugs, one common side effect was drowsiness. Paula wondered if Amanda had fallen asleep at the wheel and drifted into oncoming traffic. If that was true, the District Attorney might consider filing involuntary manslaughter charges against her. But the most important concern now was that Amanda might say something incriminating to her doctor, the nurses, family, or the police if the DA sent a detective to interview her.

After making this concern known to Reggie and Stan, they all went into the conference room to talk about it. Jodie sat in as well, because whenever there were criminal charges brought against someone a civil suit often followed. If that happened, Jodie was the firm's civil litigation attorney.

"You seriously think Amanda might be arrested?" Reggie asked.

Paula nodded and told them about the drugs found in her purse. "So, it's a definite possibility, something we need to warn her about."

"She's not our client," Stan reminded them.

"Dad," Reggie exclaimed. "You said we could represent her."

"I know, but things have changed now. She may be charged with manslaughter and there's bound to be lawsuits."

"She has insurance for the lawsuits, doesn't she?" Paula asked.

Stan shrugged. "I don't know what she has. Do you, Reggie?"

Reggie's looked down and replied, "No. I haven't even talked to her yet and the police report isn't due out for several days."

"Anyway," Stan continued. "She has no way of paying our fees. I could live with you taking on a personal injury case, but not defending her criminal case pro bono, too."

Reggie didn't say anything. Paula thought a moment. "You know, if she is charged, I could volunteer to be her court-appointed attorney. Judges usually have trouble finding attorneys willing to take on court appointments. I shouldn't have a problem getting appointed to her case.

Stan gave Paula a hard stare. "Well, if you can pull that off, fine. But she better have liability insurance because we can't afford to be defending her civil case pro bono."

"Let's just cross one bridge at a time," Paula suggested.

"Okay," Stan said. "Paula, you and Reggie go see Amanda and warn her about the possible criminal charges and see what she remembers about the accident. Get her to sign a contingent fee agreement while you're there, in case we get lucky and find someone to sue."

"She's expecting me this afternoon," Reggie said, so if Paula is free we can go then."

Paula nodded. "I'm available. I had a hearing this afternoon, but I just got a notice it was reset."

That afternoon Reggie and Paula drove to the hospital in McKinney and went to Julie's room. She was now sharing the room with Amanda after she had been released from ICU. Paula was glad to see Josh and Stella there as well, as that would save them a lot of interview time. Paula winced when she saw Amanda. Her head was bandaged such that you could only see her eyes. One leg was in a long caste and elevated. She had an IV running, a plastic tube providing her oxygen, and quite a few monitors keeping track of her vitals. Looking around the room, Paula noticed at least a dozen floral bouquets from well-wishers adorning the room. After they all introduced themselves, Paula began asking questions.

"Amanda. Why don't you start by telling us what you remember about the day of the accident," Paula suggested.

Amanda nodded, "Okay. Well, it was Friday morning. I'd worked the night shift and was getting ready to go home when my supervisor, Gus Gibson, found me and asked if I'd work a double shift. Someone had called in sick and they needed to fill a spot on the assembly line."

"A double shift?" Paula asked. "Do you do that often?"

"No. But I needed to keep my job. It took me a long time to find it, so I was afraid to turn them down."

"Who is your employer?" Reggie asked.

"Southern Battery Company. I work in their plant in McKinney. I have been with them for about a year."

"Okay, go on," Paula said.

"So, I agreed and after a 30-minute break, I went back on the assembly line. I was exhausted, so I took a nap at lunch rather than eating. During the afternoon I was very tired but struggled through the day as best I could. After the shift was over, I went to the break room to eat something and get a cup of coffee to help me stay awake on the drive home."

"Do, you usually go to the break room after your shift?" Stan asked.

Amanda shook her head. "No, but I had a little time before I had to pick up Julie from daycare and I was hungry and sleepy, so that's what I did."

"Right," Stan said. "So, after you went to the break room you drove to Julie's daycare?"

"Yes, but I made a stop at Walgreen's on the way. I had a prescription to pick up."

"What prescription?" Paula asked.

"Xanax, I have anxiety issues."

Josh sighed heavily. "Her ex-husband beat the shit out of her if he got up on the wrong side of the bed. When she tried to leave him, he stalked her and terrorized her," Josh explained. "He was an asshole."

"Yeah, I remember you telling me about that," Reggie added. "Didn't he kidnap Julie once?"

"Right, he violated their temporary orders and took her to his mother's house for Thanksgiving when it was Amanda's holiday."

"Not to mention, maxing out all my credit cards and getting us evicted from our home," Amanda added.

"If I'd have been there, I would have shot the bastard," Stella advised.

"No, you wouldn't have," Amanda spat, shaking her head. "He may be a bastard, but he's Julie's daddy!"

"Okay, we are getting off track here," Stan said.

"So, did anything happen at day care?" Stan asked. "You got Julie, okay?"

"Yeah, and we headed home on Highway 380 toward McKinney like we always do. It's about a twenty-minute drive but there was more traffic than usual cause it was a Friday night."

"It was still light out?" Paula asked.

"It was dusk, starting to get dark. I was a little tired and sleepy after the double shift, but I figured I only had to stay awake for half an hour. I'd done it a million times. We were about halfway home; I'd guess when I was blinded by headlights and ... well ... nothing after that until yesterday when they woke me up."

The room was quiet as everyone digested Amanda's limited memory of that fateful day. Reggie looked at Amanda sympathetically. Paula felt bad for Amanda. Like many women, Amanda had suffered at the hands of an irresponsible and abusive husband. She'd tried to make the best of it only to be knocked down again and again. Paula wondered if there was a chance in hell, they could help her. Now, it didn't seem promising.

Paula explained to Amanda, her mother, and Josh that there was a chance the DA might bring criminal charges against her and that she was not to talk to anyone.

"If anyone wants to talk to you or Julie," Paula said, "whether it's the police, the DA's office, or an insurance investigator, don't talk to them. Just give them my card and tell them to contact me."

Amanda choked up and tears welled in her eyes, "Okay. ... Did I do something wrong? I didn't mean to."

"No. You were just trying to take care of yourself and Julie. There's a good chance the DA won't do anything. Only if he thinks you were grossly negligent or reckless would he bring charges. I'm just trying to protect you."

"Don't worry, I won't let anyone talk to them," Stella advised. "Give me one of your cards."

As Paula was passing out her cards, the nurse came in and frowned, "What's going on in here? Only one visitor each at a time."

Paula stood. "It's okay, we're leaving. We're Amanda and Julie's attorneys."

"Well, visiting hours are over in five minutes. I need to give Amanda and Julie baths. You'll have to come back tomorrow."

Turning to leave Paula said, "Reggie. Don't forget to get the retainer agreement signed."

Reggie pulled the agreement out of his pocket and handed it to Josh. Josh looked at it and handed it to Amanda. "I've seen this already. Go ahead and sign it," Josh advised. "Should anything be recovered, you and Julie will get two-thirds, less costs, and Turner & Waters gets one-third. That's standard."

Amanda nodded and signed the contract. Reggie took it from her, put it in his pocket, and gave Paula a broad smile. Paula shook her head and couldn't help but smile back. After they'd said their goodbyes, Paula and Reggie left and Josh walked them to their car. He wanted an assessment of the case now that they had more facts.

"The PI case looks pretty grim right now," Reggie admitted, "but we don't have all the facts yet. We'll know about the insurance in a few days when the police report is released. Hopefully, the police report won't assess blame on Amanda. If that's the case, we will be able to negotiate a settlement with one or both of the insurance companies."

"We're going to need your help, Josh," Paula stressed. "This case doesn't warrant Turner & Waters fronting any investigation expense, so we are going to have to rely on you for that."

"Okay, but I have no experience as an investigator."

"You don't need any. We'll tell you what we want you to do. It will be a good experience for you. Keep track of your time and expenses and when we settle, we will make sure you get paid."

Josh nodded. "I will. Anything I should be doing right now?"

"Yes," Reggie replied. "We need to go to Southern Battery and update them on Amanda's condition. You can go to the HR department and tell them she intends to come back to work as soon as she is able. While you are there find out about her medical and disability insurance. Get her agent's name and pick up any forms we need to submit to them. While you are doing that, I'll snoop around and try to find out who was working with Amanda that Friday. They may know something."

"Okay, I've got a job interview in the morning, but I can meet you there tomorrow afternoon," Josh said.

After Josh had left, Paula said, "While we are here, we should make arrangements to talk to Amanda and Julie's doctor and get his prognosis for both of them. You're going to have to document her injuries and provide proof of her damages. You'll need a few expert trial witnesses. The doctor might know someone."

"Right," Reggie agreed. "I've got a call into Amanda's primary care physician too. She needs to explain the meds Amanda was taking."

Amanda's treating physician wasn't available until the next morning, so they left and went back to the office. When they got there Jodie was waiting and she didn't look happy.

"What's wrong," Reggie asked.

"The police report came in. Both insurance policies had minimum limits, $10,000/$20,000 with $2,500 PIP."

"Oh, crap!" Reggie exclaimed.

"That's not the worst news. The police officer cited Amanda for crossing the median and driving on the wrong side of the road. He determined that the accident was entirely her fault."

"Damn it!" Reggie screamed. "He didn't see the accident. How can he decide who was at fault?"

"He listed a witness," Jodie advised. "A Martin Gallagher. So, Mr. Gallagher must have told him something that made him decide it was Amanda's fault."

Reggie shook his head. "I can't believe this."

Paula gave Reggie another sympathetic smile and said," Well, you're on your own now kid. I'll be in court tomorrow. Welcome to the practice of law! Good luck!"

Paula turned, walked away and didn't look back, not wanting to see the disappointment on Reggie's face.

5
Missing Person

Stan

Reggie's new personal injury case had distracted Stan, so he'd momentarily forgotten about Ruben Acosta and his home invasion. When he opened the mail, however, he was pleased to see a nice fat check from him for the legal services he had provided. Stan was impressed that the check was written on a brand-new checking account for the New Horizons Trust that would be the center of Ruben's estate plan. Normally it took clients weeks to get an account opened and get new checks printed.

To make it more difficult for creditors to trace an entity back to Ruben, he didn't use Ruben's name in any of the new entity filings. Stan listed himself as the registered agent and organizer of each and he listed Medical Management, LLC as the general partner of the limited partnership.

Since the last meeting, Ruben had been acting a bit bizarre with his story of an alleged man following him and the coincidental break-in at his home, Stan picked up the phone and dialed Ruben's number hoping to follow up on that situation and make sure everything was okay. After a few rings, Ruben's voicemail picked up and allowed Stan to leave a message. He did that and then called Roger Moore to see if he had followed up with Ruben.

Roger's secretary put him through. "Hey, Ruben Acosta is a good man. I just got a big check from him. Thank you for referring him to me."

"No problem," Roger replied. "He always pays his bills the moment they come in. He can't stand owing anybody money. I have told him it might improve his cash flow if he waited a week or two to make payment, but that would drive him nuts."

"So, did he have any problems when he went back to his house after the break-in?" Stan asked.

"I don't know. I haven't talked to him since then which is unusual. We usually talk almost daily. In fact, I have several calls into him, but he hasn't called me back."

"That's odd. It's been nearly two weeks. He's apparently hard at work since he's already got his living trust all set up and checks printed."

"Let's call his actuary, Tom Rice," Roger said. "They office together."

The line went dead for a moment while Roger conferenced in Tom Rice."

"You on, Tom?" Roger asked.

"Yeah, what's up," Tom replied.

"I've got Stan Turner on the line. We're looking for Ruben. Any idea where he might be?"

"I haven't seen him for a while, but that's not unusual," Tom admitted. "As you know, he travels a lot to Phoenix and Las Vegas. MedNet has clients in both cities. He owns rental properties there, too, and he keeps one vacant, so he'll have a place to stay while he is in town."

"Well, in those markets residential property is a good investment. I guess it makes sense to invest there rather than throwing money away on a lease," Roger mused. "If he calls you, have him call me or Stan. We need to follow up on a few things."

Tom said he would and dropped off the call. Stan told Roger to call him immediately if he heard from Ruben. Roger agreed and disconnected. Several more days went by and Stan still hadn't heard from Ruben nor had any of the MedNet clients in Phoenix and Las Vegas, so Stan decided to go by Ruben's home in North Dallas to see if he had returned. Since the circumstances were a bit unusual, he took Jodie with him as a backup.

Ruben lived in an upscale neighborhood off Hillcrest Avenue. When they got there and turned down his street, Stan was impressed by the large front yards and big trees. Where Stan lived, the lots were much smaller and the homes closer together. It was an unfortunate trend as the Metroplex grew and raw land soared in value. He'd slowed down to look for the street number they were looking for when he noticed a garage door open.

"Is that his house, Jodie," Stan asked.

She looked down on her legal pad at the address she had written down before they'd left. "Yes, that's it."

They parked on the curb in front of his house beneath a big oak tree and walked down the driveway to the open garage.

"Hello! ... Hello! ... Ruben! Anybody here?" Stan yelled. There was no response, so he took a few steps inside the garage and looked around. There were no cars, only a tool bench, garden equipment, a few sacks of fertilizer, and a pile of cardboard boxes.

He knocked on the door that led from the garage to the interior of the house, but there was no answer.

"Knock on the front door, Jodie," Stan said. "I'll wait here."

A few moments later, Jodie returned shaking her head. "No response. He must be close by if he left the garage door open."

"No car, though," Stan noted.

"Maybe he went to the store," Jodie suggested.

Stan took a deep, frustrated breath, perplexed at the situation. "Let's check with his neighbors. Maybe someone has seen him today."

Jodie went to the house across the street while Stan went to the house next door to the west. No one answered when Stan knocked but Jodie had better luck. The neighbor across the street answered the door and she told Jodie that Ruben hadn't been there for over a week and his garage door had been open the entire time. She told Jodie it wasn't unusual for Ruben to be gone for long periods, but this was the first time he'd left his garage door open.

"Let's see if any doors are unlocked," Stan said. "If so, we can check inside to be sure he's not home."

"Is that wise?" Jodie asked.

"Sure. I'm his attorney and I'm concerned about his well-being, particularly since his garage door has been open for several days. We'll have his neighbor come with us as another witness."

Jodie nodded and went across the street to get the neighbor. She introduced herself as Shirley Jones. They all went to the front of his house. Stan rang the doorbell and knocked a few times, then he tried the door. It was locked, so they went to the door inside the garage. It opened right up, so they went in.

As they entered, a TV or radio could be heard in the distance. They went by a utility room where a washer, dryer, and stainless-steel sink could be seen through an opened door. A pile of dirty clothes in a basket sat in front of the dryer. A few feet later they entered the kitchen. Directly ahead was a kitchen table and to the right an island in between the sink, dishwasher, and microwave. The area was clean and tidy but there was an odd smell in the air.

"Ruben!" Stan yelled. "You home?"

There was no answer, so they continued into the family room where they discovered a big screen TV playing. Stan found the remote on a square oak coffee table and shut off the TV. Next to the remote sat an open laptop with a blank screen and a cup half full of what looked like tea. A pair of black dress shoes had been removed and tossed to one side.

"What's that smell?" Jodie asked.

Shirley took a few sniffs and went looking for its source. She went down a hallway and disappeared. A few moments later, she let out a horrible scream, "Ahhh! Oh, my god! Midas."

They all rushed toward the noise. Shirly was standing in front of an open door leading into a small bathroom. The odd smell intensified as they approached it. On the floor was a dead cat with yellowish-brown fur that looked almost golden.

Stan winced. "Oh, geez. Was it locked in the bathroom?

"No," Shirley said. "The door was open. I guess it had been drinking from the toilet bowl but there was no food. How long can a cat last without food?"

"A few days. Maybe a week," Jodie surmised.

"I would have taken care of Midas had Ruben asked," Shirley said. "I've done it before."

Stan shook his head. "Poor Midas. This doesn't make much sense."

"No, it doesn't," Shirley agreed. "Ruben loved that cat. He wouldn't have left it without food."

"Okay, let's split up and search the rest of the house. Ruben may be in here somewhere."

Jodie nodded and bounded up a spiral staircase. Stan searched the rest of the downstairs but didn't find anything unusual until he got to Ruben's home office. It was in shambles like he'd been looking for something in a hurry, found it, and ran off. Stan was about to start snooping around Ruben's desk and files when he started feeling guilty. Maybe they were overreacting, he thought. So, he decided to postpone the search.

As he was leaving Ruben's office, Jodie was coming down the stairs. "Anything up there?"

"No. Just a few guest rooms. Did he live alone?"

"I think so," Stan replied. "He mentioned an ex-wife."

"Right," Shirley said. "It was a Las Vegas marriage. I don't think it lasted six months."

"Did they have children?" Jodie asked.

"No. She had her career as a showgirl and Ruben was a workaholic. Kids were never on the radar."

"Okay, Let's lock the place up," Stan said. "We can call the police in the morning and report Ruben missing."

"If you lock up and Ruben doesn't come back, how will you get back into the house?" Jodie asked.

Stan considered this. "Okay, hope for the best, but prepare for the worst. Right." Then he remembered seeing a pile of keys on Ruben's desk and went to get them. After trying all of the keys on the front door, he found one that worked and took it from the key ring."

"Thank you, Shirley. You've been a big help."

Shirley nodded somberly. "What about Midas?"

I looked at her and asked. "Should we bury him?"

Jodie shook her head "No. If Ruben is okay, he may want to have a funeral for Midas."

"Yes," Shirley agreed. "I'll put him in a plastic bag and put it in the refrigerator.

Stan cringed at the thought but shrugged. "Okay. That should work."

On the way home Jodie and Stan speculated on what might have happened to Ruben and what they should do about it. Ordinarily, it wouldn't have been Stan's problem, but Ruben had given him power of attorney and appointed him the alternate trustee of his living trust which controlled all his assets. If Ruben was incapacitated or otherwise unable to handle his affairs, it would be Stan's duty to step in and take over his financial affairs as his attorney. If he had died or failed to act as the trustee, it would be his duty to step up as successor trustee and manage the trust in accordance with its terms.

"So, what do you think happened?" Jodie asked. "Was he kidnapped; you think?"

Stan shrugged. "It's possible. He did think someone was following him. But his car is missing, so that suggests he drove off somewhere on his own. If he got a call about a dying relative or something, he might have been distracted and concerned enough to drive off without thinking of locking up the house or getting someone to watch Midas."

"But surely he would have called someone by now."

"You would think so," Stan agreed. "In the morning, I'll call Detective Besch. Maybe he can put an APB out on Ruben's car."

Jodie nodded, "He'll probably want you to file a missing person's report?"

"Maybe. Maybe not. If he does, that's what we will do. Then I'll have to meet with Roger and Tom over the weekend to figure out what to do about his businesses until we find him."

When they got back to the office, Stan let Jodie off and then drove home to Plano. It had been a warm December so far but during the day a cold front came through and the temperature plummeted. By the time he got home, it had started to snow.

The house was empty, quiet, and dark as he pushed open the door from the garage into the house. Memories of Rebekah and his young children enthusiastically meeting him at the door and the aroma of dinner cooking on the stove drifted through his mind. The kids had grown up and Rebekah had died the previous year after a long battle with cancer, so now Stan was alone. He probably should have moved to a smaller house, but he loved this one and couldn't imagine living any place else.

The quiet solitude didn't bother him. In fact, it allowed him to relax, contemplate the day's events and develop a strategy for tackling whatever challenges were facing him. Today he had two things on his mind, Amanda Rich and Ruben Acosta. Both of them had Stan worried because each case had the potential of spinning out of control and overwhelming the firm.

Reggie had no understanding or appreciation for the amount of cash it took each month to keep the firm running. Now with his joining the firm, the situation was only going to get worse. The bankruptcy practice that he so loathed provided over fifty percent of the firm's revenue, so it couldn't be neglected. In fact, without that steady stream of income, the firm couldn't survive.

That night Stan couldn't sleep. He kept wondering what had happened to Ruben and what they would do if he didn't show up soon. He cursed his weakness in letting Ruben talk him into accepting an appointment as his attorney-in-fact and trustee. Why did I do that? Damn it! How can I run a law firm and manage Ruben's complex affairs at the same time?

As soon as Stan got to the office the next morning, he called Detective Bingo Besch of the Dallas Police Department. He had worked with Besch on several cases in the past and they were good friends. He dialed his number.

"Detective Besch," he said evenly.

"Bingo. This is Stan. How are you?"

"Stan the man. I'm fine. What have you been up to?"

"Just the usual. Trying to keep my clients out of trouble?"

"Any luck with that?" he chuckled.

"No. That's why I'm calling. One of my clients has gone missing."

Stan explained the situation with Ruben Acosta to Detective Besch and asked him if he could put out an APB on his vehicle.

"Sure, I'll do that right away. It's been long enough you should probably come in and file a missing person's report."

"Okay," Stan said.

"I'll reach out to the police in Phoenix and Las Vegas and have them go by his homes and offices there. He probably didn't drive, so I'll check the airlines to see if he bought any tickets anywhere. His car may be in the Love Field parking garage or out at DFW."

Besch was always very enthusiastic, thorough, and aggressive. Once he committed to a task, he would give it a hundred and ten percent. "Thank you. If we don't find him soon, I'll have to start operating his businesses. Luckily, he gave me a power of attorney."

"He did? That's a little unusual, isn't it?" Besch asked.

"Yeah, it is."

"Maybe his disappearance was planned," Besch suggested.

Stan didn't know how to respond. That thought hadn't occurred to him, but he could see Besch's reasoning. If Acosta knew something was about to happen and he would be out of the picture for a while, he'd set up a mechanism to deal with his sudden disappearance. But why wouldn't he tell him, Stan wondered. And was Stan to be a temporary manager, or was Ruben gone for good?

"I don't know," Stan finally replied. "All I do know is that the last thing I want to do is manage MedNet."

"MedNet?" Besch repeated.

He explained his business operation briefly stressing that it required travel since it operated in three states.

"Right. That would be quite a task. So, how's Paula and Jodie?" Besch asked. "I haven't talked to them in ages."

"Yeah, they're both fine. Why don't you stop by, and we can all catch up."

"I might do that," Besch replied. "Let me get started looking into your missing client and when I have some news, we'll all get together."

"Sounds good," Stan replied. "I'll have Ruben's actuary, Tom Rice, come see you to fill out the missing person's report. He offices in the same office suites with Ruben, and will know much more about him than I do."

"Good. Tell him to ask for me when he comes in."

After Stan called Tom Rice and asked him to file a missing person's report, he decided to go back to Ruben's house and search his office. He figured there might be some clues as to his whereabouts there, plus he needed to get a handle on his business operations in case he had to take over. When Stan told Jodie his plans, she insisted on bringing a gun.

Several years earlier, Jodie had been doing some undercover work on a wrongful death case and had been abducted by members of a drug cartel. She was held hostage for a while but managed to escape. Ever since then she'd taken personal security very seriously. After her rescue, she'd spent six months in a rigorous self-defense training program that included many hours at the gun range. Considering Ruben's sudden disappearance, Stan didn't object.

When they arrived at Ruben's house, Stan sent Jodie across the street to check in with Shirley Jones, so she didn't think someone was breaking into Ruben's house. Then he got the mail out of Ruben's mailbox and took it into Ruben's office. The office was a mess, so he cleared a spot and dropped the stack of mail there. Most of it was junk mail but there was a brokerage statement from Fisher Investments for New Horizons Trust and a letter from the City of Dallas. Stan opened the letter from the City of Dallas advising Ruben that they had impounded his automobile and were holding it at the Dallas Impound Yard. The notice didn't reveal anything about the circumstances for the city to have picked up his car, but at least they knew now that Ruben wasn't driving it.

The second letter was even more intriguing. It seemed Ruben had opened a new brokerage account for the New Horizons Trust and made initial deposits of over two million dollars! That blew Stan's mind because he hadn't seen those kinds of numbers on any of Ruben's financial statements that he'd examined.

As he was digesting this new information, Stan heard the front door open and heavy footsteps coming down the hallway. At first, he thought it was Jodie, but the person coming down the hall had to be much heavier. Fear shot through him like an arrow from a crossbow. He didn't know if he should run, hide, or find a weapon to defend himself. Then, suddenly, Ruben Acosta appeared in the doorway, and he didn't look pleased to see Stan.

"What the fuck are you doing in my house?" he spat.

"Ruben! Oh, my God. You're here."

"Yes, obviously. What in hell are you doing here?"

"Ah, well. I've been trying to figure out what happened to you. Where have you been? Everyone's been looking for you."

Ruben shook his head in disgust. "What do you mean? I took a little vacation. I can't believe you broke into my house."

"Ah. We didn't break in exactly. You left the garage door open, and the side door unlocked. We secured the place, but I took your extra key in case you didn't show up."

Ruben took a deep breath and eyed Stan warily. "Well, I guess I did leave in a hurry and wasn't thinking too clearly."

"I guess not. You forgot about Midas."

"Midas? Where's Midas?"

"I'm afraid he's dead. We found him in the bathroom."

Ruben was visually shaken. "Oh, fuck! Damn it. Where is he? I can't believe I forgot about him. Those bastards are going to pay! They have made my life a living hell."

"What bastards?" Stan asked.

Ruben squinted and rubbed his forehead like he had a splitting headache. "It's a long story?"

Suddenly, they heard a car screeching to a stop in front of Ruben's house. Ruben's face turned grim. He whirled around and ran down the hall and locked the door.

"Fuck! How did they know I was back?"

"Who is it?" Stan asked.

Car doors opened and shut, and they heard a man barking orders. Ruben looked at me and spat, "You've got to get out of here. Go out the back door. Take the alley. Go right. Run as fast as you can and hide."

"What about you?" Stan protested.

Ruben went around his desk and pulled a revolver out of the bottom drawer. "This isn't your fight! Get the fuck out of here!" Ruben demanded as someone kicked the front door hard. Stan jumped at the sound, then turned toward the back door to flee as instructed just as there was a shotgun blast that blew the front door open.

Ruben shot at the men coming through the open door as Stan escaped into the kitchen and took cover. He couldn't see what was happening, but he heard a muffled scream from Ruben like he'd taken a bullet. Stan wanted to go to his aid but being unarmed he knew he could do him no good.

Hearing a stampede of men rushing down the hall, Stan retreated farther into the kitchen to avoid detection. He heard footsteps as someone came into the kitchen. He held his breath and pressed himself behind the center island.

Suddenly, more gunfire erupted. The man retreated from the kitchen to join the others just outside the front door. Stan ducked down to avoid the bullets that were flying everywhere until the shooting stopped. Hearing screeching tires, Stan rushed over to Ruben. He was struggling to breathe but still alive.

"Stan," he moaned. "Take care of my family! Please, don't let them find them."

"What family? Who's after you?" Stan pressed. "You didn't say you had a family."

"Tell them I love them," Ruben whispered.

Ruben's eyes became fixed. Stan checked for a pulse. Feeling nothing and sure that Ruben was dead, he rushed to the front door worried about Jodie after all the gunfire. As he rushed out of the house, he saw Jodie standing in the driveway across the street with her gun pointed at the escaping vehicle. He rushed over to her. "Are you okay?"

"I'm fine," she said giving him a once-over. "How about you?"

"I'm okay, I guess, but I think Ruben is dead. He doesn't have a pulse."

"Shit!' Jodie said. "I heard the shooting and came outside immediately. I saw them trying to kick down the door and then unload the shotgun on it, so I opened fire on them. They returned the fire, so I had to take cover behind Shirley's car until they left. I didn't take any more shots in case Ruben was in the car."

"Damn it!" Stan said. "Ruben was about to tell me what was going on. If I'd had another five minutes, I might have been able to make sense of all this."

Jodie took a deep breath and then let it out slowly. "I think I might have got one of the bastards," she said. "He fell down and then limped around the car. I couldn't tell for sure."

"I hope not," Stan said. "You don't need an angry thug like that looking for revenge."

"He better not try anything," Jodie spat. "The next time I'll kill him."

"Right," Stan replied. "Ah. We better call the police."

"I'm sure Shirley's already done that. The poor lady. Her car is full of lead."

As Jodie was checking on Shirley Jones, Stan sprinted into the house. The door had been shattered and was hanging by one hinge. Inside, the walls were full of bullet holes, the floor littered with gun casings, and the harsh scent of gun powder lingered in the air. Sirens could be heard in the distance.

A moment later, Jodie and Shirley rushed in and took in the scene. We all just stared at Ruben's lifeless body, too traumatized to move. Stan thought about Ruben's last words. "Before he died, Ruben asked me to take care of his family."

"What?" Jodie said. "He had a family?"

"I didn't think so. He didn't tell me about a wife or children, but maybe he didn't want anyone to know about them."

"He never mentioned children to me," Shirley confirmed, "but I wondered about that because I have seen bags of toys and games at his house that he must have bought as gifts. I figured they must be for nephews and nieces or friend's children."

"So, who were those guys?" Shirley asked.

"I don't know. I didn't see them up close. I was too busy trying to dodge bullets. Ruben tried to protect me and, in the process, got himself killed."

"They were Hispanic males, six of them," Jodie recalled. "Probably from a gang or members of a cartel."

Stan nodded. "That would be my guess, too."

Twenty minutes later, Ruben's place was filled with police and crime scene personnel. Jodie, Shirley Jones, and Stan waited in an upstairs bedroom until Detective Besch showed up.

"So, you found your client?" Besch noted.

"Yeah, but I only had a two-minute conversation with him before he was murdered."

"Damn. That's all?" Besch asked.

"I'm afraid so," Stan lamented and then filled him in on what had happened. Besch listened with great interest and concern and then shook his head "So, are you two, okay?"

"Yeah," Stan replied. "Luckily, Jodie brought her gun and let them have a taste of their own medicine."

Besch grinned and looked over at Jodie. "So, all that time at the gun range paid off."

Jodie smiled, "You bet. I think I nailed one of the bastards."

Besch nodded. "You must have. There was a pool of blood in the driveway. Maybe the crime lab will find a DNA match when they test it. That would answer a lot of questions."

"I saw the asshole's face right after he took the bullet," Jodie explained. "He glared at me angrily before he got in their car. I was across the street, but I think I might recognize him if I saw him again."

"Good. You can go through some mug shots back at the station."

An hour later Besch let them leave the crime scene with promises they'd come in the next morning and give statements. Stan told Besch he needed some time in Ruben's office to sort through his affairs. Besch said everything would be boxed up and Stan could look at all of it at the station.

The Fisher Investment statement and letter from the city impound lot were still in Stan's pocket. He decided to forget he had them for now and give them to Besch later after he had time to check them out. It didn't make sense to give him the only lead Stan had now to try to figure out what he'd be up against as he assumed his duties as trustee. There was one thing he did know. He was going to have to start joining Jodie at the gun range if he expected to survive very long as trustee.

6
Southern Battery

Reggie

Reggie had been a history major in college and loved to read about the great empires of the world and the rulers who created them. From all his studies he believed the key to winning was preparation and an unwillingness to accept defeat. And as far as Reggie was concerned losing was never an option and the fear of failure nearly drove him crazy.

He was convinced that winners would always obtain wealth and power as a natural byproduct of their success. As a result, in college, law school, and life in general he became obsessed with preparing for the next challenge that he faced, and he'd never rest unless he was sure he couldn't be beaten.

In law school, he'd not only read all the cases assigned by the professors but also many of the cases cited in the opinions. In class, if one of his professors asked him a question, Reggie would not only answer the question but also provide a complete analysis of the decision including both the majority and dissenting opinions. This, of course, didn't make him very popular with his classmates as they were forced to work much harder due to Reggie's overachieving.

So, Reggie wasn't ready to give up on the Amanda Rich case even as it seemed to be unraveling before his eyes. He knew he wasn't even close to having enough facts to evaluate the case properly. There was lots of work to be done and he knew he'd have to do all of it himself as his father, Paula, and Jodie were currently overwhelmed with the Ruben Acosta murder and trying to untangle his affairs.

So, Reggie was optimistic as he and Josh drove out to see Gus Gibson at the Southern Battery plant in McKinney. It was in an industrial park south of downtown near the airport. Reggie drove into the front parking lot and they both got out and surveyed the layout.

It was a large rectangular building with one main entryway into the company offices in the center of the building. To the right, there was a double driveway that led along the side of the building into a chain-link enclosed yard about twice the size of the building itself. A sign advised that the loading dock was in the back and all drivers should check in with the yard manager before loading or unloading. Reggie and Josh entered the building through the front door. Inside they found the place decorated for Christmas and carols being played over the intercom system. After looking around, they spotted a directory, walked up, and studied it.

"Okay, you go to the HR department," Reggie said. "I'm going to snoop around."

Josh nodded and walked off. Reggie looked left and then right. Noticing a sign down the hallway that read Cafeteria, he headed in that direction. He stopped when he got to the door, pulled it open, and peered inside. A dozen or so employees were sitting around six picnic tables, some enjoying a quick breakfast and others coffee or a cup of tea. Two cafeteria workers were hard at work filling orders and cleaning up.

Reggie went over to the large coffee maker and poured himself a cup of coffee. He looked around and saw two women sitting across from each other talking and laughing. One had red hair and freckles and the other was a brunette with olive skin. He decided to join them. As he sat down, he nodded.

"Hi," I'm Reggie.

The two ladies stopped talking and looked up at him warily. Finally, the redhead smiled and said, "Hi. I'm Sarah." She nodded toward the brunette and said, "This is Ruth."

Reggie smiled and replied, "Nice to meet you. Is the food any good on this shift?"

Ruth rolled her eyes, "No. It's barely edible no matter what shift you work."

"Do either of you know Amanda Rich? She usually works the night shift, but sometimes she's here during the day on a double shift."

"I know who she is," Sarah admitted. "But we've never talked. They don't give you much time for socializing around here."

"Was she the one in the terrible accident the other day?" Ruth asked.

Reggie nodded. "Yes, that's why I'm here. I'm her attorney and I'm looking for witnesses. Were either of you working on December 2nd?"

Ruth looked at Sarah and then replied, "Yes, we both were."

"Did you happen to see Amanda? She was working a double shift."

"Those are brutal," Sarah said shaking her head. "But it's worth it if they pay you time and a half. Unfortunately, more times than not, they give you a shift off to compensate and avoid overtime. I hate when they do that."

"Yes, Gibson is a tightwad," Ruth agreed. "He doesn't give a shit about us girls."

Reggie thought for a moment wondering what his new friends might know that would help Amanda. Their opinion of Gus Gibson and Southern Battery wasn't much help. "So, where on the assembly line do you two work?"

"We seal the plastic bags full of battery acid after they are filled," Ruth replied. "It's a nasty job. The acid gets on your clothes, and they immediately start to disintegrate. Sometimes my blue jeans literally disappear by the time I get home."

"What? You've got to be kidding?" Reggie chuckled. "That's unbelievable. Does it hurt your skin?"

"Sure, but what really hurts is when it gets in your eyes. We're supposed to wear goggles, but sometimes they get fogged up and you must take them off to clean them. That's when it usually happens," Ruth advised. "I had to go to the emergency room once."

"Was Amanda doing the same job that day?" Reggie asked.

Ruth shook her head. "No. She was putting the plastic bags in boxes after we sealed them, stacking them on carts, and then taking them into the warehouse."

"Was she exposed to the battery acid, too?"

"Not as much, but that stuff hangs in the air. Everybody is breathing it in," Ruth replied.

"They don't make the assembly line workers wear masks?"

"No," Ruth said. "If you want to you can, but it's not mandatory."

"Did either of you see Amanda at lunch break or after your shift?"

"Now that you mention it," Sarah replied thoughtfully, "I saw Amanda asleep on the sofa in the ladies' room at lunch. I figured she must be working a double shift. I've done the same thing a time or two."

"Did either of you see Amanda talking to anyone that day? Did she have any friends she hung out with?"

Sarah looked at Ruth and shook her head, "No. It wasn't her usual shift, so I doubt she knew anybody."

Reggie thanked the girls and left the cafeteria. He thought maybe someone in the yard might have seen something. When he stepped out the back door, he saw a small metal building with a sign that indicated it was the yard manager's office. He decided to check it out.

A tall blond man in blue jeans and a T-shirt stood behind the counter. A nameplate indicated his name was Tony Smallwood. He looked up as he came in. "Hello. What can I do for you?"

Reggie introduced himself and explained he was waiting for his friend, Josh, who was the brother of one of their employees.

"Yeah, He's trying to figure out what health insurance coverage Amanda had. Her auto insurance only had $5,000 coverage and her bills were going to be over $100,000."

"Wow! That sucks. If she's got the same plan as I do, it's got a $50,000 maximum benefit. What about the other driver?"

"The police claim it was her fault, so her PIP and what she's got here is about it."

He frowned sympathetically. "So, what happened?"

Reggie explained the events of the day including the double shift, her exhaustion, and the police officer's suspicion that she fell asleep at the wheel. He told her about Julie and how she had been injured as well.

"The poor kid," he said. "Is she going to be alright?"

"Physically, she'll recover but her life is going to be a train wreck if we can't recover some money from somebody. You didn't happen to see her on the day of the accident?"

He shook his head. "No, but she would have had to check in with Gus Gibson before her second shift started. That's required by our workman's compensation carrier. Too bad she wasn't injured on the job. Then she'd have all her bills paid plus get disability benefits."

Reggie sighed. "Unfortunately, she was on her way home and she was driving her own car, so I think we are out of luck on that score."

"Too bad," Tony replied. "You should talk to Gus anyway. He would have taken notes about how Amanda was feeling after her first shift. Part of his job is plant safety."

Reggie thanked Tony and went back inside. Josh was just coming out of the HR office, so he walked over to him.

"So, what did you find out?"

"Her medical insurance will kick in as secondary coverage once the PIP is paid, but there's not much there."

"Yeah, I talked to the yard manager and that's what he said. "We need to talk to Amanda's supervisor, Gus Gibson. Amanda had to go see him after her first shift."

"Okay. His office is down the hall. I saw his name on the door."

When they got to Gibson's office, they were told he was on vacation and wouldn't be back for several days. Reggie made a note to come back later and interview him. The trip back to the office was somber as both Reggie and Josh were depressed over what little progress they'd made on Amanda's case. They were both determined to help her through this tragedy but were clueless about how they were going to pull it off.

7
The Lawsuit

Stan

It was the day before Christmas which was a rare holiday for the firm, but since Stan's kids had grown up and left home and Rebekah was gone, Christmas was no longer important to him. Stan sat at his desk thinking back to how wonderful the Christmas season had always been. Rebekah had always hosted a Christmas party for their clients and friends. It was a great celebration to thank them for their support during the year. A lot of fond memories ran through Stan's mind as well as a few he wished he could forget. Like the unfortunate demise of his friend and accountant after he slipped on the ice in front of Stan's home causing him to have a heart attack.

He sighed. What was important now was the fact that Ruben Acosta had a family. That baffled him. He couldn't figure out why he hadn't told him about them while they were planning his estate. Normally, that is why estate planning is done; to help preserve the estate for the client's family, or in some instances, to make sure certain family members never got a dime from the estate.

After racking his brain, the only reason he could come up with for Ruben's secrecy would be if knowledge of his family's existence might put them at risk. He thought about that for a while and came up with a few possibilities.

Perhaps Ruben had two families and had to keep them both secret to prevent them from finding out about each other. Could his client be a bigamist, he wondered. Or, perhaps he'd had been through a bad divorce and wanted to forget he'd ever been married. It even occurred to him that he might have fathered children out of wedlock and didn't want a previous flame pounding on his door looking for child support. These were all plausible scenarios that would have to be investigated, he decided.

His first stop after leaving the crime scene the day before had been to the Dallas Police Impound Lot. He knew the personnel there would not talk to him about Ruben's car since he and Stan weren't related, so he brought his durable power of attorney. It wasn't technically effective anymore since Ruben was dead, but he wasn't planning on bringing that up.

The clerk looked the power attorney over skeptically, but after talking to a supervisor she pulled up the file on her computer and advised Stan that the vehicle had been left in a no-parking zone for over two hours, so it was tagged, picked up, and brought to the yard.

After paying $278.22 for the ticket and towing charges, Stan called Reggie and asked him if he wanted to pick up Ruben's car and drive it to the office. He wasn't initially thrilled with the ideas since he was home wrapping Christmas gifts with his girlfriend, but when Stan told him it was a 1999 Porsche 911 Carrera, he'd agreed happily and said he'd get Jodie to give him a ride to the impound lot.

Stan knew Jodie was still at the office as she was as much a workaholic as he was. Stan told Reggie to wear gloves and not to touch anything in the vehicle as there could be some evidence as to Ruben's activities on the day he was murdered. Reggie was usually reliable and could be trusted. Still, Stan wondered if Reggie would go straight back to the office from the impound lot or take a long detour. His money was on the detour. He just hoped Reggie wouldn't try to see if the 911 really could get up to 170 mph!

His next stop was the Farmers Market where the Porsche had been illegally parked and towed away. Trying to figure out why Ruben would be visiting the Farmers' Market, Stan walked around the neighborhood hoping that he'd see a place that would stick out as Ruben's obvious destination. After an hour and a half, nothing stood out, so he gave up. Thirty minutes later when Stan drove into the office parking garage, he saw Jodie and Reggie inspecting the Porsche.

"So, how does it drive?" Stan asked,

"Like a dream," Reggie said. "Why don't you take this as part of your fee and then you can give it to me."

Stan laughed. "No. I can't do that, but I can put you in charge of maintaining it until we sell it."

Reggie frowned but then smiled. "Okay. Sure, but a car like this is going to need a lot of attention."

Jodie and Stan laughed. "Did you touch anything?" Stan asked. "There could be important evidence inside."

Reggie shook his head. "No, and I wore gloves."

"That's a good point," Jodie remarked. "Shouldn't you have let the police search it before you picked it up?"

"Maybe, but I don't think this car played a role in Ruben's murder," Stan reasoned. "Ruben must have gotten a cab or someone else brought him home the day of the murder. My guess was he was in a hurry, parked illegally, and when he came back to get it, the Porsche was gone."

Jodie gave Stan a skeptical look but didn't press the issue. When Stan didn't reply, she turned and headed back upstairs to her office. After Reggie and Jodie were gone, Stan put on some gloves and thoroughly searched the Porsche. The only things he found of interest were a laptop computer and a heavily used Mapsco with many routes and destinations highlighted.

Stan took the fruits of the search upstairs, made a copy of parts of the Mapsco, and then tried to access the computer. Unfortunately, he didn't have Ruben's password. After a while, he shut down the laptop and made a mental note to be on the lookout for it when he searched through Ruben's financial records that had been seized by the DPD.

Later that night, Stan turned his attention to the Fisher Investments brokerage statement. Ruben had made quite a few check deposits and several electronic deposits totaling $2,111,672.22. Stan was still trying to wrap his head around the large amount of funds he'd managed to deposit in the account so quickly. He couldn't tell from the statement the source of the funds, so he would have to get that information later once he had control of the account. Frustrated, he tossed the statement aside wondering what to do next.

He thought about going to see Besch and going through the stuff the police took from Ruben's office but figured it being a holiday weekend, he'd have to wait until Monday. The phone startled him as Maria had forwarded all calls to him since he was the only one in the office.

"Turner & Waters," he recited.

"Hello, Mr. Turner."

"Yes, who is this?"

"Amanda."

"Hi, Amanda, Reggie's left the office."

"Oh. I'm so glad you are still there. A Deputy Constable Bell just served me with papers. I'm being sued for 1.2 million dollars!"

Sighing heavily, Stan tried to think of what he could say to ease Amanda's shock. "Listen, this was expected. Don't worry about it. We have almost three weeks to answer the lawsuit. Jodie will call you on Monday and you can bring her the papers. Don't let this mess up your Christmas."

"Okay. I'll try not to. Thank you so much for helping us."

"Well, that's our job. Merry Christmas!"

Amanda hung up and Stan shook his head knowing it would take a miracle to extricate Amanda Rich and her daughter from their December nightmare. He got up to bring the bad news to Jodie, but she'd gone. Merry Christmas! Jodie, he thought. Then he remembered, that if the doomsayers were right, the world would be in chaos in less than a week, so it didn't matter.

8
The Tornado

Jodie

Jodie was surprised to find Stan's note when she came in on Sunday. She often worked on the Sabbath to get a head start on the week's tasks. The note indicated that Amanda had been sued and that none other than PI attorney-legend Tom 'Tornado' Tyson was handling the case. Knowing that Amanda was probably beside herself with worry about the lawsuit and having to face the TV lawyer who promised to be an insurance company's worst nightmare, Jodie figured she'd probably not object to being called on a Sunday.

She dialed the number and waited.

"Hello," a weak voice replied.

"This is Jodie Marshall from Turner & Waters."

"Oh, I'm so glad you called. Did Stan tell you about the lawsuit?"

"Yes, he did. They're suing for a lot of money, I understand."

"Yes, over a million dollars!"

"Well, attorneys are always shooting high, particularly high-profile PI attorneys like Tom Tyson."

"I've seen him on TV," Amanda said worriedly. "He must be very good."

"Not necessarily. I knew him in high school. He's a bully and very intimidating, but he still has to prove his case like the rest of us. Anyway, your insurance carrier will have to initially defend you, but they may decide to cut their losses and tender their limits of $20,000 to the court, so we will have to take over your defense."

"I don't have any money. I won't be able to pay you," Amanda moaned.

"I know. We'll worry about that later. Hopefully, Reggie will find a way to recover some money for you. You can pay us from that."

"Okay," Amanda agreed.

"How's Julie doing?" Jodie asked.

"Better. She's up and about now. I just wish I could get out of this wheelchair."

"Yes. That couldn't be much fun."

"No. I hate it."

"Sorry, honey. Anyway, I'll need you to come in tomorrow morning and see me, okay?"

"I don't have a car. It's a total loss and I haven't got a replacement yet. I'm not sure I could drive anyway."

Jodie thought for a moment. "Oh, right. That's okay. I'll have Reggie come and get you."

"Oh, but that's so much trouble," Amanda protested.

Jodie didn't think it would be. She knew Reggie would love an excuse to drive the 911. "No. Reggie won't mind. It will give him an excuse to get out of the office. Besides, he can fill you in on his visit to Southern Battery."

"Oh. He went out there?" Amanda asked.

"He did. He'll tell you about it. I'll have him pick you up at 9 a.m., okay?"

"Okay," Amanda replied. "Thanks for calling."

Jodie leaned back in her chair wondering how they were going to defend Amanda. It seemed like a hopeless case as it appeared she had worked a double shift, possibly taken medicine that would make her drowsy, and then fell asleep at the wheel. At least that's the way the DA would spin it. But at this point, Jodie knew it was all speculation.

She made a list of possible defenses such as mechanical failure; dodging a pedestrian, intervention of another car or an animal; weather conditions; and medical issues such as heart attack, stroke, fainting, epileptic seizure, sudden cramping, sneezing, etc. She'd have to check all those out and see if any came into play.

Jodie then began making a list of questions to ask Amanda on Monday. She had to know everything about what had happened. Reggie would have to sit in on the meeting, of course, since he had to find a deep pocket to sue, otherwise, the firm would spend hundreds of hours and not get paid a dime. She thought Paula might want to sit in on it as well, but knew it wasn't practical to have three attorneys involved at this stage. She'd have to tape the meeting so Paula could listen to it later if need be.

Before she left the office, she called Reggie and gave him the bad news.

"Well, we were expecting that, right?" Reggie said. "I can't believe the Tornado took the case. His card was in the stack that Amanda's mother had gathered. He must have turned down her case."

"Apparently, so let's make him regret that choice," Jodie said confidently. "If you find someone to sue on behalf of Amanda and Julie, you don't want the fruits of that lawsuit to end up going to Dr. Short, do you?"

"No! That would be a disaster," Reggie agreed.

"So, anyway. Pick Amanda up at 9:00 a.m. tomorrow, okay?"

"Sure. You think her wheelchair will fit in the 911."

"I don't know, I haven't driven it yet. We can swap cars tomorrow if you want. My BMW has a big trunk."

"No. That's okay. I'll squeeze it in somehow."

Jodie laughed. "See you tomorrow. Don't drive over the speed limit."

"Right," Reggie chuckled.

Before Jodie went home, she went into the library and refreshed her memory on the elements of simple negligence, gross negligence, and wrongful death. Then she made a list of all the possible defenses and the elements of each so that when she was questioning Amanda, she wouldn't miss anything.

By the time she was done the muscles in her shoulders and neck were in knots and she had a horrible headache. On the way home, depression began to set in as she realized the daunting task that lay ahead. A hot bath and three aspirin made her feel a little better, but she still didn't sleep well that night, tossing and turning and her mind racing over everything that might, and probably would, go wrong.

The next morning Jodie overslept, waking with a start at 8:30 a.m. She normally got up at 7:00 a.m. to run, shower, and have breakfast before leaving at eight. She couldn't believe she was already thirty minutes behind schedule and hadn't even eaten breakfast. After quickly getting dressed and putting on make-up, she grabbed a bottle of orange juice and a breakfast bar and raced to her car.

Traffic was much heavier at this late hour, so progress was slow. Luckily, she didn't live too far from the office, so she made it by 9:30 a.m. She breathed a sigh of relief when Maria told her Reggie had called, said they were running late and wouldn't get there before 10:30 a.m.

"I need some coffee," Jodie said to Maria.

"Sure. Coming right up. From the looks of the library, you were busy yesterday."

Jodie smiled. "Sorry, I should have cleaned up."

Maria laughed. "No, I just worry about you. You can't work 24/7."

"Really. Where is that law published? I must have missed it."

Maria smiled and left to get them both coffees. A couple minutes later, she entered Jodie's office with two cups of coffee and a box of donuts. She set them down. "I figured somebody would be hungry this morning, so I bought a dozen donuts."

"Thank you!" Jodie exclaimed as she grabbed one. "Hmm. You're a lifesaver, Maria. I overslept."

They talked for a while and then heard the door open and Amanda and Reggie talking. Maria got up and went back to her desk. Jodie gathered her things and headed for the conference room. She brought the box of donuts and set them on the conference table next to a fresh pot of coffee. Reggie had removed a conference chair and rolled Amanda's wheelchair up to the conference table.

"Anybody hungry?" Jodie asked.

"Yes," Reggie replied. "How about you, Amanda?" She nodded and Reggie took a donut and slid the box over to her. "How about some coffee?"

"Sure," Amanda replied. "Black, please."

Reggie poured her a cup and set it beside her. She smiled warmly at him.

"So, Amanda. Did you bring the papers that were served on you?"

Amanda grabbed her purse, pulled out a thick document gingerly, and handed it to Jodie. Jodie took it, unfolded it, and started reading. After a minute she looked up and said, "Alright, this is a pretty standard personal injury petition. The first part is a short summary of the pleadings. The plaintiffs are identified as the doctor's wife Donna E. Short and his son, David John Short. You are the defendant, of course. The suit was filed in the 299th District Court of Collin County, Texas which is the proper venue since that's the county where the accident took place.

"The next part of the petition is a summary of the alleged facts. They are claiming that you were driving without adequate sleep, exhausted from your job, and, by information and belief, that you may have taken medicine that exacerbated your drowsiness. They claim Dr. Short's death was caused solely by your crossing of the center line into traffic flowing in the opposite direction."

"So, we figured that, right?" Reggie said.

"Yes," Jodie agreed. "There's nothing new here. What will happen now is what's called discovery. They can ask us questions and we can do likewise. They will want to take your deposition."

"What's a deposition?" Amanda asked.

"That's where they question you in front of a court reporter who writes it all down. It's nothing to worry about. We will prepare you for it," Reggie assured her.

"Yes, there will be many depositions. It's how we can find out exactly what happened. Everyone is put under oath and must tell the truth."

Amanda nodded. "But what if I don't remember anything?"

Reggie shrugged. "Then that's what you tell them. You don't remember."

"They will ask a lot of questions that you will remember like everything you did that day before you drove home," Jodie interjected. "They'll want to know everything about you so there won't be any surprises on the day of the trial."

"What if I lose?" Amanda asked. "I must have fallen asleep, right? I mean, that's the only explanation there could be for what happened, right?"

Reggie frowned. "Not necessarily, but even if you lose, they won't be able to hurt you. Everything you own is protected by the Texas exemption laws, your home, your car, and all household furnishings and personal effects."

"A nurse at the hospital told me I should just file bankruptcy."

"You could do that, but then the bankruptcy trustee would own any claims you had against the insurance companies or other parties who may be liable for what happened to you," Jodie advised.

"It would also be an admission of guilt," Reggie noted. "We'd only recommend it as a last resort."

"It might also hurt you if they bring criminal charges," Jodie added. "Right now, your best defense is a strong offense. We'll try to come up with plausible defenses like last clear chance, unavoidable accident, or contributory negligence. For instance, why didn't Dr. Short swerve out of the way or put on his brakes? He might have been able to do something to avoid the accident. We won't know that until we take some depositions and find out his physical condition at that time. He may not have had a valid driver's license for all we know right now. It's too early to panic."

Amanda started breathing heavily, her hands began to shake, and she turned pale. Reggie sprang to his feet and put his hands on her shoulders. "Breathe, Amanda. It's going to be alright!"

Amanda began crying hard. "Why did this happen to me! What did I do to deserve this!"

Jodie rushed out and came back with a glass of water. "Here, honey. Have some water. It's going to be okay."

"What about Julie? Will they take her away from me?"

"No," Reggie said. "We won't let that happen. You're just going to have to be strong for her. This will be a very difficult time for you. We know that and we will do everything in our power to protect you in any way possible."

"I know," Amanda moaned. "I trust you. I'm just so scared."

After Amanda recovered, the conference went on for some time. When Reggie and Amanda had left, Jodie went back to her office to think about what she'd learned and start an outline for an answer to the lawsuit. She had to plead alternative facts to those of the Plaintiff and assert her defenses and counterclaims. She knew that would take some creativity on her part as, so far, the facts and the law looked dismal for poor Amanda.

9
Detective Besch

Stan

In years past, Stan would have taken the last week of the year off. Rebekah loved the holidays and from Christmas Eve to New Year she insisted Stan stay home and be with the family. Fortunately, clients were usually busy at this time of year, so Stan almost always complied with her wishes. But there was no way Stan could relax this year with Ruben Acosta's murder and Amanda Rich under attack.

On Monday, while Reggie and Jodie were meeting with Amanda, Stan went straight to the Dallas Police Station to meet with Detective Besch and go through the financial records that the DPD had taken from the crime scene. He brought Ruben's laptop with him. When he arrived, Besch went out to meet him and they detoured by the break room to get a cup of coffee.

"How are you holding up with Rebekah gone?" Besch asked.

Stan shrugged. "Oh. Okay, I guess. It's pretty quiet around the house these days."

"I bet. I really liked Rebekah. She was a wonderful person."

"That she was," Stan agreed.

"So, I heard you picked up Ruben's car," Besch said with a bit of irritation in his voice."

"Ah. Yeah. Right," Stan replied. "Now that Ruben is dead, as his executor, I'll have to take possession of all his assets and protect them."

"Still, you should have left it at the impound lot until our people had inspected it."

Stan swallowed hard. "Well, the murder took place long after the car had been towed. It couldn't have provided any evidence as to the murder."

Besch grunted his displeasure but didn't press the issue. Stan smiled guiltily and began telling Besch about his search through the neighborhood where the 911 had been parked when it was towed to the impound lot.

"So, was there any personal property in the vehicle?" Besch asked.

"Yes," Stan replied as he held up the laptop. "A laptop and an old Mapsco. I haven't been able to access the laptop since I don't know the password. I was hoping I'd find the password written down somewhere."

Besch nodded. "I'll ask my people about it. Maybe they'll have some ideas on how to gain access."

"Thanks. So, did your crime scene unit find any clues as to Ruben's killers?"

"Nothing definitive. The car they were driving had been stolen. We found it about a mile from Ruben's house. It had been torched. They must have planned to switch cars and had one parked there to make their escape."

"So, was this a drug cartel hit or what?"

"We don't know yet. That's one possibility but at this point, any conclusion we might reach would be pure speculation."

"Okay, well let me go through the records and I'll let you know if I find anything enlightening."

Besch nodded. "Okay, I had everything moved to a conference room. Knock yourself out."

They got up and Besch showed Stan to the conference room. Stan grabbed another cup of coffee along the way and then went to work.

The first box he opened was full of bank statements for the current year. He dug in and sorted all of them by company and date. Each of the statements had copies of the checks that had been cashed during the month. He started with the most recent which were dated October 30, 1999.

He had statements for three accounts all with Bank of America: a personal checking account, one for Med Net and another for Acosta

Less Leasing. Stan started with the personal account and noticed there were a lot of checks written to Ruben himself each for $5,000.

When Besch walked in later to see how he was doing, Stan told him about the personal checks to Acosta. "I don't think he wanted to leave a financial trail. I haven't found any evidence of him using a credit card."

"That is unusual," Besch agreed, "especially in this day and age. He must have been hiding from somebody."

Stan nodded and went back to work. Besch left and said he'd check back in a bit. After Stan finished with the box of bank statements and was about to start putting them back, he noticed a small but thick envelope at the bottom of the box. He picked it up, peered inside, and then dumped out a safety deposit box key. He examined it wondering where he'd find the the box and what he'd find in it.

In the next box, he found files for each of the MedNet locations that he was managing. If these were all the MedNet files, it meant MedNet had eleven customers in Texas, seven in Phoenix, and five in Las Vegas. Included in each file was the management contract, leasing inventories, claims files, yearly balance sheets, and profit and loss statements. Stan marveled at how profitable each of these medical practices was and wondered if he'd chosen the wrong profession.

When Besch returned Stan showed him the safety deposit box key. "I bet the box is at the Bank of America where Ruben had his bank accounts."

"Probably," Besch agreed. "I'll let you check it out. Of course, if you find out anything that might be helpful in our murder investigation, you'll tell me about it, right?"

"Of course," Stan replied.

"So, what have you learned since I was last in here?"

Stan summarized what he had discovered and then said, "All of the locations apparently were doing quite well. You wouldn't believe the cash flow going through these medical practices."

Besch's eyes narrowed. "So, do you think the numbers are legit?"

Stan shrugged. "Legit? I don't know about that, but the numbers are real. The bank statements support the profit and loss numbers."

"So, he may be legit?" Besch asked again.

Stan shrugged. "Well, he seemed like an honest guy to me, but you never know. Let's see what's in that safety deposit box before we draw any conclusions."

Besch chuckled. "You don't know if your client is legit?"

"I think he's legit. I wouldn't knowingly take on a crook for a client" Stan said irritably. "In fact, the FBI ran a sting operation against me once, and they failed."

Besch smiled. "I know?"

Stan's mouth dropped open. "You know? How would you know about that?"

Besch chuckled, "The special agent handling the operation asked me about you before they ran it. I told them you'd pass. I even made $200 on you in the betting pool."

"What the hell!" Stan exclaimed. "There was a betting pool?"

Besch bent over he was laughing so hard. "Yeah, a lot of the guys around here thought you'd fall for it."

Stan just shook his head in disbelief. Years earlier, two Arabs came to see him about filing for bankruptcy. Stan was ready to help them until one of the men confessed, he had hidden a large sum of money away and wanted to make sure the U.S. Trustee didn't find out about it. He offered Stan a bonus if he'd help him conceal it. The moment this topic came up Stan kicked the men out of his office and told them not to come back.

"I can't believe you knew about this," Stan said. "You should have told the FBI they were wasting their time. I like to sleep at night and my freedom is of paramount importance to me."

"I did," Besch said, "but they wouldn't listen. They'd just nailed one of your colleagues a few weeks earlier and were anxious for another feather in their cap."

Stan just stared at Besch as he left the conference room chuckling under his breath and closing the door behind him. Stan worked several more hours before he had completed going through everything.

When he got back to his office, he called the local branch office of Bank of America to see about getting access to the safety deposit boxes. After waiting on hold a long time and being transferred around he was told he'd have to get a court order. He cursed as he hung up the phone because that meant it might be weeks or months before he'd be able to see the contents of those boxes.

10
Inspection

Reggie

One of Reggie's friends in law school was Donnie Reeves. Reggie knew Donnie's father was an auto mechanic, so he called his friend to see if his father would look at the two cars involved in Amanda's accident to see if there was any evidence of mechanical failure or design defects. They met at the City of McKinney impound yard, where both cars were being stored as evidence.

"Hi. Thanks for agreeing to do this," Reggie said. "We don't know if there were any mechanical issues, but it's a possibility, so we need to check it out."

Marvin Reeves nodded, "Well. I'll be happy to look but I'm not optimistic I'll find anything. I checked both of these cars' recall history and didn't find anything that might cause an accident like this."

"Really. Hmm. Well, take a look anyway."

"Sure," Mr. Reeves said and then walked over to the 1999 Cadillac Eldorado. "Donnie. Get the camera out of the truck and start taking pictures."

"Okay, Dad," Donnie replied and rushed over to the truck.

Reggie watched anxiously as Reeves carefully inspected the vehicle and Donnie took pictures. While watching the inspection, he ran the accident through his mind. He imagined Amanda's car suddenly veering to the left across the median and heading straight at the Cadillac. Coming from that angle, it was unlikely Dr. Short would have seen Amanda coming at him. In his mind's eye, Reggie saw Amanda's 1992 Ford Taurus strike the front driver's side of the Cadillac. He wondered if Amanda had really fallen asleep or something else had happened.

Thirty minutes later, Reeves announced he'd finished with the Cadillac, hadn't found anything out of the ordinary, and was moving on to the Taurus.

Disappointed, Reggie sighed and nodded. "Okay. Thanks."

Reeves went to work on the Taurus and a short time later said, "Look at this."

Reggie perked up and came over to where Reeves was pointing to a silver streak along the right side of the Taurus.

"This is recent damage to this door panel. Do you know if your client was involved in another accident recently? It appears she was struck along here recently."

"I don't know," Reggie admitted. "My client didn't mention any other accidents. Do you think another car hit her on the passenger side? That would have thrown her off the road and onto the median."

"It's a possibility," Reeves acknowledged, "but I don't know how you would prove it without a witness."

Reggie nodded solemnly, "Right. But it's something to check out."

"Sure, was there any mention of a third car in the accident report?"

"No. We interviewed the police officer, but he claimed there was no evidence of a third car involved. The only witness claims not to have seen the third car either."

"Well, talk to the client about previous accidents. She may have brushed one of those shopping carts poles in the parking lot or something."

"Okay, I'll check with her. Thanks."

After the inspections were complete, Reggie went back to the office. Stan wasn't in his office, so Reggie called him on his cell phone."

"Dad. Where are you?" Reggie asked.

"Going through Acosta's records at the Dallas Police station. What's up?"

"The inspections are done. Mr. Reeves didn't find anything on the doctor's car, but he did find a long silver streak on the passenger side of Amanda's car. It might be proof that another car struck her."

"Okay. That's a theory. Now all you must do is find some proof of it. Get a sample of the silver paint. Maybe we can get it analyzed."

"Okay. Where do I send it?"

"Ask Jodie. I think she has a lab she sends stuff like that to."

"Okay, what else can I do to prove the accident wasn't Amanda's fault?"

Stan was silent for a moment and replied, "Sometimes you just have to accept the facts as they are. You can't win every case. Remember, in every case that goes to trial, one of the attorneys will lose. You have to accept reality."

"But I know it wasn't her fault."

"Reggie, you hardly know the woman. How could you possibly know it wasn't her fault? These PI cases take patience. Keep digging. Maybe you will find something, but you shouldn't have unreasonable expectations. That will only lead to disappointment and depression. Believe me. I've been there."

"Okay," Reggie said and hung up.

Reggie felt angry. He knew in his gut that this was a good case, but he didn't know how to find the truth. Reggie wondered how he could get information on Dr. Kenneth Short who lived and practiced medicine in Dallas. He knew the usual way to do that was through depositions, but Dr. Short was dead, and he didn't want to take his widow's deposition unless it was absolutely necessary. Reggie wondered if there were any public records on Dr. Short. The place to look for that would be the County Clerk's Office.

Later that day, Reggie drove downtown to the Dallas County Records building, where he looked at birth, death, marriage, county court dockets, real estate, and DMV records. It was a meticulous process that required patience, something Reggie lacked. Nevertheless, he was there all afternoon until closing. He was pleased when he reviewed his notes of what he had learned.

In the deed records, he found out that Dr. Short owned a 6,000 sq. ft. home in the Oaklawn area of Dallas with an appraised value of $825,000. He also had two properties that Reggie guessed he rented out, each valued at around $400,000. In the marriage records, he found out that the doctor had been married three times, and from the birth records, it appeared he had seven children.

Although this was all very interesting, Reggie was more interested in what he found in the county court records. Dr. Short had been sued several times and arrested twice for DWI! Was it possible Dr. Short was intoxicated at the time of the accident? Since he died, the police wouldn't have known of his intoxication. He wondered if there had been an autopsy. If so, there would be a toxicology report.

The records didn't disclose the disposition of the cases which was critical information. It would take some additional research to get the details of each, but he felt hopeful for the first time since he'd taken on Amanda's case. Now he was getting somewhere. He couldn't wait to return to the office and tell his dad and Jodie what he'd discovered.

11
New Hope Legal Clinics

Stan

The next afternoon, Stan went to the Mustang Office Suites in Las Colinas situated on the 9th floor of the Embassy Building East overlooking the Dallas skyline. Ruben and Tom both had been officing there when Ruben was murdered. The three men met in the community conference room where Ruben's records had been assembled.

Stan began the meeting. "Yesterday, I met with Detective Besch to review the evidence taken from Ruben's home on the night of his murder. Now that I have been through it, I think I understand the operation of his various businesses a little better.

"As you know, as Ruben's independent executor and trustee of the New Horizons Trust, it is my responsibility to take over the operations of all his businesses. To do that, I will need your help. So, it's my intention to retain both of your services for the indefinite future if you are both willing."

Roger nodded and said, "Sure, no problem."

Tom likewise nodded his approval noting, "Yeah, this would be a bad time to switch actuaries with compliance testing and annual reports due next month."

"Exactly," Stan agreed. "I need you both to carry on, so we don't disappoint any of Ruben's clients. In the records at the police station, I found all of the North Texas, Arizona, and Las Vegas MedNet contracts. How closely did you two deal with the staff at these local offices?"

"I rarely talked to any of them," Roger said. "Ruben hired a manager at each location, and they handled pretty much everything. I'd get weekly and monthly reports faxed to me, and if I had a question, I might call and talk to the manager, but that was rare."

"I hardly ever talked to the managers either," Tom added, "except in January of each year when all the reporting had to be done. "But I did talk to many of the employees during the year if they had questions about their 401K or health insurance."

"So, Tom. Did Ruben have health insurance through one of these companies?" Stan asked.

"Yes, he made himself manager of one of his North Texas offices and had health, life, and disability coverage as part of that group."

"So, did he have coverage for any family members?"

Tom shook his head. "No. He didn't have dependent coverage."

Stan thought for a moment. "Hmm. Before he died, he told me to take care of his family. What do you think he meant by that?"

Tom shrugged. "You got me. Maybe he considered all the MedNet locations his family."

"That's possible," Stan admitted.

Roger grimaced. "I have no idea. His cat, maybe!"

"Well, the cat is dead, I'm afraid. Did either of you help Ruben with his personal finances?"

"No," Tom said. "I only did the insurance and employee benefits for his businesses, nothing personal."

Roger nodded. "Same with me."

"I didn't see an insurance policy," Stan mused. "After the will is proven up, remind me to find out who he designated as the beneficiary of his 401K and life insurance policy."

Tom nodded. "Sure, I'll make a note."

"Okay, so did Ruben indicate to either of you why he suddenly decided to do asset protection planning. He told me it was because of the high cost of workman's compensation and medical malpractice insurance."

"That is a big problem," Tom acknowledged, "but he didn't mention to me that it was an urgent concern."

"Do either of you know why he would have been visiting the Farmer's Market in downtown Dallas on the day of his murder."

"Yeah," Roger said. "His immigration attorney runs a legal clinic there."

"What! He had an immigration attorney?"

"I don't know if it was his attorney, or he was helping somebody else get a green card. But he did complain a lot about our immigration laws. He said the laws were a disgrace, and the President and Congress could easily do something about it if they weren't always at each other's throats."

"That's probably true," Stan agreed. "Was Ruben a U.S. Citizen?"

"I don't know," Roger replied. "I didn't handle his personal affairs, so it never came up."

"Well, I didn't ask him either," Stan admitted. "He spoke perfect English. It never occurred to me that he might not be a citizen."

The meeting continued with a discussion of how they all could best keep the businesses running smoothly until Stan decided what to do with them. Under the terms of the trust, he had one year to wind things up, pay all the debts and taxes and then make a final distribution to the beneficiaries.

"So, my goal is to become intimately familiar with all of Ruben's enterprises and then put them up for sale. I don't have any desire to operate them for an extended length of time. I'm a lawyer, not an entrepreneur. So, I'll need both of you to be on the lookout for potential buyers or, if you know of any good business brokers, let me know."

They both agreed, and then the topic turned to what they should tell all of their managers and clients who were probably wondering why they hadn't heard from Ruben for a while.

"His murder didn't get much press," Tom remarked. "I don't think any managers know he is dead. I certainly haven't told them."

"Nor I," Roger agreed. "But we are going to have to tell them eventually."

"It would probably be better in person than over the phone," Stan mused.

"Right," Roger said. "We'll need to assure them their practices will continue to thrive."

"Thrive," Stan repeated. "Yes. I am amazed at how much cash each and every one of those practices generates. They all must be great doctors."

Roger shook his head. "No. They're just ordinary doctors. Ruben was incredible with the insurance companies. If they denied a claim, he was on the phone immediately. He almost always got them to reconsider and make full payment. It was uncanny."

Stan thought about that for a moment and then asked, "So, was he just tenacious, persuasive or charming? What was his secret?"

"I don't know," Roger said. "But if you don't figure out what it was, there's gonna be a huge drop in income for all our clients."

Stan took a deep breath. "Wonderful. That's all I need."

Before the meeting broke up, they decided they would all meet with the local managers, then they would go to Phoenix to meet with the managers there, and they'd go next to Las Vegas. Stan wanted to reward Roger and Tom for their loyalty and hard work keeping Ruben's empire from cratering before he could sell it off. Of course, they'd meet with the managers and doctors first, then let off a little steam on the Las Vegas Strip.

After the meeting, Tom told Stan the name of the immigration lawyer Ruben had gone to see on the day of his murder was Chistos Mejia. Stan called him, and Chistos's secretary said he could fit him in later that afternoon. When Stan arrived at the New Hope Legal Clinic, he noted it was also listed as Nueva Esperanza Clinica Legal Gratuita. It was a beehive of activity. About eight lawyers and their staff were hard at work processing dozens of clients lined up to see each attorney. Stan looked at the lines and hoped he wouldn't have to wait in one of them. He went to the receptionist and told her he had an appointment with Mr. Mejia. She nodded and pointed to a door to Stan's left.

"He's through that door. Go right in."

Stan thanked her and followed her instructions. The door led to a hallway; halfway down, there was an open door. Stan walked to the door and looked in. Christos looked up and smiled.

"Come in, Mr. Turner," he said and stood up. They shook hands, and Christos pointed to a side chair where Stan took a seat.

"So, this is a busy place," Stan noted.

"Yes, always. So many people want the American dream. Unfortunately, for many, what they get is an American nightmare."

"I bet," Stan agreed. "So, I understand you knew Ruben Acosta?"

"Yes. I read about Ruben's murder. I understand you were there when it happened."

"That's right," Stan said. "He'd come to see me about some business matters but disappeared before we were done. Eventually, we went to his house looking for him. We thought maybe he was ill or something. A few days later he showed up, but I was only able to talk to him for a few minutes before we were ambushed."

"You were lucky you weren't hurt," Christos noted.

Stan nodded. "Yes. I was. So, how do you know Ruben? Were you, his lawyer?"

"No. There was nothing I could do for Ruben. He wasn't born in America, and the government has no record of his existence. The laws are impossible for people in his situation."

So, why did Ruben come to see you the day before the murder?"

"To bring me money. He actually helps fund the legal clinic, so we can help immigrants caught illegally crossing the border."

"Really? So, he was an important donor?"

"Yes, a very generous man."

"How much did he give you this time?"

"Twenty-thousand."

"Cash."

"Yes, always cash."

"So, did you know much about Ruben's business?" Stan asked

"No. Ruben never told me much about it other than it was very profitable."

"Do you have any idea who might have wanted him dead?"

"Well, I do know his parents were recently killed by the cartel that brought them to America?"

"What?" Stan exclaimed. "Why?"

"They couldn't pay the fee for crossing the border in full when they came, so they owed the cartel. Of course, that kind of loan is never paid off. Apparently, his parents got tired of paying, and tried to disappear but were eventually caught. The penalty for trying to skip out on a cartel debt is death."

"So, you think the Cartel might have been after Ruben?"

Christos nodded solemnly.

Stan was too upset to return to the office and work, so he went straight home. For a moment, he forgot Rebekah would not be there. In the early years of their marriage, Stan had tried to keep his work and personal life separate. He told himself he wouldn't share the trials and tribulations of the law practice with Rebekah to protect her and preserve client confidentiality. But that hadn't worked, as Rebekah knew him too well and could easily detect when Stan was keeping things from her. So, he finally capitulated and began sharing the details of his more interesting cases.

This made Rebekah feel closer to him, and Stan benefited, too, by getting problems off his chest and getting a woman's perspective. Stan wished Rebekah were going to be home now. Stan needed her. She was his soul mate. They'd met in high school at an International Affairs club meeting. Stan was the club president, and Rebekah was the director of all the clubs on campus. They worked with each other for a while and then began dating.

Stan thought back to the day he knew he had found the woman who would be at his side for the rest of his life. They had decided to go on a long bus ride to support their high school basketball team that had made the state finals. They had found a seat in the back of the bus where they'd have more privacy to enjoy each other's company. After an hour or so, they fell asleep in each other's arms. It was hot on the bus, and when Stan woke up sometime later, he breathed in Rebekah's strong scent and was so aroused he had to put his jacket in his lap to avoid embarrassment.

But Rebekah was gone now. Stan couldn't believe her life had come and gone. Tears welled in his eyes as they often did when he was alone. The house was empty and dark as usual. Ever since Rebekah had died, he hadn't bothered to turn on the lights when he came home at night and often stumbled around in the dark. He'd installed a few night lights to keep from falling over furniture and injuring himself, but the darkness seemed to suit him. He took pride in his last electric bill being only $48.

When he got to his front door, he started to stick his key into the lock when he noticed the door was ajar! He froze but then figured Reggie or Marcia, his daughter, had come by and forgotten to lock up when they left. So, he stepped inside.

Suddenly, someone grabbed his shoulders while a second person pulled a bag over his head. "What the hell!" Stan exclaimed.

"Shut up, and you won't get hurt," a man ordered as he tied Stan's hands behind his back. "There is somebody here who wants to talk to you."

Stan was pushed forward hard. He stumbled but managed to stay on his feet. Another push, and he knew he was in his family room. He stepped to the left to avoid a footstool he knew was in front of him. A final push landed him on a sofa. He wiggled around into a sitting position.

"So, Mr. Turner," a deep voice said. "I understand you and Ruben Acosta have been busy here of late."

"Who are you?" Stan spat.

"You can call me Carlos."

"Okay, Carlos, take off the hood, untie my hands, and I'll be happy to talk to you."

"I'm afraid I can't do that," Carlos said. "It's for your protection, actually. I won't take much of your time. "

"Okay. What do you want?" Stan asked irritably.

"You and Ruben have been busy transferring assets into the New Horizons Trust and other various enterprises."

"So, what about it?"

"Those assets you have been transferring didn't belong to Ruben. He had no right to transfer them."

Stan's stomach twisted.

"What are you talking about? I checked all the titles; they were all in Ruben's name."

"True, but he was holding them for us. They didn't belong to him."

Stan swallowed hard and asked. "Who is us?"

"You don't need to know that," Carlos advised

"So, I'm just supposed to take your word for all of this nonsense?" Stan asked.

"Yes. Trust me, it's true."

"Trust you. I don't even know who you are. You don't have any authority over me."

"Are you sure?" Carlos asked. "Don't you have several children, a law partner, staff, and many friends?"

Stan didn't respond as a wave of fear washed over him.

"If you want to keep them safe," Carlos continued, "I suggest you listen to my instructions carefully and follow them to the letter. If you don't, they will all suffer for your disobedience."

"What in the hell do you expect me to do?" Stan spat.

"Exactly what Ruben was doing for us, managing our business enterprises. He was doing a good job, and we expect you to do the same."

Stan took a deep breath. "So, you're saying the MedNet business, the commercial properties, the rental properties, and the bank accounts, all belong to you?"

"Not to me, but the organization I represent."

"And what organization is that?"

"That's of no concern to you?" Carlos replied.

"The hell it isn't! I obviously must know the identity of the trust beneficiaries. They are the only ones I'm authorized to pay or make property distributions."

"No! There will be no distributions to trust beneficiaries. You will simply manage the properties under your control as we direct."

"I can't do that," Stan replied.

"You'll do what we ask of you from now on without question, or your family, your staff, and all your friends will die but only after they have suffered greatly."

Stan didn't respond.

Carlos took a deep breath and continued. "Listen, don't be angry at us. We were both duped by Acosta. The problem is whether you like it or not, Acosta stole our property and put it under your control. So, now you have to deal with it."

Stan sighed deeply.

"Okay, so I'll help you undo it."

"No. To do that we'd have to get lawyers and courts involved. That can't happen. Anyway, you and Ruben did all this fancy asset protection planning, and we love it. So, you are just gonna do your job as planned with a little technical supervision."

Stan said nothing.

"Listen," Carlos said softly. "This isn't a bad thing. Ruben made a lot of money handling our businesses. We will pay you handsomely for your services as well. I'll even through in a few perks, you being a widower now. By the way, sorry for your loss."

"But we'll be breaking a few dozen state and federal laws every single day. This isn't going to work."

Carlos laughed. "So, laws are made to be broken. Didn't you learn anything in law school? It's no big deal."

Stan knew he had no choice but to go along with Carlos for the moment. Otherwise, he and everyone he loved would probably end up dead. He took a deep breath. "Okay. I guess I have no choice."

"Good thinking. I knew you were a smart man," Carlos said. "We'll be in touch."

Stan felt a sharp blow to his head and then nothing.

Forty-five minutes later Stan woke up with a splitting headache. He struggled to his feet and ambled to his bathroom to look at his head. There was a large gash on the left side above his ear in the mirror. He fingered the bloody wound gingerly, cringing in pain as he examined it.

The wound looked pretty bad, so he decided he better have it checked out. He thought about calling the police or an ambulance but quickly realized that would lead to a lot of questions that he didn't want to have to answer. He finally decided to go to the Care Now clinic around the corner, where he usually went for colds and minor injuries. He'd tell them he fell down the stairs or something.

When the nurse at the clinic looked at the wound, she quickly took him to an examining room. When his assigned doctor saw the wound, he wanted to send him to the Plano Hospital Emergency Room, but Stan talked him into letting him handle it himself, with the promise he'd see his regular doctor in the morning. The doctor told Stan it wouldn't be a good idea for him to go to sleep after a head injury like that as he might not wake up.

Stan knew he was right. Rebekah had been a nurse, and he'd heard her give the same advice on many occasions, but Stan had no intention of sleeping. How could he under the circumstances? He had to figure out how to get himself out of this dire predicament and save all the people he loved from the wrath of a soulless drug cartel, and he only had a few hours to do it!

He thought about his old friend at the CIA, Mo. Stan had done a lot for the CIA in the past, so they owed him. Mo had told him to call if he ever needed anything. Stan thought about calling him, but the CIA wasn't supposed to get involved in domestic matters. That was a job for the FBI. Stan was glad he knew someone at the FBI. They might actually be able to help him.

12
Indictment

Paula

Paula felt a little guilty about abandoning Jodie and Reggie after Amanda was served on the wrongful death case. So, she decided she would help them out by starting to interview witnesses that would likely be involved in both the wrongful death litigation and Amanda's criminal trial. She had checked back with Wendy Pierce, her contact at the DA's office, and been told a prosecutor had been assigned, which meant the case was going to the grand jury.

Ordinarily, Paula wouldn't have contacted a prime witness being called by the grand jury. Still, with a pending wrongful death case, she had every right to contact witnesses who might have relevant information about the civil case. She wasn't sure what information Martin Gallagher had, but she needed to find out.

He was reluctant to talk to her when she got through to him because of the grand jury subpoena he'd received. Still, she assured him if he didn't meet with her, she'd just have to have her own subpoena issued for him. She promised she wouldn't take much of his time. She just needed to find out what he knew about the accident since their client was being sued. They met for breakfast at Denny's a few blocks from the Turner & Waters' offices.

Mr. Gallagher was a tall, stout, middle-aged man with reddish-orange hair and a pale complexion. After Paula introduced herself to him, the hostess took them to a table where they were immediately served coffee.

"So, thanks for meeting with me," Paula said. "The judge we've been assigned doesn't give us much time to do discovery, so I wanted to meet with you briefly to find out what exactly you know about the accident."

"Oh, I don't know anything about the accident," Gallagher confessed. "I only know what I saw at the plant during the day shift on the day of the accident."

Paula frowned. "Okay, what did you see?"

"Well," Gallagher began. "I was working the day shift next to Amanda. I could tell she was tired, but she was still doing okay. I totally understood how tough a double shift could be. God knows I've done enough of them myself."

"Okay," Paula said. "So, you said you saw something."

"Oh, yes. Sorry. Ah. Well, I went across the street and got something from the street vendor for lunch. The guy who comes to our plant has the best barbeque sandwiches."

"Okay," Paula said impatiently. "So, was Amanda out there too?"

"No. No. Oh, no. She didn't go to lunch. Apparently, there is a sofa in the ladies' room. I wouldn't know, of course. It's the one adjacent to the break room. She went there to take a nap."

"Really? So, how do you know this?"

"Well, when I returned to the floor, Amanda wasn't there. I covered for her for a while, but after about twenty minutes, my supervisor noticed Amanda wasn't there and asked me about it."

Paula took a deep breath, not liking what she was hearing. "So, what did you say?"

"Well, I told him she must have gone to the ladies' room. I didn't know she was there, but it was the only thing I could think of at that moment."

"So, who was this supervisor?"

"Gus Gibson," Gallagher replied.

"Okay. Go on."

"Well, I went to the ladies' room and asked a woman who had just come out whether she'd seen Amanda. Much to my surprise, she said yes and that Amanda was asleep on the sofa in there."

"So, did you wake her up?"

"Oh, no. Not me, but the woman did, and Amanda came out immediately, upset that she'd dosed off."

"What was the woman's name who saw Amanda sleeping in the ladies' room?" Paula asked.

"Ah. I'm not sure. Her first name is Lisa. She works in the office."

"So," Paula asked, "what did the supervisor do?"

"Nothing, he just shook his head when he saw Amanda, and I returned to the floor."

"Did Amanda have anything to say about all of this?"

"She apologized for the trouble she'd caused me and wanted to know how upset Gibson was. She said she'd had a headache, so she took a pill, and it put her to sleep."

Paula cringed at this revelation and immediately knew why Gallagher had been called to testify before the grand jury. Not only had Amanda worked a double shift, but she'd taken a pill that she should have known would have exacerbated her drowsiness, fully aware that she'd have to drive home after the shift ended.

"Tell me about Gus Gibson," Paula said. "Does he decide who has to work a double shift?"

"Yes," Gallagher replied. "If someone calls in sick or doesn't show up, it's his job to find a replacement. The assembly line has to be fully staffed at all times, or it will slow down or even shut down if too many workers are absent."

"Did you know about this policy when you hired on at Southern Battery?"

"Yes. It was explained to me, but I thought it would be something rare. But it's not rare. It happens all the time."

"What happens if you refuse to work the double shift."

"You might get away with it if you have a good excuse, but I know a couple of employees who refused a double shift too many times and ended up losing their job. Of course, not working a double shift would not be the official reason for the boot; Gibson would find something else as the official cause of the termination."

"In the last year, how many employees lost their job because they refused to work a double shift?"

"Oh, I don't know for sure, but at least a half dozen."

"How many employees does Southern Battery have on its assembly line?"

"There are three shifts, and each shift has twenty-four positions."

Paula thanked Gallagher and then drove back to the office. She wondered what other witnesses the prosecutor would call. She knew for sure she needed to talk to Gibson and Lisa.

When she arrived at the office, Maria advised her that Stan wanted to see her, so she went straight to his office. He appeared to be in deep thought and didn't react to Paula's presence until she sat down across from him. She could tell he was upset. Stan finally looked up.

Paula frowned when she saw a bandage on his head. "What happened to you?" she gasped.

Stan sighed. "You go first. Paula. How'd the interview go?"

"Okay. Not so good, actually."

She told Stan about Amanda's headache, taking a pill, and then taking a nap at lunch. Stan shook his head, but Paula could tell he was only half listening and had something heavy on his mind.

"So, what's up with you? You seem distracted."

He nodded. "Yes, very distracted. I just learned our client, Ruben Acosta, was working for a Mexican drug cartel. They sent a messenger last night to my house to inform me I was now working for them.

Stan rubbed the bandage gingerly and then continued, "They punctuated the message with a blow to my head. It hurts like hell!"

Paula cringed at the sight. "I bet. So, how could this be?" Paula asked worriedly. "Did Ruben mention any of this to you?"

"No. And I don't know all the facts yet, but apparently, Ruben joined the cartel to get revenge for his parent's murder. Ruben's parents bought their passage to America years ago from a Mexican cartel but couldn't fully pay for it. For years and years, they tried to pay off the debt, but it never went away due to the ridiculously high-interest rate. Eventually, they gave up trying and went into hiding. I guess the cartel found them and killed them to set an example."

"Oh, my god!" Paula exclaimed. "So, what did Ruben do about it?"

"Apparently, he infiltrated the cartel to somehow get revenge," Stan replied. "They didn't know his true identity. I suspect when he came to me and started transferring assets around, they got suspicious and did some digging into Ruben's past. If they figured out his identity, that would explain why he was killed.

"So, now they expect you to carry on with his work?"

"I guess so. It seems I was Ruben's Plan B. If he was killed all the Cartel's property would be under my control and they there wouldn't be much they could do about it since I would be compelled to administer the trust in accordance with its terms."

"That was very creative," Paula said tentatively. "Do you know which cartel?"

"No. I don't know much other than what I just told you."

"So, his bosses didn't know who he was?"

"Right. ... He came here illegally and has lived under a false identity. So, I was informed last night by a cartel messenger that I am now working for a Mexican drug cartel."

"Shit!" Paula said worriedly. "What are you going to do?"

"I don't have much choice. If I don't carry on with Ruben's work, they will kill my children, you and Jodie, and all our friends."

Paula's mouth opened, but she said nothing.

"That's why I called you in here. I need help figuring this thing out."

Paula closed her eyes and took a deep breath. "Geez, Stan. I have no idea."

"Obviously, I'm over my head here, so I'm going to arrange a meeting with Special Agent Lot. There is no way I'm doing this thing alone. Maybe the FBI can help me out of this debacle."

"That's a good idea," Paula said. "We better beef up security for everyone."

"Yes. Will you take care of that for me?"

"Sure. I'll get right on it."

After Stan had fully briefed Paula on the situation and his plans, she went to find Jodie and Reggie to give them the bad news about Amanda. They all gathered in Paula's office. After telling them about

Amanda falling asleep at work, she said it was time to focus on the criminal case and put the personal injury defense on the back burner.

"What makes you think Tom Tyson will go along with that?" Reggie asked. "He doesn't strike me as the cooperative type."

"Well, he won't really have a choice. Criminal actions take precedence over civil, and no court is going to make someone on trial for homicide defend a civil case at the same time."

"So, I should file a motion for a continuance?" Jodie asked.

"Right. The moment a criminal indictment comes down, call Tyson, and see if he'll agree. You might also suggest to him another option," Paula said.

"What's that?" Jodie asked.

"Drop the lawsuit and negotiate a no-fault settlement with the insurance companies. Tell the Tornado we wouldn't oppose that."

"Right," Jodie agreed. "That's probably the best he could do since Amanda is broke."

"And, if he goes for it," Reggie mused. "Amanda would then be free to pursue her claim against any other responsible parties, should we find them."

They all smiled. Jodie said, "You are quite the optimist, aren't you?"

Reggie frowned and replied, "What do you mean?"

Jodie and Paula laughed.

"In the meantime, we need to use this civil case as an excuse to depose everybody we can think of to get a head start on Amanda's criminal defense," Paula said. "There is no telling when an indictment will actually come down."

They continued to discuss strategy until Jodie advised them that she and Stan had a meeting to attend. Paula wasn't sure whether Reggie knew about Stan's situation with the cartel, so she didn't say anything.

"Okay," Jodie said. "After our meeting, I'm taking Stan to the gun range. It's about time he learned to shoot."

Paula gave Jodie a knowing look. Reggie perked up. "Really? Can I come?"

"No," Jodie replied. "You have a motion for continuance to draft. We need to have it ready the moment the indictment comes down."

Reggie frowned. "You're no fun."

Jodie sighed. "Sorry, but your father does have something he needs you to do. It won't take but a few minutes, but it is very important."

Reggie perked up at this news and started to leave. "Wait," Jodie said as she tore a yellow sheet off a legal pad and handed it to him. "Don't be late! Timing is critical," she said as he walked out the door.

Paula stood up. "Alright. I'm going home. Bart promised me a massage."

When Paula got home, she was delighted to hear the bath water running. Upon entering the bedroom, he said, "Right on time. Good girl!"

Paula smiled and started taking off her clothes. By the time she made it into the bathtub after their lovemaking, the water was cold, so she turned on the hot water, closed her eyes, and relaxed as the temperature rose.

"So, how was your day?" Bart asked as he stared, mesmerized by her naked body.

She responded without opening her eyes. "Not great," she confessed. "The District Attorney has it in for Amanda for some reason. He's being irrational."

"That sounds like Peters," Bart said. "He is very emotional sometimes."

"You know Preston Peters?" Paula asked.

"Of course, he was an ADA back when I was with the Collin County DA's office. They called him Porky Peters; he was so fat. I think he weighed 300 lbs."

"Wow," Paula laughed. "Too bad he's not trying the case."

"Right. You'd eat his lunch."

"So, how can I get him to be reasonable?"

Bart thought a moment. "Well, you can't talk to him directly. That wouldn't be appropriate, but I guess I could try and reason with him."

"How would you do that?"

"There's a Collin County Bench Bar meeting next week. I'll probably run into him. I could bring it up then."

"Fantastic. Maybe you can talk some sense into the jerk. In the meantime, I'm ready for that massage."

Bart smiled, turned off the hot water, and slid into the tub behind Paula. She liked that about Bart. He always fulfilled his promises. She moaned in appreciation.

13
FBI

Stan

Stan and Special Agent Lot went way back, having worked on several cases together in the past. They'd first met when Agent Lot was investigating a bank robbery. The FBI was perplexed that only one safety deposit box had been robbed, and the box had belonged to Stan. The FBI was curious as to what Stan was keeping in the bank's vault. Stan never told him what it was, but that encounter started a long and mutually beneficial relationship.

So, over the years, they had developed a protocol for meeting surreptitiously. Either one would call the other and set up a meeting at the usual place at a given time. The usual spot was Denny's Restaurant in Grand Prairie, Texas. The time was two hours and twenty minutes earlier than the verbally stated time. The only problem with the protocol was if someone followed either of them, it wouldn't work.

There was no reason to think Special Agent Lot was being followed, but it was likely Stan had a tail. To ensure Stan wasn't followed, he drove to Benihana's Restaurant a few blocks from their offices and pulled his car up for valet parking. It was cold out, so he wore a heavy London Fog overcoat and pulled it up close around his neck. A few seconds later, Reggie drove up in the 911. They then walked together into the restaurant as if they were going to have dinner.

Ten minutes later, Stan went to the restroom, leaving his coat behind, and Josh walked out of the restroom and joined Reggie, taking Stan's place. It was busy as usual, so nobody around them noticed the switch. When Stan came out of the restroom, he took the side exit, walked across the alley to the rear entrance to the Sheraton Hotel, then through the building to the front entrance, where he quickly grabbed a cab. As they pulled away, he looked for anyone who might be following him but saw no one.

Back at the restaurant, Reggie and Josh lingered after dinner and had a few drinks before they returned to the valet station, picked up their cars, and drove back to the office. Reggie then drove Josh back to the Sheraton, where Josh had parked his car. Neither of them saw anyone suspicious, but they still felt proud that they'd done their part in protecting Stan.

As Stan sank back into the cab, he wondered if he was making a mistake contacting the FBI. If the cartel found out, his kids would be reading his obituary in the *Dallas Morning News.*

Agent Lot was sitting at their usual spot in the corner of the restaurant, where they couldn't be seen from any of the windows or the front entrance. Other than a little grey hair, Agent Lot looked about the same as Stan had remembered him. Lot nodded as Stan took a seat. A second later, the waitress brought them menus and coffee.

"Stan. It's been a while."

"Yes," Stan agreed. "What, about five or six years?"

"Give or take."

"Sorry to hear about your wife."

"Thank you. We had thirty great years together, so I'm grateful for that."

"Right. Not too many marriages last that long these days."

"That's for sure," Stan replied.

"So, what's up?" Lot asked.

"I'm sorry we had to meet this way, but I've got a serious problem."

Agent Lot nodded. "Yeah, I was a little surprised to get your message. I knew it must be something serious."

Stan took a long, deep breath and then began his story. He explained how Ruben Acosta had been referred to him for some asset protection planning, what business entities he had set up for him, Stan's appointment as independent executor, attorney-in-fact, and trustee of the New Horizons Trust, and Ruben's recent murder.

"I heard about the murder," Agent Lot said. "I called Besch when I saw you were involved. He said Jodie may have wounded one of them."

"Yes. That's another reason I'm concerned. I don't want some cartel thug trying to get revenge."

"Okay, so why do you think a cartel had Mr. Acosta murdered."

Stan explained his meeting with Ruben's attorney friend and Stan's theory that Ruben had surreptitiously joined the cartel to get payback for killing his parents."

"So, you think he was out for revenge and somehow was discovered."

"Right. Of course, it's all conjecture, but why else would they kill him?"

"I don't know. It could have been a number of reasons," Agent Lot replied. "So, what's the situation now? Why contact me?"

Stan stroked the bandage on his head. "A messenger from the cartel visited me last night to let me know the cartel expected me to continue Ruben's fine work."

Agent Lot raised his eyebrows. "Yeah. I was going to ask you about the bandage."

"And because he probably was right. I'm sitting on a ton of assets, and the entire operation looks and feels like a money laundering business."

Agent Lot nodded. "Right. So, you don't want to violate any laws and go to jail?"

"Exactly," Stan said. "Nor do I want to end up in the morgue. You know the drill. They've threatened me, my kids, Jodie and Paula, and everyone we know."

"Right. What kind of money are we talking about here?"

"I have no idea, but I just opened a brokerage statement with two million dollars recently deposited. I haven't had a chance to price out all of the businesses and other assets, but it will be in the tens of millions."

Agent Lot took a deep breath. "Well, Stan. Let me look into all of this and get back to you. In the meantime, do what they tell you as long as it's just money laundering."

Stan nodded dejectedly. "Okay, I will carry on as if nothing happened."

Lot nodded. "I'll have someone go by your home and office and see if we can identify anyone suspicious hanging around. We'll also sweep for bugs at your home and in your office. You better warn your staff to be vigilant and report if they see anyone suspicious hanging around or following them."

"Right. We're ordering security for everyone," Stan noted.

"That's good."

"I'm meeting Jodie and Besch at the police gun range later tonight. They want me to carry a gun for a while."

Lot smiled. "Just don't shoot yourself or any innocent bystanders."

Stan laughed. "Right. That's why I haven't carried a gun in the past, but it looks like I better learn how to handle one now."

After dinner, Stan drove back to Dallas not anxious to begin his firearms training. He had a sick feeling in his stomach just thinking about having a lethal weapon on his person. When he got to the gun range, Jodie was waiting outside.

"How did your meeting go?" Jodie asked.

Stan sighed. "About as expected. Agent Lot will get with his superiors and see how they want me to handle the situation."

Jodie nodded sympathetically. "I'm sorry, Stan. This is so unfair. Why would someone intentionally dump this mess on you? It's unconscionable."

Stan didn't know what to say, so he just shrugged. "Well, let's get started. I've heard firing a gun can be very therapeutic."

Jodie smiled. "Yes. That it is. Come on. I'll make a marksman out of you."

They went inside and found Besch waiting with their weapons and targets. For almost two hours, they fired hundreds of rounds, and when they were done, Stan actually did feel much better. But he knew he had lots of work to do to become a proficient marksman. Still, at least now, he wouldn't be defenseless if the cartel sent him another messenger.

14
The Arrest

Jodie

Jodie drove Stan back to the office after finishing at the gun range. On the way, they stopped for dinner at the Cheesecake Factory at North Park. Stan updated her on his meeting with Special Agent Lot.

"I'm going to be very busy handling the Acosta Estate for a while and operating all his businesses until I can sell them. I'll need you to handle my Chapter 13 cases until things calm down. Reggie can handle the Chapter 7s."

"Sure, but I want to help you with the cartel, too. You'll need someone to watch your back."

Stan nodded. "Thank you, but I'm not sure how we will be handling that situation yet. Agent Lot will talk to his superiors, and then we will devise a game plan."

"Of course," Jodie replied. "I'm just worried about you."

"You're worried about me?" Stan protested. "I'm not the one who shot one of the cartel members."

Jodie smiled. "Still, you've got control of all of their money."

Stan stiffened. "True. You have a point. But they just want me to keep doing what Rubin was doing."

"Right, but you can't do that. You have to liquidate the estate," Jodie noted.

"True, but if I didn't liquidate it immediately, the only one who could complain would be the final beneficiary."

"Who is that?"

"The New Hope Legal Clinics, Inc. Ruben visited their Dallas location on the day of his murder. The man I met there might go along with the plan if I agree to keep up his funding."

"I hope you are right," Jodie replied, "but do you think he'd be willing to engage in criminal activity."

"No, and he may have people higher up who would have to make that decision. But if the FBI asks them to do it, they might."

Jodie nodded thoughtfully. "True, but it would still be perilous. Not too many people could handle that kind of stress."

"Well, let's not get ahead of ourselves. Let's wait and see what Agent Lot has to say."

Stan left Jodie at her office door, and she went inside. A neat stack of telephone messages was in the center of her desk. She sat down and started going through them. She stopped when she saw a sticky note from Paula. She got up and went to Paula's office. Paula was studying some papers when Jodie walked in. She looked up.

"Paula. You wanted to see me?"

Paula nodded solemnly. "Yeah. I'm afraid so. I wanted to give you a heads-up. Wendy called to let me know the indictment is in. The Sheriff will get the arrest warrant out on Amanda this afternoon."

"Oh. Shit!" Jodie said. "I can't believe they are going after her. She's been through so much. This is going to devastate her."

"I know. Find Reggie and get him out there right away before the Sheriff gets there. I don't want her talking to anyone."

"Right," Jodie said. "I'll go with him. She might not have a babysitter for Julie, and we don't want Julie being taken to Child Protective Services."

"No. That would be a nightmare," Paula agreed.

"Who is the prosecutor?" Jodie asked.

"Stewart Collins," Paula said, "I know him well. He was a classmate at SMU."

"Is he any good?"

She shrugged. "He's got an eighty-nine percent conviction rate, but most of those are plea deals. He probably doesn't actually try but a half dozen cases a year."

"Okay. That's good."

"It could be worse," Paula replied. "Tomorrow, you need to file that motion to abate the civil case."

"Right," Jodie said. "It's all ready to go. As soon as we have a case number, I'll call Tyson to see if he'll agree or make us fight."

"He's the type who will be vulnerable to your feminine charm. If you know what I mean," Paula noted with a grin.

Jodie smiled. "Good. I'll keep that in mind."

Jodie left and went back to her office. She immediately picked up the phone and called Reggie.

"What's up?" Reggie asked.

"Bad news," Jodie said. "The indictment came down on Amanda."

"Fuck!" Reggie replied. "I can't believe it. Those bastards!"

"Okay. Calm down," Jodie scolded. "We knew this was going to happen. Where are you?"

Reggie sighed heavily. "I'm on my way to the office. I'll be there in ten."

"Okay. We need to go out and prepare Amanda for the Sheriff. She's going to be a wreck."

"Tell me about it. Okay, see you soon."

Fifteen minutes later, Reggie and Jodie walked to the parking garage. Jodie started to get into her car, but Reggie shook his head.

"Do you have room in your trunk for her wheelchair?"

Jodie glanced at her car. "Ah. Probably not."

"Let's take mine. I've got plenty of room. I have to take Amanda to her doctor's appointments, so I'm used to getting her in and out of my car."

Jodie raised her eyebrows. "Wow. You take her to the doctor. That's nice of you."

"Well, her mom isn't strong enough to do it, so how else could she get there?"

Jodie shrugged and gave Reggie an approving smile. They went to Reggie's car, got in, and headed to Amanda's place. It was about a forty-five-minute drive, so they talked strategy while they drove.

"Did you tell Amanda we were coming? Reggie asked.

"Yes, but I didn't tell her why. I didn't want to freak her out."

"What if the Sheriff gets there before we do?"

"That won't happen. The indictment just came down, and it takes a while to get it to the Sheriff's office. We should get there at least an hour before the Sheriff's deputy arrives."

Reggie didn't say anything. Jodie could tell Reggie was upset, so she said, "So, how are we going to get Amanda out of this mess?"

Reggie frowned. "Well, Josh and I have been looking into the doctor to see if he had any health or other issues that might have contributed to the accident."

"Good."

"Josh has a friend who is a mechanic. We took him to the impound lot to inspect the two cars for evidence of any mechanical issues."

“Un huh,” Jodie said.

"He hasn't come up with anything definitive yet."

“Oh. Too bad,” Jodie moaned.

"Yeah. And we're going out to the accident site to look around, see if anyone lives near where it happened. We need to find a witness."

"Yes, that would definitely be helpful."

When they got to Amanda's place, she waited anxiously out front in her wheelchair. Julie had been riding a bike up the street, and she came racing toward them when she saw them.

"Hi, Amanda," Jodie said cheerily.

Reggie grabbed the handlebars of Julie's bike as she skidded to a stop in front of him. He smiled broadly as she jumped off the bike and stood behind her mother.

"Why are you here?" Julie asked. "Mom doesn't have a doctor's appointment today."

Amanda looked at Reggie expectantly.

Reggie took a deep breath and said gently, "Well, do you remember when we talked about the Sheriff coming out?"

"Oh, no!" Julie exclaimed. "They can't take Mommie away! No. I won't let them."

"It will just be for a little while. We'll bring your Mommie back after she sees the Judge."

Jodie wheeled Amanda back into the house. Reggie and Amanda followed.

"I'll follow you to the county jail," Jodie said. "Paula will be there to meet us. Hopefully, there will be an arraignment today, but it may not happen until tomorrow. If so, you'll have to stay overnight in the jail."

Amanda's mouth opened, and her complexion paled. "Stay overnight? Really?"

Jodie nodded apologetically.

"Okay, but what about Julie."

"Reggie will stay with Julie until your mother can get here."

Julie looked at Reggie. Reggie looked like he was going to cry, but he forced a smile. "Hey, we can play some games until your grandmother gets here."

Julie didn't say anything.

"I'm sorry," Amanda said, tears streaming down her cheeks. "I shouldn't have worked that double shift. I didn't want to. I thought I'd lose my job if I didn't."

"It wasn't your fault," Reggie assured her. "We're going to figure this out. Don't worry."

Amanda smiled softly. "I know you will try, but what if it was my fault."

"No, Mommie. It wasn't your fault. It was that biker."

Reggie looked at Julie. "What biker?"

Julie began to cry, "I don't know. The biker."

Reggie looked at Jodie. Then they heard a car pull up outside. Jodie went to the window and looked out.

"They are here?" Jodie advised.

They heard doors slam as two sheriff deputies got out of their vehicle. Jodie went to the door and opened it. The two deputies displayed their identifications. Jodie opened the door wider so they could step inside.

The taller of the two deputies said. "We have a warrant to arrest Amanda Rich."

Jodie nodded. "Yes, I am one of her attorneys. We were expecting you."

"Where is Mrs. Rich?" he asked.

Jodie led them into the family room where Amanda was sitting in her wheelchair."

Julie stood behind with a terrified look on her face.

The deputy frowned. "Can she walk?"

"No," Jodie said. "Do you have a disability van? She'll need to have her wheelchair with her."

"No. We weren't advised of her condition."

"Well, we can take her and follow you in," Reggie advised.

The officer shook his head. "No. We have to follow protocol. She'll have to ride in the back seat of our squad car."

"She can't get into your squad car without help," Reggie protested.

"We'll get her in," the officer replied.

"And if you injure her further," Jodie advised, "We'll sue the department. Let Reggie put her in the squad car. He does it all the time, and there will be less chance of further injury."

The officer took a deep breath. "Alright, but she'll have to be handcuffed."

"Oh, my god!" Reggie exclaimed.

"That's okay," Jodie said. "Cuff her once she is in the vehicle, okay?"

The officer nodded. Addressing Amanda; the officer said, "Amanda Rich. I must advise you that you have the right to remain silent, but if you choose to talk, anything you say can and will be used against you in a court of law. You have the right to an attorney; if you cannot afford one, one will be provided for you. Do you understand these rights?"

"Yes," Amanda replied meekly.

"She won't be saying anything. Her criminal attorney is Paula Waters, and she'll be at the Sheriff's Office when you get there. She wants to be present if there is any interrogation."

"I'll let the detective assigned to the case know."

"Thank you," Jodie said. "Do you know who the detective is going to be?"

The deputy looked down at his paperwork. "Yes, Detective Mark Madison."

Jodie didn't recognize the name, so she jotted it down on an empty envelope she found on the table next to Amanda.

"Okay. Let's get you in the squad car," Jodie said.

Reggie pushed the wheelchair to the squad car door, adroitly lifted Amanda out, and sat her in the backseat. After he lifted her feet and turned her around, the officer cuffed her, and they closed the door.

15
Biker

Reggie

As Jodie and the Sheriff's squad cars drove away, Reggie and Julie watched silently. Julie began to cry, so Reggie picked her up and held her. Amanda turned back awkwardly from the squad car's back seat and forced a departing smile. After they were out of view, Reggie suggested they go inside and find a game to play. While Julie was finding a game, Reggie called Julie's grandmother and told her what had happened. She said she'd get there as soon as she could.

When Reggie returned to the kitchen, Julie had set up places for a tea party. Reggie laughed, thinking back to the many tea parties he'd had with his sister Marcia. None of his brothers would participate in the parties, but Reggie always enjoyed playing with his little sister.

"Alright, Reggie. Would you like a cup of tea?"

Reggie took his seat and said, "Yes, please."

Julie pretended to pour the tea and then handed the cup to Reggie. He politely took it and pretended to drink.

"Oh, this is mint tea. It's so good."

"Yes, it's my specialty," Julie advised.

After Julie had served them some biscuits, Reggie asked, "What did Santa bring you for Christmas?"

Julie sighed heavily. "Santa didn't come this year."

"What? He didn't come?"

"No. Momma said our house is hard to find, and we don't have a chimney. So, Grandma got me a new lunch box and a coloring book."

"Well, that's good," Reggie said tentatively. "Julie. What did you mean when you said the accident was the biker's fault?"

Julie looked at Reggie thoughtfully and then back at her teacup but did not respond.

"Did you see someone on a motorcycle before the accident?"

Julie stiffened. Indignantly, she said, "This is not a proper topic of conversation for a tea party."

"I know, but it is important. You want your mother to come home to you and stay with you, right?"

Julie nodded vigorously.

"So, before the accident, did you see someone on a motorcycle?"

"No. I didn't see anything," Julie said impatiently. "I heard it."

"So, you heard a motorcycle?"

Julie nodded. "I think so. It was very loud. I put my fingers in my ears and then..." Julie closed her eyes and squinted.

"Then what?" Reggie pressed.

She removed her fingers and relaxed her face. "Then ... I don't remember."

"So, you heard a loud noise which sounded like a motorcycle, and that's the last thing you remember until you woke up in the hospital?"

Julie nodded. "Would you like another cup of tea?"

Reggie didn't respond. His mind was racing with the revelation of a motorcycle. Could this be the break he was looking for? He wondered how he could track down the driver and figure out what had happened. If a third party was involved and they had fled the scene of the accident, they wouldn't be coming forward voluntarily. He felt so frustrated he could scream.

A knock on the door interrupted his contemplation. Julie raced to the door and opened it. It was Stella Rich.

"Grandma!" Julie exclaimed. "You're here just in time for tea."

Reggie filled Mrs. Rich in on the situation with Amanda and explained she might not be back for a few days,

"What. You can't get her out on bail?"

Reggie grimaced. "It depends on the judge they assign. She'll have to post a bond. Hopefully, it won't be a very big one. I don't imagine either of you has any collateral to post, right?"

"No," Stella spat. "We don't have a pot to piss in."

Reggie nodded. Paula will try to convince the judge that she's not a flight risk in her medical condition. Still, the bond will probably be at least ten or twenty thousand."

"I guess I'll be taking care of Julie for a while," Stella moaned.

"It looks that way," Reggie agreed.

After a while, Jodie returned to pick up Reggie. Stella seemed to have everything under control and was sitting down to be served an imaginary cup of tea, so they left. Reggie told Jodie about Julie's memory of the sound of a motorcycle. So, they drove to the accident scene, hoping seeing it again might give them insight into how a motorcycle might have come into play.

"How is Julie? She seemed pretty upset," Jodie asked.

"She is, but she's a tough little girl. I think she'll be alright."

"The deputies must have called ahead when they left here. They had a nurse with a wheelchair waiting to take her in to be booked," Jodie advised.

"Was Paula there?"

"Yes, she said she wasn't going to let Amanda out of her sight."

"That's good. Amanda must be terrified to be booked and locked in a cell."

Jodie nodded. "I can only imagine."

U.S. Highway 380 was a four-lane, partially divided highway, but there wasn't a divided median where the accident occurred. The adjoining property was undeveloped agricultural land, except the southwest quadrant had an old strip shopping center that had seen better days. As they drove by, they noticed a gas station, convenience store, and a bar called Hell's Haven Bar & Grille. Parked in front of the bar, they observed several cars and a pair of motorcycles.

"That's interesting," Jodie said, looking at the two motorcycles.

Reggie nodded, pulled into the parking lot, and parked in front of the convenience store. Before they left the car, Jodie took notes on the motorcycles, including their make, model, and license numbers. When she was finished, Reggie went inside the convenience store and bought some snacks while Jodie went into the bar. As he was checking out,

Reggie struck up a conversation with the cashier, an old man with a name tag that indicated his name was Red.

"So, do you get much biker traffic in here?" Reggie asked.

"Not that much. Bikers are not much interested in food or sodas, and the landlord won't let us sell beer."

"Why's that?" Jodie asked.

"Dusty, the guy who owns the bar, also owns this place. This store is for the gas station customers," Red replied.

"Right. Makes sense," Reggie said as he turned to leave. "Thanks."

Reggie didn't need gas, but he wanted to hang around for a while and give Jodie time in the bar, so he pulled up to a pump and started filling his tank. While waiting for his tank to fill, he heard a loud rumble of engines behind him and turned to see three more bikers pulling off of 380 and stirring up a cloud of dust. One of them pulled up to the pump next to him and began filling his tank.

Reggie smiled at the man and said, "Hey, man."

The heavily tattooed man nodded but didn't reply.

"So, you local or just passing through?"

The man frowned and spat, "Why do you care?"

Reggie raised his hands, smiled, and said tentatively. "Oh, sorry. Just making conversation."

The man took a deep breath, then smiled. "Sorry, I just got pulled over by a f***ing cop. The asshole had no reason to stop me. Just did it for sport."

"Right. I can imagine that happens a lot."

"Yes. Almost every day. I live in Anna and come here for a beer after work every afternoon. I'm not speeding or driving wildly, but it doesn't matter. The cops just love to pull bikers over."

"Jesus! That sucks. ... Hey, you didn't happen to see that wreck on 380 along here a few weeks back, did you?"

Red thought a moment, then shook his head. "Not that I remember? Why do you ask?"

"I'm an attorney, and I represent one of the drivers. She and her daughter were injured pretty badly. I'm trying to figure out what happened."

"Oh. Yeah. A doctor died, right? I read about it in the paper."

"Yes. That's it."

"It's tough out there on the road," Red said. "I can attest to that. A lot of people are maniacs once they get behind the wheel."

Reggie's pump turned off, so he finished up, got in his car, and nodded to the biker. Then he pulled his car over to a parking spot in front of the bar to wait for Jodie. As he pulled up, she came out and got in the passenger seat.

Several other bikers left as they pulled out, so Reggie followed them for a while.

"So, did you learn anything?" Reggie asked.

Jodie shook her head. "Not really. The bartender heard about the wreck but doesn't remember who told him about it. I gave him my card in case anybody came in and mentioned it."

"Good. Maybe we'll get lucky."

A half mile down the road, one of the bikers suddenly did a screeching U-turn and headed back toward the strip center. The others continued, so Reggie followed them until they went northbound onto U.S. Highway 75. Reggie took the southbound entrance and headed back to the office.

When they returned to the office, they went to find Paula to get an update on Amanda's booking. She hadn't returned yet, so they went to their offices to see what calls had come in while they were out and what urgent tasks needed to be performed.

Reggie felt a wave of depression come over him. He couldn't imagine what poor Amanda was going through. His thoughts then turned to Julie. He had been lucky as a child with two loving parents who had provided him with everything he ever needed. Poor Julie hadn't been so fortunate. Her future seemed bleak at that moment, and he feared he wouldn't be able to do anything to change it.

16
The Arraignment

Paula

Paula had been at the Sheriff's office in McKinney, Texas, for over an hour before Amanda finally arrived. Amanda was met by two female Sheriff's deputies pushing a wheelchair. Paula had complained bitterly to Stewart Collins when she found out that Reggie had to put Amanda into the backseat of the squad car. The fact that he hadn't simply called her, and asked her to bring Amanda in voluntarily, galled her.

"You better make sure your officers take good care of her while she is in custody," Paula spat.

Stewart Collins smiled. "Don't worry. She'll be kept in the infirmary while she is in custody. There's a nurse there at all times," Collins assured her.

"I can't believe the DA decided to prosecute her. Hasn't she suffered enough? She's penniless and gonna be crippled for the rest of her life. I don't get it!"

Collins shrugged. "Not my call. The District Attorney assigned me the case, so I have no choice but to prosecute it."

"Well, she's obviously not a flight risk. Will you at least agree to a nominal bond or release on her own recognizance?"

"No. Negligent homicide is a serious charge, so I'll ask for the standard bond for cases like this."

"What's your idea of a standard bond?" Paula asked warily.

"Twenty-five thousand."

"What! You might as well ask for a million dollars. There is no way Amanda could come up with $25,000, and you know she has no collateral."

"Well, she'll get used to the county jail. It's not so bad. Ask your partner. He's spent some time there, didn't he?"

Collins was referring to Stan's arrest years earlier for contempt of court when he disobeyed the sitting district judge's ruling and allowed his client to testify while she was under hypnosis. The deception worked, and Stan's client was found innocent, but the judge wasn't amused and sent Stan to jail. Luckily, Stan had recently saved the life of one of the Sheriff's deputies, so the Sheriff treated Stan like a king while he did his time in the Collin County Jail. Paula knew it would be different for Amanda.

"What does the DA have against Amanda? The way you are treating her doesn't make any sense. She is a nobody and will be a burden on the state if they incarcerate her. At best, she was negligent, so she's not likely to get more than a slap on the wrist from a jury. Why go to the expense of a trial? Let her out on bond, give us a little time to investigate the accident, and then, maybe she'll agree to a reasonable plea."

Collins shrugged. "Hey. I've got an idea. Why don't we let Judge McIntyre decide on bail? The arraignment is at 10 a.m. tomorrow."

Collins forced a big smile, turned, and walked away, leaving Paula in stunned silence. She knew Amanda would be traumatized for life, having to be booked, photographed, stripped naked, her body cavities searched, disinfected, and then dressed in bright orange overalls and paraded before the court and gallery to complete her total humiliation.

Paula put a call into her bondsman to see if there was a chance in hell, she could get a bond for Amanda. Paula knew calling the bondsman would be a wasted effort, but she had to try it to assure Julie that she'd done all she could to get her mom out of jail. As expected, the bondsman was sympathetic, but he was a businessman, and, as much as he liked Paula, he told her he couldn't afford to take risks.

When Paula returned to the office, she found Reggie and Jodie and gave them the bad news. When she was done, Reggie told her about Julie's memory of a noisy motorcycle engine at or around the time of the crash and their visit to the accident scene.

"So, there's a possibility that a biker might have caused or contributed to the accident," Reggie speculated. "You know how reckless bikers can be farting around on their bikes."

Paula nodded. "Sure, but you'll have to get an actual witness or other evidence to prove that. Right now, we have nothing."

"True," Reggie agreed. "I'll go out there again and talk to some more bikers. Maybe I can find an actual witness."

"What about the inspection of the two vehicles?" Paula asked.

"Done, but nothing solid yet. Some silver paint that has possibilities," Reggie replied.

Paula looked at Jodie. "Did you get a continuance of the wrongful death suit?"

"Not yet," Jodie said. "I'll do that first thing tomorrow."

"Do you have any ideas on how we can keep Amanda out of jail? The bondsman won't post bond without collateral."

"I could guarantee it," Reggie replied.

Paula frowned. "That's noble of you, Reggie, but you don't have any assets to pledge."

Reggie nodded dejectedly. "Yeah. You're right."

"She's not going anywhere," Jodie replied. "I've got a $10,000 CD I could pledge."

Paula gave Jodie a disapproving stare. "You guys are getting too emotionally involved in this case. We can't go around posting bonds for our criminal clients. It's a bad precedent, and it puts more pressure on me. Not only do I have to worry about Amanda, but I'd have to also worry about your financial stake in the outcome."

"Come on. She's not going anywhere," Jodie repeated.

"Are you sure about that? What prevents her from packing her and Julie's bags and taking off to new horizons?" Paula asked.

"Money," Reggie retorted. "She wouldn't have money to go anywhere, and how could she take care of herself out on the road?"

Paula thought for a moment. "Okay, those are good arguments. I'll see what the judge thinks about them."

When Reggie and Jodie had gone, she called the bondsman back and told him Jodie would pledge her CD for Amanda's bond. She explained the unlikelihood that Amanda would skip out on them due to her financial and medical condition.

The following day Paula met with Amanda before the arraignment and explained the situation. "Judge McIntyre isn't sympathetic, but he is a realist and usually pretty fair, so I think he will grant you bail."

"But I thought I couldn't get bail without collateral."

"You are fortunate," Paula said. "Reggie wanted to post bail for you but wasn't able since he's just out of law school and doesn't have any money."

"Oh. That was so good of him."

"Yes, it was. So, Jodie stepped up and agreed to do it?"

Amanda's eyes widened. "What? Why would she do that?"

Paula shrugged. "I don't know. She's a good person, but I'll be honest with you, I didn't recommend it. It's against our firm policy, but it's her choice. So, don't disappear on us if you are lucky enough to get out on bail."

Amanda shook her head. "No. No way!"

The bailiff stepped in and advised them their case was up. Paula wheeled Amanda into the courtroom, and they took their places at the counsel table. Collins and an assistant were already stationed at their table. The bailiff spoke up, "All rise for the Honorable Judge Joseph McIntyre, Judge of the 199th District Court."

The judge walked in and quickly took the bench. "Be seated," he said and looked down at his docket sheet. "Alright. The State of Texas vs. Amanda Rich. Let's have announcements."

Paula and Collins both rose. Amanda tried to stand up but faltered. Paula grabbed her and sat her back down. "It's okay," Paula said, "Paula Waters for the Defendant."

"Stewart Collins for the state," Collins advised.

"Okay. Ms. Rich. You are charged with involuntary manslaughter. Would you like the charges to be read to you?"

"No, Your Honor," Paula replied. "We'll waive a reading."

"Then, Ms. Rich, how do you plead?"

Amanda cleared her throat and said, "Ah. Not guilty."

The judge nodded and then addressed Collins. "Does the state have a recommendation on bond?"

"Yes, Your Honor," Collins replied. "In light of the gravity of the charges, the state would normally recommend a bond of $50,000. But, given Ms. Rich's condition, we would be satisfied with $25,000."

The judge nodded, then looked at Paula and raised his eyebrows. "Ms. Waters?"

"Your Honor, Ms. Rich is obviously not a flight risk. She doesn't have the financial resources to go anywhere as she has lost her job and lives on food stamps, welfare, and Medicaid. She doesn't have a passport and requires constant medical supervision due to her accident. We request she be released on her own recognizance."

The judge gave Amanda a stern look and then looked over at Collins. "Mr. Collins. How could the Defendant be a flight risk?'

"Ah, well. Ah. She has a car."

"Her car is in wrecked and sitting in the impound yard," Paula noted irritably.

The judge chuckled. "Okay, it doesn't look like she'd be able to drive herself even if the car was functional. I'm not going to require a bond. I think an ankle monitor will be sufficient."

"Yes, Your Honor," Collins conceded.

"Okay. I'm setting this case for trial on the October docket. That should give both of you plenty of time to prepare, so I don't want to see any motions for a continuance."

"Yes, Your Honor," Collins said.

Paula nodded as well, and the judge excused them. She looked at Amanda and saw the relief on her face knowing she would be going home soon. As she was being wheeled out by the bailiff, Paula told her she'd wait for her to be released and Reggie would take her home.

The Sheriff's office and jail were just across the street from the courthouse, so Paula called her friend Wendy Pierce to see if she had a break coming up. Wendy said she did, so they met in the law library, where several small conference rooms were available for lawyers to meet with clients.

"So, how did your arraignment go?" Wendy asked.

"Better than I expected. I was afraid Amanda would have to stay in jail until her trial date, but then Jodie agreed to put up the necessary collateral for her bond. You've met Jodie, right?"

"No. I don't think so. She does civil litigation, doesn't she?"

"Yes, that's right."

"I've heard of her," Wendy replied.

"Well, she offered to put up $10,000 as collateral on a bond."

"Wow! Lucky for Amanda."

"As it turned out, we didn't need it," Paula said. "The judge let her out with only an ankle monitor."

"Wow! That's surprising."

"Yes and thank God. I can only imagine what Amanda has been through for the last 24 hours."

Wendy nodded knowingly. "So, how can I help you?"

Paula squirmed in her seat. "Well, I hate to keep taking advantage of our friendship, but I'm really trying to wrap my head around the DA prosecuting my client for involuntary manslaughter. She barely survived the accident herself, and her future is already pretty bleak without these criminal charges."

"Yeah, I was wondering about that myself, but I was afraid to bring it up. Everyone knows about our relationship, so any questions like that to my boss would raise a red flag."

Paula nodded. "Right. I don't want you jeopardizing your job, but if you inadvertently hear anything that might shed some light on the DA's motivation, let me know, okay?"

"Sure, I'll keep my eyes and ears open, but it's not likely I'll hear anything without directly asking about it."

"Well, don't get yourself in trouble," Paula admonished.

"I won't, but don't worry, all the legal secretaries gossip in the break room about all kinds of things, and there is a code of silence amongst us."

Paula laughed. "I bet."

"I might hear something there."

"Good. If you do, let me know."

Paula and Wendy left the library and went their separate ways. When Paula got to the jail, she saw Amanda about to be released. A deputy handed her a bag with her belongings, had her sign a receipt for them, and then buzzed her out. Paula rushed over and took control of the wheelchair from the deputy who was pushing it. Paula wheeled Amanda over to a bank of chairs, and she sat down to wait for Reggie, who was on his way to take her home.

"Thank you, so much for getting me out of this place. I would have died had I been forced to stay here until my trial."

"Well, you got lucky. Reggie and Jodie went out on a limb for you."

"I know," Amanda said with tears welling in her eyes. "You have all been so wonderful to me."

Amanda cried softly for a few moments, then looked up and pleaded, "You can't let them convict me, Paula! I didn't mean to hurt anybody. I don't want to come back here. Don't let them bring me back here."

Paula wanted to assure her that wouldn't happen, but she knew better than to make promises she might not be able to keep.

17
Hidden Secrets

Reggie

After Reggie had discovered Dr. Kenneth Short's DUI convictions, pending lawsuits, and several failed marriages, Jodie had tasked him with thoroughly investigating each of them to see if he could find anything that might be useful in Amanda's defense. Reggie had agreed with alacrity and spent several days on the task.

His first stop was the District Clerk's office, where he pulled the files on the DUI cases from the Court's archives. Short's first arrest was on January 2, 1992, when he was pulled over after attending a Christmas party. He refused a breathalyzer test, so he was arrested and jailed. During the night, his attorney arranged bond, and he was released early that morning. After that, the file was lacking in information. According to the docket sheet, the case was eventually dropped with a notation that the arresting officer was unavailable, and the blood test had been lost. Reggie pondered this for a moment and then moved to the next file.

The second arrest was after the Dallas police were called to the scene of an accident in which Dr. Short had been involved. From the file notes, Reggie ascertained that Dr. Short had been tailgating a red 1997 Buick when an approaching light suddenly turned yellow. Apparently, Dr. Short expected the Buick to rush through the intersection on the yellow light, but instead, the driver slammed on his brakes while Dr. Short was accelerating. The laws of physics prevailed, creating a nasty tangle of metal, shattered glass, and bloody flesh.

Dr. Short wasn't seriously hurt, but the driver of the Buick suffered a serious whiplash, among other injuries. While sifting through the rubble, the police officer found several empty beer cans and the butt of a joint. Again, Dr. Short was arrested. Since it was daytime, he spent only hours at the police station before his lawyer showed up and posted his bond. After that, a plea agreement was entered for a guilty plea of misdemeanor DUI with an order of defensive driving and 100 hours of community service.

As he was going through the civil litigation files, he found that one of the lawsuits against Dr. Short was filed by the driver of the Buick in the rear-end collision. The docket sheet indicated the case had been settled, but there were no details. Reggie did note, however, that the doctor's deposition had been taken during the prosecution of the case and that a copy of it had been filed and was in the Court's archives. Not seeing the deposition in the file, he asked one of the clerks about it."

"Everything we have should be in that file," he assured Reggie. "If it's not there, we don't have it."

"But the docket sheet says it was filed, so it should be here."

The clerk shrugged. "Sorry, if we had it, it would be there. Someone must have checked out the file, taken out the deposition but not put it back. The clerks are so busy, they may not have realized it."

Reggie shook his head in anger and frustration but had no choice but to move on to the following file. It was a civil case, a dispute between partners in a real estate venture in Denton County. In the complaint, the partnership complained that one of the partners had not responded to cash calls and owed the partnership $227,021. The partnership was seeking a judgment for that amount and asked that the defendant's partnership interest be forfeited if it were not paid.

Reggie left the courthouse disappointed, but he still had hope. There were two ex-wives who might know something that would help him. Although they may refuse to talk to him, he thought the odds were good that at least one of them would like the opportunity to deliver a little payback. He was right.

Cindy Black's eyes lit up after Reggie explained why he was there. When he told her he was sorry for her loss, she laughed. She explained she had been married to Dr. Short for eleven years when she discovered he was sleeping with one of the hospital nurses. Their divorce was final in 1995 after a nasty fight that had gone on for nearly two years.

Reggie explained what he was looking for, and Cindy said she couldn't think of anything helpful right off hand, but she'd answer any questions he might have.

"So, Dr. Short had a couple arrests on DUI charges," Reggie noted.

Cindy nodded. "Oh, yes. Four or five at least, but he had a good lawyer who got him out of most of them."

"I saw that. He pleaded one out and got 100 hours of community service."

"Yes, but he never did the community service. His lawyer talked his probation officer into accepting work in a free clinic where he was paid for his time."

"How did that work?'

Cindy shrugged. "I don't know. You'd have to ask his lawyer?"

"Who was his lawyer?" Reggie asked.

"Tom Tyson."

"Tom "the Tornado" Tyson?" Reggie said, "I thought he was a PI attorney."

"He is now. Back then, he was hungry and would take on any case if the client could pay his fees. Now he makes so much money fighting insurance companies that he doesn't have time for criminal work."

"You sound like you know him?"

"Yes, He belonged to Bent Tree Country Club. Ken had a membership there, and we socialized with him and his wife, Sondra."

"Are you still friends?" Reggie asked.

"God, no!" Cindy exclaimed. "After the divorce, Tom wouldn't give me the time of day. He was Kenneth's friend, not mine."

Reggie explained the facts of the accident between her ex-husband and Amanda, then asked, "What kind of a driver was your ex-husband?"

"He was a horrible driver. He was always in a hurry and had no patience. I always did the driving if we were together."

"What about his health? Did he have any issues that might impact his driving?"

"No. He was overweight, had high blood pressure, and was pre-diabetic. But I doubt that would have any bearing on your case."

Reggie nodded and talked to Cindy for another half-hour. Then he thanked her and returned to the office to report his findings to Jodie and Paula. They both considered what he found, but neither seemed excited about it.

"Okay. What about Amanda's boss. He made her do a double shift," Reggie moaned.

"True, and had she been on an errand for the company, they'd be liable. But Amanda was on her way home. An employer is not responsible for what its employees do after work."

"Yeah, but wasn't he negligent in letting her drive, knowing she was tired and might fall asleep."

"He didn't know that," Paula said. "You couldn't prove he knew she would fall asleep."

"But you might be able to prove he *should have known* she was *likely* to fall asleep and cause an accident," Jodie noted.

Paula considered this. "Well, I doubt we could prove that, and I don't see how it would help our criminal defense."

"Maybe not, but it might be a viable cause of action against Southern Battery," Reggie argued.

Paula nodded. "Okay, knock yourself out."

Reggie smiled, got up, and went back to his office to start researching employer liability. He just knew there had to be a way to go after Southern Battery. They'd have loads of insurance and never let a case like this go to trial. All he had to do was find a viable theory of liability. "Piece 'a cake," he mumbled as he got to work.

18
Undercover

Stan

It wasn't until the middle of January 2000 before Stan heard back from Agent Lot. Stan wondered if the FBI would leave him swinging in the wind. He didn't know what to do if the FBI said they couldn't help him. He was much relieved when he got the message that Agent Lot wanted to meet.

Stan drove Rebekah's old Nissan Altima to the rendezvous hoping the Cartel wouldn't recognize it. He'd driven it late one night to the office, left it in the parking garage, and then took a cab home. He didn't have a parking tag, so he informed the head of security that he would be driving it from time to time to keep the battery charged. He didn't want it being towed away.

After driving around the block several times, he decided he wasn't being followed. He got onto LBJ Freeway, heading West for the thirty-minute drive. Agent Lot was waiting for him at Denny's in their regular booth. Lot stood up when he saw Stan. The two shook hands and took seats across from each other. The waitress brought Stan coffee, and they both ordered breakfast.

When the waitress was out of sight, Stan asked, "So, have you come up with a brilliant plan? I hope."

Agent Lot stifled a laugh. "Not exactly."

Stan slumbed in his chair. "So, how am I going to extricate myself from this mess?"

"My boss is intrigued by this opportunity you've presented us. Needless to say, it is very rare to be able to put a major drug cartel out of business completely. So, we want to work with you, but we don't really know enough right now to formulate a viable plan. At this stage, we would like you to follow their instructions and carry on with their money laundering."

Stan sighed. "So, you want me to work undercover for you?"

"Yes. I presumed that was what you were offering to do."

"I guess. Do you even know the name of the Cartel?"

"Yes. It's the *Las Guías* or, in English, *The Guides.* They will guide anybody or anything into the United States for the right price. They operate out of Nogales, Mexico, and have clubs and brothels mainly in the southwestern United States. "

"So, how long will I need to do this?" Stan moaned.

"It depends. It could take some time to gather the necessary intelligence to take it down successfully. It's not hard to arrest these thugs, but it is very difficult to convict them. And you don't want any of them walking free after you have helped bust them because they will hunt you down and kill you."

"So, I've heard," Stan agreed. "So, will you have someone tailing me?"

"No. Not 24-7. If you are following their instructions, you shouldn't be in danger. Of course, if you feel your cover has been blown, let us know, and we'll have your back. The main thing we need you to do is learn as much about Las Guias and their operations as possible."

"How will I get the information to you?" Stan asked warily.

"Our technicians will set up a monitoring system so we can listen to your phone calls and get copies of your faxes, emails, and outgoing correspondence. You can supplement all of that by sending us periodic reports."

"How will I do that? I can't let you bug our law office. That would violate attorney-client privilege."

"Then you will have to work out of a private office."

Stan thought about this for a moment. "Right. I can keep the office at the Mustang Office Suites and work from there. That makes sense since Tom office there. I will be working in my individual capacity, and the firm won't be involved except for the probate. I'll hire Jodie to do any legal work I need to do. Okay, so how do I send you these reports you want?"

"You'll set up a fake vendor and include your reports with their weekly statements."

"Are you sure they won't be able to intercept these reports?"

"Yes. We'll set up a special post office box at your post office. It will be secure if you deposit the mail at any U.S. post office. Just be careful of new hires at the office suite. Las Guias may try to infiltrate their organization as insurance."

Stan nodded. "Right. I'll have to do everything myself. Luckily, I took typing in high school."

"I assume you can trust all your employees at Turner & Waters?"

Stan nodded. "Yes, absolutely."

Agent Lot stroked his chin. "We'll, keep an eye on them anyway. The Cartel may offer one of them an extra paycheck to spy on you."

Stan swallowed hard. "They wouldn't accept it, but I'll keep that in mind."

"Okay," Agent Lot said. "What's your first move."

"Ah. I'm going to have to meet with all the MedNet clients. That will involve travel to Phoenix and Las Vegas. I'll be taking along our accountant and actuary."

Agent Lot nodded. "We've checked both of them out, and they don't appear to have any connections to the Cartel."

Stan raised his eyebrows. "Wow. That hadn't even occurred to me. Good to know. Anyway, we need to advise the clients of Acosta's death and assure them that we will continue to manage their operations efficiently and his death won't impact them in any way."

"How confident are you of success in this mission? Agent Lot asked.

"I don't know, frankly. They are going to have high expectations. Their practices have been very lucrative, and I don't know if I will be able to manage them as well as Acosta did."

"Right," Agent Lot agreed, "and if you aren't able to, not only will they the clients be pissed off, but the Cartel will also be angry."

"Yeah. This doesn't sound like a fun job," Stan noted.

"Well, give us ninety days, six months tops, and we should have enough to bring them down."

Stan took a deep breath and exhaled slowly. "Right. Six months. Okay, just don't let them kill me or anyone I care about, okay?"

"No promises," Agent Lot replied, "but we're pretty good at what we do. I'm sure it will all turn out okay in the end."

Agent Lot's assurances did little to comfort Stan. He wondered how he had managed to get into such a perilous situation. Ever since he'd been visited by Carlos, he'd had an uncomfortable knot in his stomach. He'd hoped the knot would go away once he enlisted the help of the FBI, but it hadn't. It seemed to intensify with each new day.

When Stan got back to the office, he met with Maria and asked her to make travel arrangements for him to go to Phoenix and then on to Las Vegas. He told her to coordinate with Tom Rice and Roger Moore since they would need to come with him. When he was done, he found Paula and Jodie to fill them in on his situation and catch up on the latest on the Amanda Rich front.

When they all were up to speed, Stan explained, "So, I'm going to be gone for a while. You two will need to hold things together while I'm gone. Security will be of the utmost importance. There will be two private security officers assigned to the firm. Take one of them with you if you go out. You can introduce them as your assistants or paralegals. They are expensive, so you will have to share."

"What about Reggie?" Jodie asked.

"He will be sticking around the office most of the time unless he is out with one of you. If he needs to go out alone, one of you will have to stay in the office so a security officer can go with him."

"What about you?" Paula asked.

"The FBI will keep an eye on me. I shouldn't be at risk as long as I handle their business effectively."

"When will you be back?" Jodie asked.

"Hopefully, only a week or ten days, but you never know. I'll need to take whatever time is necessary to get on top of everything. The Cartel will have high expectations, and I don't want to disappoint them."

"Can't we help you?" Paula asked.

Stan shook his head. "No, I won't be able to talk to you about what I'm doing for the Cartel. I'm not even going to tell you what Cartel is involved. The less you two know, the better. If anyone asks, I'm acting as Trustee of Mr. Acosta's estate in my individual capacity and not as a member of the firm. We need to keep the firm out of this."

Paula nodded. "Okay, but if you need us to do anything, promise you won't hesitate to call us."

"I can't promise that," Stan replied. "I won't intentionally put either of you at risk."

They both looked at Stan with displeasure in their eyes. He smiled warmly and then stood up. "Okay. Thanks. I'll see you in a week or two."

They both hugged Stan, and he left to go home and pack for his trip. The moment Stan stepped in the front door of his home; his cell phone rang. It was Reggie.

"Dad. You can't go undercover for the FBI. It's too dangerous."

Stan sighed. "I know, but I have no choice."

"Yes, you do. You can decline to act as the trustee," Reggie pressed.

"Right. But then the FBI wouldn't be able to take down the Cartel."

"So. Why is that your responsibility?"

"It's not, but that's not the point. I have an opportunity to do something good here. These cartels bring in deadly drugs and engage in human trafficking. This is my opportunity to do something to stop them. Hopefully, I'll help save some lives and put some thugs behind bars."

"What about the firm and our family?"

"Don't worry. The FBI will protect me. They are experts at this undercover work."

"You're excited, aren't you?" Reggie noted.

"What? No. ... Well, a little," Stan admitted. "I think this is something that will make a difference. How often do we get an opportunity like that?"

Reggie laughed. "Oh, God! You're hopeless. Promise me you won't do anything stupid."

"I won't. And don't you worry. The firm has hired security. A well-trained security officer will be with you at all times."

"Alright," Reggie said. "Call me every day."

"I will if I can. I love you," Stan replied.

The line went dead, and Stan hung up. He felt guilty. Was he being selfish in going undercover for the FBI? What if something did happen to him? It was true; he didn't have to do this. Nobody would fault him for declining the trustee job, or would they? Did he owe a duty to his client to make those responsible for his murder pay? He wasn't sure.

Then he realized it didn't really matter; even if he didn't go undercover, the Cartel would still come after him. After all, he controlled their money and knew all the ins and outs of their money laundering operation. He was an unacceptable danger to them. No, he didn't have a choice. He had to help the FBI and make sure they took the Cartel down. He had no choice, he kept telling himself, if he wanted to live.

19
Feminine Charm

Jodie

Jodie sat at her desk thinking about approaching Tom "Tornado" Tyson about agreeing to a continuance of his personal injury case. She knew how to use her feminine charm to get what she wanted but didn't think it would work over the phone. She remembered seeing Tyson parading around like a big shot at the last Dallas Bar Association luncheon. She looked on her calendar and saw that this month's luncheon was only two days away.

"Maybe I'll accidentally run into him at the luncheon. If so, I can meet him in person and get a feel for his vulnerabilities. She wasn't optimistic, though. Ego maniacs like Tornado weren't easy to manipulate. They were too focused on themselves to be pushed in any one direction.

On the day of the luncheon, Jodie arrived early and grabbed a seat where she could observe the members arriving and getting seated. She saved a seat, hoping to lure Tornado into it as he passed. Sure enough, she saw him walk in and look around. Although Tornado knew everybody, few were anxious to sit with him and listen to his self-adulation. As he looked around for a place to sit, Jodie got his eye.

"Tom!"

Tyson turned toward Jodie and squinted. Not recognizing her, he seemed confused.

"Tom!" Jodie repeated. "There's an empty seat here."

Tyson gave Jodie a once-over and then smiled and walked over. "Hi," he said, frowning. "Have we met?"

Jodie stood up and offered her hand. "Not formally. We've talked on the phone. I'm Jodie Marshall with Turner & Waters."

Tyson took Jodie's hand but didn't let go until Jodie gently but forcibly pulled it away.

"Oh, Jodie. Right. Well, had we met, I'd certainly remembered such a stunning barrister."

Jodie laughed. "Barrister? Wow. I haven't been called that before."

They both sat as waiters began to deposit salad and rolls on the tables.

"So, we have that wrongful death case together?" Tyson said thoughtfully.

"Yes, What a tragedy for everyone. You know my client died on the operating table, but they were able to bring her back to life, luckily."

"Yes. My client wasn't so lucky."

"You know she is permanently disabled and will never be able to work again."

"My client won't be working much either."

Jodie smiled. "Right. It's too bad Amanda didn't have more than the minimum insurance limits. You've done an asset search by now and know she's penniless."

"Of course, but she's not our only target," Tyson replied.

"Oh. Have you found other culpable parties?" Jodie asked.

"No. Not yet, but I'm sure we'll find somebody with deep pockets."

"Well, I guess it's a moot point. Did you hear Amanda was arrested a few days ago?"

"No. I didn't. Was it in connection with this case?"

"Yes. The government is charging her with negligent homicide."

"Well, she did work a double shift and fell asleep at the wheel. That's gross negligence at the very least."

"Well, we don't know that for sure. We're both looking for targets with deep pockets, like a doctor. There's always more to the story than meets the eye," Jodie said.

A waiter brought the main course and deposited it in front of Jodie and Tyson. Tyson started eating immediately. Jodie figured he'd spent too much time looking in the mirror that morning and missed breakfast.

Jodie ignored her food. "So, we're debating whether to just file bankruptcy to get rid of your personal injury lawsuit. Or you could agree to take the policy limits on Amanda's insurance, and Dr. Short's widow could get some closure and get on with her life."

Tyson stopped eating and glared at Jodie. "Are you crazy? She's not settling for $20,000. I'm sorry. She's due at least a million dollars."

"Sure, in a perfect world, but you know I will have to file a motion to abate your lawsuit until the criminal case is completed, in about six or eight months. Then I'd have to advise Amanda to file bankruptcy since she'd have no money to pay me to defend her, let alone pay a judgment, should you be lucky enough to get one. So, that could delay things. What? Another year, unless we file Chapter 13, and then you'd have to dismiss Amanda out of the lawsuit or wait five years for her to complete her Chapter 13 plan."

Tyson just stared at Jodie for a moment and then laughed. "Listen, young lady, I've heard the can't-get-blood-out-of-a-turnup defense before. I don't buy it. Go ahead and file your motion. I'll fight it, and I'll win. These two cases have the same facts, so it won't be prejudicial for them to be prosecuted simultaneously. In fact, it might be more economical."

"Okay," Jodie spat. "But you can't stop Amanda from filing bankruptcy. Why don't you just let her go? If she doesn't beat the criminal wrap, you'll never be able to get a dime out of her anyway."

"But I'll have a nice big judgment waiting for her when she gets out, and I promise you I will make her life a living hell until that judgment gets paid. You don't mess with the Tornado!'

Jodie looked at Tyson, shook her head, and chuckled, "You're delusional."

Jodie suddenly realized she'd lost her appetite. She stood up and stormed off without another word. Tyson squirmed in his seat as he watched her leave. When Jodie looked back, she noticed Tyson stand up and head for the exit. Perhaps my feminine charm worked, after all, she thought. She smiled as she walked to the car and drove back to the office to tell Paula how she'd spoiled the Tornado's lunch.

20
The Gift

Stan

Stan wondered if Christos Mejia knew more about Acosta's cartel activities than he had revealed to Stan at their first meeting. He suspected he did but didn't plan to challenge him on that point, merely to let him know the New Hope Legal Clinics were the apparent beneficiary of Ruben Acosta's estate and trust. The Dallas clinic was busy, as usual, when he arrived. The receptionist told him Christos was waiting for him and to go right in.

Christos stood up when Stan entered his office. They shook hands, and Stan sat in a side chair and surveyed Christos' cluttered desk. Stan said, "So, I'm on my way to Phoenix to meet with some MedNet clients, but I needed to talk with you before I left."

"Right. That's what you said on the phone. How can I help you?"

"Well, I've got some good news and some bad news."

Christos gave Stan a knowing smile. "Right. So, what's the good news."

"Your clinic is the alternate beneficiary of Ruben Acosta's estate and trust."

"The alternate beneficiary?" Christos asked.

"Yes, the primary beneficiaries are his wife and children."

Christos frowned. "But he didn't have a wife or children, right?"

"Apparently, he didn't. So, that's the good news. Unless a wife or children show up, your organization will eventually receive all of the assets."

"Eventually?" Christos questioned.

"Right. That's the bad news. As you suspected, all this money is intermingled with Cartel money. Ruben was laundering it for them."

Christos nodded. "Okay. So, how will all this be sorted out?" Christos asked.

"That's something I have to figure out. The Cartel expects me to continue managing MedNet and the trust's money for the indefinite future."

Christo's face was blank. He said nothing. Stan continued. "So, I need your consent to do this. As the sole beneficiary, you could insist that I liquidate all the assets within a reasonable time and distribute them to New Hope Clinic. The problem is that the Cartel won't like it, and we might end up dead if I tried to do that."

Christos stiffened but still said nothing.

"So, that's the dilemma. What should I do?" Stan asked.

Christos swiveled around in his chair and looked out the window behind him. After he'd thought a moment, he swiveled back around, shrugged, and replied. "So, you are willing to go along with this charade?"

Stan swallowed hard and replied, "I'm not happy about it, but I am if you are. I could resign as trustee and let you worry about the consequences."

"No. Don't do that. I guess we have no choice."

"Exactly," Stan agreed. "Don't worry, though. I'm sure you'll keep getting your funding plus added bonuses from time to time. There is plenty of money to go around, assuming I'm as good at laundering money as Ruben was."

Christos smiled faintly. "Well, you better be, or we are both in trouble."

Stan inhaled deeply and let the air out slowly. "Yeah, I'm a little worried about that, actually."

Christos stood up abruptly and extended his hand, "Well, if there is anything I can do to help, let me know. I've got to be in Court in ten minutes."

Stan stood, and they shook hands. He was a little shocked at Christos's sudden termination of the meeting. Still, he understood if Christos indeed had a hearing appearance in ten minutes. He wondered about that but quickly forgot about it as his attention turned to his flight to Phoenix, which was due to depart in less than two hours. He just had time to go by the office and head to the airport.

Maria had everything ready for him when he arrived. Reggie had put all his luggage into his car and was ready to take Stan to DFW Airport. After Stan said his goodbyes, they were off. The airport was only twenty minutes away, so it was a quick trip. Stan could tell Reggie was upset, so he tried to ease the tension.

"So, you think the Mavericks will do better under Mark Cuban than Ross Perot, Jr.?"

Reggie nodded. "I hope so."

"Dirk has been looking good this season," Stan noted.

"Yeah, he's the best."

"Some guy called me last week and wanted me to sue the Mavericks for him?' Stan chuckled. "He didn't get the season ticket seats he wanted."

"What did you tell him?" Reggie asked, slightly amused.

"I told him to save his money. It was a lost cause."

"So, Dad. Are you expecting to run into any cartel thugs on this trip?"

"No," Stan assured him. This is routine business. I need to establish contact with our clients and assure them nothing will change with Ruben Acosta out of the picture. It will no doubt be quite boring."

Reggie helped Stan check his luggage when they got to the airport and then escorted him to his gate. When they arrived, they saw that Tom and Roger were already there. Stan introduced them to Reggie, and then Reggie left as their flight was already being called. As Stan waited with his colleagues, he wondered what they would think if they knew they would be unwitting participants in an FBI sting operation. Fortunately, that information was confidential, and he wanted to keep it that way.

After they arrived at Sky Harbor Airport in Phoenix, they boarded a bus to the rental terminal to pick up a rental car. Then they took I-10 to a suburb called Chandler, where they had reservations at a Hilton Phenix

Chandler Hotel. Later that evening, they were to meet several of the MedNet doctors for cocktails.

"So, who are we meeting tonight?" Stan asked.

"Dr. Kent Keating and his partner Dr. William Bright. They have a digestive disease consulting practice," Tom said.

"Right. Colonoscopies?" Stan asked.

"That's one of the things they do, but they cover the entire spectrum of digestive diseases."

"Anyone else?"

"Their accountant, Larry Gillis, will be there. He's our main contact and represents several other of our clients as well. One of them is Dr. Denton Derby, DDS. He's operated a medium-sized dental practice for over forty years. About five years ago, he had a heart attack and was about to go out of business when Ruben heard about his situation and convinced him he could turn things around. He was one of Ruben's first clients."

"Okay, I will introduce myself and explain the legal situation, and then you two can assure them we are in full control of everything, and they have nothing to worry about,"

Tom and Roger agreed, and when they got to the hotel, they went to their separate rooms to clean up and prepare for the meeting. Stan's room was a standard tourist-grade room with two double beds. He wasn't one for wasting money on large, extravagant accommodations when all he was going to do was sleep there a few hours. The only reason he'd booked them in a nice hotel was that Tom and Roger were with him. He suspected they wouldn't appreciate staying at the local *Motel Six*. Plus, he had doctor clients to impress; they would expect nothing but the best.

He ordered dinner from room service and, when he was done, took a shower and dressed casually for their meeting. By 8:00 p.m., he was ready and went downstairs to the hotel bar. The decor was old southwest, with cream-colored stucco walls, four burnt orange chairs around eight small cedar tables. The long bar had eight stools facing large windows overlooking the pool area. The bar was staffed by three male and two female bartenders working from an impressive inventory of wines and liquors.

A hostess smiled as he approached. "Hi. I'm expecting some guests. Can you put a couple of tables together? There's going to be seven or eight of us."

"Sure," the hostess said and immediately accommodated Stan's wishes. When the tables were ready, Stan took a seat where he could observe when his guests arrived. A waitress immediately came over to him, and he ordered a drink. A few moments later, Tom and Roger showed up and joined him.

Larry Gillis and Dr. Derby were the first to show up. Tom introduced Stan to them, and the waitress took their drinks.

"So, how was your flight," Gillis asked.

"Uneventful, fortunately," Tom replied. "The last time I came to Phoenix, a man got on the plane who had spent too much time in the airport bar before boarding. After he sat down, he asked the flight attendant for a drink. When she told him he'd have to wait until they had taken off, he got belligerent and demanded the drink immediately. Things escalated from there, and the guy had to be forcibly removed from the plane. The whole affair delayed our flight by forty-five minutes."

They all laughed. As they were talking, Dr. Keating and Dr. Bright arrived. Tom got up and escorted them to the table. Stan stood and, after Tom had introduced him, shook both of their hands. The waitress then showed up with some drinks and took the orders from the new arrivals.

Once everyone had their drinks and the chit-chat was over, Stan began the meeting.

"Well, gentlemen. It's nice to put some faces to your names. I have been going over all of your financials and am impressed with what I have seen. As you know by now, Ruben Acosta was murdered and left me with the task of operating MedNet for the foreseeable future as his executor and trustee.

"You have worked with Tom and Roger in the past, and they will continue in their same capacities for MedNet in the future. I have no plans to make any changes in your operations as Mr. Acosta has everything running smoothly and efficiently.

"I don't know how much you know about trusts and probates. I'm sure you've heard the usual horror stories of endless conflict and court proceedings as beneficiaries duke it out."

Several heads nodded, and their faces were glum. Stan continued. "I want to assure you that isn't going to happen here. I have already talked to one of the managers of the New Hope Legal Clinics, which I believe is the ultimate beneficiary of Mr. Acosta's estate and trust, and he doesn't see the need to make material alterations to MedNet."

Dr. Bright raised his hand. "Excuse me. You said you believe?"

Stan nodded. "Yes, the will and the trust name Ruben's wife and children as the primary beneficiary, but as I understand it, he wasn't currently married and had no children. This means the New Hope Legal Clinics, Inc. would be the ultimate beneficiary. The good news is, the NHLC has agreed to keep all of the assets in trust so there will be no disruption in the management of MedNet."

"Will you also stay on as trustee?" Dr. Bright asked, "or will you hire someone else to run MedNet. I've had managers before, but no one was near as good as Ruben."

Stan smiled. "That's a fair question. I don't know what the future holds for me. But I will manage MedNet until I understand every aspect of its operations. Then, at that time, I will evaluate my future role. But you can be assured that I won't relinquish my management role until I'm sure someone else can be hired to operate it as efficiently and effectively as Ruben Acosta."

"That might take a while," Larry Gillis said. "Ruben had an uncanny ability to process claims, submit them, and get them paid in full. If you know anything about this business, that's our biggest problem. So many of the insurance companies will routinely deny your first claim. They will always find something wrong and make you resubmit it two or three times. Then, if they pay half of it, you're lucky."

"I'm aware of that," Stan said, "and that is a skill I will endeavor to learn quickly."

Stan knew their Las Guías affiliation had something to do with their impressively high collection rate with insurance companies. Still, he didn't know exactly how that worked, so he could say no more. Stan then turned the discussion over to Tom and Roger, who took individual questions from the clients who were present.

After the meeting, Stan thanked Tom and Roger and told them he'd meet them in the lobby at 8:00 a.m. to go back to the airport for their flight to Las Vegas. He left them and went back to his room to watch the news before going to bed.

After kicking off his shoes and collapsing onto his bed, he flipped on the TV, where a news anchor was reporting on breaking news.

"Alaska Airlines, Flight 261 crashed in the Pacific Ocean off Point Mugu, California, killing all 88 aboard. The MD-83, experienced horizontal stabilizer problems, which authorities believe contributed to the crash."

"In sports, the St. Louis Rams beat Tennessee Titans, 23-16 in Super Bowl XXXIV held this year in Atlanta, Georgia. Kurt Warner, the St. Louis QB, received the MVP award for the game. Congratulations..."

There was a knock at the door. Stan muted the TV and looked at the door suspiciously. He hadn't ordered room service, so he couldn't imagine who it would be. There was another knock, this time more persistent. Stan sighed and got up to answer it, but before opening it, he looked through the peephole and was shocked to see a beautiful Hispanic woman in a short skirt and halter top. She tossed her hair nervously as she waited. Then Stan noticed she had a bottle of champagne in her hand. He figured she must have gotten the wrong room, so he opened the door slowly and smiled. "Hi. Can I help you?"

"Hi. Are you Stan Turner?"

Hearing his name sent a shiver down his spine. "Ah. Yeah. I am."

"Can I come in? Carlos sent me."

"Carlos?" Stan repeated warily.

"Yes, from Dallas. He said you and he were good friends, and he wanted to make your day. I don't know exactly what that means, but I'm sure we can figure it out," she said with a broad smile as she slipped by him and stepped into the room. Stan closed the door, turned and gazed at the woman's fine slender legs in disbelief.

She turned, forced a smile, and extended her hand, "I'm Rosa Méndez."

Stan looked at her hand blankly and then tentatively accepted it. She squeezed it firmly, causing Stan's heart to race. This was so unexpected he was at a loss for words. Then alarms went off in Stan's head.

"Oh, that was nice of Carlos, but I can't accept his gift. It wouldn't be right."

Rosa grimaced and replied, "I don't know about you, but I don't want to piss off Carlos. He's not a man you want as your enemy."

Stan knew she was right, so he smiled and asked if he should open the bottle of champagne. She agreed that would be a good way to start their evening together.

21
Abatement

Jodie

Jodie knew Amanda couldn't file bankruptcy unless she was willing to give up any chance of receiving the proceeds of a personal injury claim. But many attorneys were ignorant when it came to bankruptcies, so she hoped that was the case with Tom Tyson. Unfortunately, bankruptcy would not impact Amanda's criminal trial, so filing bankruptcy was a strategy that would only come into play if she was convicted and sentenced to jail.

When she returned to the office, Jodie visited Paula to report on her meeting. Reggie was there, so she filled them in on the aborted luncheon. Reggie thought the whole thing was hysterical. Paula just shook her head and smiled.

"I would have loved to have seen Tornado's face when you outlined your strategy to him," Reggie said.

"Yeah. His expression was priceless," Jodie replied.

"You know, Amanda could file Chapter 13 and, if down the road if we figured out who to sue, she could voluntarily dismiss the case or forget to make a Chapter 13 payment."

"Couldn't the U.S. Trustee object to that as bad faith manipulation of the bankruptcy system?" Paula asked.

"Technically, yes, but as a practical matter, a lot of Chapter 13s get dismissed long before completion anyway. It most likely would slip through the crack." Jodie noted.

"Well, let's keep that idea on the back burner for now," Paula said. "Go ahead and file your motion to abate, and let's see how Tyson responds. If he is smart, he won't oppose it. The last thing he wants is for Amanda to file bankruptcy. That would complicate his case dramatically, and the Tornado does not like complications which might delay or hinder his total annihilation of his opponent."

Jodie nodded and went back to her office. The next day, Jodie finished her Motion to Abate and filed it with the District Clerk. She then sent a copy by courier to Tyson's office. She wondered if he'd call her when he got the motion. He did, but it was two days later.

"I got your motion," Tyson said. "Like I told you at lunch, there is no reason why we can't try these cases simultaneously, so I'm going to oppose your motion."

"You sure?" Jodie asked. "I noticed Dr. Short had a drinking problem. Was it two or three DUIs filed against him?"

"Two, but he was sober on the day of the accident."

"How do you know that? There wasn't an autopsy. I guess we could find out during discovery if you force us to try the cases together. I wonder how the jury will feel about it, should it come out."

"It's not relevant," Tyson argued. "The judge won't let it in. Besides, your client crossed the median and was going the wrong way, against traffic."

"So, if your client was on drugs or drunk, that would explain why he made no effort to avoid the collision."

"Like I said, it's not relevant. The judge won't let it in without convincing proof."

"Maybe he will, maybe he won't. Oh, and then there are all those lawsuits filed against the Doctor. I haven't had time to thoroughly research each one, but I'm sure the plaintiffs will be happy to fill me in on the facts of each claim. Was the Doctor depressed? Could this have been suicide by automobile?"

"That's all nonsense!" Tyson spat.

"Oh, did I tell you about the streak of silver paint on Amanda's vehicle? It seems there may be a third party involved. Wouldn't it be better to sort all those things out in the criminal trial, so you won't be blindsided during our civil trial? But it's your call."

"Alright. You make some good points. I won't oppose your motion to abate, but you can bet I'll be following Amanda's criminal trial like a fox on a rabbit,"

"Okay, and I'll keep my other offer on the table until the day of the criminal trial, and then it will be rescinded."

"What was the other offer?" Tyson asked. "I've forgotten."

Jodie laughed. "You should pay more attention. It was a pretty generous offer."

"Okay, don't bust my balls. Refresh my memory," Tyson replied irritably.

"The offer was to advise the insurance carriers that Amanda has no assets, any judgment against her would be uncollectable, and you will accept her policy limits and release her from all liability," Jodie replied.

"Oh, right. So, would the release be mutual?"

"Yes, but there would be no admission of guilt or liability, strictly a convenience settlement to avoid the time and expense of further litigation."

"I'll give that some thought,"Tom said, "but my clients will not likely agree. They are not going to let your client off the hook that easily."

"Thanks. I'll inform the Court you don't oppose my motion to abate."

"You do that, and I'll get back to you on the other offer."

Jodie hung up the phone and then went straight to Paula's office. Paula was working intensely on her computer. She looked up when Jodie walked in.

"Well, it worked. The Tornado agreed to the abatement."

"Wow! Thank you, Jodie. Good job."

"I think I even have him thinking seriously about taking the policy limits and leaving Amanda alone."

"That would be nice, but I doubt he'd be that stupid. I'm glad we don't have to worry about him for now and can concentrate on keeping Amanda out of jail."

Jodie nodded and went back to her office. She called Reggie and gave him the good news. He was delighted, as expected.

Now the real work begins, she thought, digging up more dirt on Dr. Short, finding the illusive biker, developing other viable defenses and presenting it all to the jury. Then, if Amanda escaped a criminal conviction, she'd have to find a target with deep pockets and come up with a viable theory of liability. A tall order, she knew, but with Reggie's help, it wasn't beyond the realm of possibility."

22
The Understanding

Stan

Stan's mind was spinning. He knew Carlos was trying to compromise him. If Stan accepted his gift, it would show moral weakness and Stan's willingness to be corrupted. On the other hand, if Carlos believed Stan had accepted Rosa, it would give Carlos a false sense of security, which would make his undercover work less risky.

Stan opened the bottle of champagne, took a swig, smiled, and handed the bottle to Rosa. She frowned but reluctantly accepted the bottle and took a long drink herself. When she offered the bottle back to Stan, he took her in his arms and kissed her hard while pushing her back onto the king-size bed. As she fell back onto the bed, the contents of the bottle of champagne fell from Rosa's hand and emptied onto the bedspread, soaking all the way through to the mattress.

Stan suddenly let Rosa go and stood up. "Oh, shit! We've spilled the champagne all over the mattress."

Rosa gave the mattress a cursory glance and chuckled, "Don't worry about it. It's a big bed. We don't need all of it. "

Stan shook his head. "No. I don't want anything spoiling our fun. I'll call down to the front desk and get them to give us another room."

Rosa reluctantly got up and replied. "You sure? It's no big deal."

"Yeah. Maybe not. But it's been a long time since I've been with a woman, and I don't want the memory of it to be of spilled champagne."

Rosa was quiet as Stan called down to the front desk. The desk clerk on duty offered to send someone up to clean up the spill, but Stan insisted they give him a new room. He wasn't happy about Stan's demand, but he eventually agreed.

Thirty minutes later, Stan and Rosa entered a new room, and Stan closed the door. Rosa immediately edged toward Stan to continue where they'd left off, but Stan stopped her.

"Wait a minute," Stan said. "We don't know each other. Let's talk a bit. I like to know something about the women I sleep with. Not that I've slept with that many. How do you know Carlos?"

Rosa looked intently at Stan but said nothing. Stan said, "Don't worry. This room isn't bugged. We can be honest with each other, and I would never intentionally hurt a woman."

Rosa's eyes lit up. "That's why we switched rooms?"

Stan nodded. "Exactly. We need to come to an understanding. This is an unusual situation for me. I don't know about you."

"What do you mean?" she asked.

"Well. You were sent here by Carlos, so what's your assignment?" What did he tell you to do?"

Rosa looked around nervously. "I'm supposed to make you happy and, you know, well..."

"Well, what?"

"Slip some pills into your drink to make sure you have a good time."

Stan took a deep breath. "Right. So, does he make you take pills too?"

She nodded. "Yes, sometimes."

"So, how did you come to work for Carlos?"

Rosa looked down dejectedly and replied, "Well, it's a long story."

"That's okay. We've got all night. I assume you were planning to stay with me all night."

"Yes. Of course."

"So, go on," Stan pressed.

"Well, I came to America with my brother six years ago when I was seventeen years old. The gangs were out of control in my hometown. I'd been raped the previous year by several gang members and had a new baby."

"Oh," Stan groaned. "I'm so sorry.

Rosa shrugged. "It was a long time ago."

What's your baby's name?"

"Mariana."

"Oh. That's a pretty name.

"Anyway, my parents had died in a car wreck years earlier, and we were living with our grandparents. They were afraid of what would become of my brother and I if we stayed, so they insisted we go to America. They'd heard that life was much better here and we'd be safe. My baby was too young to travel, so my grandparents agreed to raise her until I got settled and could bring her to America."

"That must have been hard," Stan said. "I've heard the journey to America can be a nightmare. How did you and your brother manage it?"

"My grandparents raised all the money they could, packed us as much food and clothing as possible, and helped us find a caravan going North. We paid the people running the caravan to join it and began our journey. It took us about three months to get to Mexico. Those were the worst three months of my life, but I thought everything would be okay once we got there. Man, was I wrong about that."

"So, how did you get hooked up with Carlos?"

"When we were nearly at the U.S. border, some men tried to kidnap me. My brother tried to stop them, and they killed him."

Stan closed his eyes and took a breath. After a moment, he said, "So, these men were from the Las Guías Cartel?"

"Yes," Rosa replied softly.

Stan stepped forward and embraced Rosa. At first, she was stiff, but after a moment, she melted into his embrace and began to sob.

"I'm so sorry you have had to endure all of that," Stan said softly. After a few seconds, he let her go and sat at the end of the bed. Rosa took a seat on the sofa across from him.

"So, we both find ourselves in a place we never wanted to be, right?"

She nodded. "No. I thought living in America would be wonderful."

Stan smiled. "Maybe there is a way I can at least make it tolerable for you. I am a lawyer from Dallas, and I got involved with Carlos accidentally when the Cartel had one of my clients killed."

Rosa gasped. "Oh, no! Did you know him well?"

"No, but I was there when he got killed and was lucky, I wasn't killed as well."

"You were fortunate, indeed."

"Yes, but unfortunately, my client had appointed me trustee and executor of his estate."

"What does that mean?" Rosa asked.

"It means I was forced to finish his work for the Cartel. That's why I'm here; to figure out how to continue his work."

"So, how can you help me?"

"Well, I could accept you as Carlos's gift. Not that I believe you are a commodity. I don't believe in slavery, but if you were with me, I would treat you with respect, and you wouldn't have to please me in bed. I would never force a woman to have sex against her will."

"Really?"

"Yes. It would be a partnership of sorts. My wife died a few months ago, and it's been hard being alone. I would enjoy your company, and you could help with my work for Carlos."

Rosa considered this and replied, "It sounds too good to be true."

"Well, it's your choice. I can thank Carlos and tell him I had a great night, and you can go back to your life with the Cartel."

"No. I only do their bidding, so they won't kill my grandparents and my baby."

"Right. That's why I think this would be a good plan for both of us. You will be doing the Cartel's work but not have to be under their thumb. And, you won't have to lie to them. We know they will be watching and listening to us, so the only secret we'll have to keep is our mutual agreement. As far as the Cartel will know, you are my girlfriend and the Cartel's spy."

They both laughed.

"There is one other issue. You will need to promise that you won't ever drug me. I have never taken drugs, and I'm not going to start now."

Rosa looked away.

"I know Carlos probably has you hooked on drugs. I had a client who owned a strip club once. They all worked voluntarily and could quit whenever they liked, but they were all hooked on drugs, so it was difficult for them to get any other type of work. So, am I right?"

Rosa looked back at Stan and nodded. "Yes, but Carlos gave me a good supply."

"You should consider getting clean. I know that's no easy task, but will you try? You can't truly be free if you are on drugs."

Rosa nodded and then started to cry again. They talked for several hours before succumbing to exhaustion and going to bed. They agreed Rosa would report to Carlos in the morning as she was supposed to and tell him that they'd had a night of wild sex, and Stan wanted to see more of her. If Carlos agreed, which Stan thought he would, then Rosa would become Stan's official girlfriend and the Cartel's spy.

That night Rosa took the bed, and Stan slept on the sofa. Neither of them could sleep, though, as their minds were excitedly contemplating their future relationship together. During their talk, they'd gotten to know each other. Stan liked Rosa and felt she was a good person who had suffered through unspeakable circumstances. He felt he could trust her and thought she was beginning to trust him.

The following day Tom and Roger were stunned when Stan brought Rosa to have breakfast with them. They both stood up at seeing the attractive young woman.

Stan introduced them. "Rosa, this is Tom Rice, and that's Roger Moore."

"Nice to meet you," they both echoed, and they all took their seats.

"I met Rosa last night, and we really hit it off. She'll be joining us for the rest of the trip."

"Ah, okay," Roger said. "Ah, what do you do, Rosa?"

Rosa looked at Stan.

Stan smiled and replied, "She's going to be my assistant. She's from El Salvador, so she speaks Spanish as well as English. I'll have to train her, of course," he laughed, "or, I guess, we will learn the business together."

Rosa smiled broadly.

"You two just met last night?" Roger asked.

Stan laughed again. "Yes, it was quite the chance encounter. We were having a drink, got to talking, and discovered we had a mutual acquaintance."

"Really? Who was that?" Roger asked.

"Oh, you wouldn't know him. The important thing is I found out Rosa wasn't happy in her current job, so I offered her this one."

"Huh," Roger said skeptically. "I didn't know you were looking for an assistant."

"I didn't either, but I got to thinking I would need someone to run my office. Oh, by the way, I'll be keeping Ruben's office suite in your building so we can be close. It wouldn't be appropriate to run MedNet out of my law office."

"That's true," Tom agreed, "and having an interpreter will come in handy. Can we borrow her for other clients if we need her?"

"Of course," Stan replied.

"Good. Our MedNet clients have lots of Hispanic patients."

"True," Stan agreed, "and many of the tenants in our rental properties are Hispanic, so her language skills will come in handy."

Rosa smiled and said, "I am very excited about this opportunity. I hope I don't disappoint you."

"Oh, I'm sure you won't," Tom replied.

"Oh, no," Roger agreed. "It's just Stan didn't mention he was looking for someone."

The waitress came over and took their orders. While they were eating, Stan explained the business to Rosa, with Tom and Roger chiming in from time to time. After breakfast, Stan announced he and Rosa were going to stay another day in Chandler and join them in Las Vegas the next morning.

"I want to check on the real estate we own here in the Phoenix area. So, I thought Rosa and I could do that this morning and catch the red eye to Vegas. We should be able to join you there by noon. That way, you can gamble tonight and sleep in tomorrow morning."

Roger and Tom were taken aback by the change in plans but managed to smile awkwardly as they got into their rental car and headed for the airport. Stan knew they hadn't bought his claim that Rosa would be his assistant. He was sure they thought he'd found a girlfriend, but that remained to be seen. He and Rosa had work to do on the details of their relationship, and it might take some time to accomplish that.

After Tom and Roger were gone, they returned to their room, and Rosa called Carlos to check in. Carlos was very upset that they had changed rooms and wanted a minute-by-minute account of the evening. Stan listened to Rosa and thought she had done a good job explaining everything, but he'd only heard her side of the conversation, which was in Spanish.

When she had hung up, he asked, "So, what did he say."

"He said I'm a valuable piece of property, make him lots of money, and it would be expensive to give me up."

"I don't doubt that," Stan said.

"He said you haven't earned a bonus yet, and your partner shot one of his men, but he was a reasonable man, and as long as you do well handling the Cartel's investments, he'd let you have me. But he did want me to advise you that if you betrayed the Cartel, you'd not only lose me, but they'd, of course, kill you."

Stan swallowed hard and nodded. "Right. That was a given."

"So, I guess I'm now officially your girlfriend."

"Right," Stan agreed. "At least that's what the Cartel and the rest of the world will think."

"So, you don't want me to be your real girlfriend?"

"No. I'm not saying that, but let's be realistic. I'm too old for you, and if you weren't owned by the Cartel, you'd never dream of being my girlfriend."

Rosa thought about that for a moment. "That's true, I suppose, but right now I am owned by the Cartel, and if you can save me from a life of slavery and protect my family, I would owe you my life and gladly do anything for you."

"I believe you, but I'm not doing this for my benefit. I'm doing this to try to right a wrong and give you back your freedom. Only then should you make commitments about your future. Besides, I can't promise how this will all turn out. For now, we should just concentrate on staying alive.

Rosa nodded as tears flowed slowly down her cheeks. Stan felt guilty that he'd upset her. He was already starting to fall in love with this woman he'd just met, and he prayed he'd be able to protect her.

23
The Girlfriend

Paula

Paula sat at her desk, staring at Amanda's file. She had a status conference with the Court in less than two days, and she was considering her trial strategy. In a criminal case, the prosecution had the burden of proof, and it was a difficult one. They had to prove beyond any reasonable doubt that Amanda had been criminally negligent. Under the Texas Penal Code, a "person commits criminal homicide if he intentionally, knowingly, recklessly, or with criminal negligence causes the death of an individual."

To prove criminal negligence, the prosecution would have to show that Amanda was aware of the risks associated with the actions that led to the other person's death and that the defendant acted or failed to act appropriately in a dangerous situation. That action or inaction caused the victim's death, and finally that there was a direct link between the defendant's conduct and the victim's death.

Paula wrote down the uncontested facts. Amanda knew she had a sleeping disorder. She knew that the medicine she was taking would make her sleepy. She had to know that taking a double shift would make her tired and sleepy and that there was a risk that she'd fall asleep while she was driving home. That left causation. She thought her best defense was to attack the link between her actions and the victim's death. This was the prosecution's week link. With no actual witnesses, the prosecution would have to convince the jury that there was no other explanation for what happened except Amanda falling asleep.

As she was thinking, the phone rang. It was Stan. "Hi. How are things at the office?"

"Oh, fine. I'm working on my strategy for defending Amanda. I think causation is the best point of attack."

"Right. I think Reggie has dug up some good stuff on that."

"Yes, he has. If there was a biker involved, that could easily cause reasonable doubt."

"Exactly. Hey, I wanted to alert you to a new development."

"Okay, what's that?"

"I think I'm in love?"

Paula nearly dropped the phone. "What did you say?"

Stan laughed. "I know. It's crazy, right? But I met this girl at my hotel in Chandler, and she's amazing. I'm bringing her back to Dallas, so I wanted to give you a heads up."

"Aren't you being a little rash?" Paula noted. "I mean, you just met her?"

Paula found herself overcome with jealousy. For years, she'd had a thing for Stan when they first started Turner & Waters. Still, Stan remained faithful to Rebekah no matter how hard Paula tried to sabotage their marriage. She'd finally given up and married Bart, but those old feelings came rushing back.

"True. We're not rushing into things, but I'm too old to miss an opportunity like this. It's lonely with Rebekah gone."

Paula knew that to be true, so she didn't argue further. She'd spent many nights alone and hated it. "No, you're right. Tell me about her?"

"She's beautiful, smart, and way too young for me," Stan laughed.

"Hmm. Watch out. She may be after your money."

"What money? You know I don't have any money, and that's the last thing Rosa cares about."

"Rosa, that's a pretty name."

"It is. So, anyway, I just wanted to give you a heads-up. You should tell Reggie and Jodie, so they won't be surprised. I don't want Rosa being embarrassed by their reaction to her sudden arrival in my life."

"Sure, I'll tell them to be on their best behavior when they meet her."

"Thanks. As usual, you're the best, and I will need your feminine take on the situation. Remember in the old days when we'd get on the phone and talk for hours?"

Paula frowned. She couldn't remember ever having long telephone calls with Stan about anything but work, but she played along anyway. "Yeah. Those were the days."

"Alright. Talk to you again soon. Take care," Stan said and hung up, leaving Paula alarmed and concerned. What was that all about? She immediately got up and rushed to find Jodie. She found her in the library. Jodie could see she was upset.

"What's wrong?"

"Stan just called. He's got a girlfriend!"

"Huh?"

"Yeah, he just met her a day or two ago, and they are already together!" Paula said, her face flushed with emotion. Paula didn't know if she was jealous, scared, or just angry.

"That makes no sense," Jodie said. "Stan is so level-headed."

"I know. It's like an arctic blast hitting you on the beach in August, so unexpected. I think there is something very wrong here. He mentioned something about our long phone calls in the past and my feminine advice. He said he'd talk to me soon."

Jodie thought a moment. "Oh!" Jodie exclaimed. "Wait a minute. He wants to talk to you privately. The Cartel must be monitoring his calls."

"Oh! So, what should I do?"

"You need to get a burner phone. I suspect Stan will call you once you have it, and he knows the number."

"How will I get him the number?" Paula asked.

"Leave that up to me," Jodie said. "Get the phone, and while you're gone, I'll figure a way to get the number to him."

Paula nodded. "Okay, I'll be right back."

Paula rushed to her car and drove to a CVS Pharmacy down the street. She purchased a phone and made it back in less than fifteen minutes. When she returned to the office, she read the instructions and activated her service. Then she brought the phone to Jodie.

"Okay, girl. How do I get him the number?' Paula asked.

"We need to come up with a code," Jodie said, "something only he will remember. Any ideas?"

"A code. We've never ... wait. There is a code Stan deciphered during a murder trial once. The murderer typed a message, but she accidentally got her fingers on the wrong keys. The message looked like total garbage, but Stan figured out the intended message by moving his fingers to the correct positions."

"Perfect!" Jodie said. "I'll have Maria forward a few faxes that came into him and insert the fake number somewhere inconspicuous. I'm sure Stan will figure it out."

After Maria had sent the faxes to Stan at his hotel and with her burner phone on her desk, Paula continued to work on Amanda's defense. While she was working, her office phone rang. She considered not answering it in case Stan called but didn't think he'd had time to decipher her number yet, so she picked it up.

"Hello. This is Paula Waters."

"Paula. This is Wendy."

"Oh, hi, Wendy. How are you?"

"Great. I've heard some interesting gossip. I think it will be quite revealing."

"Really? What is it?"

"You know you were wondering why the DA had his panties in a wad over Amanda Rich allegedly falling asleep at the wheel of her car?"

"Yes, given her medical condition and financial situation, it doesn't make sense."

"Well, it seems the DA's mother was killed in a car accident where the other driver fell asleep at the wheel after spending too much time at Happy Hour."

"Oh, my god! That explains a lot."

"Yes, Apparently, he has become a real hard ass since that happened."

"But Amanda didn't stop for Happy Hour. She wasn't drunk. She just had a headache and took a pill for it. It was just an unfortunate accident."

"I agree. Now, maybe you can figure out a way to convince the DA of that."

"Yes. Thank you. You've been a big help."

Paula hung up the phone and looked down at her notes. She'd have to show that Amanda did what any ordinary person would do in the same or similar circumstances. She had to work to support herself and Julie. If she'd refused to do a double shift, in her mind, she thought she'd be fired. She had a headache, so anybody in her shoes would have taken a pill for it. She may have been borderline negligent but certainly not reckless. She was in pain, after all. The burner phone buzzed. Paula quickly picked it up.

"Hello!"

"Paula, you are so smart. I wasn't sure you'd understand my call."

"Well, Jodie helped. What's up with the girlfriend?"

"Yeah, that."

Stan explained about the gift from Carlos and the awkward position in which he found himself.

"Anyway, I think Carlos made a big mistake giving me Rosa. She could be the key to bringing him down. The Cartel kidnapped her in Mexico and smuggled her into the United States. They have her grandparents and baby as human collateral to keep her in line. The FBI may have their key witness if I can gain her trust and protect her."

"Yes. Why did he give her to you?"

"To spy on me, probably. She has to call Carlos every day and report on what I'm doing."

"So, you're in bed with a spy? Isn't that a bit dangerous? She could turn on you at any moment."

"I know that. I'm not going to do anything that can't be reported back to Carlos."

"What about this call?"

"She's taking a shower, and I'm in the closet, so the Cartel can't see or hear me."

Paula laughed. "Okay, but don't get caught."

"I won't. Her name is Rosa Méndez. Pass all this on to Agent Lot. Okay?"

"Will do. Now hang up before you get caught."

"Bye."

The phone went dead, and Paula put it down. Her mind was spinning from Stan's revelations. She wondered how she'd get the information to Agent Lot. The Cartel could be watching their offices. The muscles in her neck and shoulders began to ache. She could feel a headache coming on, so she dug through her drawer and found some Motrin. Then she remembered she had a burner phone now.

She picked it up and called the local FBI field offices. When Special Agent Lot answered, she filled him in on the situation, gave him Stan's new burner number, and told him about Rosa. Lot listened and thanked her without comment. Paula hung up, wondering if the FBI would protect her partner or would Stan be acceptable collateral damage to them. She worried that it was the latter.

24
Burner Phone

Stan

Stan had made an appointment with the real estate agents hired by Ruben Acosta to manage his Phoenix rental properties. The rental properties had turned out to be quite a lucrative investment as real estate values had been climbing steadily in recent years.

Sunrise Realty was owned by Margie and Raul Rojas, a husband-and-wife team of some twenty-five years, so they claimed. They told Stan over the phone that they specialized in retirement properties and had hundreds under contract. They went on to explain that home ownership was everyone's dream, but many retirees didn't have the substantial credit necessary to get a mortgage loan. So, many rented, at least temporarily, they told themselves.

Their offices were in a high-end strip shopping center in Sun Lakes, Arizona. Margie greeted Stan and Rosa warmly and escorted them to a small conference room. While they were waiting for Raul, Margie, a talkative woman of Nordic descent, told them how she and Raul had met at the University of Houston when they were freshmen. She was from Wisconsin, and Raul lived in Mexico City at the time. Margie claimed to be five feet two in heels and had to stand on her toes to kiss her husband at their wedding. A few minutes later, Raul joined them.

"So, I was sorry to hear about Ruben," Raul said. "We really liked him, didn't we, Honey?"

Margie nodded vigorously. "Yes. He was so easy to work with and anxious to find new properties. He was one of our best customers."

"What a way to die, huh?" Raul said.

"Yes, it was. That's one of the reasons I wanted to come by. Do you know of anyone who would want to hurt Ruben? The Dallas police are investigating, but I doubt they will come to Arizona or Nevada to check on his business relationships there."

"No," Raul replied. "Everyone liked him as far as I know."

"How do you handle repairs and maintenance of his properties? Do you use your own contractors, or does Ruben handle that?"

"Ah," Margie said. "That's what's so nice about our arrangement with Ruben. He has a list of contractors for us to use. All we have to do is call them if something needs repair. And they bill him directly, so that saves us a lot of work."

"He didn't have any disputes with any of them?"

"No. Not that I ever heard about," Raul replied.

Stan nodded. "I'm just grasping at straws, trying to figure out why he was killed."

"I bet," Margie agreed.

"Okay," Stan said. "Can I get a list of those contractors? I'll need to contact each of them to update their records and let them know I will be taking over."

"Sure," Margie said. "I'll print it out for you."

"What about tenants. To your knowledge, did Ruben interact with any of the tenants?"

"No, I don't think so," Margie replied.

"Well, there was one," Raul interjected. "His very first tenant. He signed her up himself before he hired us."

"Oh. So, her info will be on our rental inventory?'

"Yes, her name is Leira, I think. Leira Corrales."

"Well, great. Thanks. I hope we can continue to use your services in the future," Stan said as he got up. "From Ruben's records, it looks like you're doing a great job."

Margie and Raul looked at each other curiously then back at Stan.

"Well, thank you," Margie said, coming to her feet as well. "So, if there is ever anything we can do for you, let us know."

"Ah. I just wanted to meet you and introduce you to Rosa. She'll be helping me out in the future. Keep looking out for new properties for me."

"Well, we will, and we appreciate your business," Raul said. "It's always nice to have an image of the people you work with. We never see so many of our clients."

"Yeah. I bet in this day and age. Anyway, have a nice day."

"It was nice to meet you," Rosa said as they exited the building.

After their meeting, they went into an adjacent grocery store and bought some drinks and snacks for the road. It was a pleasant seventy-seven degrees, and the sky was clear. Rosa looked at Stan and smiled warmly.

"I don't think I have been this relaxed in months. It is so pleasant riding around with you and not having to worry about Carlos or his thugs manhandling me."

Stan smiled back. "Well, I'm glad to hear that. I can't imagine the life you've led since you came to America."

"So, what now?" Rosa asked.

"Now. Let's go see if Ruben's first tenant knows anything about him. I'd like to talk to someone who knew Ruben Acosta. She might be able to give me another perspective on his life."

"Sounds good. Can we have lunch first? I'm starving."

Stan laughed. "Sure. I bet we will pass some restaurants along the way. What do you like?"

"Anything. At the club, they usually bring us fast food like pizza, hamburgers, or chicken nuggets."

"Well, we can do better than that," Stan promised.

A few miles down the road, they stopped at an Italian restaurant and enjoyed a long leisurely lunch. While they were waiting for the order, Stan looked on a street map he'd purchased to see how to get to Leira Corrales' house. He figured it was about ten miles from their current location. After he had memorized the route in his head, he looked at Rosa and smiled.

"So, where are you living now?" Stan asked.

"Carlos has a club in Phoenix. I've been working there the last few months."

"Do they move you around a lot?"

"Yes. Carlos says, in this business, you have to rotate the merchandise, so the customers think they are always getting something new. Plus, I don't think he likes the girls to get to know each other too much."

Stan nodded. "Well, that makes sense from his perspective, I'm sure. It must be tough for you, though."

"Yes," Rosa replied. "I have made friends with so many girls only to have them disappear without warning. I don't know if they are still alive or dead."

"Where were you before Phoenix?"

"Albuquerque."

"And before that?" Stan asked.

"Dallas."

"Really? Dallas? Huh. What was the name of the club in Dallas?"

"The Empire Club," Rosa replied.

"So, where do you eat and sleep when you are at these clubs?"

Rosa shrugged. "It varied. Sometimes the club had sleeping quarters attached, and other times we were housed in a nearby residence. Phoenix and Albuquerque had adjacent rooms, but in Dallas, we had to walk a few blocks to a house where we ate and slept."

"Did you have your own rooms?" Stan asked.

Rosa laughed. "No, we slept several girls to a room. Sometimes we had one big king-size bed for three or four girls. At one place, seven of us slept on mattresses lined up across the room."

Stan slowly shook his head. "You would think with the kind of money you made for them that they would treat you better."

Rosa sighed deeply. "Yeah, they treated their toilet paper better than they treated us," she said bitterly.

An hour later, they pulled into a nicely manicured suburban neighborhood with palm and Joshua trees, prickly pear cactus, agave, and bristle brush. It was obviously tract housing with only four or five different floor plans. When they found the street name they were looking for, they turned right and quickly found the address they wanted. As they stepped out of the car, they heard voices in a courtyard to the left of the white stucco home. A rod iron gate prevented them from entering the courtyard. Stan unlatched the gate, and they walked in cautiously. A little girl looked up at them as they entered.

"Hi, there," Stan said. "Is your mommy home?"

The girl nodded and ran to the front door and went inside. A minute later, a Hispanic woman who looked to be in her thirties appeared. She gave them a curious smile and said, "Can I help you?"

"Hi. Sorry to bother you. I'm Stan Turner, and this is Rosa Méndez. We're taking over Ruben Acosta's properties and wanted to meet you."

Leira frowned. "What? Taking over?"

"Yes, I'm an attorney, and Ruben appointed me as Trustee over all his properties."

Leira just stared at Stan for a moment and then said, "Why?"

"Oh, I guess you didn't hear," Stan said, "Ruben was murdered."

"Murdered!" Leira gasped. "What? No!"

Leira grabbed the doorjamb to steady herself.

"I'm sorry," Stan said. "I didn't mean to upset you. Did you know him well?"

She shook her head. "No, but he was such a nice man. It's just upsetting to find out he's dead and to know he was murdered. Why did they kill him? I mean, do you know who killed him?"

Stan shook his head. "Not exactly. The police have their suspicions, but at this point, it is just speculation. Did you two ever talk? Did he ever tell you about his work?"

Leira didn't respond right away. Finally, she shook her head and said, "No. We never talked about his business. Ruben liked to talk, but only about other things like the weather, politics, movies, and everyday stuff."

"Right," Stan said. "Well, nothing is going to change. If you need any repairs or anything, just call the same number. It will be taken care of right away."

Leira smiled and replied, "Thank you," and then shut the door.

As they walked out of the courtyard, Rosa said, "She really liked Ruben."

"Yes, she did," Stan agreed. "Well, everyone I have talked to who knew Ruben said he was a great guy. It's a real tragedy that he's dead. What a waste."

"I hate Carlos. What a bastard!" Rosa spat. "I'd like to put a stick of dynamite up his ass and lite it up!"

Stan laughed. "Go for it, girl!"

They both laughed as they pulled away. The rest of the afternoon, they drove by their other properties and stopped and talked to anyone they found at home. None of them, however, were the actual tenants, just family members or friends living on the premises temporarily. On the way to the airport, they stopped at a place called the Longhorn Steakhouse and killed a couple of hours until their flight took off at 11:30 pm.

"It's funny not one person, other than Leira, knew Ruben or anything about the property lease."

Rosa thought about that a moment and replied, "Well, they didn't have to pay the rent, so I guess it didn't matter to them."

Stan nodded, "Yeah, maybe. We'd have to come at night to catch one of the actual tenants."

"None of them were old," Rosa added. "Didn't you tell me they specialized in renting homes to retirees?"

"Right," Stan replied. But I'm sure Ruben instructed her not to turn any willing renters away."

It was a short flight to Las Vegas, so by 2 am, they had checked into their room at the Luxor Hotel. The room had two double beds, so they slept separately. At least, that is what Stan had intended. However, when he woke up during the night to go to the bathroom, he found Rosa sleeping next to him. He wondered how that had happened but didn't wake her to ask. He remembered her telling him she was used to sleeping several girls to a bed, so he figured she felt uncomfortable sleeping alone. He thought about mentioning it but couldn't bring himself to do it. He kind of liked having her next to him, even though it took all his willpower not to touch her.

The following day they slept late and were hungry when they got up, so they went down to the hotel cafeteria and had breakfast. A copy of the *New York Times* had been slipped under the door during the night, so Stan grabbed it to read at breakfast. In a small article on the front page, a headline caught Stan's eye.

Law Firm Charged In Aiding Smugglers of Chinese to U.S.

By Susan Sachs

Federal prosecutors yesterday accused one of the city's busiest immigration law firms of working hand in hand with the smugglers who bring illegal aliens from China, and then keep them as virtual indentured servants in the United States until the price of their passage is repaid.

In a 44-count indictment filed in Federal District Court in Manhattan, the government described the Manhattan law firm . . . as a racketeering enterprise that had been paid over 1.2 million dollars in fees over the years. ...

"I'm done," Rosa said with a smile. "That was good. So, do you want to explore this gorgeous hotel and the mall before our afternoon meetings?"

"Sure," Stan replied as he folded up the newspaper. "Let's go back to our room first, though. I want to save this newspaper article and I should call the office before we start exploring."

They took the escalator up to the lobby floor and then weaved their way through banks of slot machines, numerous blackjack, roulette and poker tables and hundreds of eager gamblers before they finally got to their elevator. They entered and pushed the up button. The elevator quickly rose to their floor and then opened onto a corridor that overlooked the Casino below. It was a breathtaking sight and Stan and Rosa gazed down at it as they walked to their room. After lingering a moment, Rosa opened the door and was shocked to see three men milling around. Rosa looked at the smaller of the men and said, "Carlos?"

Stan's mouth fell open. He had never looked Carlos in the eyes and had hoped he never would. He rubbed his forehead where Carlos or one of his bodyguards had struck him after their first meeting.

"Yes, Rosa, it's me. How's my girl?" he said as he grabbed her wrist and pulled her to him violently.

Stan stiffened but managed to force a smile. "Carlos. I was hoping to meet you. I wanted to thank you for Rosa. She's a great companion and a lot of fun."

Carlos looked at Stan, seeming amused. "Yeah, I'm sure you've never had a woman like Rosa. She'll wear you out."

Stan laughed tentatively.

"Anyway," Carlos continued. "After your little accidental spill last night, I wanted to let you know that no matter what kind of tricks you might try to get a little privacy, they won't work. I will be always watching and listening to you. So, don't fuck around with me. Got it!" he said letting Rosa go.

She pulled away and rubbed her wrists where Carlos had grabbed her.

Stan raised his hands. "Hey, there's no need for that. And it wasn't a trick. I was just a little nervous around such a beautiful woman. Don't worry. We're all on the same team, right? I'm going to handle all of your business satisfactorily. It will take a little while for me to get up to speed but having Rosa will help."

Carlos gave Stan an assessing stare, smiled, and said, "Alright, sorry. I just wanted to check in on you, Stan, and see how you were doing. I've got a lot riding on your performance, so don't disappoint me."

"I won't," Stan assured him.

"Okay, guys," Carlos said cheerily. "Let's go see who's playing high stakes poker."

Carlos and his two bodyguards left, and Stan closed the door behind them. Rosa had gone over to the window and was staring outside. Stan came up behind her, put an arm around her, and whispered, "I'm sorry."

"I'm never getting away from him, am I?" she moaned.

Stan took a deep breath. "I don't know, but you have to try. I'll do my best to help you. In the meantime, let's do the shopping I promised you."

Rosa nodded and pointed to a blinking light on the telephone. Stan picked it up. It was a message from Tom and Roger with the time and place of their next meeting with MedNet clients.

Stan hung up and said, "Well, we have two hours to shop and explore. We better get moving. Rosa nodded, and they left, but the joy and excitement they had both been feeling over the past twenty-four hours had gone. Now they were both distracted by the reminder that the Cartel would be watching them, ready to pounce if they made the slightest misstep.

That afternoon, Stan, Rosa, Roger, and Tom met with the MedNet clients and then hit the casinos one last time before driving to the airport. It was after midnight when Stan and Rosa made it to Stan's home in Plano. Rosa was impressed by the size of the house and loved Stan's big kitchen. She promised to cook him some spectacular meals.

That night they both slept soundly. Stan didn't set an alarm, so they didn't wake up the next morning until after 10 a.m. Stan was excited to have Rosa staying with him, so he made them a big breakfast. Although, they had lots to talk about, Stan reminded Rosa that the house was likely bugged, so to watch what she said.

Later Stan took Rosa on a walk through the neighborhood so they could talk freely. "So, how are you feeling?" Stan asked. "Did you sleep good?"

Rosa nodded. "Yes. I love your bed. The mattress is so comfortable."

"Yes, it is. It's extra firm," Stan noted. "So, I know you are going to run out of your drugs soon. How was Carlos going to handle that?"

"He said I could go to the Empire Club in Dallas when I needed a refill."

"Okay. That makes sense. Are you going to try to ween yourself off the drugs?"

Rosa nodded. "Yes. I never wanted them. We were required to take them."

"Well, I have a friend who is a nurse. I'm sure she would be happy to come stay with you while you are going through withdrawals. It will be a tough time, so I'll stay away and give you privacy if you want."

"No," Rosa said. "There are many rooms in your house. I'd rather you be here."

Stan smiled. "Sure, whatever you want. While you are in detox. I will get our offices up and running so, when you are feeling up to it, you can come help me manage Med Net and New Horizons. It's going to be a lot of work."

"Sure, that sounds good. Hopefully, it won't take too long before I can come help you."

"Yeah. I guess it will depend on your pain tolerance and how badly you want to get clean."

"Well, I'm very highly motivated. I promise."

Stan smiled. "I know you are."

"So, how do you know this nurse who will be helping me?" Rosa asked.

"My wife was an RN. She is one of her old friends and is like a sister to me. I helped her through her divorce and a child custody battle. "

"How will she feel about me living with you?"

"Ahh. It will be a bit uncomfortable at first, but she's encouraged me to date, so I don't think it will be a problem. She'll like you, I'm sure."

"I hope so," Rosa said.

The next three weeks were very difficult for Rosa but her motivation to get her life and her daughter back pulled her through it. After that ordeal, she was at Stan's side everyday helping him get MedNet and the other businesses running smoothly. While they were working hard laundering the Cartel's money, they prayed that the FBI was gathering all the evidence needed to put Carlos and the Las Guías Cartel out of business.

25
New Theory

Reggie

Reggie was depressed. He knew he was running out of time. Amanda's murder trial was just a few weeks away, and he still hadn't found the biker or any admissible evidence that a third party had been responsible for the accident that resulted in the death of Dr. Kenneth Short. Nor had he found any admissible evidence that Dr. Short was drunk or on drugs at the time of the accident.

It was late July 2000, and his father had been working undercover for the FBI for over six months. Reggie thought back to when he picked up his father at DFW airport in January. He stared at the stunning woman holding Stan's arm as they walked into the baggage claim area. He knew the scene wasn't real and had been supposedly staged for the benefit of the Cartel, but the image was still shocking.

He wondered if his mother was watching from heaven. What would she think of this? Would she understand, or would she feel betrayed? He knew his father's marital promise had ended at Rebekah's death, but it still didn't seem right that his father had another woman in his life.

As it turned out, Rosa wasn't the woman Reggie had imagined when he first heard about her. He'd expected a glamourous but shallow woman who was only suitable as arm candy. But, on the way home, they'd stopped at a noisy Steak & Ale restaurant, found an isolated booth, and had dinner. While they ate, Stan explained Rosa's perilous situation and her role in their undercover operation.

The meeting quickly changed Reggie's perspective on Rosa. After listening and talking to her, he found her intelligence and determination to be as stunning as her beauty. He'd heard much about human smuggling and sex slavery, but it had not seemed real or possible in America. Now, he felt sickened by the harsh reality of it. He couldn't imagine there were thousands, even tens of thousands of women in America, just like Rosa. It seemed surreal.

In the following weeks, he'd helped his father set up the management offices in the Mustang Office Suites. It was a small, two-office arrangement but had all the necessary computers and equipment to effectively handle the MedNet management business and other New Horizon enterprises. Rosa would always be there during office hours, and his father would split time between there and the law office.

The phone rang, interrupting his thoughts. "Reggie Turner," he said.

"Hey, Reggie, this is Amanda."

"Oh, hi," Reggie said. "What's up?"

"That friend at work, Melissa, finally called me back. She said she'll talk to you now."

"Really? That's good news. I have called her several times, but she never answers."

"Well, she didn't know who you were. If you come early tomorrow to pick me up for my doctor's appointment, I'll have her stop by so you can meet her face to face."

"That would be great. I'll see you at noon tomorrow then."

"Good. Have you talked to Paula lately?" Amanda asked. "Are we definitely going to trial on August 18th?"

Reggie sighed. "It looks that way. We are still number one on the docket."

"Do you think the jury will convict me?"

"I don't think so, but you never know about a jury. Each juror has had unique personal experiences that impact how they think about a case. It's hard to predict how they will react to your situation. And Judges are unpredictable as well."

"Has Paula decided if I'm going to testify?"

"No, but I doubt she'll let you. Prosecutors are good at intimidating witnesses and twisting their words."

Amanda fell silent. Reggie continued, "I'm sorry I can't be more definite, but going to court is a crapshoot. You need to be prepared for the worst. Who knows, maybe your friend will know something important."

"Okay," Amanda replied meekly.

"See you tomorrow."

Reggie felt horrible after he hung up the phone. Fate had dealt Amanda one tragic hand after another. It seemed she was destined for a life of pain and suffering. He wanted to do something to help her, but he was at a loss as to what that would be.

The following day when he rolled up to Amanda's house, he noticed two cars parked in front. He wondered who the second car belonged to. When he stepped up to the front door, he heard laughter. He couldn't ever remember hearing Amanda laugh, so his spirits were immediately elevated. He knocked on the door, and Julie quickly answered it.

"Hi. Reggie," Julie said and then opened the door wide to let him in.

Reggie walked in and nodded to the two women sitting on the sofa across from Amanda's wheelchair. They were all smiling. He said, "What's so funny?"

"We were just gossiping about our bosses?" Amanda said. "They're a bunch of losers."

Reggie smiled. "So, you both work at Southern Battery?"

They both nodded. Amanda said, "Yes, Melissa works on the assembly line with me, and Ruth works in HR."

Reggie's eyes widened. "HR?"

"Yes," Ruth said. "I'm a secretary there. Amanda was a regular at HR, so we got to know each other."

Reggie chuckled. "A regular. What does that mean?"

"I guess I never mentioned this to you, but I was sexually harassed when I first went to work for Southern Battery. It was a while ago, and the matter was resolved, but I spent a lot of time in HR back then."

"I see," Reggie said. "So, what do you know about Amanda's current situation, Ruth?"

"Well, when I heard about the accident and what happened to her, I felt horrible. The company never should have made her work a double shift."

"Why do you say that?" Reggie asked. "Don't many line workers have to work double shifts?"

"They do," Ruth agreed, "but none have sleep apnea."

"Are you sure about that?" Reggie asked.

Ruth nodded. "Absolutely, I do most of the paperwork involved in overtime compliance. If anybody didn't want to do a double shift and had an excuse, they would certainly tell HR about it."

"Did Amanda tell them she had sleep apnea?"

"She did. I checked her file, and it was right there in black and white."

Reggie thought about this a minute and then turned to Amanda, "So, when they asked you to do the double shift, did you remind them of your sleep apnea?"

Amanda thought a moment. "No. They knew about it already, so I figured they didn't care."

"Well, that could help us. The fact that you were being forced to do a double shift should mitigate your culpability in your criminal trial."

Amanda frowned.

Reggie elaborated, "Ah, you didn't want to do the double shift, but your boss made you do it. Some of the blame has to shift to Southern Battery. This could really help you on both fronts, civil and criminal."

Reggie liked what he was hearing and couldn't wait to tell Jodie and Paula, but he still had to talk to Melissa and then take Amanda to the doctor. He took a deep breath to calm himself and then turned to Melissa.

"So, Melissa," Stan said. "You worked on the assembly line, right?"

"Yes, I did."

"So, on the date of the accident, where were you?"

"I was at home," Melissa replied.

Reggie frowned. "At home? Okay, so you didn't hear or see anything on the day of the accident?"

"No. But the next day, when I heard about it, I was shocked and appalled at what had happened."

"You and Amanda were close?"

"No. We hardly knew each other, but I could have easily come in and worked that shift. There was no reason Amanda had to do it!"

"Seriously," Reggie questioned. "Do you know why he didn't call you?"

Ruth answered. "I do. He didn't want to pay time and a half. Amanda works fewer hours than Melissa, so they wouldn't have had to pay time and a half for her. So, Amanda was their cheapest option for covering that shift on the line."

Reggie's eyes widened. Then he frowned and asked, "Are you both willing to testify against your employer?"

"Why not?" Ruth said. "They can't retaliate if we are called as a witness. If they do, we can hire you to sue them."

Reggie laughed. "That's true. But their attitude toward you will change. They could make life at work uncomfortable."

Melissa shrugged. "I don't really care. I have thought about quitting anyway. There are other, better jobs available."

Reggie was in good spirits when he took Amanda and Julie to see their doctor. While they were with the doctor, Reggie called Jodie and gave her the good news. When he got back to the office, Jodie and Paula had already put Melissa and Ruth on the witness lists and were working on an outline of each's testimony.

On his way home, Reggie stopped at Stan's office in the Mustang Office Suites. He told him the good news about Amanda's co-workers.

"Wow! I bet Paula is thrilled."

"Yes, she is," Reggie said. "What do you think about suing Southern Battery."

Stan shrugged. "It's a theory, but it will not be a slam dunk. You will have to show their actions were intentional or, at least, reckless. Your witness can't read her boss's mind. She's speculating as to their motives at best."

Reggie didn't like his father's response but decided not to argue about it then. So, how are things going here?"

Stan looked around and said, "Let's get a cup of coffee. I'm getting tired and need some caffeine to keep me alert."

Reggie nodded, and they went downstairs to the building cafe, and each bought a cup of coffee. Then they took a walk. They found some benches at a bus stop and sat.

Stan took a sip of his coffee and said, "You asked how things were going? Well, to be honest, they are not going well."

"What's the problem?" Reggie asked worriedly.

Stan shook his head. "I'm not sure. We have been submitting our client's insurance claims each month, but the insurance companies are dragging their feet on paying them and turning many of the claims down."

"Really? Have you talked to them?"

"Yes, I call them all the time but get nowhere. They always have some ridiculous issues, so we have to resubmit the claim. The weird thing was when Ruben submitted the claims, they were almost always paid within thirty days."

Reggie thought about this. "Huh. So, what are you going to do?"

"I don't know for sure. I'm going back through old files to see if there is something in them to explain the problem. In the meantime, the clients are up in arms because their incomes have plummeted since I took over management. Some of them are threatening to pull their business."

"That's not good," Reggie noted.

"Yeah," Stan agreed. "Carlos would have a stroke. He might decide to fire me. "

"You mean to kill you?"

Stan nodded. "So, who's the alternate trustee if something happens to you?" Reggie asked.

Stan's face paled. "I'm afraid it's you. When I was setting things up, I couldn't think of anyone else."

"Shit!" Reggie exclaimed. "You better fix this problem and do it fast!"

Stan took a deep breath. "I'm sorry, Reggie. I never dreamed I'd ever end up having to act as the trustee. If something happens to me, you can decline to act. They can't make you act as trustee."

"Like they gave you a choice," Reggie noted. "Let me look at those old files. Maybe you missed something."

"Okay," Stan agreed, and they went back to the office. Rosa looked up and smiled when she saw Reggie."

"Hi. Reggie," Rosa said, cheerily. "Haven't seen you in a while."

"Yeah, I've been busy doing bankruptcies and helping Paula and Jodie defend Amanda Rich."

"Rosa. Where are the old claims files? I want Reggie to index them for me."

Rosa frowned, but when Stan put a finger to his lips, she got up and went to a file cabinet. "They are all in here," she advised, and Reggie went over to have a look.

Reggie went through the files while Rosa and Stan continued working on other things. The office was quiet, but that was the norm since they all knew the room was bugged, and both the FBI and the Cartel were likely listening. Reggie found it to be an unsettling environment, so he rarely visited his father there.

That night Reggie went over to Stan's house, which was also as still as a mortuary. After he had engaged in chit-chat with Rosa, he suggested they take a walk. After they rounded the corner of Stan's cul-de-sac, Reggie said, "So, I went through the files, and I did notice one thing that you might have missed."

"What's that," Stan asked excitedly.

"I know all the claim forms have a name and address where the claims are supposed to be submitted, but in each file, there is also a handwritten post-it note stapled to the file entitled Claims Adjuster with a different name and address."

"Yeah, I saw that," Stan said. "I think it is just the correspondence address."

"I don't think so," Reggie replied. "The names are different than the person who ends up handling the claim."

Stan thought a moment. "So, you think we have been submitting our claims to the wrong adjuster?"

"Maybe. You said yourself, Ruben had an uncanny ability to get insurance companies to promptly pay the claims submitted."

"That's true," Stan agreed. "So, you think this alternate address is where we should submit the claims?"

"I don't know. But you should check it out?"

"How?"

"Call one of the names on the file and ask what's going on with your claims. The Cartel may have compromised a claims agent at each insurance company."

"Okay, that makes sense. Thank you, Reggie. I should have thought of that."

"Well, you are too closely involved to be thinking clearly."

Stan laughed. "You've got that right."

Reggie felt good as he drove to his apartment. It had been a good day for him. He'd contributed to the firm, but he knew he couldn't quit yet. He had to find other ways to help the firm, his father, Amanda, and Rosa survive the perilous predicaments in which they found themselves.

26
Set Up

Stan

After Reggie had gone, Stan got back to work. There were always bills to pay, checkbooks to balance, invoices to send out, and dozens of phone calls to answer. Stan wouldn't have minded the job so much if he could have hired some clerical help, but that was out of the question when he was under such intense scrutiny by the Cartel and the FBI. While lamenting the situation, Rosa advised him he had a phone call.

"Hi, this is Stan."

"Mr. Turner, this is Carlos."

Stan stiffened as he felt a jolt of fear shoot through him. "Oh, hello. How are you?"

"Not so good. I have been looking at last month's financial reports, which are very disappointing."

Stan sighed. "Yeah. I know. I'm having problems with the insurance companies. They are being very bureaucratic; if you know what I mean."

"No. I don't, and I don't care. Figure it out quickly, or we'll have to find someone else to handle it."

"What do you mean? Who else could handle it? As I told you, I'm the duly appointed independent executor, and the Probate Court has accepted the will. If something happened to me, you'd be tied up in the Probate Court getting a substitute appointed."

"Don't lecture me on the law," Carlos spat. "I have a string of lawyers to advise me. They say the beneficiary could appoint a substitute trustee if something happened to you."

Stan knew he was right.

"Okay. Don't worry. I'm working on it," Stan assured him.

"Just to make sure you understand that I don't make idle threats, I'm sending someone over to pick up Rosa."

"No!" Stan protested. "Don't do that. I need her. It will just make matters worse if I don't have her help."

"What's the matter, Stan?" Carlos snarled. "You in love?"

"No. She's a smart woman and very good with the clients. I don't want to waste time looking for someone to replace her. Plus, hiring someone else would be dangerous for both of us."

"Two weeks!" Carlos snapped. "That's it. No excuses, no extension."

The phone went dead. Stan stared at the receiver for a moment and then hung it up. Stan didn't know Carlos had attorneys advising him. In retrospect, he realized, how could the Cartel operate without attorneys? Stan knew the beneficiaries could replace him by petitioning the Probate Court to appoint someone else as Independent Executor and Trustee, but he couldn't let that happen since that would mean he would soon be dead.

Stan dropped everything, went through the pending claims files, and searched for the post-it notes. After going through some of them, he quickly realized each insurance company had the same alternative adjuster. This made sense, and Stan berated himself for not figuring it out immediately. Ruben had been paying a kickback to one of the adjusters at each insurance company. Stan figured Carlos must have known this. He wondered why he hadn't told him.

Stan felt a little better now that he understood Ruben's methods. Now all he had to do was find out how the kickback scheme worked. After giving it some thought, he decided to call one of the designated claims adjusters and see if they would enlighten him on the procedure. He wasn't optimistic any of them would talk, but he had no choice but to try.

Stan ended up calling four of the names on the post-it notes before he convinced one of them to talk to him. Her name was Laura Matos, and she suggested lunch rather than talking over the phone. They met at the Highland Park Cafeteria the next day. In their phone call, Stan explained that Ruben had died and he was taking over. Laura Matos turned out to be a petite, middle-aged woman of Portuguese descent with long dark hair and brown eyes. They took their trays through the line and then found an empty table.

"You're not a cop, are you?" she asked.

"No. I'm an attorney and had the misfortune of having Ruben Acosta as a client."

"Ah. That explains it. You shouldn't have called me," Ms. Matos complained. "You should have sent a note or dropped by for a private chat."

"Sorry, I didn't think it through."

"Well, you better get your act together, or we will both get into serious trouble?"

"That's what I'm trying to do. So, tell me, how did you and Ruben handle the MedNet claims?"

"It's simple. Send all the claims to my address, and I will take care of them. Don't ask me how?"

"Okay, but I need to know how you are compensated for your special handling? I assume you're not doing this out of the kindness of your heart."

Ms. Matos gave Stan a puzzled look, then shook her head and said, "Ruben, didn't tell you how this worked?"

"No," Stan replied. "I didn't expect him to die right away."

"Okay. Well, I take my cut from the cash you deliver. Ten percent. That's how I pay for my kids' college tuition and room and board. Thank you very much."

Stan shook his head apologetically. "Of course, I'm an idiot. Sorry."

She rolled her eyes. "It's okay."

"Just out of curiosity, how is the money delivered to you?"

"It comes by Federal Express Overnight?" Ms. Matos replied.

"And who does the Fed Ex package say is sending it."

"I don't know. Some investment company, Global Insurance Equities, I think they call it."

"Okay, thanks," Stan said, nodding. "Good to know. That should make it easy then for me to get the ship righted."

"Easy for you. I'm going to have to deal with all your fucked-up claims."

"Sorry," Stan said. "What are you going to do?'

"I'm not sure. I will probably have to figure out a way to reject them all. Then you'll have to resubmit each and every one of them."

Stan cringed at the thought of having to redo all that work, not just for this insurance company but for all of them! He and Rosa had submitted claims to dozens of insurance companies, but at least now he knew how to fix this problem, get the cash flowing again, and keep his clients and the Cartel off his back. He thanked Ms. Matos and went back to his office to get started.

The next day he got a call from Paula wanting to strategize about Amanda's upcoming trial. He felt guilty that he couldn't help her more on her defense. In the past, they had worked hand in hand on her criminal trials, but this time he'd been too distracted for such collaboration.

"So, you're definitely going to trial next week?" Stan asked.

"It looks that way," Paula replied worriedly. "I was hoping to convince the DA to drop the case. It's a waste of the taxpayers' money to prosecute someone like Amanda who was simply a victim of circumstances."

"So, you've pointed that out to the ADA prosecuting the case?" Stan asked.

"Yes. Stewart Collins is the prosecutor. I've discussed it with him, but he refuses to bring the issue up with Preston Peters, the District Attorney."

"Wonderful," Stan sighed.

"Bart's going to talk with Peters at the Bench Bar conference this week. Hopefully, he can get him to take a realistic look at the case."

"So, you're worried about losing?" Stan asked.

Paula hesitated. "Maybe. They don't have to prove intent, so technically, the jury could find Amanda guilty."

"Is there anything I can do to help?" Stan asked.

"No. You've got your own problems. Jodie is going to be second chair."

"Well, let me know if you need me for anything."

Stan hung up the phone, and his thoughts quickly returned to his own perilous situation. The only thing positive about his mishandling of the MedNet claims, he thought, was the fact that the FBI would soon know the identity of dozens of the Cartel's co-conspirators. He'd be sure to relay that information to Special Agent Lot.

With that thought, he wondered how and when the FBI would make their move on the Cartel. He hadn't talked with Lot for nearly six months. He'd said they needed time to gather information on the Cartel, but how much time, he wondered. Did they expect him to carry on this charade indefinitely? He hoped not because it was getting very old and starting to seriously impact his law practice.

There was Rosa, too. She'd turned out to be a great partner in managing the Cartel's money laundering operation, and he enjoyed her company, but she was becoming attached to him, and he worried when it came time for them to part company, it would be too much for both of them.

He decided it was time to set up another meeting with Special Agent Lot. He had to bring things to a head, no matter how dangerous that might turn out. He arranged for the meet for the following morning. That night he had trouble sleeping. Between all his fears and worries, a line of thunderstorms had rolled through during the night, awakening him every time he managed to doze off.

He awoke the next day to a dark sky and heavy rain, which made the commute to work long and difficult. When he finally arrived, he checked all his messages in case any critical ones had arrived. Finding none, he went straight to the parking garage where he had left Rebekah's car. Unfortunately, when he tried to start the old car, nothing happened. After cursing himself for not realizing the battery might die and driving the old car occasionally to prevent that, he pondered his options. As he was thinking, a woman walked by that he recognized. She worked in the building cafe, so he knew it would be safe to talk to her. He got out of the car.

"Wanda!"

Startled, she turned and looked at him expectantly.

"Hey, you got a minute. I need a jump."

She relaxed and smiled. "Sorry, I don't have cables."

Stan shook his head. "I've got some."

Wanda looked at her watch.

"Please," Stan pleaded.

"Okay," she replied, but you'll need to hurry; I'm already late coming back from my break."

"It won't take a minute," Stan assured her.

Five minutes later, Stan was on his way. He looked behind as he pulled out of the parking garage, praying that no one was following him. As an extra precaution, he took a shortcut through the Medical City Hospital parking lot and came out onto the main cross street, Forrest Lane. If anybody had been following him, he was sure he would see them coming out of the parking lot. While he was focusing on his rearview mirror, the car in front slammed on his brakes, and Stan nearly rear-ended him.

"Damn it!" he exclaimed as he slammed on his brakes. "Take a breath!" he chided himself, trying to relax.

He started thinking about the upcoming meeting when he was finally on LBJ heading West. He prayed the FBI was ready to move as his nerves were about shot.

When he got to the Denny's, Special Agent Lot wasn't waiting for him. This rattled Stan as Agent Lot had always gotten to their meetings first. Stan began to imagine a host of different scenarios as to why Lot wasn't there. Had the Cartel figured out the FBI was involved? Had they ambushed him along the way?

As Stan imagined the worst, Special Agent Lot walked through the door and strolled toward him. Relief overcame Stan as he stood up and shook Lot's hand vigorously. Lot seemed amused by Stan's enthusiasm.

The waitress suddenly appeared and asked them if they wanted coffee. They both nodded, and she left.

"I'm so glad to see you," Stan said, stating the obvious. "This undercover work is exhausting and terrifying. I don't know how you guys do it."

Lot shrugged. "It's definitely no fun. Luckily, I don't have to do it too often."

"So," Stan asked. "Have you got enough to take down the Cartel?"

Lot took a deep breath. "Well, we have a lot, but the brass isn't sure it's enough."

"Why not? You have Rosa. She'll testify to the Cartel kidnapping her and murdering her brother."

"Yes, but she doesn't know for sure Carlos did it. She assumed it was Carlos and the Cartel since that's where she ended up. The best she can provide is testimony that she was forced into prostitution and sex slavery."

The waitress appeared with two cups of coffee and took their orders. When she had gone, Stan continued. "Isn't that enough?"

"No, we need to bring down all the Cartel leadership."

"Carlos as much as admitted to me that he killed Ruben Acosta. Did you tape all his phone calls?"

"Yes," Lot admitted, "but he didn't come right out and say it. You could interpret what he says as an admission, but any good defense counsel would argue it wasn't clear at all."

"What about the kickback to the claims adjusters?"

"You're the only one who dealt with the claims adjusters. Carlos is clean on that score."

"Damn it! So, we have nothing?"

"I didn't say that," Lot replied. "We just need a little more. What if you let the Cartel take Rosa?"

"What? Are you kidding?" Stan protested.

"No. If we have her under surveillance and document the kidnapping, then, along with Carlos' threats on tape, we'll have a slam dunk on at least one of the charges. Hopefully, we'll be able to get some of the Cartel members to flip and help us prove the other charges."

Stan grimaced. "What if Rosa gets hurt?"

"She won't. As soon as they lead us to the Cartel hideout, we'll go in and arrest the bunch of them."

"I don't know. It's a big risk to Rosa."

"It's the best option if you want this nightmare to end."

"Okay. So, you want me to intentionally piss off Carlos, so he takes Rosa?"

Lot nodded. "Right."

Stan frowned. "What if he takes her and kills me?"

"You'll have to be careful. Just irritate him enough that he takes Rosa. You're smart enough to figure out how to do that."

Stan stared at the Special Agent. "I've never liked playing with dynamite."

"It's the best option," Lot assured him.

Stan nodded tentatively. "Okay, should I alert Rosa to the plan?"

"Does she know we are involved?" Lot asked.

"No. I don't think so. I've never told her the FBI was watching us, but she's no dummy. She may have figured it out."

"Better to keep her in the dark. It will make her a better witness."

The waitress brought them their breakfasts. They ate in silence, pondering the ramifications of their conversation.

Stan finally said, "There is one complication."

"What's that?" Lot asked.

"If you expect Rosa to testify, you'll need to put her in witness protection."

"Sure, no problem," Lot agreed.

"Not just her, but her grandparents and her baby."

Lot gave Stan a stern look. "Well, they're not in the United States. How could we do that?"

"I don't know, but you better figure it out because neither she nor I will testify unless I know she and her family are protected."

"About that," Lot said. "Are you willing to go into witness protection yourself?'

Stan's mouth opened, but no words came out. "Ah. Do you think that would be necessary?"

"Yes. Even if everything goes as planned, there will be members of the Cartel out in the wind. You will be their number one target if you testify."

Stan hadn't thought of that. He squirmed in his seat. "Maybe you won't need my testimony," Stan reasoned.

"Don't count on that," Lot said. "Are you ready for a new life? You'll have to change your name, move to a small town somewhere, and you'll never be able to contact your family or friends for the rest of your life."

Stan thought about that. If he did have to go off the grid for a while, it was a good time to do it with Rebekah gone and Reggie now working for the firm. The firm could get by without him. He knew he wasn't essential anymore. Paula and Jodie were quite capable of keeping the firm alive, and they'd look after Reggie.

"Let's try to keep me off the witness stand, if possible," Stan urged.

Special Agent Lot nodded, and the two men called over the waitress, paid their bills, and went on their separate ways. On the ride back to the office, Stan began to worry about Rosa. How could he intentionally betray her? Or was it a betrayal? He tried to rationalize what he had agreed to do, but it didn't help. He knew he was intentionally risking Rosa's life and the lives of her family. He was sick inside.

After checking in at Turner & Waters, he called Rosa to tell her he would be there soon. When she didn't pick up, he went into a panic. He was about to rush over there when his phone rang.

"Stan. You called?" Rosa asked.

Relieved, Stan exhaled slowly. "Yes, just making sure you were okay."

"I'm fine. I was in the ladies' room when you called."

"Right. I just wanted to tell you I'd be over soon. I've got a few things to finish, and then I'll be on my way."

"Okay, see you soon," Rosa said cheerfully.

Stan's heart sank. He wondered how he'd be able to go through with the FBI's plan. If anything happened to Rosa, he didn't know if he'd be able to live with himself. Tears began to well in his eyes. He started taking slow, deep breaths to calm himself, but it did little good.

When he got to his car to go to the MedNet offices, he turned on the radio to get a traffic report. He wasn't sure if he should take LBJ Freeway or go on surface streets to the Tollway.

"This is Margie Moore with the KRLD traffic report at 5pm. For commuters on Eastbound I-20 near Carrier Parkway in Grand Prairie, traffic has been at a standstill for the last hour as a black Chevrolet SUV apparently collided with a green Ford F-150. The F-150 was entering the freeway when one of its tires blew out causing the driver to lose control, and cross two lanes into the path of the SUV. Police and ambulances are on the scene now, and police are detouring traffic onto surface streets. Expect a delay of 22 minutes,"

In today's news, Vladimir Putin was inaugurated as the President of Russia today..."

The location of the accident caught Stan's attention. He knew he was just at that very location. The Denny's where he met Special Agent Lot was just blocks away. He told himself it was just a coincidence and put the thought out of his head. He had to focus on Rosa and what he should say to her. He didn't know if he should alert her to what was about to come down on her or leave her in the dark.

When he got to the office, Rosa welcomed him with a hug, and they kissed as was their practice when they knew someone from the Cartel was watching them. Stan enjoyed this role-playing and looked forward to it. He wondered how Rosa felt about it but didn't have the nerve to ask.

"So, how is the claims report looking? Are we on target?"

Rosa grimaced. "It's up 20%. Is that going to be enough?"

"Not really, but it's definitely an improvement," Stan replied. "Hopefully, Carlos won't pull the plug on us."

Rosa licked her lips nervously. "So, what happens if he pulls the plug?"

Stan shrugged. "I don't know," Stan lied and looked away. A jolt of fear and remorse washed over him. He couldn't look at Rosa, knowing what would happen to her. Tears began to well in his eyes.

Sensing something was wrong, Rosa went over to him and put a hand on his shoulder. "What is it?'

Stan wiped his eyes, turned, and smiled. "I'm just getting used to having you around, and I know one day it will have to come to an end."

She nodded. "I know, but let's not think about that now. What do you want for supper? Enchiladas?"

Stan laughed. "Sure. You know that's my favorite."

On the way home, Stan prayed the FBI would protect Rosa as they promised. He knew their plan was the only way they could put Carlos away and shut down the Cartel, but he hated putting Rosa at risk. That night he tossed and turned, unable to sleep. When he did finally doze off he had nightmares, each ending with Rosa lying on the floor, lifeless and in a pool of blood.

27
The State vs. Amanda Rich

Jodie

The weekend before Amanda's trial, Paula and Jodie had a full schedule of activities planned. Paula wanted to practice her opening statement and have Jodie critique it. They also needed several hours to prepare Amanda in the event Paula decided to call her as a witness. Then they needed to go through all the expected exhibits and prepare witness outlines. It would be a long and exhausting two days that Jodie wasn't looking forward to facing.

On Saturday morning, while Paula was working with Amanda on her testimony, Jodie decided to take one more shot at Tom Tyson. She had given him a deadline on her last offer and wanted to put some pressure on him to accept it. If she could pull that off, that would take a lot of pressure off her and Paula. She put a call into Tyson's office but got the weekend voicemail. She left a message in the firm's mailbox knowing somebody would check messages frequently.

"This is Jodie Marshall, Tom. Just wanted to remind you of our offer in the Amanda Rich case. It's about to expire, and I thought you might want to hear some new information that has come to my attention. It's something significant that you should consider before you let the deadline pass. Call me back."

Jodie hung up, wondering how long it would take to get a callback. Much to her surprise, her phone rang almost immediately. She picked it up.

"I told you I wasn't interested in your offer," Tyson spat.

"I know. But I have new information that might make you change your mind."

"There's nothing you can say that will change my mind," Tyson said impatiently.

"Hear me out. I think you're wrong about that."

Tyson sighed heavily, "Okay, spit it out; I don't have all day."

"One of our associates did some digging into your client's past. He had a lot of issues, lawsuits, DUIs, marital problems, and I could go on."

"I know all that," Tyson acknowledged. "That's ancient history. It won't have an impact on our lawsuit."

"I'm not so sure about that, but I don't know the facts, and, at this point, I don't want to know them. If I did, I might be considered a co-conspirator."

"What the fuck are you talking about?" Tyson asked angrily.

"Okay, relax. I'll get to the point," Jodie said evenly. "Do you remember the lawsuit your client recently settled with some business partners? "

"Of course, I do," Tyson admitted.

"Well, one of our associates had the clerk pull the case file and discovered something quite interesting."

"What's that?" Tyson asked.

"Your opposing counsel took Dr. Short's deposition, and a copy of the transcript was part of the Court's file. What's interesting is that the deposition transcript is missing."

There was silence on the line. "So," Tyson finally said.

"Well, I'm wondering what's in that deposition transcript you don't want anyone to see."

"You're nuts," Tyson spat. "I had nothing to do with the transcript's disappearance. Some clerk probably misfiled it."

"Maybe, but I thought it was interesting who checked the file out last."

Tyson didn't respond. He finally said, "It wasn't me."

"No, it probably wasn't you, but it was someone you or your law firm hired."

"You can't prove that?" Tyson argued.

"Maybe not," Jodie agreed, "but I can get a copy of the transcript from the court reporter or your opposing counsel and read it."

Jodie heard heavy breathing and muffled curses. "I don't know what you think you know, but it's bullshit!"

"Is it? You're not worried about life expectancy?" Jodie asked. "Shall I spell it out for you?"

There was more heavy breathing, then reluctantly Tyson replied, "No. Don't bother. I'll take your shit offer. Your client is about to get locked up anyway, so what's the point. Send me a proposed settlement agreement, and I want an air-tight confidentiality clause."

"Yes, sir," Jodie agreed. "I'll have it to you by the end of the day."

Jodie hung up and let out a scream. Paula heard her and came rushing in.

"What's going on?" Paula asked.

"The Tornado just got deflated!"

Paula smiled excitedly. "Okay, how did you pull that off?"

Jodie reminded Paula of Reggie's discovery that a deposition transcript had gone missing from the archives of one of the civil suits against Dr. Short.

"So, why did that matter?"

"Well, I finally got a copy of the transcript last night from the court reporter. It cost me $455, but it was well worth it. It turns out Dr. Short was dying of lung cancer and only had six months to live when he was killed in the accident."

"Okay, so what?" Paula asked, trying to connect the dots in her mind.

Jodie smiled. "Well, the good doctor's policy has a one million dollar uninsured or underinsured motorist coverage. Amanda qualified as an underinsured motorist since she has minimum coverage. Ordinarily, the Tornado would have no problem proving a loss of income of one million dollars over the expected lifetime of a doctor of Dr. Short's age and income. But, if the doctor's expected lifetime is six months, he'd be lucky to convince the insurance company to give him a hundred grand."

Paula laughed. "Very clever," Paula said. "Wow! I'm impressed."

"Thank Reggie," Jodie said. "He found the needle in the haystack; I just shoved it up the Tornado's ass."

They both laughed.

"So, now we can file Amanda's personal injury lawsuit against Southern Battery," Paula noted.

"Reggie is already working on it," Jodie advised. "We should be able to file it on Monday."

"Good. Just in time for our dear District Attorney to see it before the trial begins," Paula replied. "I wonder what he'll think of it."

Jodie gave her a wry smile. "He won't like it, I suspect."

They both laughed harder this time, then went back to trial preparation. They hoped for the best, of course, but they knew they couldn't rely on the District Attorney acting rationally. Amanda's freedom was at stake, and they couldn't stand the thought of Julie having to live with her grandmother in a doublewide and having to visit her mother in prison. That just wasn't an outcome they could accept.

28
Gutsy Move

Reggie

Reggie nervously worked on the original complaint against Southern Battery. It wasn't an easy lawsuit because usually an employer was not liable for what their employees did off the jobsite unless they were on an errand or official company business. He tried valiantly to come up with some sort of argument along those lines but finally decided it was impossible.

Reggie finally settled on two counts, ordinary negligence, and gross negligence. His theory was that Southern Battery owed a duty to Amanda as an employee to act with reasonable care in assigning her work at Southern Battery. They breached that duty when they assigned her a double shift knowing she was being treated for sleep apnea and that she would not be in any condition to drive after working the extra shift. The second count of gross negligence was added so Amanda could ask for punitive damages.

Gross negligence had been defined by the courts as an act or omission that involved an extreme degree of risk and a "mental state" of actual awareness of the risk coupled with conscious indifference to the welfare of others. He was hopeful they could meet that burden with the evidence he had uncovered.

He looked over the complaint one last time, printed it out, and took it to Jodie for her review and input. She took it from him and promised she would review it soon. When he got back to his office, he noticed Stan had called and wanted him to call him back. Maria had written IMPORTANT in capital letters at the bottom of the message, which was unusual,

Curious, Reggie called his father immediately.

"Dad? You called?" he asked.

"Yes," Stan replied. "Come to the house. We need to talk."

"What about?" Reggie asked.

"It's too complicated to talk about over the phone. Just come home immediately. Okay?" Stan said sternly.

"Okay. Okay. I'm on my way." Reggie replied.

Reggie returned to Jodie's office and told her his father was acting weird, and he had to go home to see what was up. Jodie was concerned at hearing this news and said if they needed her, she'd try to get away and join them.

Being the weekend, traffic was light, so Reggie made it to his dad's house in less than twenty minutes. As he walked in the front door, he found his father pale and disheveled, pacing in front of the fireplace.

"What's going on, Dad?" Reggie asked worriedly.

"They've taken Rosa. She's gone."

"What? Who's taken her?"

"The Cartel," Stan moaned. "They threatened to take her if I didn't perform as well as they expected handling the MedNet accounts. I was working on it and had gotten everything ironed out, but I was late with one report, and they came and got her."

"How do you know they have her?"

"She never leaves the house without letting me know she's going out. Besides, they took her clothes and jewelry."

"Did you call the police?"

“No, I called the FBI to check in with Special Agent Lot, but they told me he had been killed in a car accident, and no surveillance had been set up on Rosa."

"Agent Lot is dead?"

"Apparently, the accident occurred right after our last meeting. They don't know if the Cartel had anything to do with it. It could be a coincidence, but I doubt it."

"You're not a cop or private investigator," Reggie reminded his father.

"I know, but the longer Rosa is gone, the less chance we'll ever get her back."

"So, what are you going to do now?" Reggie asked worriedly.

"I'm not sure. I just wanted you to know that some weird shit may be coming down on me, so don't be surprised."

"Jodie said she could come if you needed her," Reggie said. "There must be something we can do."

"If I had a clue where they took her, we could try to rescue her, but I have no idea."

"You don't know where the Cartel hides out?"

"Well, not for sure. Rosa did tell me about a private club they owned and operated. She worked there for a while as a stripper and escort. She said there was a large house several blocks away where the girls lived when they weren't working."

"What was the club called?" Reggie asked.

"The Empire Club, it's on Northwest Highway near Walnut Hill. I've driven past it a few times."

"I've heard of it," Reggie said. "Let's call Jodie and meet her over there. We can talk to one of the girls and get the address of the residence."

"I don't want you going," Stan said. "You need to stay here in case Rosa shows up. They may have just taken her for a ride to scare me. If she shows up here, call me immediately.

Reggie nodded and then called Jodie and told her the plan. She told him she'd get her gun and be on her way. Reggie passed on the message as he walked Stan to the garage.

Let me take the Porsche," Stan said. "They may be on the lookout for my car."

Reggie fished the keys out of his pocket, and they traded car keys.

"Be careful," Reggie pleaded. "Call the FBI if you find them. Don't try to be a hero."

Stan nodded, got in the Porsche, and sped off. Reggie prayed his father would be okay. When he returned to the house, he called Paula to fill her in on what was happening.

"Jodie just left here in a hurry. What's up?"

Reggie explained about the kidnapping, Special Agent Lot's death, and Stan's hope of finding Rosa at the Empire Club.

"They should have waited for the FBI," Paula moaned.

"They couldn't. The FBI is still reeling over Agent Lot's murder and is in disarray. They were supposed to be watching Rosa, but they totally dropped the ball. Stan had no choice."

"What a mess," Paula lamented. "I have Amanda's trial on Monday. I need Jodie."

"She'll be there, I'm sure," Reggie promised. "If they can't find Rosa today, they'll have no choice but to turn the matter over to the FBI."

Paula sighed. "If they do find her, the Cartel's not going to give her back without a fight."

"Right," Reggie said. "That's what I'm afraid of, too. ... Hey, did Jodie finish editing my complaint against 'Southern Battery?"

"Yes," Paula replied. "She signed it and gave it to Maria to get filed before the end of the day."

"Good," Reggie said and hung up the phone. He walked over to the front window where he could see any cars coming down the cul-de-sac. The street was quiet, so he decided he'd call Amanda while he was waiting and see how she was holding up. He couldn't imagine what she'd be feeling with her life in the balance. She picked up immediately.

"Amanda. Hey. I just wanted to check on you. You, okay?"

"I guess so," Amanda said softly.

"Good. Hey, I'll pick you up at 7:30 a.m. Monday, okay?"

"Un-huh. I'll be ready."

"What about Julie? Is your mom going to take care of her?"

"No. She wants to come to the trial. Julie wants to come to."

Reggie felt sick. "Do you really want her there?"

"No, but what choice do I have?"

"We can drop her off at daycare on the way to the courthouse."

"She'll be mad."

"Well, it's your call, but it could be traumatic for her."

"You're right. We'll stop at daycare."

"Okay," Reggie said. "Try to get a good night's sleep."

"I'll try," Amanda said. "No promises. Every time I fall asleep, I dream of being in prison, pushed around the yard by demented inmates, and dumped out onto the pavement."

"Oh, my god!" Reggie exclaimed. "I'm so sorry."

"I know they are just dreams, but they are still scary."

"Right. Well, this will soon be over. Paula and Jodie have been working hard to give you the best defense possible. They are very optimistic that the jury will be sympathetic to your situation. Just hang in there."

"Thank you," Amanda said and hung up.

Reggie went back to the window, but the street was still quiet. He wondered what was happening and prayed his father and Jodie would be okay. He remembered when he was growing up several times that his father had gotten into some sticky situations, but his parents had kept the details of those events secret. Only now did he understand how dangerous the practice of law could be.

Reggie looked at his watch and saw it was nearly 3:00 p.m. He decided he'd waited long enough for Rosa and decided it was time to go back to the office. When he arrived there thirty minutes later, he went straight to Maria's desk and got two copies of the Original Petition that had just been filed with the District Clerk. On his way home, he dropped one of the copies off to a college buddy he knew who had gone to work at the *Plano Star Courier*. His buddy promised he'd make sure his editor saw it before he left for the day.

29
Rescue

Stan

Stan went into his home office and retrieved the revolver Jodie had bought him. It came with a handy ankle holster for easy access. He had continued practicing at the shooting range weekly with Jodie and Besch and felt comfortable with the weapon but hoped he wouldn't have to use it.

When he pulled into the Empire Club's parking lot, he saw Jodie standing in front of her car. Several men had already gathered around her. He figured they probably thought she was a stripper or an escort for hire. Stan parked the Porsche and strolled over to her.

"Jodie. You made it here quickly."

"Well, I was closer than you. Besides, I didn't want to miss out on the fun."

Stan rolled his eyes. "You consider this fun?"

"Not, really. I'm just trying to lighten the mood. Anyway, I talked to one of the bouncers, and he said he hadn't seen Rosa in the Club for months. He said I should check the residence. He gave me directions."

"Good, let's go," Stan replied.

They both got into Jodie's car and took off, following the directions she had been given. When they got to the three-story Victorian home, they drove past it and parked down the street. Three cars were parked on the street in front and a white van in the driveway as they went by.

"So, how are we going to do this?" Stan asked.

"Why don't I go in and inquire if Rosa is there. They probably won't come right out and tell me she's there, but I will be able to tell by their reaction if they're lying."

"I don't know," Stan replied. "Maybe we should sneak around and look in the windows first."

"That might work, but we'll be in trouble if we get caught. Can you call the FBI and tell them we think we've found her?"

Stan thought about that for a moment and then shook his head. "Nah. That's probably not a good idea. We don't know if she is here, and I don't know who to call at the FBI and how long it would take them to respond. If she is here, right now, we have the element of surprise."

Suddenly, two large Hispanic males came around from the back of the home and went straight to the van. Stan and Jodie assumed they were Cartel thugs. The men opened the vans' back doors, and Stan and Jodie saw a half-naked woman, tied and gagged, lying motionless in the truck bed.

"That's Rosa," Stan whispered.

"Is it? She's still. I hope she's still alive."

"Me, too!"

The two men pulled Rosa out of the truck and carried her around to the back of the house. Stan and Jodie followed them at a safe distance. Behind the house was a shed where they observed the men open the door and take her inside. After a minute, they came out, closed the door, and locked it with a padlock.

When the men had left, Stan and Jodie went to the shed and surveyed the situation. As they were snooping around, one of the Cartel thugs spotted them through the house's back window and rushed out, screaming, and waving his gun at them.

Without hesitation, Jodie pointed her gun and shot the big man in the shoulder. He fell to his knees and dropped his firearm. A second man suddenly rushed out and pointed his revolver at Jodie. Before he could fire, Stan fired his weapon and grazed the man's arm, causing him to curse and point his gun at Stan. Stan dove into the bushes and rolled behind a concrete bench. A barrage of bullets sailed harmlessly over his head.

Jodie rushed over to the fallen man and held her gun to his head. Looking at the second man, Jodie screamed, "Put your gun down, or your amigo is dead!"

Stan stood up and pointed his gun at the second man. "Put down the gun!" Stan commanded.

The second man surveyed the situation briefly, then finally tossed his weapon aside and lifted his hands in the air. Stan rushed over and kicked the gun away.

"Give me the key," Jodie demanded of the man at the end of the barrel of her gun, and he quickly complied.

Hearing the commotion, several women came out the back door of the residence to see what was happening. Jodie got the keys from the first man and rushed to the shed and opened it. Before going in, she looked back at the women standing around and yelled, "Help me!"

Two of the women rushed over and helped Jodie untie Rosa and carry her out to Jodie's car. Stan held the Cartel thugs at bay with his revolver until Rosa was safely in the car, and they were ready to go. As Stan walked by the van, he shot both passenger side tires out so the men couldn't pursue them.

Soon, they were speeding off toward Northwest Highway. "Where to?" Jodie asked.

"Rosa is still unconscious. We better take her to the hospital. Parkland is the closest, I think," Stan said.

"Okay," Jodie replied.

"I'll call the FBI and see if I can get them to meet us at the hospital."

As Stan was talking to the FBI dispatcher, Jodie looked in her rearview mirror and saw a car approaching them from behind.

"Shit!" Jodie spat. "They must have taken one of the girls' cars."

Stan turned and saw a black sedan on their tail. He noted the license plate read: SHO GRL. He recognized the driver as the man he shot in the arm. A third man in the passenger seat stuck his head out the window and pointed his gun at them.

"Duck!" Stan yelled.

They both ducked as a bullet shattered their back window. Jodie glanced back, then accelerated and adroitly passed two cars in front of her. Their pursuers mimicked the move and moved in close behind them again. Two more bullets hit the trunk of Jodie's car, causing her to weave in and out. At Northwest Highway, Jodie went left and pulled away from her pursuer.

"This car has a lot of pick up," Stan observed.

"Yeah. I got the high-performance package. I hate wimpy cars."

"Good choice," Stan said holding on tightly as Jodie raced up the on-ramp to I-30.

Stan looked back, and their pursuers were dropping back. He also noted smoke was coming out of the trunk.

"Oh, my god!" Stan screamed. "We're on fire."

Moments later, they got to the exit for Parkland Hospital and exited the freeway.

As they drove into the emergency entrance to the hospital, Stan saw two police cars and a big black SUV, which he assumed belonged to the FBI. Jodie pulled in front of the entry door and stopped. Two orderlies pushing a gurney rushed toward them.

Stan and Jodie got out and opened the back door to let the orderlies get at Rosa. Within seconds they were rushing her into the Emergency Room.

As two special agents approached them, Stan yelled. "Get away! We're on fire." Seeing the smoke pouring out from beneath the car, everyone scattered and dove for cover. Jodie's car exploded in a fiery inferno.

Moments later, Jodie peeked from behind a bus stop bench and said, "Damn. I loved that car."

Stan shook his head and replied, "I hope you have insurance."

"No. I hope the firm has insurance. We're on the job."

Stan didn't argue. After the two agents had dusted themselves off and checked for injuries, they introduced themselves as Special Agents Alice Thompson and Roger Wilson.

"How did you manage to rescue Rosa?" Agent Thompson asked.

Stan shrugged. "We got lucky. Rosa worked at the Empire Club several years ago. She had told me about it, so I figured this would be where they would take her. I tried to contact Agent Lot to tell him, but when I found out he was dead, I figured Rosa's only chance would be if I acted immediately."

"Yes, Agent Lot's death has been a jolt to our local field office. I'm sorry, we let you down."

Stan shook his head. "No, I was upset as well. I've known Agent Lot for years. I considered him a friend."

"The funeral is tomorrow if you want to attend."

"Yes. Absolutely!"

"Okay, go on. So, what did you do then?" Agent Wilson asked.

"I called Jodie, and we met at the Club. She got there first, so she pretended to be one of the girls and got a bouncer to tell her where the residence was located."

Stan explained the events at the Empire Club's residence and the car chase along the way to the hospital."

"Well, we will need you to come in and make a statement, but for now, let's go see how Rosa is doing? Was she injured in the escape?"

"No. I don't think so. Rosa was unconscious when we found her. With help from some of the girls, Jodie carried her to our car. You should get someone over there to identify and secure any witnesses."

"The police got there shortly after you left the scene on reports of gunfire by neighbors. Our agents are already on the scene as well. It seems everyone had fled the scene."

"Damn!" Stan exclaimed in frustration.

"Oh, also, we will need your firearms as evidence."

Stan looked at Jodie. She pulled a revolver out of her purse and handed it to agent Thompson. Stan did likewise. When they got inside, a nurse told them that Rosa was being examined and that they should go into the waiting room until the doctors were through with her.

While they were waiting for the doctor, Stan asked. "So, did you catch the driver who killed Special Agent Lot?"

Agent Wilson shook his head. "No. It was a hit and run, and no witnesses have come forward."

"What? I thought it was a tire blowout."

"No. That was a false report. The truck drove across the median and fled the scene."

"Damn!" Stan exclaimed. "I can't believe the Cartel killed him."

Agent Wilson nodded. "It certainly has been a blow to our investigation of the Cartel. Special Agent Lot had spent a lot of time putting a solid case together, but unfortunately, much of his plans and strategy were in his head and not written down. It will take us some time to get back on track."

"Do you have any witnesses lined up?"

"We have a couple of Cartel members in custody and hope one of them will flip. What about Rosa?" Agent Wilson asked. "Is she loyal to the Cartel?"

"No. She hates the Cartel. They've threatened to kill her grandparents and daughter if she steps out of line."

"Why was she with you?" Agent Thompson asked.

"She was offered to me as a companion, but I think they just wanted to spy on me. So, knowing that I never told her anything about the FBI, and, honestly, I don't think she would have intentionally told them anything useful. She hates the Cartel with all her heart and soul."

Agent Wilson raised his eyebrows. "Well, I hope that's true. We need her as a witness if we have any chance at bringing down the Cartel."

"She'll be a good witness," Stan assured them, "if she's alive."

Agent Wilson nodded and asked, "So, Ms. Marshall, I understand you shot one of the Cartel members when Ruben Acosta was murdered."

Jodie nodded. "Yeah. I wish I'd have killed him."

"You're going to be an important witness, too, if we are able to bring charges against Carlos Herrera."

"I figured as much," Jodie replied. "Whatever you need me to do, let me know."

As they were talking, a doctor walked into the room and looked around. When his eyes fell on the FBI agents, he said, "Ah. Are you here for Rosa Méndez?"

Stan said, "Ah. We're all here for her. How is she?"

The doctor looked at Stan and replied. "She's awake now. It appears she was just heavily sedated. She'll be fine."

Relief flooded over Stan's face. "Thank God!"

Jodie put her hand on Stan's shoulder and said, "You saved her life."

Stan turned to Jodie, "Ah, I think we both saved her life."

Jodie nodded, and they embraced. A second later, they turned to the two Special Agents. Stan asked. "So, how will we protect Rosa from now on?"

"That will be the U.S. Marshal's job. We'll take her to our field office and interrogate her. Then we'll turn her over to the Marshals."

Stan nodded.

"You two may want to go into protective custody as well after your little rescue," Agent Wilson noted. "The Cartel's gonna be pretty angry. They may come after you two."

Stan frowned. "Is that really necessary?"

Agent Wilson nodded. "Yes, both of you must stay alive so we can nail these bastards."

"I have to help Paula with a murder trial starting Monday," Jodie noted. "I can't go into protective custody."

"Sure, you can. The Marshal will bring you to Court each day and return you to the safe house. It will be a pain in the ass for them, but that's what they get paid to do."

Jodie swallowed hard. "Well, okay. I guess."

Stan felt a bit deflated, knowing he wouldn't have Rosa's company anymore, but he knew it was for her own good. He didn't know how he could operate the Cartel's businesses without Rosa while in the US Marshal's custody. After mulling this over in his head, he said, "I need a few days to secure all of Ruben Acosta's assets if you don't want the Cartel to get control of them."

The two special agents looked at one another. Agent Wilson said, "Okay. We'll have the Marshals protect you while you take care of that. Then you'll have to disappear until Carlos, and his lieutenants are arrested and put on trial."

Stan nodded dejectedly. A few hours later, Rosa was discharged and went with Special Agents Wilson and Thompson. Stan and Jodie were driven by a police officer back to her apartment, where they were picked up by two U.S. Marshals. Neither were happy with their lives being turned inside out, but they were relieved they would be safe. At least, they hoped the Marshals could protect them.

During the next few days, Stan met with Tom, Roger, and a business broker they had previously dealt with. Stan knew he couldn't manage MedNet or the trust from witness protection, so his only option was to sell the businesses and do it quickly. The problem with such a sale was timing. Usually, it would take thirty to ninety days to sell this type of business. This amount of time was necessary to obtain financing and conduct due diligence. Stan knew to speed up the transaction, he would have to either cut the price severely or offer seller financing with a right-of-recission should the buyer later discover any legitimate misrepresentations. Selling cheaply wasn't an option, as Stan had a duty to get a reasonable price for any trust assets he sold.

Stan told the broker he had decided to sell MedNet as he didn't have time to operate it anymore. When the broker saw the financial statements, the reasonable asking price of $1.2 million, and Stan's offer of seller financing, he got very excited. Even though the offer was only good for 48 hours, the broker said he knew of several entrepreneurs who would jump at this opportunity. Of course, the fact that the broker would make over $67,000 in commissions in just a few days gave him the necessary incentive to get the job done in a timely manner.

While Stan was waiting for the business to be sold, he safely put the rest of Ruben Acosta's assets away in long-term investments that didn't require constant monitoring. He didn't know how long it would be before Carlos was caught and the Cartel was put out of business.

Stan and Jodie attended Special Agent Lot's funeral along with their U.S. Marshal bodyguards. It was a memorable event as hundreds of officers from the Dallas Police and Sheriff's offices, and dozens of FBI and other federal agents gathered to ride in a motorcade from Love Field to the Cathedral Guadalupe in Dallas where a memorial service was to be held.

Stan was sad over the loss of his long-time friend. While he listened to the accolades about Agent Lot, he vowed to do everything in his power to bring Carlos Herrera and the Las Guías Cartel to justice. That would be the least he could do for his fallen friend, who had come to his rescue and saved his ass on more than one occasion.

30
Amanda's Trial

Paula

As usual, Paula had trouble sleeping the night before Amanda's trial. At 5:00 a.m., she finally quit trying and got up and took a shower. She was due in Court at 9:00 a.m. for jury selection which she anticipated would take most of the day. While putting on her makeup, she was thinking about who an ideal juror would be.

She presumed women would be more sympathetic to Amanda's situation because they were more compassionate and forgiving. Older people would be better as well since they would have had more experience with pain and adverse reactions from medications. She figured she needed to keep young men off the jury as they often had little patience for female drivers. She'd also have to find out who on the jury panel had a loved one killed or injured in a car accident. She didn't need anyone like District Attorney Preston Peters on her jury.

After she showered, she got dressed and took a good look in the mirror. She knew her appearance was essential, so she always took the time to look good. Bart smiled when he saw her walk into the kitchen in her royal blue Fringe-Trim Midi Dress and GG Marmont Silver Stud Earrings he'd bought her at Neiman Marcus.

"You look great," Bart noted. "Ready to give them hell?"

Paula shrugged. "That breakfast looks great, but I don't think I should overeat. You know how nervous I get before the trial begins."

"Well, you'll need your strength, so eat something."

Paula sat down and started nibbling on a piece of toast. "I can't believe Preston Peters wouldn't listen to you. This case is ridiculous. Poor Amanda having to go through all of this."

"I know. Talking to him was like talking to a brick wall," Bart complained. "He wouldn't even look me in the eyes."

"The bastard!" Paula spat.

"Make him pay," Bart suggested with a grin.

Paula smiled. "I might just do that if I can pick a good jury."

"Jodie has good instincts on jury selection. She'll help you out."

"I don't know. She'll be there, but the Marshals have her in protective custody. I'm not sure she'll be on the top of her game."

"Oh, I think she will be. If she can handle herself in a gunfight, picking a jury should be a piece of cake."

Thirty minutes later, they were on the way to the Collin County Courthouse. When they arrived, Bart let Paula off at the side entrance so she could avoid the press and then went to park the car. He had promised he'd be there in the gallery for moral support.

Paula took the back stairs to the second floor and caught the first elevator to the 4th floor, where the 199th District Court was situated. When she stepped out, she saw a mob of reporters but managed to stay out of their sight and walked through the swinging doors to the clerk's office and entered the courtroom through the Judge's door.

The courtroom was packed with spectators. She immediately spotted Amanda in her wheelchair in front of the defense table and Reggie standing nervously by her side. She walked over quickly.

"Hi, Amanda. I see you got here okay."

Amanda smiled and said, "Yeah. Reggie came and got me bright and early."

Paula smiled at Reggie and said, "Thank you, Reggie."

"No problem. Do you need me to do anything?"

Paula shook her head. "No. Today we just pick the jury. I might need you tomorrow to help keep track of witnesses."

"Okay. Just let me know what you need."

"Have you seen Jodie?"

"Not yet, " Reggie said.

There was a commotion outside, causing everyone to turn and look toward the door to the courtroom. After a minute, two U.S. Marshals walked in and surveyed the courtroom. When they were done, Jodie stepped inside and walked toward them.

"Hey," Jodie said. "Quite an entrance, right?"

They all laughed.

"Yeah. Now you know how the President feels," Reggie joked.

"Yeah. It feels good," Jodie said. "So, are we ready to go?"

"Just waiting for the judge," Paula said.

As they were talking, the Bailiff handed them an envelope. Paula grabbed it and pulled out the packet of completed jury questionnaires inside.

"You've got thirty minutes," the Bailiff advised. "You'll have six strikes."

"These are our potential jurors," Paula said as she divided the stack into two parts and gave Jodie one of them. Reggie watched them for a moment and then walked away.

They each grabbed legal pads and started going through the list and jotting down notes on each one. The questionnaire asked each prospective juror their name, occupation, place of birth, education, previous jury experience, and other basic information about themselves. When they finished, they traded piles of questionnaires and repeated the process.

Ten minutes later, they compared notes and agreed on seven jurors they didn't want on the jury. Since they only had six strikes, they hoped the Prosecution would strike at least one of the persons on their list.

Five minutes later, the Judge's door opened, and the Judge walked in. The Bailiff stood and stated, "Please rise for the Honorable Judge Joseph McIntyre."

The Judge took the bench and looked down at his docket sheet. "All right. We will proceed with the matter of the State of Texas vs. Amanda Rich. Bailiff, please bring in the jury panel."

The Bailiff went out into the hallway where sixty potential jurors were seated, brought them into the courtroom, and seated them in the first three rows. Jodie quickly filled in a juror seating chart so Paula could address each juror by name, which was essential to establish rapport with each juror.

When the jurors were all seated, the Judge said," Okay. Earlier today, I explained why you are here today and what would be expected of you. Now the Prosecution and the Defense counsel will ask you questions to ensure each of you can be a fair and unbiased juror. Listen to all their questions and answer them truthfully. If you don't understand a question, feel free to ask questions.

The Judge introduced Amanda, Paula, and Stewart Collins to the jury panel and explained each's role in the trial. Then he looked at Collins, nodded, and said, "Mr. Collins, you may proceed with a short explanation as to what this case is about."

Collins stood, walked over to the jury box, and with his hands behind his back, began, "Ladies and gentlemen of the jury. This case is about a traffic accident involving the Plaintiff, Amanda Rich, and Dr. Kenneth Short, deceased. The uncontested facts are pretty simple. Ms. Rich worked at a business called Southern Battery Co. and had just come off of a double shift and was driving home in her own car. On the way home, she picked up her daughter, Julie, from daycare and was proceeding onto State Hwy 180 going northbound when her vehicle veered out of her lane, crossed the median, entered the southbound lane where she struck the vehicle being driven by the decedent, Dr. Kenneth Short. As a result of the accident, Dr. Short died from his injuries sustained in the accident.

"Additionally, it is uncontested that the Defendant suffers from an ailment called sleep apnea and that after her shift, before she got into her car, she took medicine for a headache that has a common side effect of drowsiness.

"As the Judge pointed out, your job will be to determine the contested facts in the case as to the cause of the accident, the reasonableness of the Defendant's actions, and other factual questions that the Judge will explain to you later. For now, I will ask you some questions to determine if you can be fair and unbiased, which is a requirement for all jury members."

Collins looked down at his Jury Seating Chart and asked, "Mrs. Wendel Jones. Do you know the Judge, the Defendant, or any of the counsel in this case?"

A tall, lean, middle-aged woman with black hair stood. "Ah. No. I don't think so."

"Mrs. Jones, have you or a family member ever been in an auto accident?"

Mrs. Jones nodded and replied, "Yes, I have been rear-ended a few times."

"Were you injured?"

"Yes, I had whiplash and had to go around with a neck brace for weeks."

"Did you sue the driver that hit you?"

"Ah. I don't know. My insurance company handled everything."

"Now, Mrs. Jones, you've heard my brief rendition of the facts, in this case, so I ask you, will your experience as a victim of a negligent driver influence your thinking about this case. In other words, are you biased at all when it comes to victims of negligent drivers?"

She shook her head. "No, of course not. Every case is different."

"So, as a juror, you would listen to the evidence and make your decision based on the facts and the instructions from the Judge?"

"Right. Of course."

'Thank you, Mrs. Jones. You may sit down."

Collins looked out over the jurors and said, "Has anyone else been or had a family member in an auto accident? If so, raise your hand."

Several people raised their hands. "Okay, based on the questions I asked Mrs. Jones, would anyone of you not be able to be unbiased based on the facts of this case."

Everyone's hand went down, so Collins continued. "Now, did any of you witness this accident, read about it in the newspaper, or hear about it from friends or acquaintances?"

Almost every hand was raised. Collins stepped back in shock. "Wow! Okay," he muttered. "Let's see. Mr. Howard Edwards, please stand."

A short, stout man with greying hair rose, "Yes, that's me."

"Thank you, Mr. Edwards. Ah. How did you read or hear about this case."

"I read the article in Sunday's Star Courier?"

Collins looked over at his assistant and frowned. The assistant shrugged. Then he looked at the Judge, who was looking at him expectantly.

"Your Honor, I wasn't aware of an article in the newspaper about this case," Collins said, looking accusingly at Paula and Jodie."

The Judge said, "Mrs. Waters, do you know anything about this newspaper article?"

"No, Your Honor. It's news to me."

Jodie stood. "I'm perplexed as well, Your Honor."

Collins said, "Your Honor, perhaps we should take a brief recess and find a copy of this newspaper article so we can ask the jury intelligent and relevant questions about how this article might impact them."

The Judge nodded. "Alright. I think I have a copy of that newspaper in my chambers. We shall take a thirty-minute recess to review the article. Counsel shall meet me in my chambers at once."

The Judge banged his gavel and left the bench. The Bailiff yelled, "All rise!"

Paula and Jodie each grabbed their purse and a legal pad and headed to the Judge's chambers. Collins and his assistant followed right behind them. When they entered the Judge's chambers, he was rifling through a stack of newspapers.

"Here it is," the Judge advised and started reading it. When he was done, he shook his head.

"Ms. Waters, you just filed a lawsuit against Southern Battery."

Paula said, "Well. Ah. Yes, Your Honor."

"Well, the *Plano Star Courier* got wind of it and published an article about it. Since it involves the same auto accident, the article is highly prejudicial."

Jodie stiffened. "We had a perfect right to file that lawsuit, Your Honor. We believe Southern Battery is responsible for the auto accident."

"Your Honor," Collins spat. "This was an intentional act to sabotage this case."

"No," Paula replied indignantly, "that is not the case at all. The same facts in our complaint will come out during this trial, so it doesn't matter how or when the jurors hear them. They still will have the job of determining what they believe the facts to be."

"Alright," the Judge said. "Mr. Collins, you can ask the jurors whether this news story will prevent them from being unbiased. If they answer affirmative, I'll strike them for cause."

"That's well and good, Your Honor. But many of them will say they can still be unbiased, but they will be deceiving themselves."

"Then you have six strikes, Mr. Collins," the Judge reminded him. "Now, let's get on with it!"

They all got up and filed back into the courtroom. The Judge looked at the Bailiff and said, "Bring in the jury."

After the potential jurors were back in their seats, Collins resumed questioning. "Alright, sorry for the delay. Now, Mr. Edwards, after reading the article you mentioned in the *Plano Star Courier*, do you think you can still be fair and impartial?"

"Well, the facts in the article are very different than your summary?"

"That's not the question? As the Judge advised you, as a juror, you can only consider the evidence presented during this trial. You can't consider anything in the news article."

"But Ms. Rich almost died on the operating table, was in a coma for days, and will be in a wheelchair for the rest of her life. You're saying I can't ..."

"Objection, Your Honor. "Mr. Edwards, please just answer the question. Can you be fair and unbiased as a juror in this case?"

"Fair, yes. Unbiased, I don't know. It depends."

Collins looked at the Judge, "Your Honor, I think this juror has shown he should be stricken for cause."

"Objection, Your Honor,' Paula said. "Don't I get an opportunity to question this juror?"

The Judge shook his head. "Counsel, approach the bench."

Collins and Paula went up to the bench, and the Judge whispered. "Mr. Collins, you are about to spoil this juror panel, and the taxpayers of Collin County have spent a lot of money getting these jurors here today. Although it will be time-consuming, I have no choice but to conduct the remainder of the voir dire individually."

"Thank you, Your Honor," Paula said.

"Very well, Your Honor," Collins grumbled.

Collins and Paula returned to their counsel tables and sat. The Judge said, "Ladies and gentlemen of the jury. I apologize, but to avoid subjecting you to any undue influence, we will have to question you separately.

"Bailiff, please remove the jury except for Mr. Edwards, who will stay."

The Judge stood up and escorted all the jurors, except Mr. Edwards, out of the courtroom. When they were gone, the Judge said. "Ms. Waters. You may cross-examine the witness."

"Mr. Edwards. If you are selected as a juror, would you be able to follow the Judges instructions in determining the facts of this case?"

"Yes, of course."

"Okay. So, if you were selected as a juror and the Judge instructed you to only consider the evidence presented at trial, could you do that?"

"Yes."

"So, you realize the newspaper article is not evidence, right?"

"Ah. Right. I guess not."

"So, you wouldn't consider the newspaper article, just the facts presented to you in court."

"If that's what the judge instructed me to do, yes."

"Thank you, Mr. Edwards. Pass the witness."

The Judge nodded. "Okay, I'm going to deny the Prosecution's motion to strike this witness for cause."

After Mr. Edwards, the other jurors were brought in one by one and examined. At noon the Judge recessed the case for lunch and told everyone to return at 1:30 p.m. Paula, Jodie, Amanda and Reggie went downstairs to the cafeteria for lunch. After they were seated, Jodie looked at Reggie.

"Ah. Reggie, do you know anything about the *Plano Star Courier* article?"

Reggie turned red and looked away. "Ah. Well, I may have dropped off a copy of our complaint to a friend I know there."

"That was brilliant," Paula said. "Wow. I'm impressed. I hadn't thought of that."

They all laughed.

"But the Judge doesn't seem too happy about it," Reggie noted.

"Too bad," Paula said. "The lawsuit is a public record. Collins can't do anything about it."

When they were about to finish eating, Paula saw Bart approaching. He looked happy, if not gleeful.

Paula frowned as he sat down. "Why are you so happy?"

"You won't believe this, but I just ran into the District Attorney. He's pissed about the Plano Star Courier article. He says it was a low blow and not appreciated."

"So, too bad," Paula said defensively.

"Anyway, the good news is he was going to tell Collins to dismiss the case. They will blame it on us for polluting the jury pool."

A broad smile came over Paula's face. She turned to Reggie. "Reggie, you're a genius."

Everyone laughed and had the cafeteria served champagne; they'd of ordered a bottle.

When they returned to the courtroom, Paula was summoned to the Judge's chambers, where Collins was already seated.

The Judge didn't look happy. "So, Ms. Waters, it seems Mr. Collins has decided to dismiss this case without prejudice. He thinks the jury pool has been hopelessly poisoned by Sunday's news article. Since a jury was not seated, double jeopardy will not apply should the District Attorney decide to bring charges later. Is that agreeable?"

Paula considered the matter and couldn't imagine the District Attorney trying a second time to prosecute Amanda, so she replied. "That is agreeable, Your Honor."

The Judge nodded. "Well, then, I guess we are done here. Thank you both. You are both dismissed."

"Thank you, Your Honor," Paula said, stifling a broad smile.

Collins stood and stormed out without a word. Paula thought she saw the hint of a smile on the Judge's face as she followed Collins out the door.

31
Safe House

Jodie

After the Judge dismissed Amanda's criminal case, Jodie wanted to go out and celebrate with them, but the two U.S. Marshals responsible for her safety would not have it. After hugging Amanda, she embraced Reggie.

While in his embrace, she whispered, "That was a pretty gutsy move. Your Dad would have been proud."

Reggie smiled, let go of her, and replied, "Reckless is what my dad will probably say."

"No. Your father would have done the same thing, trust me."

Reggie raised his eyebrows and added, "Luckily, it worked out okay. When will we see you again?"

Jodie shrugged. "Weeks or months. Who knows? You know how long it will take the Feds to round up, indict and prosecute the Cartel."

Reggie sighed. "Well. Be safe. We'll miss you two."

Jodie said goodbye to Paula and Amanda and then was led away by the U.S. Marshals. They drove East on State Hwy 380 and passed the site of Amanda's accident. From the back seat of the big SUV, Jodie carefully scanned the area as they passed wondering what actually happened on that fateful day. They continued East past Tyler for several miles and then turned down a gravel road. At the end of the road, they stopped at a ranch house surrounded by white fencing. Several horses were grazing in an adjacent field.

Jodie got out and surveyed the rural landscape. A moment later, the front door opened, and another marshal stepped out and greeted them. Jodie hadn't been to the safe house since she had to participate in Amanda's trial. She knew Stan and Rosa were already there.

Jodie followed the Marshals into the spacious home and spotted Stan and Rosa anxiously waiting.

"Hi," Stan said. "I didn't expect you here so soon."

They embraced, and then Jodie explained, "Well, I have good news. The Judge dismissed the case!"

Stan's eyes widened, "Really? What happened?"

Jodie smiled and then looked at Rosa. "Hi, Rosa. How are you feeling?"

Rosa smiled. "Fine, now that I'm far away from Carlos."

"What about your family? Are they safe?"

Rosa nodded. "Yes, they are safe at the U.S. Embassy. They're going to go into witness protection with me."

"Oh. That's wonderful," Jodie said.

Stan smiled. "Yes, now all the FBI has to do is find Carlos and his men and arrest them."

"Hmm," Jodie said and then explained how Amanda's case was dismissed.

"Damn. Reggie's got a lot of guts," Stan said. "I knew he was tenacious, but I didn't know how he'd do under fire. I guess I got my answer."

"He takes after his dad," Jodie noted.

Stan blushed. "Well, I don't know about that."

Rosa smiled broadly, "I like Reggie. He's a nice boy."

"I don't think the Collin County DA would agree with you, Rosa," Stan chuckled.

They all laughed.

A woman wearing an apron stepped out of the kitchen and said, "I'm Sarah. I'm your cook. I have lunch ready for anyone who is hungry."

Jodie smiled at Sarah and said, "I'm famished. Lead the way."

Sarah turned and went back into the kitchen. They all followed her and found a long table that seated eight diners. Across from the table was a smaller table where plates, glasses, utensils, and plates of food had been placed. Stan, Jodie, Rosa, and the three U.S. Marshals each grabbed and filled a plate, then took a place at the table. After a few minutes, when they were all gathered around the table, they began eating heartily. A few moments later, Special Agents, Wilson and Thompson joined them.

When they had finished eating and were drinking coffee, Stan asked, "So, what's the plan now to bring down the Cartel?"

Agent Thompson wiped her mouth and replied, "Well, we've finally found Carlos Herrera in Santa Fe, New Mexico. He's currently held up in an Indian Hotel and Casino North of the city, where he runs a prostitution ring for hotel visitors. We're not sure how long he'll be there. Are you familiar with that operation, Rosa?"

Rosa shook her head. "I've heard of it, but the closest I ever got to it was the ShoGirl Strip Club in Albuquerque."

"Well, we plan to arrest him there first thing tomorrow morning and then extradite him here to Dallas where we can try him for the murder of Ruben Acosta, Rosa's kidnapping, human trafficking, and a long list of other charges."

"That's good to hear," Stan said. "Will you have enough evidence to convict him?"

"We think so, and after we arrest him, we will shut down the Cartel's operations all over the Southwest and try to flip some of his lieutenants. If we can get a couple to play ball, that should be icing on the cake."

Rosa frowned. "I don't know if his men will testify. They know if they do, they will be hunted down and killed for their betrayal."

"Well, you may be right, Rosa," Thomson replied, "so we have a couple of spots available in witness protection to offer them; first come, first serve."

They all laughed.

"What about all your surveillance of the MedNet and New Horizon Trust's operations?" Stan asked. "Did you get some good evidence of their money laundering?"

"Yes, but we need to figure out how the New Hope Legal Clinics fits into the picture," Thompson said. "I understand they are the ultimate beneficiary of the Acosta estate and his trust, right?"

"It looks that way. I'm not sure if Cristino Mejia is part of the Cartel, but I suspect he is," Stan replied. "He had no problem with Carlos's plan to delay a final distribution indefinitely. If the non-profit legal clinic were truly independent, they wouldn't so readily have agreed to such a delay."

"We're checking into him as we speak," Thompson noted. "We're also looking into the lawyers that work in the clinic. They may be on the Cartel's payroll as well."

"Don't you have a case like that in New York," Stan asked.

"Right, the Chinese law firm in Manhattan who we think are bringing in illegal immigrants from China and exploiting them as indentured servants," Thompson replied. "How did you hear about that?"

"I saw an article in the *New York Times* about it." Stan replied. He thought for a moment and then added, "Carlos told me once that he had a string of lawyers. That surprised me then, but it makes sense for an operation of that size and scope."

"What we are missing to be certain of nailing Carlos is testimony from one of the thugs that kidnapped Rosa," Thompson advised and looked over at Rosa.

"They sedated Rosa, so she can't help identify them. I'm sure you and Jodie had never seen them before, right?"

"Right," Jodie said, "but I could pick the bastards out of a lineup if you ever find them,"

"We are working on getting together an album of all known Cartel members, Rogers interjected. "Hopefully, these two guys will be included in the collection."

"What about the license plate number, SHO GRL, I gave you," Stan asked. "Did you track the car down?"

"Yes," Thompson replied. "It was found Sunday in a vacant lot. It had been torched. The vanity plates were purchased by a woman who died in 1966."

"Oh! Great," Jodie exclaimed. "So, we were chased by a ghost?"

"It seems so," Thompson agreed.

"Those bullets flying through the back window of Jodie's car seemed pretty real," Stan noted.

"That reminds me," Jodie said. "I need to file an insurance claim."

"I hope you had uninsured motorist protection," Stan said.

Jodie nodded, "Oh, yeah. I'm not an idiot. I know a lot of people can't afford auto insurance, and those who have it only get the $20,000 minimum limits."

After lunch, Agents Wilson and Thompson left, leaving Stan, Jodie, Rosa, and three U.S. Marshals. There were two of the Marshals stationed outside to watch the perimeter of the safe house, and one stayed inside and worked at a desk with a computer, printer, fax, radio, and telephone.

By 3:00 p.m., Jodie was bored and jittery and couldn't imagine being locked up in the safe house for weeks or months. All she could think about were all her cases back at the office that needed attention. Jodie had asked if she could at least call the office and work by telephone but was told that was too dangerous. She thought the Marshals were being a little paranoid on that score, but they insisted she not contact anyone.

That night the three witnesses went to their respective bedrooms. However, Jodie could not sleep and decided to make a cup of tea. While on her way to the kitchen, she saw Rosa slip out of her room and enter Stan's bedroom. She chuckled to herself, wondering how that relationship was going to end. She couldn't imagine Stan and Rosa staying together after all this Cartel mess was over.

Two days later, Wilson and Thompson showed up for breakfast with good news.

"We've arrested Carlos," Thompson advised. "He's in the Dona Anna Detention Center in Las Cruces, NM. They caught him trying to flee into Mexico. The extradition is expected to take a week to ten days."

"That's good news," Stan replied. "Did he put up a fight?"

"No. We had an inside man at the Indian Casino who put a tracking device in his luggage when he checked out. We set up a roadblock ten miles north of the border crossing, and when his driver saw it, they tried to turn around, but we had him trapped. He wasn't dumb enough to try and shoot his way out of it."

"Too bad," Jodie noted. "If you'd have killed him, it would have saved the taxpayers a lot of money, and I'd have been able to get back to work."

"Sorry," Agent Thompson said with a grin.

"Will the detention center be able to hold him? Stan asked. "Can they hold off an all-out assault on the facility by the Cartel?"

"Oh, yes," Thompson replied. "It's a new facility, state-of-the-art. There are no bars, just glass partitions between the guards and the inmates. We will have eyes on him at all times."

"Glass. Seriously?" Jodie asked. "I hope it is bulletproof."

Agent Thompson laughed. "It is, don't worry."

With Carlos behind bars, Jodie felt some relief, but she knew they still had a long road to go before the government could indict, try, and convict him.

That night she had nightmares of her kidnapping years early by a different, but no less vicious, Cartel that operated a sweatshop in South Dallas. She had gone undercover and dated the Cartel bosses' son to get intel on the Cartel, but when he discovered what she was up to, he ordered his son killed and took her prisoner.

Jodie felt much safer with the protection of the U.S. Marshals but still had difficulty falling asleep. She missed having her gun on her nightstand and it pissed her off that the FBI had taken it from her and not replaced it.

32
The Arrest

Stan

Several weeks went by at the safe house, and the three guests of the U.S. Marshals were getting a bad case of cabin fever. Agents Wilson and Thompson had come by every few days to keep them updated on the investigation and to see how they were doing. On this day, they were dressed in casual attire and brought with them a federal prosecutor, Assistant U.S. Attorney Beverly Burns.

After everyone had been introduced and gotten a cup of coffee, they took seats at the kitchen table.

Agent Thompson started the meeting. "So, we have Carlos in custody now in the Grayson County Jail. He arrived here yesterday, and the judge denied him bail given the seriousness of his alleged crimes and the fact he was caught fleeing to Mexico."

"That's a relief," Stan said. "Does that mean we can get out of here?"

"No. I'm afraid not," Agent Thompson replied. "We've arrested several of his lieutenants, but many others are still out there. It wouldn't be safe."

Stan sighed and looked at Jodie, who shook her head in disappointment. Finally, Stan asked, "Okay, so how long do you think it's going to be?"

Beverly Burns spoke up, "That's why I'm here," she said. "I will be putting the case together against Carlos and the other Cartel members.

"Right now, we are evaluating the evidence, our witnesses and working on our prosecution plan. Everything is looking good, but there are a few holes."

"What kind of holes?" Stan asked.

"Well, we are not sure how all the money flows. The Cartel is obviously laundering a lot of money, but we don't know all the details of how they are doing it."

Stan frowned. "Yeah. That took me a while to figure out. There were three sources of income, property rents, management fees and investment income."

"How much was coming in from rents?" Burns asked.

"About a quarter million a month?" Stan replied. "Have you interviewed any of the managers yet?"

"You mean Margie and Raul Rojas at Sunrise Realty?"

"Yes. And we have a local manager here in Texas, Amos Washington, and a manager in Las Vegas, Otis Jones."

"We have someone watching each of them, but we haven't interviewed them yet. That's one of the things we might need your help with."

"Oh, okay," Stan replied. "How can I help?"

"We need to convince one of them to testify. Also, we need one or more of the insurance adjusters to tie Carlos to that part of the laundering operation. Unfortunately, in all the conversations between you two, he has never admitted to having a connection to the insurance adjusters. You and Ruben are the only ones with a connection."

"I met with one of them; Matos was her last name. I think her first name was Laura. She's a single mom and uses the Cartel money to pay her kids' college tuition. I'm sure she'd cooperate to keep from going to jail."

"Good. You and I will need to meet with her."

"Sure," Stan agreed.

"And we don't know how the New Hope Legal Clinics fits in."

Stan frowned. "Yeah. I don't know either, but I have my suspicions."

"So, we can count on you to help figure it all out?"

Stan nodded. "Yeah. I don't have anything else to do. Why not?"

"What can I do?" Jodie asked.

Burns looked at Jodie. "We need you to go back to the Empire Club and see if you can identify any of the girls who witnessed Rosa's kidnapping and the gun battle you and Stan had with the Cartel members."

Jodie smiled. "Yeah. Let's do it. I'm bored to tears sitting around here."

"First, I have some photos of known Cartel members I need you two to look through," she said and pulled out a file from her briefcase. She divided the stack of photos into two parts and handed one to each.

Stan looked through his stack but found no one he recognized. Jodie pulled out one photo and said, "This is the guy I shot." She handed it to Burns and then showed it to Stan."

"Yeah, I think you're right," Stan agreed.

Burns turned the photo over and read, "Gabino Escalona, male, 34 years of age, a truck driver from Mexico City, suspected of human trafficking, last seen in Del Rio, Texas about six months ago."

"Well, he obviously made it to Dallas," Stan said. "Maybe he brought a load of girls up here, and Carlos recruited him for Rosa's abduction."

Burns nodded and replied, "Good. We'll put an ABP out on him. Maybe we'll get lucky."

Thompson said, "Why don't Wilson and I take Stan and Jodie to the Empire Club. When we are done there, we will split up. I'll take Stan to meet with Laura Matos, and Rogers can take Jodie over to the abduction scene, and she can explain exactly how that went down."

Burns nodded. "That sounds good. I will take Rosa with me so she can identify Carlos in a lineup. Call me when you get back," she said and started gathering her things together. Stan and Jodie went to their rooms to get ready while Wilson and Thompson talked to the Marshals on duty.

Right around noon, they pulled into the Empire Club parking lot. Two other agents, also in casual attire, were there to meet them and provide backup. Thompson paid the cover charges, and they all entered together. Once inside, they split up into two groups of three. Stan, Thompson, and a female special agent named Roxanne Polk went to the buffet, and Jodie, Rogers, and a male special agent named Kurt Ventura took a seat around the stage where two girls were working the poles.

Stan scanned the room but didn't recognize anyone. He was hungry, so he grabbed a plate and filled it up from the buffet. The others filled their plates and then followed Stan to a table. A topless waitress came over and took their drink orders. They all ordered beers and took in their surroundings.

Ten minutes later, Stan turned when he heard a loud voice. He saw an obviously drunk man grab the waitress's boob. "Get your hands off me!" she spat.

A few seconds later, a bouncer grabbed the drunk by his collar. "Ven Conmigo gilipollas!" the bouncer spat as he dragged the drunk toward the exit. As the bouncer went by, Stan thought he recognized him. He knew he'd seen him but couldn't recall where. Then he remembered. The man had been with Carlos in Las Vegas.

Stan nodded to Thompson and Polk and pointed toward the bouncer. They both rose and followed him out of the club. Stan trailed them at a safe distance, and as he stepped outside, he observed Thompson show her badge to the bouncer.

"You're under arrest!" Agent Thompson barked. "Put your hands up."

The bouncer gave Thompson a shove and turned to run, but from behind, Polk pulled her gun and pointed it at his face. Reluctantly, the bouncer raised his hands." Agents Polk and Ventura then took the bouncer into custody and drove him to the FBI field office, while the rest of them went over to the residence to go over Rosa's rescue and look for witnesses. Unfortunately, the residence was locked up and appeared to be deserted.

Stan and Agent Thompson's next stop was the offices of People Care Insurance Company, where they hoped to find Laura Matos. It was located in downtown Dallas near Neiman Marcus. The company occupied the top six floors of the thirty-story office building built in the early 1920s.

The old brass elevator still had an attendant who greeted them as they entered.

"Where to?" he asked.

"Claims department," Stan replied.

"Oh, coming to collect some money, huh?"

"Ah. Not exactly," Stan said. "Just needing a little help from one of the claims adjusters."

The attendant laughed. "Don't hold your breath."

Stan laughed as the elevator came to a stop. The man opened the door for them.

"Twenty-nine," the man announced.

They got out and walked over to a directory mounted on the wall. According to the directory, the Claims Department was in Room 2932, which was to their right. When they got to the room, Thompson opened the door, and they went inside. A receptionist looked up as they entered.

"Hello, can I help you?" she asked.

Thompson started to pull out her badge, but Stan stopped her.

"No. We don't want Laura to lose her job."

Thompson stuck her badge back in her purse and let Stan take the lead.

"Hi. I've got an appointment with Laura Matos to review some claims we submitted."

The receptionist nodded and announced our arrival. Five minutes later, Laura came out looking a little perplexed. "Stan, I wasn't expecting you."

"Oh, I left you a message. I just need a few minutes. It's very important."

Laura sighed and then said, "Well. Okay. I'm a little busy, but come in."

Stan and Thompson went to Laura's small, cluttered office. Laura removed a pile of file folders from one of her two side chairs and invited them to take a seat.

"What's up?"

Stan nodded toward Thompson and said, "Ah. This is Special Agent Alice Thompson of the FBI."

Visibly shaken, Laura's jaw dropped open. "Oh, my God!"

"It's okay," Stan assured her. "She's not here to arrest you. We know you were coerced into working with the Cartel. She's here to offer you a deal."

Laura nodded. "Oh. Okay. I can't go to jail. I've got kids in college."

"We know," Stan said.

Thompson said, "Stan has briefed us on the money laundering you've been doing for the Las Guías Cartel."

"Really. Is that its name? The man who forced me to do it didn't bother to tell me their name."

"If you cooperate and testify against the Cartel, we can offer you immunity and witness protection."

"Witness protection? Will I need that?" Laura moaned.

Thompson shrugged. "We would recommend it. I think it would be wise, but it's your decision. You know how ruthless these cartels can be."

"Oh, Jesus. My girls. I won't be able to see my girls?"

"They can come with you if they don't mind relocating and changing their names."

"Okay, how does it work exactly."

"You have to be interviewed and they'll do a background check to make sure the program will work for you. If you pass the interview, you will have to settle your affairs, then you are given a new identity, relocated and given a stipend until you can get a job and are able to take care of yourself."

Laura took a deep breath and closed her eyes. "Okay. I guess I don't have a choice. What do you need me to do?"

"Don't tell anyone, particularly your employer, that you are cooperating with the FBI. They have no idea what you are doing, right?"

"No. My employer doesn't have a clue. If they did, they'd fire me."

Agent Thompson explained to Laura that she'd need to let them monitor her activities for a few weeks so they could gather evidence.

Then she'd need to testify to the grand jury and at the trial. She agreed and thanked them both for giving her a way out.

When Stan returned to the safe house, Rosa had just returned from the Collin County Jail, where she had positively identified Carlos Herrera as the person she believed was the head of the Las Guías Cartel.

"So, how did it go?" Stan asked. "Were you scared seeing your old boss?"

She shook her head. "No. Carlos couldn't see me, thankfully. I was behind a one-way mirror. I recognized him immediately. It was a great relief to confirm the FBI had the right man. I was worried they had captured an impersonator."

"Really? Does he have a double?"

"Yes. The cartels are always fighting rival cartels, so the bosses use impersonators as decoys to make it harder to find them."

"Gees. I wouldn't want that job," Stan chuckled.

As they talked, Sarah came out and announced that dinner was ready. Stan and Rosa immediately followed her into the kitchen, where they smelled cheese enchiladas, rice, and beans. Stan smiled and grabbed a plate. Five minutes later, everyone was seated around the table, eating and talking about the day's exciting events.

"So, I heard from Polk a minute ago," Thompson said. "They think the man they arrested today is going to flip. His name is Pepe Díaz. He jumped on it when they told him we only had one more witness protection slot open."

"I hate to give thugs like that a free ride," Rogers said.

Thompson shrugged. "It's a necessary evil. We'd never get convictions without snitches."

The kitchen door opened, and the Marshal on inside duty stepped in. "We have reports of a convoy of vehicles heading this way. Everyone get your weapons and take your positions." Jodie jumped up and exclaimed. "You took my weapon!"

"Sorry," Thompson replied. "Witnesses go to the basement."

"What!" Jodie exclaimed. "I want to fight."

"No way! You're no good to us if you're dead. Rogers, take Jodie, Stan, and Rosa to the basement."

"What if they overrun you? We have no weapons."

Agent Thompson looked at Jodie and replied, "Fair point. Wait a minute," she said, rushing out of the room. A minute later, she returned and handed Jodie and Stan each a gun and some ammo."

Stan reluctantly took the weapon and ammo and watched Jodie quickly load hers, and then he loaded his. A moment later, someone yelled. "They are here!"

Rogers barked, "Come on!" Stan, Jodie, and Rosa followed Rogers to the basement door. He opened the door and descended a long stairway. At the bottom, Rogers said, "I'll lock the door. If they somehow make it down here, make them pay!"

Jodie nodded and replied. "Will do. Good luck up there."

Rogers smiled, turned, and ran back up the stairs. They heard him lock the door and looked around their surroundings, which included two sleeper sofas, cabinets, a table, a pool table, a refrigerator, a sink, and a bathroom. There was also a door with a sign indicating it led to the furnace.

"This must have been somebody's rec room," Stan observed.

"Pretty nice," Jodie noted as they suddenly heard gunfire above them. "Shit! It sounds like they are already inside."

Rosa's face turned pale as she scanned the ceiling worriedly. Stan grabbed her and led her to a sofa where they sat. "It's going to be okay," he said. "They are trained in combat."

"So are the Cartel thugs," Jodie noted as she inspected her weapon again.

An explosion rocked the house. Rosa squeezed Stan's hand hard and began to shake. "We're okay down here. They can't touch us," Stan assured her.

Rosa gave Stan a skeptical look as smoke began to pour into the room from cracks in the ceiling. Stan stood up and looked worriedly at Jodie. "I hope they stocked this place with gas masks!"

Jodie opened all the cabinets and rifled through them but found no gas masks or anything else useful. "We better get out of here, or we'll die of carbon monoxide poisoning," she said somberly.

Stan nodded and rushed up the stairs. He tried to open the door, but it was locked, and he quickly realized he wouldn't be able to open it even with a crowbar and a sledgehammer. He rushed back down the stairs and shook his head in frustration." Sorry, I guess they didn't anticipate the Cartel setting the place on fire."

33
The Massacre

Reggie

Reggie and Paula were very busy suddenly being saddled with Stan and Jodie's workload in addition to their own. Still, they felt pretty good with Amanda's criminal and wrongful death cases both out of the way. Their mood quickly changed, however, when Maria ushered them into the conference room and turned-on Channel 4.

This is Christine Sommers with breaking news! Earlier today, five federal agents and three witnesses were killed in an attack at a federal safe house near Wolf City, Texas. The federal officers were protecting three witnesses scheduled to testify in the trial of Carlos Herrera, the alleged kingpin in the Las Guías Criminal Cartel. Five of those who attacked the compound were also killed.

Upon arriving on the scene, Hunt County Sheriff's deputy, Hal Logan, began the press conference. "Hal. What did you see when you got there?"

"It was like a war zone. Bodies were lying everywhere. The main ranch house was on fire. There had obviously been an explosion. I think a small airplane crashed into the farmhouse. Its tail could be seen protruding from the roof."

"Were there any survivors?" Christine asked.

"I didn't see any. I don't know how anyone could have still been alive inside that house. It was completely engulfed in flames."

"Thank you, Deputy."

We have reached out to the U.S. Marshal's office and the FBI but have yet to receive any comments. The big question on everybody's mind is whether the trial of Carlos Herrera is still on since three key witnesses are apparently dead.

Reggie looked at Paula as tears began to well in his eyes. "No. This couldn't have happened. They were supposed to be safe."

Paula embraced Reggie, struggling to keep her own composure. "It's not confirmed. They may not be dead."

"You heard the deputy. He said no one inside could have survived!" Reggie wailed, tears streaming down his face.

"I know. I know," Paula cried out, squeezing Reggie tightly.

Maria said, "You think that bastard will get off now?"

Paula let Reggie go. "No. No way! He's gonna pay. They can't let him get away with this."

Reggie wiped the tears from his eyes and spat, "I'll kill the bastard myself if they let him get away with this."

"I'll contact the FBI and the prosecutor," Paula said. "You go tell your brothers and sister. They're going to be devastated."

Reggie returned to his office and called his family after he had regained his composure. They agreed to meet at Stan's house to monitor the situation and console one another. However, when Reggie drove down Stan's cul-de-sac, he was shocked to see the street filled with news vans and reporters. The congestion forced him to park up the street and walk to his dad's house. When he exited his car, nearby reporters advanced on him.

"Mr. Turner, do you know if your father is alive?" a reporter asked as he shoved a microphone in Reggie's face.

"All I know is what has been reported on the TV," he said as he walked briskly down the street.

"Mr. Turner, do you think the government will still prosecute Carlos Herrera?"

"They better," Reggie replied as the reporters pressed around him. "Let me through! I need to get to the house."

A police officer spotted Reggie and rushed over. "Alright. Let him through! They just murdered his father. Cut him some slack, for god sakes!"

The crowd backed off, and Reggie made it through the crowd to the front door. The door immediately opened, and he saw his sister, Marcia, whose eyes were red and swollen. She pulled him in and slammed the door.

"Reggie. Is Dad dead?"

Reggie shrugged. "I don't know. That's what they said on the news. Have you heard anything new?"

"They haven't found his body or any of the other witnesses. They say the intense fire may have completely consumed the bodies."

"Or they weren't killed and somehow escaped." Reggie replied.

"Maybe," Marcia said. "I don't know what to think."

As they talked, Reggie noticed his grandparents and some neighbors had arrived. Over the next few minutes, they came over one by one and gave him their condolences. After a while, Reggie became so distraught that he went upstairs to his old room to be alone. He closed the door, stared out the window at the crowd below, and wondered how he'd live without his father.

As he was grieving, his cell phone rang. "Reggie, this is Beverly Burns, Assistant U.S. Attorney."

"Yes," Reggie said. "I remember you. Any word on my father?"

"No. The firefighters haven't found a body, but the heat was so intense after the explosion it's likely they will never find them. They did find a man's wedding band, though. It could be your father's. If you saw it, would you recognize it?"

"Yes. It's very distinctive. I'd know if it was his immediately."

"Alright. When it's convenient, you can come in and take a look at it."

"I'll come now. Where do I go?"

"I'm at our McKinney office. I'll wait here for you."

Reggie went downstairs and told Marcia where he was going. She insisted she come with him, so they went out the back door, sneaked down the alley, and came through a neighbor's yard to get to Reggie's car. Reggie backed out of the cul-de-sac and took off toward McKinney.

Twenty minutes later, they pulled into the FBI parking lot and went inside. The dispatcher took their names and notified Burns that they were there. A moment later, Burns emerged and took them back to an interview room where a small box had been displayed. They all took a seat.

"Okay," Beverly said as she opened the box. "Take your time."

Marcia gasped when she saw the ring. Reggie stood up abruptly and turned away.

Beverly said, "I guess this is your father's ring."

Marcia nodded between sobs.

"I'm sorry for your loss," Beverly said solemnly. "Your father's sacrifice will not be in vain. We're going to take down the Las Guías Cartel. I promise!"

"Don't make promises you can't keep!" Reggie spat. "How can you possibly take down the Cartel when you've lost your most critical witnesses."

"I'm sorry this happened," Beverly replied sternly. "But five federal officers lost their lives trying to protect your father. They took every precaution."

"I know, but they failed miserably, didn't they?" Reggie spat and stormed out of the room.

34
U.S. vs. Carlos Herrera

Paula
Six months later

In the aftermath of the Wolfe City Ranch Massacre, as the press dubbed it, Paula and Reggie struggled to keep Turner & Waters from crumbling. Neither of them was fully functioning even six months after the loss of Stan and Jodie. Paula knew they needed to hire a new attorney to handle part of the load, but she didn't have the stomach to start the recruiting process.

It was day three of the Carlos Herrera trial, which Paula felt she had to attend in person if she was ever to get any closure from the tragic events of Y2K. It hadn't been the cataclysmic computer disaster she expected, but every bit as devastating to her life. While she sipped a cup of coffee at her breakfast table, she turned on the morning news.

This is Christine Sommers with breaking news! Day 3 of the Carlos Herrera murder, kidnapping, and racketeering trial resumes today after a jury was finally picked and seated yesterday. Opening statements begin at 10:00 a.m. today at the Federal Courthouse in Sherman, Texas.

Many legal experts are criticizing the government for proceeding with this RICO prosecution without their three-star witnesses who were murdered while in witness protection. They say the U.S. Attorney is being reckless in his attempt to bring justice for the three slain U.S. Marshals and two FBI Special Agents. The officers were murdered in an assault on the safe house last October. If the government can't meet its heavy burden of proof without these critical witnesses, Carlos Herrera may never pay for his crimes, and the Las Guías Cartel will get even stronger.

To date, the government has been unable to determine how the Cartel found the government safe house. Critics believe there must be a mole in one of the government agencies for this to have happened.

So, stay tuned for updates throughout the day as this sensational trial gets underway with opening statements and perhaps one or two key witnesses on the stand.

In other news, Republican George W. Bush appears to have narrowly lost the popular vote to Democrat Al Gore in Tuesday's presidential election but appears to have defeated Gore in the electoral college. Gore initially conceded to Bush but later retracted his concession. The matter is now in the hands of the Florida Supreme Court.

This is Christine Sommers, Channel 4 News. Now back to our studios.

Paula finished her breakfast and shut off the TV. She looked at her watch. It was 8:35 a.m. Knowing it was at least an hour to the Paul Brown Federal Courthouse in Sherman, she had to hurry if she was going to get a seat. Five minutes later, she was on Highway 75 going North.

It was a cold rainy day, and traffic was heavy. Near Anna, Texas, there had been a wreck, and traffic was at a crawl. She cursed herself for not getting up earlier. If she couldn't get a seat, she'd be pissed. Finally, at 9:40 a.m., she and her bodyguard arrived and found a parking spot down the street from the Courthouse.

The courtroom was packed when she stepped through the double doors. Scanning the room, she didn't see a single seat left vacant. Then a hand rose, and she recognized a face. It was Marcia, so she rushed over and sat next to her.

"I figured you'd be late, so I saved you a seat," Marcia said.

"Thank you, you are a lifesaver," Paula said. "I would have slit my wrists had I not got a seat."

"No problem. Let's just hope we don't leave disappointed."

Paula nodded as she scanned the room. She saw the prosecutor, Assistant U.S. Attorney Beverly Burns, was there along with her second chair, Assistant U.S. Attorney Lincoln Jenson. At the defense table were noted Austin defense counsels Marcus Mann and his partner, Shelly Peters.

The Judge had denied a request for the proceeding to be televised, so many reporters and sketch artists were situated in the front row.

"Looks like everyone is here and ready to go," Paula noted.

Before Marcia could respond, the rear door to the courtroom opened, and the tall, grey-haired Judge entered the courtroom. The bailiff rose and announced, "Please rise for the Honorable Willard P. Samuels, Chief Judge of the United States District Court for the Eastern District of Texas, Sherman Division."

Everyone got to their feet as the Judge took his place on the bench and shuffled through some papers. Then he looked up and forced a smile. "Alright. Let's get started with opening statements. Bailiff, bring in the Defendant."

The bailiff went out a side door and returned with Carlos Herrera dressed in tan slacks and a long sleeve, dark blue shirt. His long black hair had been trimmed, making him almost look respectable had it not been for the tattoo of a rattlesnake's head protruding onto his neck. There was a murmur of displeasure from the gallery.

When Carlos was seated, the Judge said, "Bailiff, bring in the jury."

The bailiff went back out, and a moment later, the jury filed back into the courtroom and took their seats. The Judge forced another smile and said, "Alright. Ms. Burns. You may make your opening statement.

Assistant U.S. Attorney Beverly Burns, smartly dressed in a black skirt, white silk blouse, and black flats, stood up and said, "May I approach the Jury, Your Honor?"

"You may," the Judge replied.

Burns smiled. "Ladies and Gentlemen of the Jury. Over the next few weeks, you will finally have the opportunity to stop years of violence, intimidation, murder, kidnapping, human trafficking, drug dealing, and money laundering by the Las Guías Cartel across Texas, New Mexico, Arizona, and Nevada.

"The Prosecution will bring credible witnesses who will testify that the Defendant, Carlos Herrera, who was thought by many to be the kingpin of the Las Guías Cartel, is actually second in command of this criminal organization. The identity of the actual leader of the Las Guías Cartel will be exposed later in the trial at the appropriate time.

There was a murmur in the gallery. Reporters jotted down this new revelation. The bailiff stood up and glared at the crowd.

"The evidence will show that the Defendant was in charge of the Cartel's day-to-day operations and ordered the murder of many people including U.S. Marshals and FBI special agents who were charged with the safekeeping of crucial witnesses in this trial.

"The evidence will further show that the Las Guías Cartel engaged in extensive human trafficking across the U.S. and Mexican border to staff its strip club and prostitution businesses and operated an extensive money laundering operation for the benefit of the Defendant and other Cartel leaders.

"The evidence I speak of will consist of live witness testimony, documents, and affidavits. Some of the testimony will be graphic and shocking, so brace yourself. But, by the end of the trial, the Prosecution will prove, beyond any reasonable doubt, that the Defendant is guilty of murder, kidnapping, and racketeering.

"Finally, the identity of some of the Prosecution witnesses will be shocking, so the Judge will now explain who they are and how it is they are here today ready to testify."

Burns turned and nodded to the Judge. "Your Honor."

There was a murmur in the courtroom as the Judge stiffened and cleared his throat. "Ladies and gentlemen of the jury. This is quite unusual, but it was necessary to protect the witnesses in this trial. It has been widely reported that three key prosecution witnesses were killed in the attack on the safe house. Fortunately, the press was mistaken, and these witnesses are alive, well, and ready to testify."

Everyone in the gallery stared at the Judge for a moment in stunned silence. Then chaos erupted; reporters rushed out of the room and cameras flashed as everyone tried to process the Judge's words.

Reggie's mouth fell open. "Does that mean ..."

"Dad's alive!" Marcia exclaimed as she embraced her brother.

Tears were pouring out of Paula's eyes as she nodded and added, "And Jodie too, apparently."

Marcia and Paula embraced and danced in each other's arms.

Tears of joy were flowing from all of their eyes. Several people looked at them and gave a thumbs up.

"I'll have order!" the Judge demanded as he pushed the button that simulated a pounding gavel.

The bailiff raised his hands and screamed at everyone to be seated. After a few minutes, the gallery was silenced, and the Judge continued.

"So, to be fair to the Defendant, he was advised shortly after the attack on the safe house that these witnesses were alive and that he would have the standard access to them to prepare for trial. To protect these witnesses from further attempts on their lives, I signed a gag order prohibiting anyone from advising the press or public of their status.

"Now, Mr. Mann. You may proceed with your opening statement," the Judge said.

Marcus Mann stood and replied, "Thank you, Your Honor. May I approach the jury?"

The Judge nodded and replied, "You may."

Mann was a handsome man, tall and muscular, with dark brown eyes, jet black hair, and a mustache. He smiled and began, "Ladies and gentlemen of the Jury. Don't let the Prosecution's theatrics fool you. Even with their key witnesses arising from the dead, they still cannot prove beyond all reasonable doubt that the Defendant murdered or kidnapped anyone or engaged in racketeering.

"We will show during the course of this trial that Defendant was simply a manager of businesses engaged in perfectly legal enterprises throughout Texas, New Mexico, Arizona, and Nevada. We will show that his employees all worked voluntarily, and that each business entity possessed all the required licenses and permits to engage in these many businesses, complied with all labor laws, and paid all legal taxes.

"You will soon come to see that much of the Prosecution's evidence is circumstantial, conjecture, innuendo, and outright lies. Don't let the Prosecution's brutal and baseless attack on Carlos Herrera blind you to the fact that they cannot and will not prove the elements of these charges beyond all reasonable doubt.

"We are confident if you hold the Prosecution to their burden of proof, you will find the Defendant not guilty of all these charges.

Thank You," Mann concluded.

Mann took his seat, and the Judge said, "Thank you. Ms. Burns, you may call your first witness.

"Thank you, Your Honor," Burns said. "The Prosecution calls Stan Turner."

There was excited chatter in the courtroom and then gasps as Stan Turner walked in and took a seat on the witness stand. Some spectators stood and clapped.

"Order," the Judge spat. "Take your seats."

Burns began, "Mr. Turner. It's so nice to see you alive and well."

Stan smiled and nodded. "Yes, it feels good to be alive."

There was laughter in the gallery.

"I bet," Burns agreed. "So, briefly tell us how it is you survived the attack on the Safe house."

"Objection!" Mann exclaimed. "Irrelevant and prejudicial. There is no proof that Defendant had anything to do with that."

"Overruled," the Judge said. "The question is only about the escape. The jury is entitled to have that information. Keep it brief, however."

"Thank you, Your Honor," Burns said. "You may answer the question."

Stan cleared his throat and then explained how he, Jodie, and Rosa had managed to escape the fiery inferno that had erupted overhead as they huddled in the smoke-filled basement of the farmhouse on Wolf City Ranch.

35
The Deception

Stan
Six months earlier

Stan felt helpless as the basement filled with smoke, making breathing harder and harder. Scanning the room, he hoped to find something that might save them and noticed the furnace room again and bolted for it.

Opening the door, he was excited to see shelves stacked with towels and rags. "Come here!" he shouted. "Grab some towels or rags, wet them in the sink, and let's fill all the gaps in the ceiling, doors, and windows."

Everyone rushed over, and they all started frantically working to stop the flow of toxic fumes into the basement.

"Put a wet rag over your nose to filter the fumes, too," Jodie screamed, and they all took her advice.

Ten minutes later, they had sealed the room as best they could and were huddled in a corner where the smoke was thinnest.

"If we could just get some fresh air in here," Stan said. "I think we would be okay."

The shooting upstairs had stopped, and Stan feared the Cartel had won the battle. Suddenly, there was pounding on the door, and Stan knew it wasn't from someone friendly.

"I hope that door holds," Jodie said.

Stan replied, "It will. It's steel reinforced. I couldn't get it to budge. Besides, reinforcements should be here soon. The Cartel can't hang around for long."

Rosa began to cough incessantly. "Shit, if we don't get some fresh air in here, it won't matter how strong that door is," Jodie noted.

Stan nodded his acknowledgment of her concern, got up, and crawled to the furnace room again. Upon seeing the towels, he had been distracted from inspecting the room thoroughly. He stood up and carefully scanned the room's perimeter but found nothing but concrete. He was about to leave the room when he noticed a rectangular outline behind the shelves where they'd gotten the towels. It looked like a panel of some sort.

Stan pulled the shelves out from the wall and saw there indeed was some sort of passageway that had been boarded over.

"Hey, guys! I found something." Stan yelled.

Jodie rushed in and helped Stan remove the wooden panel. A cool breeze began spilling into the room. "Fresh air! Thank God," Jodie exclaimed as she drew in a deep breath.

"This might even be a way out," Stan suggested. "It's pretty small, but it might be big enough."

"We don't know who is waiting outside," Jodie noted. "The Cartel could still be out there."

"Right," Stan agreed. "The fact that we haven't heard any friendly knocking at the door would indicate help has yet to arrive."

"Oh, I feel so much better," Rosa said. "I thought I was going to die."

Jodie walked out of the furnace room and smiled at Rosa. "Yeah. This is much better. Now it's just a matter of time before help shows up.

Suddenly there was a cracking sound, and the ceiling began to cave in. "Fuck! Jodie exclaimed. "The ceiling is collapsing!"

Stan looked up where the noise was coming from and frowned. "Damn it! We need to get out of here!"

A different noise from the furnace room made Stan spin around. He pointed his gun at the door, as did Jodie. "Don't shoot," a voice said. A minute later, Agent Thompson stepped out of the furnace room.

"Come on. We need to get out of here," Thompson said, motioning them to follow her.

"You got that right," Stan exclaimed, looking up at the sparks flying from the ceiling.

Jodie quickly followed Thompson with Rosa right behind her. Stan took one last look up and saw a beam come crashing down through the ceiling. He quickly caught up with the others. Special Agent Thompson and Rosa had already disappeared through the opening, and Jodie was just bending down to climb through.

"It will be close," Jodie said, "but I think you can fit through."

Stan hesitated, not so sure that he could fit through the hole, but finally bent down and tried it. Halfway through, he got stuck and couldn't move. Luckily, Jodie had waited for him and helped pull him through. 'When they exited the structure, it looked like a war zone with burning vehicles, the house ablaze, and bodies everywhere.

"This way!" Agent Thompson yelled from an outbuilding twenty yards away. "They're all inside."

Everyone rushed to the outbuilding, where Agent Thompson pointed to two four-wheelers. Agent Thompson jumped on the first one, and Rosa jumped in the passenger seat. Jodie took the second one, and Stan jumped in next to her; she sped away. Soon they were rapidly leaving the ranch in the dust.

When they were almost a mile away, Agent Thompson stopped and looked back. A wall of smoke was rising rapidly from the ranch house and the vehicles that had exploded. They looked for any sign of pursuers but saw none.

Stan said, "So, now what?"

"We need to find a phone," Agent Thompson replied. "I need to get you to our backup safe house."

Jodie said. "What happened? How did they find the safe house?"

Agent Thompson shook her head. "Someone at the Empire Club must have put a tracker on our vehicle. I meant to sweep it but got distracted."

"What about a mole?" Stan suggested. "The Cartel may have someone in the Marshal's office or at the FBI on their payroll."

"Anything is possible," Agent Thompson said, "but that's an investigation for another day. Right now, we need to get you to a new safe house."

"What makes you think the Cartel won't find the backup safe house?" Jodie asked.

Thompson smiled, "Because the backup safe house is on a military base with twelve thousand troops surrounding it."

Stan smiled appreciatively. "That should work."

An hour later, they were picked up by a Hunt County Sheriff's deputy and taken back to the Sheriff's office. On the way, Special Agent Thompson explained what had happened.

"One of the marshals walking the farm's perimeter saw a caravan of eight vehicles turn onto the gravel road that leads to the farm. He immediately called in the intrusion but then noticed a small aircraft approaching from the North.

"I was inside and went out immediately to help defend the house, but we were not prepared for an air assault. Soon, what looked like an old crop duster flew by. When it was directly overhead, it dropped a bundle on the roof that exploded upon impact and immediately engulfed the building.

"I rushed inside to tell everyone to vacate the building. When they all rushed out, they were sitting ducks for the Cartel members who had overwhelmed the three Marshals outside. Seeing no other option, I went to the master bedroom and managed to sneak out a window.

"I knew it wouldn't be too long until the fire had consumed the entire building, including the basement, so I opened the escape tunnel and crawled in. I don't know if any of the marshals or special agents survived," Agent Thompson concluded soberly.

A wave of despair washed over Stan. He closed his eyes, wondering if there was any chance in hell that they'd ever bring down the Cartel or were their days numbered. He felt like the situation was hopeless, and perhaps they should give up. Then a thought came to him?"

"Agent Thompson, the world probably thinks we are all dead, right?"

Agent Thompson nodded and replied, "Probably."

"So, as long as we are dead, we are safe, right?"

Agent Thompson nodded and smiled broadly.

36
Key Witness

Paula

Paula sat mesmerized by Stan's account of their rescue from the safe house. When he was done, the crowd buzzed with excitement. Reporters dashed in and out of the courtroom to keep their media outlets updated.

Burns continued her examination. "Mr. Turner, do you know Defendant Carlos Herrera?"

"Yes," Stan replied.

"Is Carlos Herrera in the courtroom here today?"

"Yes," Stan replied and pointed to the Defendant. "Yes, that's him."

"How did you two meet?"

"I had recently been retained by a client, Ruben Acosta, to do some estate planning. He didn't have anyone he trusted to be the executor and trustee of his estate, so he asked me to do it. Shortly after the documents were signed, he was murdered. His death left me as the executor of his estate and trustee over a trust he had created.

"Shortly after my appointment, the Defendant and others broke into my home, ambushed me, put a hood over my head, and informed me that Ruben had been working for his organization and that I should continue the arrangement in his place."

"I see," Burns said. "So, was he claiming the assets of the trust belonged to his organization?"

"That was the implication; however, legally, the assets belonged to Ruben and would transfer to the trust beneficiary at his death."

"Objection," Mann exclaimed. "The trust document will speak for itself."

"Sustained," the Judge ruled.

Burns looked at the Judge, nodded, and continued. "So, did this man identify himself?"

"He said I could call him Carlos."

"Okay, but you never actually saw him since you had a hood over your head."

"That's correct."

"So, what happened next?"

"He threatened to kill me, members of our law firm, and my children if I didn't continue Ruben's work."

There were gasps from the gallery.

"Did you agree to do that?"

"Yes, I didn't want anyone to die, so I agreed."

"So, did Carlos and his men leave at that point?"

"Yes, but not before knocking me out with a blunt instrument. It took thirteen stitches from the nurse at the hospital to close the wound."

"After this first encounter with Carlos, did you two ever meet again?"

"Objection. Mr. Turner admits he never saw this man, so we don't know if it was the Defendant."

"Sustained," the Judge ruled.

"I'll rephrase. Mr. Turner, did you later meet Defendant Carlos Herrera?"

"Yes. Carlos and two of his men broke into my room at the Luxor Hotel and Casino in Las Vegas. They were waiting for Rosa and me."

"Who is Rosa?" Burns asked.

"She was a companion that Carlos provided for me."

There was a murmur in the crowd. The Judge glared at the gallery, and the noise stopped.

Burns continued. "Okay, we will talk more about Rosa later. So, the Defendant and two of his men were in your room without your consent when you opened the door?"

"Yes," Stan replied.

"So, how did you know it was the Defendant?"

"He introduced himself, and, of course, Rosa knew him. She had been sent to me at his request."

"I see," Burns said, looking over at the jury and raising her eyebrows. "So, did the Defendant say anything to you?"

"Yes, he said he didn't like the stunt I had pulled the night before. I was trying to talk to Rosa privately, and I figured the room we were in was bugged, so I spilled a bottle of champagne on the mattress and requested a new room."

There was laughter in the gallery. The Bailiff stood up and glared at the offending parties. The Judge said. "I'll have order. The Bailiff will remove anyone who refuses to keep their emotions to themselves."

"Go on, Ms. Burnes," the Judge said.

"Yes, Your Honor," Burnes replied. "Mr. Turner, what was the purpose of assigning you Rosa as an escort?"

"Objection," Mann protested. "Calls for speculation."

"Sustained," the Judge ruled.

Burns continued questioning Stan about Rosa and their relationship as it developed over time. Stan explained how he had helped her get off drugs and put her to work, helping him manage the trust businesses. He admitted they lived together and had bonded but denied any sexual involvement with her. Evans then asked him to explain how he laundered money for Carlos.

"The Trust owned single-family residences, office buildings, office equipment, computers, medical equipment, and other assets. The leases called for much higher rent than was commercially reasonable, so the lessees were given a substantial discount. The difference was paid in cash by a third party, so it looked like the lessee had made the full payment."

"I see," so how else was money laundered?"

"The trust had a business called MedNet which managed medical practices for doctors and dentists. MedNet handled everything, including claims, which were a huge problem for them. Typically, many claims were never paid, but MedNet paid every claim in full, in cash provided by the Cartel."

"Objection," Mann spat. "There has been no evidence of where this alleged cash came from."

"Sustained," the Judge said.

Evans thought a moment and continued, "So a third party provided the cash, but you don't know where the cash came from?"

"No. I was told it was delivered by Federal Express from a company called Global Insurance Equities."

"Objection, hearsay," Mann said.

"Sustained," the Judge ruled.

Burns continued questioning Stan about all the methods used to launder money and was able to introduce substantial tangible evidence of many transactions. She was having difficulty, however, linking the Cartel to the trust.

"Alright, who was the trust beneficiary?" Burns asked.

Stan shifted in his chair. "Ruben Acosta's wife and children were the primary beneficiaries, but if he had no wife or children, the New Hope Legal Clinics, Inc. was the sole beneficiary."

"Did Mr. Acosta have a wife and children?" Burns asked.

"He told me he didn't," Stan said.

"Objection," Mann argued. "Hearsay."

"Overruled," the Judge said. "He can tell us what the decedent told him."

"So," Burns continued, "to your knowledge, the decedent never had a wife or children."

"To my knowledge, he did not," Stan agreed.

"Okay, so the New Hope Legal Clinics is the sole beneficiary of the property owned by the trust?"

"Yes, it would seem so."

"Have you talked to anyone at the New Hope Legal Clinics or NHLC about the trust?"

"Yes," Stan replied, "right after Ruben's murder, I met with the managing attorney at the clinic, Christos Mejia. He told me Ruben Acosta had been financing the clinic and that they depended on his support."

"Did you ever inform him that the NHLC was the beneficiary of Mr. Acosta's trust?"

"Yes, later on, I met with him again and explained it might be a while before I could wrap up the estate administration and trust and make a final distribution to him."

"What was his response?" Burns asked.

"He was very amenable and told me to take my time; there was no hurry as long as I kept making monthly contributions to the clinic so it could pay its bills."

Burns next shifted to the topic of Rosa's kidnapping. After having Stan explain what happened, she asked. "So, what makes you think Carlos Herrera was involved in the kidnapping?"

"He had threatened in a telephone call to pick her up if I didn't meet certain performance requirements."

"And you took picking her up to be kidnapping?"

"Yes, because he knew Rosa was clean, happy working with me, and didn't want to go back to being an escort or dancer under his ruthless thumb."

"Okay, so what kind of performance requirements are you talking about?" Burns asked.

"I didn't know how the insurance claims worked, and Carlos wouldn't tell me, so I had to figure it out myself. Consequently, claims were well below expectations."

"Right, you explained earlier how that worked."

Stan nodded. "Yes, so I was late on a report, and claims were way down, so that pissed him off and set the kidnapping in motion."

Burns went on for the rest of the day to ask Stan more about Rosa's kidnapping and many other topics before wrapping up and passing the witness. The Judge looked at the clock and said, "Alright, Mr. Mann, you can begin the cross-examination of the witness tomorrow morning at 10:00 a.m. We are in recess until then."

"All rise," the Bailiff yelled as the Judge got up and left the courtroom.

Paula stood up and stretched. Marcia sighed and asked, "So, how do you think it's going?"

Paula shrugged. "It's a very complicated case, and the prosecution's burden is tough, but so far, so good. She has a long way to go, but I think she'll get there with a little luck."

"I hope so. I just want this all to be over," Marcia groaned.

"Well, at least your dad is alive," Paula noted.

Marcia smiled. "Yes, that's true." Then her smile faded. "But, if we never see Dad again after this trial is over, it will seem as if he is dead."

Paula shook her head as that harsh reality set in.

37
Cross Exam

Reggie

With half the staff in witness protection, Reggie and Paula both couldn't attend the Carlos Herrera trial, but Reggie wasn't complaining since he had heard on the news the previous day that his father was alive. He was so happy, relieved, and excited that he broke out one of his dad's bottles of champagne for him and Maria to enjoy.

Today was his day to attend the trial, so Paula was back at the office holding down the fort. He and his bodyguard had gotten there early and had met Marcia for breakfast. She filled him in on the previous day's proceedings and talked excitedly about their father and Jodie's unexpected resurrection.

At 10:00 a.m., the bailiff stood and barked, "All rise for the Honorable Willard P. Samuels, Chief Judge for the United States District Court for the Eastern District of Texas."

The Judge entered the courtroom and told the bailiff to bring in the jury and the witness. When they were all seated, the Judge said, "Mr. Mann, you may proceed."

Mann stood up and took the podium. "Mr. Turner, you testified that Ruben Acosta came to you for estate planning, which resulted in the elaborate estate plan you allege is a money laundering operation."

Stan frowned. "I never characterized it as a money laundering operation. I thought it was a defensive estate plan for someone in a high-risk profession or business who expected frivolous attacks."

"Did you know Ruben Acosta before you set up this plan?"

"No," Stan replied. "When he came in, it was the first time I had met him."

"Why did he come to you?" Mann asked.

"He said someone referred him to me, but I wasn't ever able to figure out who it was."

"Are you sure?"

Stan hesitated, then said, "Yes. I don't know who referred him to me or if he just found me in the phone book."

"Don't you screen your clients?"

Stan shook his head, "No. I give the client a free 30-minute consultation, and if I think I can help them, a retainer agreement is signed, and the only checking I do is for conflicts of interest."

"Aren't you the expert in what you called defensive estate planning?"

"I'm not board certified in any area of the law. I do a lot of estate planning, but I do many other things too."

"You testified that Mr. Acosta didn't have anybody to be executor and trustee, so you volunteered for the job?"

"No. I didn't volunteer. I reluctantly agreed to accept the appointments since Mr. Acosta didn't have any family and didn't trust banks."

"Now, Mr. Acosta paid you to set up this elaborate defensive estate plan? Right?"

"Yes," Stan agreed. "He paid $7,500.00 plus costs."

"And now, as trustee, you get paid as well, right?"

"Of course, the trust pays me for my time."

"And how much do you get paid for your time?"

Stan thought a moment. "$300 per hour."

"Since Mr. Acosta's death, how many hours a day have you been working?"

"Pretty much full-time, unfortunately. There was plenty of work to do."

"So, if you worked ten hours a day, you would get $3,000 per day or $90,000 per month?"

Stan shook his head. "No, I billed a maximum of eight hours per day, five days a week, and half my regular rate for travel."

"Oh, okay. So, how much did you bill the trust last month?"

Stan thought a moment. "I think the bill was for about $52,000."

"Oh, okay, just $52,000 last month," Mann chuckled. "So, you've done alright as trustee, haven't you?"

"The money goes to the firm, not me. I just get my regular paycheck. And it doesn't seem like that much when bullets are flying overhead, and bombs are exploding," Stan spat.

"Oh. I'm glad you reminded me of that," Mann interjected. "You were there when Ruben Acosta was murdered, weren't you?"

"Yes, I almost got killed myself," Stan retorted.

"So, how do we know you didn't kill Ruben Acosta? You had motive and opportunity."

"What!" Stan exclaimed. "Are you nuts?"

"Objection!" Burns exclaimed.

Mann pointed his finger at Stan and said, "You were with Acosta when he was killed. How do we know you didn't kill him and then make it look like the burglars did it?"

"Objection!" Burns spat. "The witness is not on trial here."

"Well, he should be!" Mann shouted.

"Sustained. Mr. Mann, you know better than that!" the Judge admonished. "The jury will disregard counsel's statements."

The attack on his father upset Reggie. He knew Mann would be aggressive and challenging but didn't expect him to accuse his father of murder. Reggie looked over at the jury and saw shock, confusion, and suspicion on their faces. He looked over at Marcia, who sat stone-faced.

Mann spent the rest of the morning cross-examining Stan and when he was done, the judge recessed for lunch. After lunch, Burns took Stan on redirect, and when she was done, it was clear Stan had nothing to do with Ruben Acosta's murder; still, the jury seemed confused, which was a bad sign for the Prosecution. Burns next called Jodie to the stand, and the clerk swore her in. Burns had Jodie explain how she fit into the picture and went through her memory of Ruben Acosta's murder. Then the issue of Rosa's kidnapping came up.

"Ms. Marshall, how did you come to meet Rosa Méndez?"

"Stan called me and told me, Carlos, the Defendant, had hooked Stan up with her. Stan said he knew she was a spy for Carlos, but once he got to know her, he wanted to protect her from further abuse, so he decided to pretend to accept her as his girlfriend."

"So, when did you physically meet Rosa?" Burns asked.

"A few days later, when Stan returned from Las Vegas. He brought her by the office and introduced her to us as his girlfriend."

"But you knew that wasn't true at that point, correct?"

"Yes, but we went along with it because we didn't know Rosa's state of mind. Stan had told me she was reporting to Carlos each day, so we had to assume everything we said would get back to Carlos."

"When did you first hear Rosa had been kidnapped?"

"Stan had told me that Carlos was threatening to take Rosa away from him as punishment for the poor performance of his money laundering duties, so it didn't surprise me when I got the call that Rosa was missing.

"Stan had tried to reach Special Agent Lot, his handler for his undercover work, but he couldn't make contact with him. So, Stan asked me to help him look for her."

Burns took Jodie through the events at the Empire Club, and the residence just blocks away. Then she asked the Judge to bring in an inmate the U.S. Marshals had in custody. The bailiff went out and returned with a man dressed in an orange jumpsuit.

"Ms. Marshall, the bailiff has brought in a man who is now standing before you. Do you recognize this man?"

Jodie nodded and said, "Yes, this is one of the men who took Rosa Méndez from a van and locked her in a shed behind the Empire Club residence. The residence is where the waitresses, dancers, and escorts reside when they are not working."

"For the record," Burns stated, "the witness has identified Gabino Escalona as a participant in Rosa Méndez's abduction."

Burns continued questioning Jodie for some time but finally passed the witness late in the afternoon. The Judge looked at his watch and said, "Okay. Mr. Mann, it's getting late, but you can at least get started on your cross-examination.

Mann nodded, jumped to his feet, and strolled to the podium. "Ms. Marshall, you've never met the Defendant, have you?"

"No," Jodie agreed.

"So, you have no personal knowledge of his business or who he works for, isn't that correct?"

"Right, no personal knowledge."

Mann smiled wryly. "Before the night of the alleged abduction, you had never met Gabino Escalona, had you?"

"No," Jodie said.

"So, again. You have no personal knowledge of any relationship between Defendant Carlos Madera and Mr. Escalona, correct?"

"That's true," Jodie conceded.

"You were present when Ruben Acosta was murdered, were you not?"

"I was," Jodie replied.

"You engaged in a gun battle with the robbers who invaded Mr. Acosta's home. Isn't that, right?"

"They weren't thieves; they were assassins," Jodie replied.

"Objection! Speculation," Mann said. "That hasn't been established."

"Nor that they stole anything," Jodie shot back.

"Sustained," the Judge said. "Move on!"

"Did you get a good look at any of the intruders at Ruben's house where the gun battle took place?"

"No. I was too busy ducking for cover."

"You did manage to wing one of them? Right?" Mann pressed.

"So, I'm told."

"But again, you have no personal knowledge as to whether Acosta's murder had anything to do with Rosa's kidnapping, the Empire Club, or the residence it owned a few blocks away?"

"That's correct," Jodie conceded.

"So, to summarize, you know nothing to tie the Defendant to the kidnapping, the alleged murder of Ruben Acosta, or the Las Guías Cartel?"

Jodie shrugged. "I stand by my testimony. I'll let the jury draw its conclusions."

"Sure, Ms. Marshall," Mann snickered. "I think they got the picture. Pass the witness."

The Judge looked at the clock again and said, "Okay, we'll recess until tomorrow at 10:00 a.m., at which time the Prosecution will call its next witness.

Reggie and Marcia stood up and stretched as the courtroom emptied. A U.S. Marshal came, got the defendant, and escorted him out of the room. Mann and his assistant left the courtroom. Jodie walked over to Burns, and Reggie and Marcia joined her.

"So, how do you think it's going?" Jodie asked.

"Well, we are slowly connecting the dots, but the proof is a little thin. Carlos has been clever in not talking specifically about his role in the Cartel. He manages the clubs and the girls, but that's about it. All he told Stan was to keep doing his job as trustee. Unfortunately, the estate and trust Stan set up are not directly tied to the Cartel."

"So, how do you prove that he runs the Cartel?" Reggie asked.

"We have several more witnesses that will help with that. I'm not at liberty to disclose them."

"Sure," Jodie said. "Anyway. I hope my testimony helped."

"It did," Burns said. "It was nice to meet you, Reggie."

"Likewise," Reggie said, and they all left.

When they were out of earshot of Burns, Jodie said, "I'm worried. I thought this Prosecution would be a slam dunk, but now I realize Carlos may walk, and if that happens, Stan and I may have to stay in witness protection indefinitely."

Reggie's face paled. No. No way. We can't let that happen."

"Well, I hope your father has a rabbit he can pull out of his hat. If not, Turner & Waters is going to be short two attorneys!" Jodie warned.

Marcia looked worriedly at Jodie and then at Reggie as they silently walked to the elevator.

38
The Connection

Stan

After Jodie's testimony, Burns asked Agent Thompson to come to visit her along with Stan Turner. It was almost seven o'clock before they arrived since traffic between Dallas and Ft. Worth during rush hour was always heavy.

Burns thanked them for coming and told them to take a seat. She offered them coffee which they both declined.

"So, how's the trial coming?" Stan asked.

"Well, that's why I asked you two to come in."

"We all assume that Carlos Herrera is tied into the Las Guías Cartel, but that's not good enough. We must prove it. Stan has testified he was laundering money for somebody, but he doesn't know who it was. It seems the ultimate beneficiary of the money laundering is a non-profit corporation helping illegal aliens get work permits to stay in the United States. That's not going to sit well with the jury.

"Unless you can show the non-profit corporation is just a front for the Cartel, like the Chinese law firm in Manhattan," Stan interjected.

"Right. We need some direct evidence that Carlos is tied in with NHLC or benefiting from the money laundering, and I need you two to find it pronto."

Agent Thompson thought a moment and then replied. "So, you think this so-called, non-profit is part of the Cartel?"

Stan nodded. "That wouldn't surprise me. The Cartel killed Carlos's parents, so the only reason he would be doing money laundering for them would be to be in a position to get revenge."

"How would he expect to get revenge?" Burns asked.

Stan stroked his forehead a moment and then looked up. "Well, he could kill the boss who ordered his parent's death or expose the Cartel and enjoy watching the government take them down. Kind of like what is happening right now."

Burns raised her eyebrows. "Do we know how the Cartel discovered his plans?" Burns asked.

Stan shook his head. "I have thought a lot about that, and only one thing makes sense."

"What's that?" Burns asked.

Stan smiled and replied, "It's only speculation right now. Give Agent Thompson and me a day or two, and we may be able to figure it out. We'll need to take a road trip."

"Okay, I have enough witnesses to get me through Monday, so you better have something by then. I don't know if Mann will put on a defense or just argue we haven't proven our case. So, time is of the essence."

Stan stood up. "Okay, we need to get to the airport,"

Agent Thompson frowned and asked, "Where are we going?"

"Phoenix, for starters," Stan replied. "If we don't get what we need there, we may need to go to Las Vegas."

Burns smiled and walked them out, "Good luck. Don't let me down."

Stan and Agent Thompson split up and agreed to meet at DFW Airport at 6:00 p.m. for a 7:00 p.m. flight to Phoenix. Stan went back to the safe house and packed a suitcase. After calling Reggie to tell him he was going out of town, he drove to the airport. Agent Thompson was waiting for him at the gate when he arrived. Their flight was uneventful, and they arrived in Phoenix at 9:00 p.m. local time. They both rented cars so they would have maximum flexibility. By 9:45, they had checked into a LaQuinta hotel for the night.

The next morning, they met for breakfast and discussed strategy. Stan said, "When I was here last, I tried to visit some of the tenants of the rental properties but didn't have much success. You, however, have a badge, so I think you will have better luck."

Stan then gave Agent Thompson the rent roll for twenty-seven properties located in the Phoenix area. "You should interview as many of these people as you can today, and we'll meet back here at 7:00 p.m. for dinner."

Agent Thompson frowned. "What are *you* going to do?"

"I'm going to visit the managers and see if I can get one of them to flip on the Cartel. Can I promise them witness protection?"

"Yes, if they can tie Carlos to the Las Guías Cartel or implicate the NHLC to the money laundering."

Stan nodded. "Good. Then we best get moving. We don't have much time."

Stan took one last sip of his coffee and motioned to the waitress that they wanted their bill. She came over, and Stan gave her his credit card. A minute later, she was back with his receipt. They stood up, wished each other luck, and were on their way.

Stan's first stop was Sun Lakes, where his Arizona property managers had their offices. He had called ahead to make sure they would be around to meet him, but the storefront was dark, and the door locked. Stan knocked on the door in frustration, but there was no answer. He was about to leave when a big Cadillac pulled up. A disheveled Margie Rojas stepped out smelling of booze.

Stan smiled and stepped back. She walked over and unlocked the door. "Sorry about that. I wasn't expecting your call."

Stan smiled. "Thanks for meeting me."

They walked into the office, and Margie turned on the lights. Stan watched her as she went to a cabinet, opened it up to a minibar, and poured her a drink.

"Want one?" Margie asked.

"No thanks, it's a little early for me."

Margie took a swallow and asked, "So, what's up? I thought you were dead."

Stan laughed. "Yeah, that was a ruse for the Carlos Herrera trial. Where's your husband?"

"Oh, he's in Mexico visiting family."

"Really? I didn't know you had family there?"

Margie bit her lip. "He does. My family is in Minneapolis."

"Hmm. So, when will your husband be back?"

"He didn't say," Margie replied and looked away.

"So, why didn't you go with him?"

Margie shrugged. "I don't like Raul's family much."

"Okay. Let me get to the point. I guess you've been following the Herrera trial in Dallas?"

She nodded. "It's been on the news."

"Well, we need your help. I've figured out how you've been laundering money for the Cartel."

Margie swallowed hard. "Have you? How's that?"

Stan sighed. "Don't play dumb. The prosecutor can subpoena you, and you can talk or plead the fifth, your choice. Still, a smarter thing to do would voluntarily appear, tell the truth and go into witness protection."

Margie took a deep breath, then walked over to the minibar and poured another drink. She gulped it down and then looked back at Stan.

"That's all I'd have to do?"

Stan nodded. "Testify, and there will be no charges against you, no jail time or probation, and you get a free reboot of your life."

"Is this one of those offers I can't refuse?" Margie chuckled.

Stan shrugged. "No, you can refuse if you are prepared to suffer the consequences."

"Alright, I'm in. What now?"

"You'll have to come back to Dallas with me, and we'll need to bring some evidence with us."

Margie went to the liquor cabinet and poured herself another drink. "Sure, my files are your files," she chuckled.

Stan and Margie spent over an hour reviewing their records and filling up a big briefcase. While Margie was busy going through papers, Stan made a phone call to Beverly Burn's office. Forty-five minutes later, two FBI special agents showed up and took Margie into protective custody.

Stan thanked them and drove to his next destination. He was there all afternoon, confirmed his theory to be correct, and returned to the

LaQuinta. He was in a good mood when he met Special Agent Thompson for dinner.

The following day they flew back to Dallas, met briefly with Beverly Burns, and then Stan went back to the safe house, praying what he had done would be enough to put a nail in Carlos Herrera's coffin.

39
The Bodyguard

Reggie

It was Reggie's day to attend court on Friday. In the morning, Burns called Detective Besch to describe the crime scene after Ruben's murder. Besch was followed by a doctor from the coroner's office who had done an autopsy on Ruben Acosta. Then she called FBI Special Agent Kurt Ventura, who described the scene of the kidnapping.

In the afternoon, Burns called Pepe Díaz, and he took the witness stand. He was a short, muscular man in his mid-twenties with a mustache. He wore jeans, a red, long-sleeved shirt, and black boots.

"Please state your name," Burns asked.

"Pepe Diaz," the witness replied.

"Mr. Diaz. Do you know the defendant, Carlos Herrera?"

Diaz nodded and replied, "Si."

"Is that a yes?"

"Yes, I know him."

"Who is he to you?"

"The boss man," Diaz replied. "I'm one of his bodyguards."

"You say he is the boss man. So, the boss man of what organization?" Burns pressed.

"The Cartel."

"Which Cartel?"

"Ah. The Las Guías Cartel, I think it is called."

"Objection!" Mann exclaimed. "Lacks foundation, speculation."

"Overruled. He is stating his understanding. You can challenge him on cross," the Judge ruled.

"So, how long have you been one of Defendant's bodyguards?"

"About six months, I think."

"What were your duties for Defendant as a bodyguard?" Burns asked.

"I drove him wherever he wanted to go and stayed by his side in case there was trouble."

"While you were with him, did he go to Las Vegas earlier this year?"

Diaz nodded. "Si."

"Did you have occasion to accompany Defendant to a room in the Luxor Hotel rented to Stan Turner?"

"Yes, Carlos wanted to surprise Stan Turner and his girlfriend Rosa, so I paid the maid a hundred dollars to let us in his room."

"Was that girlfriend Rosa Méndez?"

"Si."

"Did you know her before that day?"

"Yes, she was an escort at the Empire Club in Phoenix. I had seen her around when Carlos went to that club."

"Did you know Stan Turner prior to the confrontation you testified about in Las Vegas?"

"No.

"Did you ever take your boss to Dallas to confront Stan Turner?"

"No."

"Does the Las Guías Cartel own the Empire Club in Phoenix?"

"I think it owns all the Empire Clubs in Phoenix, Albuquerque, Dallas, and Las Vegas."

"Objection! Lacks foundation. Speculation."

"Overruled," the Judge replied.

"Was Carlos the boss at all those clubs?"

"I don't know that, but the managers of each of those clubs always did what he asked them to do. No one dared challenge, Carlos."

"So, was this meeting between Carlos and Stan Turner friendly?"

"No. Carlos was pissed off. I'm not sure why, but they were okay when the meeting was over."

"Now, you were arrested at the Empire Club in Dallas, is that correct?"

"Si."

"How did you end up there?" Burns asked.

"Carlos told me to help take some girls from Phoenix to Dallas. They move the girls around a lot. While I was in Dallas, they needed a bouncer because the regular one was sick. So, the manager told me to stay that night and return to Phoenix the next day.

Burns continued questioning Diaz about his background, other jobs he'd held with the Cartel, and what he knew of their operations. Then Mann took Diaz on cross-examination.

"Mr. Diaz. Do you have any proof that you work for the Las Guías Cartel? Does the Cartel give you a paycheck every Friday, or do you have a badge or something?"

"No. I get paid in cash," Diaz replied meekly.

"So, when you were hired, did Carlos or someone else say, come work for the Las Guías Cartel?"

"No."

"So, when you say you work for the Las Guías Cartel, that's just your opinion, right?"

Diaz nodded. "Si. That's what I thought."

"The truth is, you don't know anything about the Las Guías Cartel, do you?"

Diaz shrugged. "It's just what I thought. I don't know for sure."

"Did Carlos ever tell you he worked for the Las Guías Cartel?"

"No, sir."

"Were you paid weekly?

"Si."

"Who actually handed you the cash?"

"Carlos."

"So, you worked for Carlos, right? That's really all you know for sure, isn't it?"

Mann nodded. "Si."

"You mentioned Stan Turner? How do you know him?"

"He got me arrested at the Empire Club. He remembered me from Las Vegas."

"Did you make a deal with the government in exchange for testifying today?" Mann asked.

"A deal?"

"Yes, did the government promise you anything if you testified here today against Carlos?"

"Si. They said they would protect me from the Cartel and give me a new life."

"What about prosecuting you? Did they agree not to bring charges against you?"

Carlos nodded and replied, "That is true."

"So, you want Carlos to be found guilty by the Court, isn't that, right?"

"No, it doesn't matter. I get witness protection; either way, my attorney assured me of that."

Mann chuckled, continued his cross for some time, and then Burns took the witness on redirect. When she was done, the Judge called a twenty-minute recess, so Reggie and Marcia went downstairs to the cafeteria to get a snack.

"So, what do you think?" Marcia asked.

Reggie thought a moment. "Well, Diaz definitely thought there was a connection between Carlos and the Cartel, and that the Cartel owned the clubs. It helps, but it isn't conclusive."

"She hasn't proven the Cartel's existence or that Carlos is its boss, has she?"

Reggie shook his head. "Not really. I hope she's got some better witnesses coming up."

When the Court resumed Burns came through when she called her next witness, Gabino Escalona, one of Rosa's abductors. Not only did the thirty-four-year-old truck driver turned bodyguard know he worked for the Las Guías Cartel, he claimed Carlos worked for it as well.

"So, prior to being assigned to Carlos Herrera what did you do for the Cartel?" Burns asked.

"I drove a truck across the border from Nogales to Tucson." Escalona replied.

"How often did you do that?"

"Back and forth, Monday through Friday?"

"What about the weekends?"

Escalona shook his head. "No, never on the weekends."

"Why not? "Burns asked.

"It wasn't safe. Manuel didn't work weekends."

"So, the Cartel paid Manuel to make sure the Cartel trucks were not properly inspected."

Escalona nodded, "Si."

"What's Manuel's last name?"

"I don't know. I never met him."

"What kinds of cargo did you take across the border?" Burns asked.

"Coke, marijuana, and immigrants mostly. cash, sometimes."

"Okay, how was your cargo concealed?'

"There was a false back to the trailer," Escalona explained. "It was about 6' by 8'. Drugs were put in spare tires, too, or carried by immigrants being smuggled across the border."

"And all this property belonged to the Las Guías Cartel?"

"Si. That's what I think."

When Burns was finished, Mann took him on cross examination. He made Escalona explain the non-prosecution and witness protection deals he had struck with the government, but Mann wasn't able to damage his testimony in any other way. Reggie felt much better when the Judge recessed the case for the day.

40
Witness Protection

Paula

Paula was anxious to get to the Carlos Herrera trial on Monday as Stan had told her Burns would be calling some surprise witnesses. After taking a shower, she joined Bart for breakfast. The news was on as she sat down.

This is Christine Sommers with the Morning Report. Day 7 of the Carlos Herrera murder, kidnapping, and racketeering trial resumes at 10:00 a.m. today at the Federal Courthouse in Sherman, Texas.

Assistant U.S. Attorney Beverly Burns will continue her presentation of the government's case with the kidnapping victim, Rosa Méndez, who is expected to describe the murder of her brother, abduction by the Las Guías Cartel, and forced labor as a dancer and escort.

On Friday, Pepe Diaz testified he acted as a driver and bodyguard for Carlos Herrera and believed Herrera was the boss of the Las Guías Cartel. However, upon cross-examination, he admitted he was only speculating and had no proof of Herrera's involvement in the criminal organization.

Following Diaz, Burns called Gabino Escalona, who knew exactly for whom he worked, testifying he worked for the Las Guías Cartel as a truck driver transporting cash and drugs as well as immigrants from Nogales to Tucson, Arizona as well as later becoming a bodyguard for Carlos Herrera.

In other news, nine remain missing after a U.S. sub hits a Japanese fishing boat off the Hawaiian coast..."

Paula looked at Bart and said, "I may lose my law partner over this murder trial if Stan has to go into witness protection."

Bart raised his eyebrows. "You could. What would you do if that happened?"

"I don't know. It seems so surreal. He was dead, and then he's alive, but now he may have to disappear. I don't know how much more of this I can take."

"You know Stan, he always manages to get in over his head but somehow survives."

"Yeah, but this time he might get us all killed. The attack on the safe house was brutal. I mean, who bombs a federal safe house? That's insane! Millions of dollars are at stake, and these people will do anything to protect it. I'm not sure the FBI and Marshals will be able to protect us."

Bart nodded. "You may be right. Stay close to your bodyguard today."

"I always do, but my bodyguard can't take his gun into the courthouse."

"The courthouse is probably the safest place to be," Bart said. "It's coming and going from the courthouse that is dangerous."

Paula looked at her watch and said, "I've got to go. See you tonight. They kissed goodbye and then Paula left. Her bodyguard was waiting outside. A few minutes later, they were back on Central Expressway heading North. The commute to Sherman was getting old, and Paula just wanted her life to return to normal.

When she arrived, the courthouse was buzzing with activity. Reporters and cameramen were milling around, waiting to ambush attorneys and witnesses as they entered the building. As Paula approached, her bodyguard tried to clear a path for her, but she was surrounded by several reporters anyway.

"Ms. Waters, how do you think the trial is going?"

Paula smiled and replied, "Very well. Beverly Burns is doing a great job,"

Paula didn't stop as her bodyguard pushed through the crowd of reporters and led her to the elevators. Marcia was waiting there for her, so they all entered it together and pushed the button for their floor.

"Is Dad going to testify again?" Marcia asked. "I heard he might be called again."

"I don't know. Where did you hear it?"

"Burns came by a minute ago and talked to her assistant about it."

"Hmm. That should be interesting," Paula replied.

When they made it to the courtroom, they rushed in to get the last two seats. Paula's bodyguard told her he'd wait outside and to get him before she left. Burns and Mann were there and appeared ready to go. The Bailiff stood up and yelled, "All rise!"

The Judge entered the courtroom, took his place on the bench, and told the Bailiff to bring in the Defendant and the jury. When they were all seated, he said, "Ms. Burns, call your next witness."

"Yes, Your Honor. The prosecution calls Rosa Méndez."

Rosa entered the courtroom wearing a conservative blue skirt, white blouse, and blue flats. Wearing glasses, she looked more like a college professor than an escort. The jury eyed her closely as she took her seat at the witness stand.

Burns smiled as she approached the lectern. "Ms. Méndez, where do you currently reside?"

"At the old Carswell Air Force Base in Ft. Worth."

"Are you under the protection of the U.S. Marshals?"

"Yes."

"So, where were you before Carswell?"

"At a safe house in Hunt County, the Wolfe City Ranch, I think they called it."

"And why aren't you still there?"

"Because the safe house was attacked and burned to the ground. We barely escaped with our lives."

"Do you know who was responsible for the attack?" Burns asked.

"No. I was in the basement and was almost suffocated. Luckily, an FBI agent rescued us."

"So, where did you work before being taken into witness protection?"

Rosa gave Carlos a stern look, then said, "I worked for the Empire Clubs International?"

"And who was your boss?"

"Each club had a manager, but Carlos Herrera was everyone's boss. He told the manager what to do," Rosa replied.

"So, just before you were taken into witness protection, where were you working?"

"With Stan Turner, the trustee of Ruben Acosta's estate and New Horizon Trust."

"How did that come about?" Burns asked.

"Carlos told me he was giving me to Stan Turner so I could keep an eye on him and report back each day about what he was doing?"

"When you say giving you to him, what do you mean."

"I was supposed to get close to him, be his girlfriend, you know."

"So, you were a spy?"

Rosa nodded. "That's not what he called it. He said I was to be his eyes and ears and needed to call him daily to report what Stan was doing."

"Okay. So, how did that work out?"

"Stan didn't want me as a girlfriend but to help him manage Ruben Acosta's businesses instead?"

"Why did Carlos care about Stan Turner's activities?" Burns asked.

"Because Stan had taken over the money laundering operations for the Cartel from Ruben."

"Objection! There has been no proof that Defendant had any relationship to the Cartel or any money laundering."

"Until now," Burns noted.

"Overruled," the Judge said.

"Did Stan ever talk to Carlos by telephone?"

"Not often. Stan knew what had to be done, but if Carlos was unhappy, he'd call."

"Why would Carlos be unhappy?"

"If the reports he was getting weren't right, he'd call and want to speak to Stan."

"Did you overhear any of those conversations?"

"Only Stan's side of the conversation, but he usually filled me in after he hung up.

"Now, you were abducted recently, correct?"

Rosa nodded solemnly. "Yes, two men took me from the parking lot where our office suite is located. I saw them coming, so I ran to my car, but they were too fast."

"So, what happened after they grabbed you?" Burns asked.

"They put a hood over my head, bound and gagged me, then put me in the back of a van."

"Did you get a good look at them?"

"Yes."

"Had you seen them before?"

"No, but I was expecting them?" Rosa replied.

"How so?"

"Carlos had told Stan he would take me back if the reports he was getting didn't improve. Stan told me about the threat, so I was being extra careful not to be alone."

"So, if you were on loan to Stan, why wouldn't you just go back voluntarily to Carlos if he asked you to."

"I wouldn't have gone back voluntarily, and Carlos knew it. Stan had helped me get clean and treated me like a human being, so Carlos knew he'd have to kidnap me to get me back."

"Objection!" Mann barked. "Speculation. The witness doesn't know what the Defendant was thinking."

"Sustained," the Judge ruled.

"Did you know Stan was working with the FBI?"

"No. He didn't tell me about that, but I suspected something was up."

"So, after the two men put you in the back of the van, what happened?"

"I'm not sure; they drugged me. I woke up later at the hospital."

"So, were you hurt?"

"No. Thanks to Jodie and Stan."

Burnes continued to question Rosa and had her explain how she had come to the United States, the murder of her brother on the way, and how she had ended up as an escort for Empire Clubs International. Then Mann took her on cross-examination.

"Ms. Méndez, do you have any personal knowledge as to the ownership of the Empire Clubs International?"

Rosa shrugged. "Only what I saw?

"Right. Did you see any stock certificates?"

"No."

"Did you see and board of director minutes?" Mann asked smugly.

"No."

"Did you attend any board meetings?"

"No."

"Ah. How about tax returns or anything else that might tell you who owned Empire Clubs International?"

Rosa shrugged. "No, sir."

"Did you ever see an employment contract between Defendant and Empire Clubs International?"

"No," Rosa replied, "but I know he worked for them because I lived at the club, and he told me when I had to dance, go out on a date, or suck his cock!"

"Objection!" Mann spat.

"Your Honor," Burns said. "The witness is simply answering the question."

The Judge looked a Rosa and asked, "Were those the actual words the Defendant used?"

Rosa nodded. "Yes, sir."

"Overruled," the Judge replied.

Mann continued to cross-examine Rosa for some time, and then Burns took her on redirect. After another hour, Rosa stepped down from the witness stand, and the Judge asked for Burns' next witness.

Burns stood. "The Prosecution calls Margie Rojas."

Margie was sober and dressed to impress in a white knit top and dark blue skirt. As she took the witness stand, she flipped her long blond hair out of her face and smiled at the jury. Burns asked her some background questions and the basics of her employment, then she got to the salient points.

"Ms. Rojas, you said you managed rental properties for Ruben Acosta, correct?"

"Yes."

"How did you find your tenants?"

"Ah. They were referred to us."

"Referred by whom?" Burns pressed.

"The NHLC," Margie replied.

"What does NHLC stand for?"

"The New Hope Legal Clinics, it's a non-profit organization that helps illegal immigrants settle once they make it to America."

"I see. So, explain how a typical rental referral would be handled."

Margie took a breath and replied, "Well, we'd get a telephone call or fax from the NHLC with the information about the prospective tenant, and then we'd set up an interview to do the paperwork."

"I see. So, what were the typical terms of each rental?"

Margie thought a moment and then replied, "The rent depended on the unit's square footage, but I would say about $1,500 per month with a one-year term, auto-renewal, and two months security deposit."

"I see," Burns said. "So, how were the payments made?"

"They were paid in cash either by the tenant or a representative of the NHLC."

"So, you never received a rental payment by check?"

"No," Margie agreed.

"How was the cash handled once it was delivered to you."

"We were instructed to make a daily deposit but not over $9,500."

"Why the limit?" Burns asked.

"They said something about the government meddling in our affairs if a deposit was over $10,000."

"So, how much would you deposit in your rental account in a typical month?"

"About $200,000 in each account?"

"Each account?" Burns asked.

"Yes. We had to have accounts at several banks since we could only deposit about $200,000 in any one account each month."

"Alright. What about repairs and maintenance?"

Margie shrugged. "The tenants had a maintenance number they could call if there were any problems. We didn't get involved in that."

"Okay. So where is your husband now?"

Margie shrugged again. "The last I knew; he was in Mexico City. He left about the time this trial started, and I'm not sure he's coming back."

"Why do you say that?" Burns asked.

"Because he was summoned by his brother and seemed panicked when he left."

"Panicked about what?"

Margie smiled. "This trial, I guess."

'So, why would this trial spook him and his family back home?"

"Because his brother runs the NHLC," Margie confessed.

"Objection!" Mann said. "Counsel has not laid a predicate for this line of questioning. This is pure speculation at this point."

"I'm sorry, Your Honor. Let me have the witness provide that predicate. It will only take a few questions."

"Alright, overruled," the Judge said.

"Ms. Rojas, do you know the owners of the NHLC?"

"Yes, it's owned by its members, and my husband and his brother are two of the three directors."

"How do you know this?"

"I've seen the tax returns and attended board meetings."

"When did you see their tax returns?" Burns pressed.

"Many times. I help prepare them each year, and I have had to include them in financial disclosures when they buy property."

"So, who is the third member of the Board of Directors of the NHLC?"

"The defendant, Carlos Herrera," Margie said evenly as she stared at the Defendant.

The crowd buzzed, and several reporters left the courtroom. The Bailiff stood and glared at the unruly crowd. The buzz died down.

"Alright, what's your brother-in-law's name. He's the other board member, right?"

"Yes. His name is Cristino Mejia. At least that's the name he goes by. His real name if Cristino Rojas."

The gallery erupted in conversation, and many reporters quickly left the room to report to their media outlets.

The Judge banged his gavel. "I'll have silence."

The courtroom became quiet again, but tensions were high as it was apparent, they had arrived at a critical stage in the trial. Mann glared at Burns and opened his mouth, but no words came out. Burns smiled and continued.

"So, Mrs. Rojas, why are you testifying here today? Isn't it going to be dangerous for you?"

"Yes, I'm sure there is already a contract out on my life."

The courtroom buzzed. A woman let out a gasp. The Bailiff stood up once again and looked out at the gallery. The woman put her hand over her mouth apologetically.

Margie continued. "Luckily, the government has offered me witness protection."

"Okay. So, does that include non-prosecution for any crimes you may have committed?"

"Yes," Margie agreed.

"So, you realize that your life is still in danger even in witness protection, correct?"

"Yes, they have explained that to me."

"So, is everything you have testified to today true and correct?"

"Yes, ma'am," Margie said solemnly.

"Pass the witness," Burns said.

Mann took the witness on cross and tried to get her to waiver from her testimony but with very little success. After forty-five minutes, he finally gave up and passed the witness. Burns said she had no further questions, and the Judge asked her to call her next witness.

Laura Matos was Burns' next witness. She explained how cash was laundered through several insurance companies, with her help along with other corrupt agents, by paying rejected claims with dirty money.

Burns then called one of the illegal immigrant tenants of the rental properties. The tenant confirmed that immigrants were assigned rental units at no cost for a year while they got settled if they signed the lease agreement that contained a promissory note to repay the amount advanced at 18% interest and a non-disclosure agreement forbidding them to discuss or disclose the terms of the lease with anyone, ever.

Burns had subpoenas issued for Cristino Mejia and Margie's husband, but there was no effort to try to serve them in Mexico. She thought about re-calling Stan to further solidify her case but then decided against it. Nor had the Marshals been able to serve subpoenas on any of the attorneys at the NHLC's offices in Dallas, Albuquerque, Phoenix, or Las Vegas, all of which had shut their doors. Finally, she had no choice but to rest.

The Judge looked at Mann and said, "Counsel, you may call your first witness."

Mann looked around the room nervously, then smiled. "Your Honor, the defense rests. We feel strongly that the prosecution has not met its burden of proof; therefore, any further evidence is unnecessary.

The Judge gave Mann a skeptical nod and replied, 'Very well. Any further witnesses, Mrs. Burns?"

"No, Your Honor. The prosecution closes."

"Alright. We will adjourn for the day and resume with closing arguments tomorrow at 10:00 a.m.," the Judge said as he stood up and left the courtroom."

Paula stood up, stretched, and smiled at Marcia. "Well, that went well, don't you think."

Marcia nodded. "I can't believe Mann didn't put on a case."

"No. He was right. That would have made matters worse. There is little doubt Herrera will be convicted. What I'm worried about is that Stan and Jodie are now at risk with two Rojas brothers on the loose."

"So, will Stan have to go into witness protection?" Marcia asked worriedly.

"I'm afraid he has no choice."

"What about Jodie?"

"She told me she wouldn't go into hiding for anyone. She'd take her chances. But she will not be as much of a prime target as Stan."

"Oh, my god! I won't be able to see my father ever again?"

Paula sighed. "I'm afraid not."

Tears began to flow down Marcia's cheeks. "I can't believe this!"

Tears began to well in Paula's eyes, and soon she, too, was crying. They embraced, trying to provide what little comfort to each other as they could under such tragic circumstances.

41
Closing Arguments

Stan

On Tuesday, Burns and Mann were to give their closing arguments. Stan and Jodie were in the gallery since their testimony was over and the courtroom was secured. The Judge took the bench at 10:00 a.m. and told the bailiff to bring in the Defendant and then the Jury.

The bailiff and a U.S. Marshal left the courtroom. A minute later, there were gunshots and a commotion in the hallway behind the courtroom. There were yells and screams in the gallery, then a stampede for the exit doors to the courtroom. Two Marshals rushed out and escorted the Judge off the bench and out the back door of the Courtroom. Stan and Jodie looked at each other and then ran to the Judge's door to see what was happening. They peered out cautiously.

At the end of the hallway, a bailiff stood over two bodies. A grey haze hung over the scene, and there was a strong scent of gunpowder. Stan figured one of the bodies was Carlos Herrera and the other his assailant. Both appeared to be dead as no one was attempting to revive them. Stan felt nothing as he looked at the two corpses. He wondered how the assailant had gotten a weapon into the courthouse.

Agent Thompson joined them at the open doorway and said, "Well, that guy saved the taxpayers a lot of money."

Marcia and several others joined them in the doorway. A door at the end of the hallway opened, and two detectives came in. "Alright. This is a crime scene; everybody out," they ordered.

Thompson excused herself as she wanted to find the Judge and find out what he was going to do about this unexpected turn of events. Stan, Jodie and Marcia stayed in the now deserted courtroom waiting for the Judge to return and continue the trial or recess the case.

Agent Thompson rushed back into the courtroom and walked over to them and reported. "The Judge is recessing the case until 10:00 a.m. tomorrow. You don't have to wait around."

Stan frowned. "Okay. Is Carlos dead?"

Agent Thompson nodded. "Yes, he took two bullets to the head. He died instantly."

Marcia gasped.

Stan sighed. "So, if Carlos is dead and the Judge dismisses the case, I'm stuck with millions of dollars that I will have to give to the NHLC which we now know is a front for the Cartel."

Agent Thompson frowned and replied thoughtfully. "You're right. We can't confiscate the Cartel's assets without a court order. I'll get with Burns and see if she has any ideas."

"Okay. In the meantime, I have another avenue I want to explore."

"What's that?" Agent Thompson asked.

Stan shrugged. "It's just an idea. Let me explore it a little more, and then if it works out, I'll explain it to you."

"How will you explore it if you are in witness protection?" Jodie asked.

"I can't go into witness protection until I sort this out and distribute the corpus of the trust or get another trustee appointed."

"Good luck finding someone to be trustee," Jodie said dryly.

They all laughed.

The next day Stan had a meeting with Beverly Burns and Paul Dotson from the U.S. Marshal's office. They discussed Stan's theory and his need to make another trip to Arizona. Thompson reluctantly agreed to accompany Stan to ensure his safety. Then they discussed Stan's entry into witness protection.

"So, we have a location for Rosa and her family. Do you want to go to the same location or somewhere different?" Dotson asked.

Stan stiffened. "Oh, God! I don't know. I'm fond of Rosa and would love to be with her, but now that she is free, I don't want to tie her down or restrict her freedom in any way. She may regret it later, and then she'd have to go through more heartache getting rid of me."

"So, a separate location then?' Dotson pressed.

Stan nodded. "Yeah. I think that's best."

"Okay. You'll need to say goodbye to Rosa today because she's leaving tonight to join her family at her new home."

Stan felt a surge of regret at this news. He would miss Rosa and didn't relish saying goodbye. Stan sighed deeply. "Okay. I'll pay her a visit."

Later that afternoon, Stan saw Rosa back at Carswell. She told Stan she was excited to finally have her nightmare over and couldn't wait to see her grandparents and Mariana.

"I doubt I will recognize her. She was so tiny when I left her. Now she's almost old enough to go to school," Rosa said excitedly.

"I know they change so quickly at that age," Stan replied.

"I wish you could meet her," Rosa said. "She'd love you."

Stan smiled and felt a pang of guilt and remorse. "I'd love her too, I am sure."

"So, you're going to be all alone?" Rosa noted with a frown.

"Right, but that's something I'll just have to get used to. It comes with old age."

"You're not that old," Rosa objected.

"I don't feel old until I look in the mirror, then I get depressed."

Rosa laughed. "After all I have been through, I feel very old myself."

Stan smiled. "That will change once you're safe and can get some decent sleep at night. Having your grandparents and Mariana around will do wonders for you, too."

They continued to talk until Stan had to leave for the airport. He met Agent Thompson at the gate, and they were soon in the air and on the way to Phoenix. Stan had called ahead and told Leira Corrales that he needed to talk to her. She didn't object or question the purpose of the visit. That reaction spoke volumes to Stan. He knew his gut feeling had been right.

Leira opened the door quickly after they knocked. It was still warm in Sun Lakes this time of year, so she was dressed in blue shorts and an Arizona Wildcat t-shirt. She let them in and escorted them to a small living area where they all sat.

"So, how was your flight?" Leira asked.

"Good. No problems," Stan replied.

"So, what can I do for you?" Leira said. "You've come a long way. It must be important."

Stan raised his eyebrows and said, "Yes. It is. When we met the last time, I got the impression you knew Ruben Acosta pretty well."

Leira looked back at Stan and sighed. "You noticed, huh?"

"Yeah. He was more than a landlord, right?"

Leira nodded. "So, this is all confidential? I mean, if the wrong people find out about the kids and me, they will come and hunt us down."

Thompson nodded and replied, "Everything you tell us will be confidential, and we can provide you protection for now. I can't say exactly how we will do it, but we'll figure it out."

"But we need to know the full extent of your relationship with Ruben in order to help you," Stan added.

"Okay," Leira said. "Ruben was my husband, and we have two children together."

Stan smiled broadly. "I am so glad to hear that," Stan said excitedly. "I didn't want to turn over millions of dollars to the Cartel or the government."

"Millions of dollars?" Leira asked.

"Yes, many millions," Stan replied. "You and your children are the beneficiaries of the trust and estate, so all I need is proof of your marriage and birth certificates for your children. Then I won't have to give any of the money to the Cartel."

"Well, the government may confiscate some or all of it," Agent Thompson warned.

Stan nodded. "Well, we will have to sort all that out, but I know you are the beneficiary of a million-dollar insurance policy. I can't see how the government could take that away from you."

Leira began to cry. "I was so upset when you were here last time because Ruben had just been murdered, and I had no one to talk to about it. It was hard to explain to the children that their father was dead. I didn't even dare tell my priest."

"I felt that when we talked," Stan said. "You did a good job concealing your emotions, but I knew something wasn't right."

The next day Leira and her children accompanied Stan and Thompson back to Dallas to meet Paul Dotson and Assistant U.S. Attorney Beverly Burns. Dotson had arranged for Leira and her children to stay at Carswell AFB, where she'd be picked up as soon as arrangements had been made for her new home. Dotson told Stan he'd have the rest of the week, and then he'd be picked up and taken to the McKinney airport, where a jet would be waiting to take him to his final destination.

"Can you pick me up from my house? My family wants to give me a going away party."

"That's not a good idea," Dotson replied. "We don't want anyone from the Cartel knowing when you are leaving."

"I'll tell my family to keep the party to themselves. Besides, even if they followed us to the airport, they couldn't follow the plane once it took off."

Dotson shrugged. "Alright. We'll pick you up from your house at 7:00 p.m. on Friday. Be ready."

Stan smiled. "I will be. No problem."

During the following week, Stan arranged for a new trustee to take over his duties and sort out any claims the government might have over the trust corpus. He also managed to convince Burns not to interfere with Leira's insurance claim, so she wouldn't have any future financial worries.

On Friday night, Dotson showed up at Stan's house right on schedule in a black SUV. Stan asked him to give him a minute to say his final goodbyes. The going away party hadn't been a funeral, but that's what it felt like to many. Although Stan could live for decades, his loved ones would not be able to share that life. There was not a dry eye in the house. Before he left, Stan had a few last words.

"Before I go, I wanted to thank all of you for the many wonderful years we've had together. A man couldn't ask for better friends or family.

God has been good to me, so I have no complaints now. Apparently, he has other plans for me now. So, don't worry about me, and I'll try not to worry about any of you, although that won't be easy.

"Though I'll be gone, I can still follow your lives from afar. So, be on your best behavior."

Everyone laughed tentatively.

"Anyway. Keep your fingers crossed that the FBI can track down enough of the Cartel that I can safely return home someday."

Stan looked at Jodie. "You be careful, girl. Keep your bodyguard close. I don't want to read about you in the newspaper."

Jodie nodded and smiled, holding back her tears.

Stan gave Marcia and Paula one last hug then shook Reggie's hand and slapped him on the back. "Take care of the firm. I'm counting on you, son!"

"Take care of yourself, Dad," Reggie replied solemnly.

"I will. I'm going to miss you all. God bless!" Stan said, turned, and walked briskly out of the house to the awaiting SUV. Dotson held the door while Stan got in but said nothing. The SUV took off briskly, heading for the McKinney Airport, where a private jet was waiting to take Stan to his new home.

As they drove away, Stan wondered if he'd ever make it back home. Would Jodie be safe, or would she be the Cartel's next victim? He wished she'd have gone into witness protection, but he knew she loved the law too much to give it up. On the other hand, he wouldn't mind a more tranquil life, at least for a while.

The airport was nearly deserted at this time of night. The SUV drove right up to a jet that was fueled and ready for take-off. A crew member took Stan's luggage and loaded it into the jet's storage compartment. Stan thanked the driver and then boarded the plane. The captain came out and introduced himself and then went back into the cockpit.

Stan found a seat and suddenly realized he was the only passenger. The crew member took a seat behind him and buckled up. Stan wondered why Dotson or someone from the U.S. Marshals wasn't traveling with him. Within seconds his thoughts were interrupted by the rumble of the jets' engines, the plane jerked, and they began taxiing to the runway. Stan looked out the window as the plane turned onto the runway and started accelerating. Soon they were in the air and flying back over Plano. Stan looked down, hoping to see his home one last time, but all he saw were indistinguishable lights that got smaller and smaller with each passing second.

Stan searched to see landmarks telling him which direction they were flying. But the jet kept banking in one direction and then another making it difficult to figure out in which direction they were flying. He finally gave up, laid back, and closed his eyes, wondering where they were taking him and what his new life would be like. Eventually, he fell into a deep sleep and didn't wake up until the jet's landing gear dropped with a jerk, and he felt the jolt of the jet's tires hitting the runway.

It was still dark, and the only lights he saw were those outlining the runway. When the jet came to a halt, Stan looked around for the crew member, but he had disappeared. Stan waited patiently for the cabin door to open, but nothing happened. A jolt of fear suddenly came over Stan as he realized something had gone seriously wrong. This wasn't his new home. It couldn't be. There were no lights, buildings, roads, cars or people. Then the cabin door finally opened, and he saw a familiar face, confirming his worst fears.

"Hello, Stan," Christos Mejia said with a huge grin. "Welcome to Mexico."

Stan stiffened, then swallowed hard.

Raul then stepped aboard and pointed a gun at Stan. "Have a nice flight?" Raul asked.

"Shit!" he mumbled looking around in disbelief. "How did you pull this off?"

Christos grinned. "Impressive, huh?"

"Yes," Stan agreed dejectedly.

"Well, we've been wrestling with your government for decades. We've planted plenty of moles over the years, so our intel is pretty good."

"But Dotson put me in the SUV at my house. How did he not know it wasn't the right car?"

"He did know, but for the right price, he didn't care," Christos replied.

Stan rubbed his forehead to try to soothe a rapidly developing headache. "So, why kidnap me? Why didn't you just put a bullet in my head? You could have saved a lot of jet fuel."

"Well, that would have given us great pleasure, but you have our finances entangled in a nasty web. We needed something or somebody to trade to get it all sorted out," Christos noted.

As they were talking, the cockpit door opened, and the captain walked out. He nodded and quickly exited the plane. While they were distracted, the door to the rear restroom opened and the missing crew member stepped out and yelled, "Hands up!"

With Christos and Raul focused on the crew member, Stan reached down, pulled out the revolver Jodie had given him from his ankle holster and pointed it at them as well.

"Drop your gun!" Stan ordered.

Stunned, Christos and Raul froze. Stan reached over and took Raul's gun away from him. The crew member rushed over to assist.

"Okay, off the plane!" The crew member spat.

Christos started to protest but the crew member quickly subdued him.

"Don't even think about it," he said. "I'd like nothing better than to put a bullet in your head."

Christos stood up and then smiled at Stan. "How in the hell do you think you're going to escape. We have fifty men outside."

Just then, the sound of approaching helicopters could be heard.

"What's that?" Raul asked as he scanned the sky.

"That would be a U.S. Special Operations team coming to take you back to Dallas," the crew member advised.

Gunfire could be heard as the special ops team engaged with the few cartel members who hadn't fled when they saw the helicopters descending on them. A minute later, two soldiers entered the plane.

"Here you go," the crew member said to the soldiers. "These are your packages, Christos Mejia and Raul Rojas."

The soldiers grabbed Christos and Raul and searched each of them. Several other soldiers entered the cabin and assisted in the arrests. Stan sat back in his chair and relaxed for the first time since he'd left his house.

When Christos and Raul were gone, Dotson stepped aboard and smiled wryly at Stan. "So, that went pretty well, huh?"

Stan shook his head. "I'm still breathing, so I guess it did."

Another civilian entered the plane, and Stan squinted in the dim light to see him. Then recognition came over him. "Mo?"

Mo nodded, and Stan stood to embrace him and shake his hand. Tears welled in his eyes. "So, this was a Company operation. I wondered how the Marshal's Service could have pulled it off."

"Yeah. When we got the call that there was an opportunity to simultaneously put a cartel out of business and save your ass; how could we refuse?"

"Thank you," Stan replied. "I'm glad this nightmare is over. Now I can return to Dallas and resurrect my law practice. It has been a nightmarish year."

"Alright," Mo said. "Our work is done here. The pilot will fly you and Dotson to wherever you want to go. We will take the prisoners to a maximum-security prison until the U.S. Attorney decides what to do with them."

Stan and Mo shook hands again, and then he and the soldiers left. The same pilot returned and entered the cockpit. Stan gave Dotson a stern look.

"Okay, what the hell just happened," Stan spat.

Dotson laughed. "Sorry about that, Stan, but we all wanted the entire cartel put out of business, right?"

"Yeah," Stan agreed.

"Well, several months ago, we discovered a mole in our witness protection division. Rather than arresting the corrupted agent, we have been using him to gather intel and spread disinformation. When the mole was asked for information about your placement in witness protection, we knew they would try to somehow intercept you.

"During your party, our driver stepped out for a smoke, and while he was away from the car, he was grabbed, gagged, and tied up. A cartel driver then took his place. We were expecting him, so Dotson pretended not to notice. He didn't want to alert you to the switch. You needed to act normal."

Stan took a deep breath, not believing what he was hearing. "Okay, what happened at the airport?"

"The cartel driver took you to a different hanger with a Cartel plane fueled and ready to go. Before you arrived, we had raided the hanger, taken everyone into custody, and were ready when your SUV arrived. We had our pilot now on board and one crew member."

"Yeah. It didn't feel right. You're lucky I didn't protest, but I was so exhausted from all the intrigue over the past year that I didn't have the energy to complain."

"We hoped you would figure out what was going on since there was a note in the file that the Company would help if things went south."

"I suspected that might be the case," Stan said, "but I wasn't sure."

"So, what's your connection to the Company."

Stan smiled. "Sorry, that's classified."

Dotson chuckled. "Oh, I see. You're gonna play that card."

Stan nodded and smiled. "Sorry. You know our government has to protect its secrets."

They suddenly heard helicopters taking off. Dotson said, "Okay, let's get out of here before the Federales show up. We don't want to have to explain to them what we are doing here.

"Do we have enough fuel to get back?" Stan asked.

"Yes, don't worry. We have carefully planned this operation. We are not going to run out of fuel."

As they heard sirens in the distance, the jet was airborne again and heading North this time. Stan felt better at that moment than he had for years. Then his mind was filled with questions.

"So, do I need witness protection now with all the Cartel leaders in custody?" Stan asked.

"Yeah. I'm afraid so. When one leader falls, another takes his place."

"Damn it!"

"But it's your choice. We can't force you into witness protection."

"So, where are we going then?"

"Craig, the county seat of Moffat County, Colorado, population 9,189."

"That's pretty small."

"Well, it's growing, and that's kind of the point. We don't want you in a heavily populated area where you could accidentally be spotted."

"So, what I'm I supposed to do there?"

"We've set you up as a real estate agent. Since you are an attorney, that shouldn't be too difficult for you."

Stan nodded. "I guess not, but I don't have a license."

"You will be sitting for the exam next week. We have a book for you to study."

"Wonderful," Stan groaned.

"There's good news, though."

"What's that?" Stan asked hopefully.

"You won't be alone."

Stan smiled broadly. "Rosa changed her mind?"

"Apparently, she did. She's been begging her handler to contact you and tell you to come to Colorado."

Tears welled in Stan's eyes. He could hardly keep his composure. He silently thanked God for this turn of events. He so much didn't want to be alone. When they got to the airport, Dotson gave Stan a briefcase full of papers documenting his new identity, including a passport, driver's license, title to a 1999 VW Passat, birth certificate, discharge papers from the U.S. Marines, cash, and a personal history that he was to memorize, then destroy.

Dotson gave him the address of his destination and hand-written directions, then got back on the jet. Stan watched it take off, then got in his Passat, excited to see Rosa again and started the engine. The directions were a bit complicated, but Stan finally found the mini ranchette the Marshals had rented for Rosa. It was dark, so he couldn't see much.

As soon as he pulled up and shut off the engine, the door opened, and Rosa came running out.

Stan got out of the car and took her into his arms. He kissed her long and hard, and when he finally let her go, he turned and saw a small child standing in the doorway. Rosa smiled and said, "Come here, Mariana. I want you to meet someone."

Mariana walked over timidly and stood before them.

"This is mommies' friend I told you about. He's going to be staying with us."

Stan smiled and then squatted down to Marianna's level. "So, how do you like America?" he asked.

"It's okay, but I miss my grandpa and grandma."

Stan stood back up. "What happened?"

"They changed their minds and decided to stay since Carlos was killed. They didn't think the Cartel would care about them anymore."

Stan nodded. "They are probably right. There wouldn't be much point in hurting them now with you out of their control. So, what made you change your mind about us?"

Rosa shrugged. "I went out on some dates and to a church social, but most of the boys were only interested in drinking, having sex, and partying. They were all so immature I could barely stand being around them. And, of course, when they found out, I had a child, anyone that might have been the least bit interesting suddenly disappeared."

Stan chuckled. "Well, I love children, obviously, since I have four of them. So, a child doesn't scare me in the least."

Stan bent down and said, "Can I hold you, Marianna?"

She looked at him a moment and then nodded. Stan picked her up and let her settle in his arms. Rosa smiled at them.

"I think I'm going to like my new life in America," Rosa said as a tear rolled down her cheek.

Stan smiled. "Me, too. When I left college, I thought about being a real estate agent."

Rosa laughed. "You did not!"

"Well, I did think about it for a minute or two."

As they walked into their new home, a strange, surreal feeling came over Stan. He felt like an intruder who had taken over someone else's body. It was unsettling, and he wondered how long or if he'd ever get used to it. When Rosa showed him their bedroom, he looked in the mirror and was almost surprised that he saw himself staring back.

42
The Slap

Reggie

Several months had passed from Stan's entry into witness protection. At first, Reggie had been so depressed over the fact that he'd never see his father again that he barely ate or slept. This was detrimental to the firm, but Paula and Jodie didn't have the heart to complain about it. Finally, Jodie walked into his office and sat down across from him.

Reggie raised his eyebrows expectantly. "Yeah. What's up?"

"So, have you given up on the practice of law now that your dad is gone?"

Reggie frowned. "No. Of course not. What are you talking about?"

"Well, since your dad left, you've been acting like a zombie. You're barely keeping up with the old bankruptcies, let alone trying to get any new ones filed."

Reggie shrugged. "Well, you know how much I hate bankruptcies."

"Well, you have to generate revenue somehow. If you're not going to follow up on new bankruptcies, you better start getting some new PI cases."

Reggie frowned. "Yeah, you're probably right. I just can't get enthusiastic about anything anymore."

"What about Amanda's case. You've got a trial coming up pretty soon. It might be a good time to schedule a mediation, don't you think?" Jodie said sarcastically.

Reggie thought about it. "Yeah, I guess; as good a time as ever."

Jodie's face flushed. She stood up abruptly, came around the desk and slapped Reggie across the face. "Wake up! You're not a kid anymore. Move on! Your Dad will be back as soon as the threat level dies down. You don't really think he can stay away indefinitely, do you?"

"Huh?" Reggie said rubbing his face gingerly. He glared at Jodie for a moment, but then sighed deeply. "You're right. He'll be back!"

"Yes! So get your fucking act together and make him proud."

Reggie smiled as he stood up, grabbed Jodie's arm, and tried to pull her in for a kiss, but she managed to break away. They both started laughing.

"You owe me a kiss after that slap! Get back here!"

Jodie ran off, leaving Reggie standing in the doorway thoughtfully. A minute later, he returned to his desk, picked up the phone, and called the attorney for Southern Battery, Jeb Walters.

"Hey Jeb, our trial is fast approaching. Do you think a mediation might be in order? Or does your client want to throw the dice."

Jeb sighed. "Yeah. I don't think your client will have a prayer at trial, but the insurance company has asked me about mediation. I think they would be inclined to give it a try."

"Excellent. I'll prepare a joint motion for mediation, okay?"

"Sure. Sounds good. Send me some dates and proposed mediators, and I'll get with my client."

"Will do," Reggie said and hung up. A wave of relief came over him. Dad will be back. Jodie's right. He couldn't stay away from his family and the practice forever. He'd be back.

His next call was to Amanda to tell her about the mediation and how the process worked.

"You mean we won't have to go to trial?" Amanda asked.

"If we settle, we won't, but there are no guarantees. We will still have to go to trial if we don't settle."

"So, do I have to testify?"

"No. You just sit there and look pretty."

She laughed. "Yeah. I'm so beautiful in my wheelchair."

"Anyway," Reggie continued. "The mediator will make a statement, then both attorneys will outline their cases, and finally, the mediator will ask questions. Once all that is over, we will split up, and the mediator will do his magic."

"Magic?"

"Yes. He'll go back and forth and tell us how horrible our cases are and that the only intelligent thing to do is to settle for an amount that both parties can live with but won't like."

"I hope it works. I don't want to testify. That would be so scary and embarrassing."

Reggie smiled. "I know. Mediations have a high rate of success, so keep your fingers crossed. You'll need to bring Julie too. She's also a plaintiff, and I want them to see her. The insurance adjuster will worry about how the jury would react to both of you."

"Okay, whatever you say. I trust you."

Reggie said goodbye and hung up. He hoped and prayed the insurance company would make a reasonable offer and not some ridiculous lowball number. He'd been through a few mediations that turned out to be a waste of time. He'd know they weren't serious about settling if the first offer was less than $10,000.

His problem now was to come up with his initial demand. That would require getting together all the medical expense records, calculating lost time, the value of pain and suffering, mental distress, past and future income loss, and the cost of future medical services. This was all very complicated, so he'd need the services of an accountant and actuary.

Since Turner & Waters had not been practicing personal injury law, they didn't have a list of these types of experts. Then he thought of Roger Moore and Tom Rice. They could probably do it. He dialed Roger's number.

"Mr. Moore," Reggie said. "This is Reggie Turner."

"Oh," Reggie. "Have you heard from your father?"

"No. I guess he is safely tucked away somewhere."

"Yeah. That's so sad. I really miss him. This new trustee is a jerk. I hate working with him."

Reggie chuckled. "Sorry. Anyway, I'm calling to see if you and Tom can help me on a personal injury case we have coming up for trial."

"Sure, I can. I'm sure Tom would be happy to help, too."

Reggie explained the situation and what would be needed. Roger said he'd get with Tom, and they'd get started on it. Reggie thanked him and said he get them all the information they would need to do their work.

Several weeks later, all the parties showed up at Turner & Waters and met in the large conference room. Additionally, three small meeting rooms were available for the mediator, the plaintiff, and the defendant. The initial meeting was called the general session. The mediator began the meeting, explained the mediation process to everyone, and got each's commitment to act in good faith.

"Alright, Mr. Turner. Why don't you tell us your client's position."

"Sure," Reggie said and began, "In December 1999, Amanda Rich went to work at her job with Southern Battery located near McKinney, Texas. She was working the night shift from 11:00 p.m. to 7:00 a.m. When the shift was over, she was told she needed to work a second shift as a worker had called in sick.

Now prior to this time, when Amanda had been asked to work a double shift, she had told her supervisor that her doctor did not want her working more than eight hours per day as she had sleep apnea. It would be dangerous for her to be working or driving back and forth to work in such a tired state.

Amanda protested the assignment of a double shift. She reminded them of her doctor's advice, but they insisted she work anyway. Since Amanda is a single mom and lives paycheck to paycheck, she couldn't afford to lose her job, so she worked the second shift.

During her shift, she got a terrible headache and took some medicine prescribed for her for headaches. Tired and in pain, she did not think about the side effect of her medication, sleepiness.

Consequently, after her second shift, she got in her car and drove to Julie's daycare center, where her mother had left Julie that morning. After picking up Julie, on the way home, they got into an accident. It was a head-on collision causing the death of the driver of the car they hit. Amanda also died but was resuscitated, and Julie was severely injured. Whereas Julie has fully recovered, Amanda will never walk again and will require extensive medical attention for the rest of her life.

Now I know the defendant will contest its liability in this matter and has alleged that Amanda was contributorily negligent in not refusing to work the second shift, but do you think a jury will buy that argument. We don't think so. Considering these facts, I have prepared an initial demand of 2.7 million dollars which I have itemized in this settlement brochure.

Reggie handed copies of the settlement brochure to the mediator, Jeb, and the insurance adjuster.

"Thank you," the mediator said. "Mr. Walters. What's the defendant's position?"

Walters nodded. "Well, as tragic as this whole situation was, it is well-settled law that an employer is not responsible for the acts of its employees when they are off the job. However, I have been told by our adjuster to try to settle this case anyway in the spirit of goodwill.

So, I'm going to let our adjuster explain the offer."

The mediator nodded and said, "Very well, Mr. Snyder.

Snyder smiled at Amanda and Julie and then began. "We agree with our counsel that there is no liability here, but we are not so naive to think a jury might believe otherwise. So, rather than spend hundreds of thousands of dollars on attorney's fees for defending this case and then for appeals all the way to the Texas Supreme Court, we will make one and only one offer, take it or leave it.

"If we can settle this case today, we will pay the equivalent of $999,999.99 to Amanda and Julie Rich. I have prepared a settlement brochure that explains how we arrived at this figure. The offer is effective now but will be withdrawn at 5:00 p.m. today. So, we will hang around to answer questions about our offer but will not negotiate further at this time."

The mediator smiled and said, "Okay. Let's break out to our separate rooms to consider these offers. I will shuttle back and forth as needed to help facilitate a final settlement. Thank you."

The general session broke up, and the parties went to their separate rooms. Each room had coffee and snacks to help settle nerves while the negotiations went forward. Reggie rolled Amanda in and asked her if she wanted coffee or a soda. She opted for a soda, as did Julie. Jodie poured herself a cup of coffee. Jodie's bodyguard remained outside the room.

"Okay," Reggie said. "This is a bit unusual to get an offer during the general session, but I think it's a positive sign. They've offered almost a million dollars."

"Yes, but it is only good today," Jodie reminded them.

"Right," Reggie agreed. "And if we make a counteroffer, they could consider their offer rejected, and we are back to square one."

"What?" Amanda said. "You mean we can't negotiate for more money?"

"Technically, no," Reggie said.

Jodie frowned. "Attorneys always say that," she pointed out. "Even if you reject it, they usually will honor the offer until the expiration date."

Reggie shook his head. "This isn't a typical situation. We can't afford to turn down almost a million dollars. We could end up with nothing at trial."

Jodie nodded. "Well, let's go through the offer and make sure we understand it. We don't need to make a counteroffer right away."

For the next hour, they read the settlement brochure and asked the mediator questions about it. When Reggie thought Amanda understood it, he asked her what she wanted to do.

"As I understand it, I'll get a guaranteed income for life, my future medical bills not paid by insurance or Medicaid will be covered, and Julie's college expense will be paid."

Jodie and Reggie nodded. "It's not a bad deal," Jodie admitted.

"What about your fees?" she asked.

"Twenty-five percent will be paid in cash, which will be our fee under our contract. So, you won't owe us anything.

"Take it then!" Amanda said. "I want this nightmare over."

Reggie looked at Jodie, and she smiled back at him. "Okay. I'll tell the mediator we will take their offer."

The lawyers and mediator hammered out the paperwork for the next hour, and the settlement was completed. For the last time, Reggie took Amanda and Julie home and said goodbye.

"You've been so wonderful," Amanda said with tears rolling down her cheeks. "I don't know what we would have done had you not come along."

"Well, it turned out okay for both of us," Reggie replied.

Julie ran over and hugged Reggie. He smiled broadly and said, "It worked out well for all of us. Even Julie gets an education."

"You better not be a stranger," Amanda warned. "I consider you a good friend."

Reggie nodded. "Me too. I'll be talking to you a lot. Don't worry."

Reggie felt good as he drove home. His only regret was that his father hadn't been there to see him successfully prosecute his first personal injury case. When he got back to the office, Jodie and Paula were waiting for him in his office.

"Well, how do you feel, champ? Your first million-dollar settlement," Paula said.

Reggie smiled proudly. "Yeah, what a way to wrap it up, huh?"

Jodie stepped up and planted a big kiss on Reggie's cheek. He brightened up, and his eyes sparkled. Jodie laughed. "There's another kiss for you every time you bring in a million-dollar recovery."

They all laughed.

"But I did want to point out to you that the quarter million dollar fee goes to the firm, not to any individual lawyer."

Reggie nodded his realization of that fact.

"But, as managing partner, I can give out bonuses for merit," Paula said. "Jodie, do you think I should give Reggie a bonus?"

Jodie frowned. "I don't know. That might be a bad precedent."

Reggie glared at her and realized she was kidding.

"Ah, what the hell," Paula said and handed Reggie a check for $50,000.

Reggie looked at the check and stammered, "Whoa! That's a big check."

"Yes, it is," Paula agreed. "But it may be a while before you get another one, so put in a savings account or invest it in the stock market, don't go out and buy a new car on some other frivolous waste of money."

"You're right," Reggie agreed. "I'm going to use it for the down payment on a house. I hate living in an apartment."

"Yeah," Jodie agreed. "As long as you like mowing the lawn, painting, repairs, and all that good stuff."

"What about your dad's house? Why don't you live there?" Jodie asked.

"He's coming back," Reggie said. "Remember what you told me?"

Jodie closed her eyes and took a deep breath. "Right. But I'm sure he wouldn't mind if you lived in it until he got back."

The door to Reggie's office opened, and Maria rushed in. "You need to come into the conference room. There's some news on the TV about Stan. They all rushed into the conference room, where Maria had the report on pause. Maria grabbed the remote and pushed the button.

This is Christine Sommers with the News at Five. The FBI held a news conference today to announce the Capture of Christos Mejia and Raul Rojas, the last of the bosses of the Las Guías criminal organization. As you might remember, Carlos Herrera, was recently on trial for murder, kidnapping, and racketeering in the U.S. District Court up in Sherman, Texas.

Before a verdict could be rendered, Herrera was gunned down and killed as he was being brought into the courtroom for closing arguments. No suspects have been arrested in connection with that murder.

Assistant U.S. Attorney Beverly Burns will be handling the prosecution of these two fugitives who were arrested at an unknown location. Apparently, attorney/witness Stan Turner was involved in capturing these fugitives. However, details of his involvement have not been released. Stan Turner is currently in the Federal Witness Protection Program, as is Rosa Mejia, a cartel victim. Both will be witnesses in the government's case against these two defendants.

"See," Jodie said. "I told you he'd be back."

Reggie smiled and nodded. "Yeah, but I hope it's not just for the trial. With those two thugs in prison, he should be able to stay home."

A broad smile came over Paula's face. "I bet you fifty bucks; when Stan returns, he and Rosa will be together."

"No," Jodie said, shaking her head. "I'll take that bet. I heard him tell Dotson he didn't want to take advantage of her. She was too young for him and needed to find someone her own age."

"Reggie. What do you think?" Paula asked.

"I think that's gonna be up to Rosa. If she wants them to be together, I can't see my dad turning her down," Reggie replied.

Paula looked at Jodie and said, "He is pretty smart for a guy."

Jodie nodded her agreement and gave Reggie a wink.

Reggie rolled his eyes. "My dad needs to get back here soon to rescue me from you two."

They all laughed.

About the Author

WILLIAM MANCHEE

William Manchee makes a living as a consumer lawyer practicing in Dallas, Texas with his son Jim. Originally from Southern California, he lives now in Plano, Texas. Writing is his passion, and his novels are in the genres of mystery, science fiction, and suspense. His works to date include the Stan Turner Mystery series, the Rich Coleman novels, the Tarizon Saga and two stand-alone novels, Uncommon Thief and the Prime Minister's Daughter. He's also written a non-fiction work for small business owners, *You Can Save Your Small Business.*

Other Works

www.ingramcontent.com/pod-product-compliance
Lightning Source LLC
Chambersburg PA
CBHW020600310726
48979CB00008B/1282/J

* 9 7 8 1 7 3 3 3 2 8 3 4 0 *